BOUND

In my left hand I'd drawn a dispel focus, a slender silvery wand able to neutralise a single spell. In my right hand I'd drawn my dagger. Neither would have been much use against Vihaela. 'You okay?'

Anne didn't answer for a second and I was about to ask again, but she took a deep breath and seemed to shake it off. When she turned to me she looked normal again, but there was a distant look in her eyes, and I wondered what she and Vihaela had shared in those few seconds. Life mages see the world very differently from other people. 'Is she always like that?'

'Only with the people she's interested in.'

The far door opened and the dama reappeared. It was still wearing that same empty smile, and when I saw what it was going to say, Vihaela went right out of my mind. 'Mage Drakh will see you now.'

By Benedict Jacka

BENEDICT JACKA

BOUND

www.orbitbooks.net

ORBIT

First published in Great Britain in 2017 by Orbit

1 3 5 7 9 10 8 6 4 2

Copyright © 2017 by Benedict Jacka

Excerpt from *Chasing Embers* by James Bennett
Copyright © 2016 by James Bennett

A CIP catalogue record for this book is available from the British Library.

ISBN 978-0-356-50719-4

Typeset in Garamond 3 by Palimpsest Book Production Limited, Falkirk, Stirlingshire
Printed and bound in Great Britain by CPI Group (UK) Ltd, Croydon CR0 4YY

Papers used by Orbit are from well-managed
forests and other responsible sources.

1

January

Walking through Richard's mansion felt like broken glass under my skin.

The inside was well lit, though the dark walls and floor made it feel shadowed. Candle-shaped bulbs in chandeliers shone down onto russet tiles, and thick rafters crossed the ceiling overhead. The walls were panelled, engraved in neat geometric patterns. Our footsteps echoed faintly off the wood, and from time to time a whisper of sound would hint at movement deeper within. Shades of brown and yellow blended into a dark gold.

For me, this was a place of horror and madness. It had been a little more than fourteen years since I'd first passed these doors, and on that day, Richard had introduced me to my fellow apprentices, Rachel and Tobruk and Shireen. He'd explained our duties, then left us to do as we pleased. After a while, there'd been a job. And then another job. And within two years Shireen and Tobruk were dead, Rachel was insane and I was half insane too, fleeing and hiding and trying to rebuild my shattered life. It had taken years, and once I was whole again, I'd sworn I'd never return. Now I was doing exactly that.

The creature leading us was walking two paces in front. To a casual glance it would have looked like a young woman, golden-haired and beautiful, dressed in white.

Only the eyes gave it away: when it had greeted us at the door, I'd met its gaze, and the eyes looking back at me had been blank and empty. I'd heard of these kinds of constructs – they were called 'dama'. They were physically weak and nearly mindless, with only enough intelligence to obey simple commands, but they did have one particular trait that certain mages valued highly. Dama had no long-term memory: any command given to them, once executed, faded from their minds. Back when I'd lived in this mansion, Richard had used house-slaves for these kinds of tasks. The fact that the slaves had apparently been replaced was an improvement from one point of view, but it had ominous implications.

I stole a glance at Anne, walking beside me. Her hair had grown out a little while we'd been on the run, and it brushed her shoulders now as she glanced from side to side, reddish-brown eyes searching the walls. I knew she was sensing the living creatures in the mansion, seeing them through the walls and doors, but I didn't dare ask her about it, not here. Her weight was towards the balls of her feet, and she looked ready to fight or flee. I was glad she was there, and ashamed of that gladness. There are few people I'd rather have at my side in a tight spot than Anne, but I couldn't shake the feeling that she was here because of me.

The construct led us into a sitting room, also panelled in wood, with red cushions and no windows. It turned to us with an empty smile. 'Please wait here. You will be summoned soon.'

'How soon is "soon"?' Anne asked in her soft voice.

The construct's smile didn't change. 'Please wait here. You will be summoned soon.'

Anne opened her mouth again. I caught her eye and gave

a tiny shake of my head, and she stopped. The construct, still smiling, turned and left the room, shutting the door.

'Feels like talking to the people at the Department of Work and Pensions,' Anne said under her breath, then looked up sharply.

'There you are!' a voice said from my right. 'I was wondering how long I'd have to wait.'

I was glad my precognition had given me some advance warning. The woman who'd just walked into the room wasn't the person I *least* wanted to come face to face with, but she was definitely in the top five. 'Vihaela,' I said, turning.

'Verus,' the woman said with a slight smile. 'You're looking well, considering.'

Vihaela is one of the tallest women I know, taller even than Anne and able to stand eye to eye with me. She's dark-haired and dark-skinned, with the build of an athlete and the grace of a raptor, and she dresses in brown and black and red. Vihaela draws attention from people who don't know her, and draws even more attention from the ones who do. Like Anne, she's a life magic user, but Vihaela's magic is a blend of life and death and she puts it to much darker uses than Anne does. Right now, she looked happy. Vihaela often looks happy, though I get the impression that the things that make her happy aren't so pleasant for the people around her.

'Could say the same of you,' I said. 'Although that never seems to change very much.'

'Was that a compliment? Points for trying, but I'm more interested in what you've brought me.' Vihaela glided past, apparently forgetting I was there.

Anne stood her ground as Vihaela approached. Most mages won't come close to a life mage, but if Vihaela was afraid of Anne, nothing in her movements showed it. She came to a stop within arm's reach of the younger woman, looming so that Anne had to tilt her head up slightly. 'I've been looking forward to meeting you,' Vihaela said, her voice like silk. She reached up to stroke Anne's cheek.

It's easy to forget just how fast Anne can move. One moment her arms were by her sides, the next her left hand was clasped around Vihaela's wrist, halting the older woman's fingers just short of her face. 'Please don't do that,' Anne said. Her voice was soft and clear.

'Lovely,' Vihaela said. She smiled at Anne. 'Has anyone ever told you you're a very beautiful young woman?'

'A lot of Dark mages have.' Anne held Vihaela's gaze. 'It was never for a reason I liked.'

'So suspicious,' Vihaela murmured. 'How strong do you think those spells are?'

'Strong enough.'

Vihaela's smile widened. 'Let's find out.'

'Anne!' I snapped.

A wall of black energy flashed up, separating me from Anne, and green-black light leapt from Vihaela's hand into Anne's arm and down into her body. The spell was one I'd never seen before, malignant and deadly, and the attack was quick as lightning. Most mages would have been overwhelmed in the first second.

But Anne is almost as fast as Vihaela, and my shout had given her a heartbeat's warning. A barrier of leaf-green light flashed into existence around Anne's body, holding Vihaela's magic back. Black tendrils twined and snapped, but that thin, fragile-seeming shield of green held them away.

Vihaela stared down at Anne. She'd twisted her hand around to grasp Anne's wrist and now leant forward, bearing down on the younger woman. Anne slid back a step, then steadied, and for a moment the two of them were still, the muscles in Anne's arm straining. Then slowly, gradually, the green light of Anne's magic began to push Vihaela's spell back. The green-black snakes receded, fighting every inch of the way. Soft green tendrils twined their way up to Anne's elbow, then up her forearm. Anne's eyes gleamed red in the light as she held Vihaela's gaze. The tendrils of Anne's magic reached for Vihaela's fingers, and I saw a flash of surprise on Vihaela's face, just before her eyes narrowed and black light burst outwards.

I stumbled back, shielding my eyes. My skin stung from the energy discharge, and I had a weapon in either hand, but as my eyesight cleared I saw that the fight was over. The wall was gone, as were Vihaela's spells, and Vihaela was standing three steps back. From beginning to end the whole thing had taken less than ten seconds.

'So Sagash *did* teach you something,' Vihaela said.

'Stay away from me,' Anne said softly and clearly.

'Touchy, touchy.'

'Vihaela?' I said. I made an effort to make it sound like a suggestion rather than an order. 'Maybe it might be a good idea if we left this for another time?'

'Hm?' Vihaela didn't look at me. 'Oh. I suppose.' She looked at Anne for a moment longer, then gave her a smile. 'Be seeing you.' She walked past and out through the way we'd entered, both of us swivelling to watch her go. The door clicked shut behind her.

The room was silent. Ten seconds passed, then twenty. 'Is she gone?' I asked once I was sure Vihaela was out of earshot.

Anne nodded once.

I resheathed my weapons. In my left hand I'd drawn a dispel focus, a slender silvery wand able to neutralise a single spell. In my right hand I'd drawn my dagger. Neither would have been much use against Vihaela. 'You okay?'

Anne didn't answer for a second and I was about to ask again, but she took a deep breath and seemed to shake it off. When she turned to me she looked normal again, but there was a distant look in her eyes, and I wondered what she and Vihaela had shared in those few seconds. Life mages see the world very differently from other people. 'Is she always like that?'

'Only with the people she's interested in.'

The far door opened and the dama reappeared. It was still wearing that same empty smile, and when I saw what it was going to say, Vihaela went right out of my mind. 'Mage Drakh will see you now.'

Flashback fourteen years

'. . . on the first floor,' Richard was saying. 'Pick an empty bedroom for your own. I believe the other three have already settled in.'

It was the beginning of winter. I was seventeen years old and had just left home, cutting ties with my mother to move into Richard's mansion. I'd spent most of that first visit staring open-mouthed. I'd never seen a house so big. 'This place is huge,' I'd said.

'Yes.'

'How much did it cost?'

Richard smiled slightly. With hindsight, I know he was

amused. 'The value of money in the magical community is somewhat less than it was in your previous life.'

I looked at Richard. 'How much do I get?'

'As much as you need, within reason. What would you use it for?'

'What do you mean?'

'There really isn't much for you to buy. Food will be provided from the kitchen, and there is a selection of clothes and other necessities in the first-floor storeroom. Take what you need. If you need something else, ask Tristana or Zander. Oh, treat them with courtesy, please. I've instructed them to follow your orders, but if I discover you've harmed them, I'll be upset.'

'What if I want to go somewhere?'

'Travel expenses?'

'Yeah.'

'You're in the middle of Wales, Alex,' Richard said. 'You can't exactly flag down a taxi. I suppose you could walk to the nearest bus stop, but it's several miles of woods and fields and I doubt it would take you anywhere you especially wanted to go.'

'Then how do I get anywhere?'

'Use a gate stone.'

'I don't know how to use a gate stone.'

'Then I suggest you learn.'

I paused again. Now that I look back on it, I can see that Richard had already started teaching us. Most of his lessons weren't direct; it was all done by implication. Here's the playing field; here are the rules. If you want anything more, get it yourself. 'Your introduction and first lesson will be in the living room at eight o'clock,' Richard said. 'I'll see you then.'

It was a dismissal, but I didn't leave. 'Why are you doing this?' I asked.

'Excuse me?'

'You're giving us all this, and you're helping us,' I said. 'What do you get out of it?'

Richard smiled, and for the first time, he looked genuinely pleased, as though I was beginning to ask the right questions. 'Everyone wants to leave something behind.'

I stared at him a moment longer before turning to go.

The whole memory flashed through my head as I stepped through the door of Richard's study, there and gone in barely a second. Then it was forgotten as I focused on the man sitting behind the desk.

As far as looks go, Richard Drakh is average in almost every way. He's neither short nor tall, neither thin nor fat, not particularly handsome or ugly or plain. His hair is medium brown, his eyes don't draw attention and he wears an understated suit that doesn't look especially cheap or expensive. Put him on a London train, and he'd disappear into the crowd without a ripple. In the stories, the greatest Dark mages are always terrifying to look at, tall or striking or monstrous or all three at once. Richard was none of those things – in fact, Vihaela looked the part of a Dark master mage far more than he did. Yet it was Vihaela who obeyed Richard, not the other way around, and Richard struck more fear into me than she ever could. It was Richard who'd recruited me and trained me and taught me to be a Dark mage, and it had been Richard who'd watched as I'd fallen from grace and been dragged away by Tobruk to the cells below.

Richard was writing in a plain black notebook, and he

kept writing as we walked in and stopped in front of his desk while the door swung silently back behind us. Only when it closed with a soft *click* did he close the book and look up. 'Alex.' He nodded to me. 'Anne. How was your trip?'

Anne and I stared at him.

'I asked you to visit today to give you an overview of your duties,' Richard said. 'I understand you've been somewhat out of the loop, so I thought it best to give you the opportunity to ask any questions.' He looked between us, his eyebrows raised. 'Before we begin, is there anything you'd like to bring up?'

Richard's voice is deep and powerful, almost hypnotic. Standing, he blends into the background, but when he speaks he dominates any room he's in. Sometimes, back when I was an apprentice, I'd go into a session with Richard meaning to argue with him, then come out an hour later thinking about everything he'd told us, and only afterwards would I remember what I'd planned to say.

But I wasn't an apprentice any more. 'We aren't here because we want to be,' I said.

Richard paused. 'Excuse me?'

A part of me – actually, *most* of me – didn't want to say anything. I was still terrified of Richard, and the part of me that remembered being his apprentice wanted to avoid anything that would provoke him. But if I stayed silent, I'd be accepting his authority. There wasn't much I could do, but I could do this.

'You know how Morden *motivated* us,' I said. 'We didn't come because we wanted to work for you. We're here because Morden told us that if we didn't, he'd kill our entire families.'

'You have some quarrel with Morden?' Richard asked.

'Yes,' I said. 'We have a quarrel with Morden.' At my side, Anne nodded.

'And yet it's because of Morden that you're alive.'

'That doesn't matter!'

'Really?' Richard said. 'As I understand it, without Morden's intervention, you would have been turned into a fine mist of blood and body parts approximately two days ago. Assuming Levistus's men didn't manage to take you alive, in which case your death would have been considerably slower.' Richard looked at Anne. 'Not you, of course. Though I believe you have reason to owe Alex some loyalty. Which suggests to me that both of you should be grateful to Morden rather than the reverse.'

Anne was silent, and I knew why. I'd had to trick her to get her to go along with that plan, and that conversation was one that was still hanging over my head. But I wasn't going to let Richard deflect this onto her. 'Morden didn't help us to be nice,' I said.

Richard shrugged. 'He is entitled to a measure of payment.'

I remembered Morden's words, how he'd explained in detail that if I refused, he'd kill everyone I knew or cared about, one by one, saving the closest for last, and white-hot anger flooded through me. 'Screw his payment,' I said through clenched teeth.

'You'd prefer that Morden had stayed uninvolved?'

I glared at Richard silently.

'As you wish,' Richard said.

I flinched, but all Richard had done was to reach down into a drawer. His hand came back into view holding a dagger. It was a short, heavy-bladed fighting knife with a hilt wrapped in black leather, and my mind raced as I looked through the futures. I couldn't see any trace of combat, but—

Richard laid the dagger down on the desk, pointing towards me, and withdrew his hand. He nodded down at the blade. 'Take it.'

'For what?'

'For yourself.'

I stared at Richard.

'I'm sure you know where to strike,' Richard said. 'Though I'd appreciate it if you picked somewhere neat. Opening the throat or the wrists tends to make a mess, and I'd rather not replace the carpet.'

'You expect me—'

'To kill yourself?' Richard said. 'If that's what you want.'

'Why would you—?'

'You would prefer to die than be in Morden's debt?' All of a sudden Richard's voice was cold and hard. 'Then here is your chance. Take that blade and turn it on yourself. There will be no retaliation, no reprisal killings. All that will happen is that you will be dead – exactly as you would have been had Morden left you alone.'

'That's your idea of a choice?' I demanded.

'What did you expect, Alex? That Morden would solve your problems for free? And make no mistake, they are *your* problems. Your enmity with Levistus is entirely of your own making. You chose to provoke him, expecting . . . what? That there would be no consequences? There are *always* consequences. This is one of them.' Richard's eyes held mine as he reached out to tap the dagger. 'I have no use for children, nor for those without the will to live. Choose.'

Anger flashed up inside me, both for the tone of Richard's words, and for the fact that I didn't have an answer. Because I'd already understood what he was saying, and he was right. Only a few days ago, I'd been about to let Levistus's men kill me. Oh, I'd have made a fight of it, but there was only one way that it could have ended. If I used that knife on myself, all I'd be doing would be resetting the status quo.

But there was no way I was going to do it, and Richard knew that. And the anger had done one useful thing: it had burned away most of my fear. Right now I wasn't seeing Richard as the teacher out of my nightmares; he was just another Dark mage, and I looked into the future to see what would happen if I turned that knife on him instead.

It was . . . closer than I'd expected. Much closer. In fact, to my surprise, as I looked at the futures of combat playing out before us, I actually thought that I might win. It was true that Richard wasn't as defenceless as he looked, and I knew his reactions would be lightning-quick, but none of the futures ended with him simply blasting me with magic. He would use weapons and tricks and combat skill, and those were all things I could counter.

For the first time, I let myself wonder if I *should* be so scared of Richard. When I'd fled this mansion I'd still been a child. I'd had a long time to grow stronger. Maybe it was all in my head . . .

No. Richard wouldn't have handed me a weapon if he hadn't been prepared for me to use it. Besides, even if I could beat him, what then? Richard could have his victory of words. I could wait.

'Good,' Richard said when I stayed silent. He glanced at Anne. 'I assume your answer is the same? Yes?' He put the knife back in the drawer and shut it. *That's that*, his manner seemed to say. *We've settled who's in charge.*

We hadn't, but I wasn't about to tell him that.

'Now as to your duties,' Richard said. 'For the moment, both of you will be assigned to Morden. You're now his liaisons to the Keepers and to the medical corps, respectively. As I'm sure you know, Morden has been working to expand the recognition and acceptance of Dark mages within the Light Council. I expect you both to act in accordance with that.'

'How?' I said.

'I am sure you are both quite able to figure that out for yourselves.'

'Where are we supposed to be staying?'

'Wherever you like.'

That wasn't what I'd expected, and it must have shown because Richard raised an eyebrow. 'Neither of you are apprentices. I'm not responsible for your accommodation.' Richard turned to Anne. 'You've been quiet so far. Do you have any questions?'

'Just one,' Anne said in her soft voice. 'What do you want?'

'As I said, you're to work with Morden.'

'You could have recruited a Dark healer or a Dark diviner,' Anne said. She didn't raise her voice but her eyes stayed steady, and I had the feeling she was watching Richard very closely. 'Why us?'

'Competent life mages and diviners are rarer than you might think.'

'That's not an answer.'

For the first time, Richard smiled. 'How long has it been since you joined the Light apprentice programme, Anne?'

'I'm not a member any more.'

'Regardless, how long ago did you join?'

'Five years.'

'How many years would you say a Light mage usually spends as an apprentice before graduation?'

'Three to seven.'

'But the only Light apprentices who spend the full seven years are those who join the programme in their mid-teens,' Richard said. 'The seven-year-apprenticeship tradition is rare nowadays. Almost all Light mages graduate by twenty-one, twenty-two at the latest. You are . . . twenty-four, was it?'

'There are apprentices in the programme older than me.'

'Let me put this another way,' Richard said. 'You spent a little over three years in the apprentice programme. After the first six months, how often were you taught anything about the use of your magic that was genuinely new?'

Anne was silent. I looked at her, slightly puzzled. Somehow Richard had her off-balance. 'What's your point?' I asked Richard.

'The point is that she should have been raised to journeyman rank within three months,' Richard said. 'Instead she was required to waste her time in classes far below her level of ability. I expect that it wasn't uncommon for her to know more about life magic than her teachers.' Richard turned back to Anne. 'Do you know why they resented you so much?'

Anne didn't answer.

'Because you were an embarrassment,' Richard said. 'Apprentices aren't supposed to outperform their masters, especially apprentices trained outside the programme. They were never going to let you graduate. Your argument with that apprentice was simply a pretext. If they hadn't expelled you for that, it would have been something else.' Richard looked back at me. 'A similar story with you. You only achieved the status of auxiliary because of your friends in the Order of the Star. They would never have allowed you to become a full Keeper.'

'The Council doesn't like us,' I said. 'What are you getting at?'

'Unlike the Council, I do not believe in wasting talent,' Richard said. 'The two of you are highly competent. Your skills were being under-utilised. I viewed that as an opportunity.' He looked at Anne. 'I hope that answers your question.'

Anne hesitated. 'I suppose.'

'Good. One last thing.'

Here it comes, I thought.

'From time to time, I will have additional tasks for you. When I do, I will send someone with instructions. I will expect them to be carried out promptly and thoroughly. Is that understood?'

It was what I'd been afraid of, and I didn't have an answer. There was no point arguing. I stayed silent, and so did Anne.

'Then if there's nothing else, you're free to go.'

I looked at Richard.

Richard sighed. 'Yes, Alex, you are free to go wherever you wish. Stay in Wales, return to London, travel to another country if you like. As long as you fulfil the duties assigned to you, then where you spend your time is your own decision.' Richard glanced at the clock. 'Morden will be expecting the two of you at the War Rooms tomorrow at nine a.m. In the meantime, I have another appointment.'

We looked at Richard, then at each other.

'You can go now,' Richard said.

We left. The construct was waiting for us in the next room, empty eyes and an unchanging smile. 'Please follow me.'

As we walked back through the corridors, I searched through futures of us staying in the mansion, scanning for any signs of danger. Nothing showed, but I still couldn't help wonder whether Richard was going to just let us walk away.

'Is that it?' Anne asked.

We passed an intersection and I glanced left and right. 'For now,' I said, keeping my voice down.

'I was expecting . . .' Anne said.

'Expecting what?'

'I don't know. Something worse.'

'We're not out yet,' I said. Ahead of us, the dama kept to its steady pace. I wasn't sure if it was even hearing us at all.

The dama reached the front door, opened it, then stood with its hands clasped, looking at us with its empty smile. Through the open doorway I could see green grass and trees. The cold January air blew in, making me shiver.

I walked out through the door. The front of the mansion held a porch, with three concentric steps leading up to the doorway and pillars supporting a balcony above. Beyond the porch was nothing, not even a path. A grassy slope dipped down into a valley before rising up to a treeline. Around us, the green hills of Wales rose up into an overcast sky.

Anne followed me out and I walked down the steps. I was still looking through the futures in which I turned and went back inside, looking for any signs of danger in the mansion behind us.

The attack came from ahead.

A green ray stabbed from the trees on the other side of the valley, down towards where I would have been if I'd taken that last step onto the grass. I jerked back just in time, seeing the air flash sea-green an arm's length away, and I had an instant to identify the spell before I was darting back for the cover of the doorway. A second ray cut me off, passing between us to strike the side of the door, and I saw Anne's eyes go wide as a whole section of the masonry puffed into nothingness, then Anne jumped back and I had to twist to dodge another ray which hit the pillar supporting the left-hand side of the porch and turned the bottom half of it to dust.

With a creaking groan, the porch collapsed. The natural reaction would have been to jump backwards, but I knew that would leave me exposed to my attacker so instead I darted forward under the falling stone. Bricks smashed onto the steps all around, then I was through just as an avalanche of stone and masonry crashed down behind me.

All of a sudden everything was still. Choking dust filled the air. 'Alex!' Anne shouted from inside.

'I'm okay!' I shouted back. 'Stay there!'

Anne stayed quiet. The left side of the porch was a pile of broken rubble, shielding me from the line of fire, and the jagged remains of the balcony ended abruptly overhead. I crouched behind the debris, looking ahead to see if I'd get shot at if I stuck my head up. For a moment, shadowy images of violence played through the futures, then they were gone.

I checked again, then stood up with a grunt. 'We're clear.'

Anne appeared in what was left of the doorway. She'd dodged back into the entrance hall when the balcony had fallen, and now picked her way over the rubble. 'Look,' she said, nodding back into the hall.

I did. The dama was still standing there, still looking at us, still smiling. The balcony's collapse had ripped one of the double doors off its hinges, but the rubble had missed the dama by a few feet. 'Why's it just standing there?' Anne asked.

'It's programmed to wait for us to leave, then close the door,' I said. I pointed at the remains of the door beneath the rubble. 'It'll sit there until someone gives it new orders or until it runs out of batteries.'

Anne looked at the construct and shivered.

A movement in the futures made me turn. Richard had appeared in the hallway. He looked at the ruins of his front porch, then up at me. 'Your doing?'

'No.'

'Then whose?'

I wanted to ask if he didn't know everything already, but thought better of it. 'Oh, I don't know,' I said. 'Who lives around here, uses disintegration spells and really doesn't like me?'

Richard's eyes narrowed and I felt a flash of fear, but the next moment his face was smooth again. 'Move along, please.'

'Are you going to——?'

'You are not my Chosen, Alex.' Richard's voice was level, but his eyes stayed fixed on me. 'Do not take liberties.'

Anne looked at me, and I held my tongue. We walked away down the hillside. The dama watched us go.

2

Only when we were most of the way down into the valley did I begin to relax. I'd searched for danger in all the futures that I could see and found nothing. 'I suppose that was the something worse,' Anne said at last.

'I think you're being optimistic.'

A cold wind blew across the hillside, making the grass ripple and Anne's hair flutter, and I shivered. The fight hadn't been long enough for me to warm up. 'Keep scanning with your lifesight,' I said. 'We're not out yet.'

'Was that Rachel?'

'Safe bet,' I said. Rachel is the other survivor of Richard's apprentices, though she goes by Deleo now. Disintegration is her speciality and she *really* hates me. Anne's never met Rachel, but she's heard the stories.

'Why didn't you see her coming earlier?'

I looked at Anne and she coloured slightly. 'I didn't mean it like that,' she added. 'It's just that you can usually—'

'Spot things further ahead,' I said, and sighed. 'Yeah, that's one of the problems with divination. The crazier someone is, the less predictable they are.'

'I thought Rachel was Richard's Chosen,' Anne said. 'If he wanted us here . . .'

'Yeah,' I said. Now that I thought about it, that flash of anger had been the only moment today that Richard hadn't seemed in control. Maybe Richard had ordered Rachel *not* to attack us, and she'd disobeyed. If that was true, it was the first crack we'd been able to find in Richard's forces. Was there some way to exploit that?

'You were thinking of using that knife on him, weren't you?' Anne asked.

'Was it that obvious?'

'I saw your adrenalin levels,' Anne said. 'You were gearing up for a fight, then . . .'

'It wasn't the right time,' I said. 'Maybe it'll never be, but . . .' I shook my head. 'What did you see when you looked at him?'

Anne frowned, diverted. 'He's . . . strange.'

I looked at Anne. 'Strange how?'

'He's human,' Anne said. 'But his body seems . . . enhanced, somehow? It's like there's more output than there should be input. I'd have guessed it was a boosted metabolism or something, but those accelerate ageing, and he looks like the opposite if anything. From his bones, he has to be fifty at least, but he's got the cellular and muscular structure of a man of thirty.'

'Longevity magic?'

'I think so, but not one I've seen.' Anne looked up at me. 'You never did tell us Richard's magic type.'

'That's because he doesn't give it away,' I said. 'Uses items and general spells . . .' I tailed off as a movement in the futures caught my attention. We were halfway up the other side of the valley and almost to the trees, but as I looked ahead I saw that the woods we were about to enter weren't empty. 'We're about to have company,' I said. 'Someone in the trees.'

Anne looked upwards towards the treeline, narrowing her eyes slightly. 'Hostile?'

'No, or I would have seen earlier. What can you see?'

'It's just one,' Anne said after a moment's pause. 'Male, early twenties. He's healthy I think . . . oh.'

'What?'

'He's got an artificial leg,' Anne said. 'Left side from the knee down. Might be a construct graft.'

'Anyone you know?'

'I'd remember something like that.'

I'd had time to check out the futures more thoroughly, and I was as certain as I could be that the person waiting for us wasn't here to fight. 'Then let's see what he has to say.'

The guy waiting for us wasn't hiding. As we entered the woods, he stepped out from behind a tree, keeping his hands in plain view. Tall and athletic, with blue eyes and a crew cut, he had the look of a fighter but wasn't carrying any weapons or magic items that I could see. There was a woven bracelet on his wrist. 'My boss wants to talk to you,' he told the two of us.

Anne had come to a stop and was staring at the guy. I wasn't quite sure why – okay, he could have been good-looking, but I wouldn't have thought Anne was the kind to get caught up on that. 'You had anything to do with that?' I asked, jerking my head back towards the distant debris across the valley.

'Wouldn't be hanging around if I had.'

'So what, you stood around and watched?' I said dryly.

Crew Cut shrugged. 'You did all right.'

'Who are you?' Anne asked.

'Just the messenger.' Crew Cut nodded back over his shoulder. 'My boss is a quarter-mile that way. He says you'll be able to find him.'

I noticed that he hadn't asked who either of us were. I

was more interested in how he'd known that we'd be coming here. 'And how did you—?' I began.

'I know you,' Anne said suddenly.

Crew Cut looked back at Anne, then to my surprise dropped his eyes. 'Two and a half years ago,' Anne said. 'It was you, wasn't it?'

I glanced at Anne. 'You know this guy?'

'So do you,' Anne said. 'He tried to kill you.'

'Doesn't narrow it down much.'

'As in, more than once.'

'You're going to have to be more specific.'

'Three years ago.'

'More specific.'

'In the summer.'

'More specific.'

'Oh, come on,' Anne said in exasperation. 'Your memory's not *that* bad. The Nightstalkers. Remember?'

'I don't—' I started to say, then stopped. The Nightstalkers had been a group of adept vigilantes looking for vengeance on Dark mages in general and Richard's apprentices in particular, and by the time they arrived on the scene, the only apprentices of Richard still alive had been Rachel and me. They did okay against me and really badly against Rachel. Most of them had died in the basement of the mansion behind us.

But now that I thought about it, I hadn't seen *all* of them die. A seeker adept called Lee had escaped. And there'd been another, a weapons and explosives expert, who'd gone by the name of . . .

'Kyle,' I said, and saw the slight reaction on Crew Cut's face. 'That was your name, wasn't it?'

'Still is,' Kyle said.

'Okay,' I said. 'I'll admit, having you talking to me rather than trying to cut me in half with a sword is an improvement. However, given that the *last* time I saw you, you were trying to shoot me, I'm not too inclined to follow anywhere you lead.'

'Not just you,' Anne said. 'He nearly killed me as well.'

A trace of embarrassment showed on Kyle's face. 'That was an accident.'

'You put a bomb on the roof of the flat we were sleeping in!'

'It wasn't aimed at you,' Kyle said.

'Yeah, you're kind of just digging yourself deeper at this point,' I said.

Kyle exhaled slightly. 'All right,' he said. 'I'm not going to say I'm sorry and that I didn't mean it.' He turned to Anne and seemed to brace himself. 'But I am sorry about planting that bomb. It was wrong, and I knew it was wrong when I did it. You want to come after me, I'm not going to blame you.'

Anne stopped, looking at Kyle in surprise. 'Wait. You think I'd want to . . . ?'

Kyle didn't answer. 'Okay,' I said. 'I think Anne and I need to have a word.'

Kyle stood with his arms folded as I touched Anne's shoulder to lead her away through the trees. 'Is he telling the truth?' I asked once Kyle was out of earshot.

'I think so,' Anne said. One of the side effects of Anne's abilities is to make her pretty good at reading people. Few people are cold-blooded enough to lie to your face without tensing up. 'You don't think the Nightstalkers are still around?'

'No, they're gone.' The leader of the Nightstalkers had

been an adept named Will; he'd died in that mansion, and without him, the group had fallen apart. 'I think I know which boss he's talking about. You haven't met him, but his word is good. Do you want to go?'

'With Kyle?' Anne thought for a second, then shrugged. 'Well, he said sorry. That's more than most of the people who've tried to hurt me have ever done.'

We walked back to the adept who'd once tried to kill me. 'Okay, Kyle,' I said. 'Let's go.'

We walked through woods and across fields, tall grass brushing against my trousers as we picked our way between gnarled trees. The air was bitterly cold and my coat did little to keep away the chill. Anne stayed close by my side, quick and alert, and from her reactions I was able to tell exactly where the person ahead came into range of her lifesight. The trees opened up into a small clearing, and standing at the centre, a man was waiting for us.

Cinder is as tall as me and a good deal heavier. Not much of it is fat; he's got the look of a weightlifter, with a thick neck and a barrel chest, though it isn't his muscles that make him dangerous. He's also Rachel's partner, but while Rachel is crazier than a coked-out wolverine, Cinder is trustworthy, more or less. Piss him off and he'll kill you, but his word is good and if he'd invited us to talk, I was pretty sure we were safe.

'Verus,' Cinder said in his deep voice.

'Cinder.'

Cinder looked at Anne, waiting. 'You can call me Anne,' Anne said.

Cinder nodded. Most people would have missed the fact that by waiting for Anne to introduce herself, Cinder was showing good manners. It's a point of etiquette among Dark mages to only call each other by a name that they've told you. 'Need to talk,' Cinder told me. 'Alone.'

I glanced at Anne. She gave a small motion, and I started walking.

'Wait here,' Cinder said to Kyle as I reached him. Kyle nodded and Cinder turned to walk by my side. We disappeared into the trees, leaving Kyle and Anne alone in the clearing.

'First things first,' I said once we were out of earshot of the two younger spellcasters. 'Did I miss something, or is Kyle working for you now?'

Cinder nodded.

I thought back to the last I'd seen of Kyle, lying in the basement of Richard's mansion, crippled and cornered. Cinder had warned me off, and I'd taken the out. I hadn't had any reason to believe that Kyle was still alive. 'Why?'

'Bonded.'

I stared at Cinder in surprise. 'You *bonded* him?'

Bonding is an odd and very specific tradition among Dark mages. If a Dark mage defeats someone in combat, then he can offer to bond them. If the defeated party says no, they're killed. If they accept, they become the Dark mage's servant. Under Dark customs they're considered property of their owner, and from the point of view of the Council they'd be a slave, but calling the relationship master–slave isn't quite accurate. A bonded servant is closer to an apprentice or a junior partner – if a Dark mage chooses to bond someone, it's a sign they respect them enough to want to keep them around.

Not many Dark mages take bonded servants. The only ones who still follow the tradition are the more martial and honour-orientated types, and they're a minority. Of course, now that I thought about it, that described Cinder pretty well, so maybe I shouldn't have been surprised.

But there was one thing I couldn't understand. 'Don't you have to agree to be a bonded servant?'

'Yeah.'

'Kyle and the rest of those adepts were on a crusade to kill as many Dark mages as they could,' I said. 'How the hell did you persuade him to say yes?'

Cinder shrugged.

'What's that supposed to mean?'

'Ask him.' Cinder looked at me. 'You done?'

We'd walked fifty yards or so. 'All right,' I said. Cinder wouldn't have called me here unless he had something important to say. 'Let's hear it.'

Cinder stopped and turned to face me. 'You're working for Morden.'

'Yeah, that's not exactly a secret.'

'So's Del.'

I raised an eyebrow. 'Thought she reported to Richard.'

'Less now.'

'Huh,' I said. The last I'd heard, Del – a.k.a Rachel – had been first among Richard's servants. For her to be reporting to Morden sounded a lot like a demotion. All of a sudden, her trying to kill me made a bit more sense.

Though come to think of it, of all the people I'd laid eyes on today, the only one who *hadn't* tried to kill me or do something horrible to me at some point or other was Anne.

My life is really messed up.

'So what about you?' I said.

Cinder raised an eyebrow.

'You working for Morden again?'

'If I have to.'

'You don't sound that enthusiastic.'

'I'm with Del,' Cinder said simply.

And that was Cinder's problem in a nutshell. 'So I gathered,' I said. 'Were you around when she took that shot at me?'

Cinder shook his head.

'And I'm guessing you're not here to finish the job.' I folded my arms. 'So what do you want?'

'Split her from Richard.'

I stared at Cinder. 'Are you out of your mind?'

Cinder just looked at me.

'In case you didn't notice, your *partner* just tried to turn me into a dust cloud,' I said. I almost said 'girlfriend' instead of 'partner', but changed my mind at the last second. 'And you want me to do her favours?'

'Tried talking,' Cinder said. 'Didn't work.'

'What, and you think she'll listen to me?' I was pissed off now. Only a month ago, I'd had Shireen tell me the same thing. She'd been Rachel's best and closest friend while she was alive, and now both she and Cinder were expecting the same impossible task. 'I have met Deleo exactly twice in the past year. The last time she saw me, she didn't make it five minutes before trying to kill me. *This* time she didn't make it five *seconds*. Expecting me to talk to her is one of the stupidest plans I've ever heard in my life.'

'Isn't anyone else.'

I looked away, frustrated and angry. Rachel showed up and tried to murder me, and now not only was Cinder expecting me to put that aside, he wanted me to help her.

I had more enemies than I could handle in a lifetime, and both Shireen and Cinder were expecting me to pick a fight with yet another. 'Maybe you should *find* someone else.'

'You're smart and you've known her the longest,' Cinder said. 'Besides. Doing shit that's supposed to be impossible is your thing.'

'Doesn't feel much like it at the moment,' I muttered. 'What's in it for me?'

'You help Del; I'll watch your back,' Cinder said. 'Long as it takes.' He looked at me. 'Well?'

I wanted to say no. I didn't have the slightest clue how I was going to get Rachel away from Richard. I didn't even know how to stop her from trying to kill me on sight. Shireen (or Shireen's spirit, or whatever that creature who'd spoken to me in Elsewhere had been) had asked me to redeem Rachel, and I had no idea how to do that either.

Except . . . Shireen had *also* told me that if I didn't succeed, then I was going to die. And given where she'd got that prediction from, I had a nasty feeling that it wasn't the kind I could dodge. Which meant that I really didn't have a choice: I was going to have to help Rachel anyway.

If I was going to do an impossible task, I'd need all the help I could get. I've fought both with and against Cinder, and I much prefer the former. 'Fine,' I said. 'I'll try. But if you want me to get anywhere, I'm going to need your help.'

Cinder nodded, turned and started walking. And as simple as that, I had an ally. *I wonder how long it'll last.*

Anne and Kyle had been talking quietly; they fell silent as we appeared through the trees. Cinder drew Kyle to his side with a jerk of his head, then opened up a gate between the trees and stepped through into darkness. Kyle followed. The gate closed behind them and we were left alone.

'What did he want?' Anne asked.

'The same thing that Shireen did. I'll tell you about it on the way.' I looked at Anne. 'You ready?'

Anne gave me a nod. I took out a gate stone and began the process of opening a gate to take us back to London. I'd faced my enemies. Now I had to face my friends.

We made the journey back to London in silence.

Now that we were away from Cinder and Kyle, my thoughts kept going back to Richard. I suppose, to an outsider, it might seem a little bizarre that I was worrying about Richard and not the people who'd actually attacked us. Vihaela had gone for Anne and Rachel had come far too close to assassinating me, while all Richard had done was give us some orders. But Richard frightened me in a way that Rachel and Vihaela couldn't. That mansion is a place of horror to me, and being connected to it, even at one remove, felt like all of my old nightmares come to life. Maybe Richard hadn't seemed to ask much, but then, it had been the same way all those years ago. One of the lessons my apprenticeship taught me is that it's the things with no price tag that end up costing you the most.

Anne stayed at my side but didn't speak. Anne can be very quiet sometimes and she was quiet now, her eyes downcast and shadowed. I knew it wasn't the first time that she'd been forced to work for a master that she'd rather avoid, but from her expression it was hard to know what she thought of it. Maybe she saw it as just more of the same. I hoped not. I hated that Anne was involved in this almost as much as I hated that I was, and I wasn't sure she was ready for what was coming.

A gate stone took us to a park in Camden. Variam had told us to meet him near Great Portland Street, and so we walked south across the wide expanse of Regent's Park, skirting the edges of London Zoo where birds roosted in the aviary. Even in the winter cold, the park was crowded, tourists and locals strolling along the paths and sitting on the benches. The place that Variam had directed us to was on the other side of Marylebone Road, next to the big hotel, and we walked around to the front of the building.

And there was Variam, pacing up and down the pavement, a small wiry brown-skinned figure wearing street clothes and a turban. He made a beeline for us as soon as he saw us. 'You okay?' he asked Anne.

'For now,' Anne said quietly.

Variam looked at me. 'We're fine,' I said.

Variam nodded and then to my surprise gave me a quick hug and clapped me on the back. 'Glad you made it.'

'Uh, sure,' I said. Displays of affection make me uncomfortable, though I'm pretty sure that's less to do with my personal issues and more to do with me just being English. From the corner of my eye, I could see that Anne was hiding a smile. 'You're all right?'

'Come on, let's get out of the street.' Vari started towards the hotel. 'Too many prying eyes.'

The inside of the building was white and antiseptic, with the vaguely soulless look that all hotels seem to have. We took the lift up to the sixth floor. 'So what happened?' I asked Variam once the doors had closed.

'When?'

'Back on Boxing Day.'

Variam looked startled. 'That long ago?'

'We've spent the last month being hunted,' I told him. 'It was kind of hard to get news bulletins.'

'Yeah, that might not have changed as much as you think,' Variam said. 'I wasn't kidding about being watched. That escape of yours from Canary Wharf got a *lot* of attention and it turns out Keepers don't like it when you make them look stupid. You were right up there on the most wanted list.'

'I'm hoping not any more.'

'The notices went out, but right now you're kind of the mage equivalent of O. J. Simpson. Might want to keep your head down.'

I grimaced. Meeting Morden in front of the War Rooms tomorrow was really not going to help with keeping a low profile.

The lift stopped with a *ding* and we walked out into a carpeted hallway. Variam led us to the left. 'What about you?' Anne asked.

'Oh, I was fine.'

'Didn't sound like you were that fine,' I said. The last I'd heard, Variam had been in custody.

Variam shrugged. 'Got knocked about a bit. Could have been worse. At least Anne got away.'

'Thanks to you,' Anne said.

'Eh. Landis sorted it out.'

Variam came to a halt in front of one of the rooms which looked exactly the same as all the others. 'By the way,' I said. 'What's with the hotel?'

'What do you mean?'

'I thought you were living with Landis.'

'Course.'

'Then why . . . ?'

'It's not for me,' Variam said. 'It's for Luna.'

I looked at Variam, puzzled. 'Wait,' Anne said. 'You said she got out safely.'

Until a day and a half ago, Anne and I had been on the run from the agents of a member of the Senior Council, a mage called Levistus. We'd stayed far enough ahead to force a stalemate, which had been broken when Levistus's principal agent, a slimy little bastard called Barrayar, rigged Luna's flat with explosives while she slept. I'd shown up ready for a last stand, but before Barrayar could finish me off, Morden had stepped in. He'd appointed Anne and me as his liaisons, giving us a place with the Council and putting our death sentence on hold. I hadn't had the chance to see or speak to Luna since then. If something had happened to her . . .

'She did,' Variam said. 'But she wasn't exactly going to stay in that flat afterwards, was she?'

'So can we see her?'

'Yeah,' Variam said. 'About that.'

'What?'

'There might be issues.'

'What kind of issues?'

Variam hesitated, then seemed to give up and knocked on the door. 'Hey,' he called. 'Luna?'

Silence.

'Luna! You there?'

I gave Anne a questioning look. Anne nodded, and from her manner I knew that Luna was inside and unhurt. But she wasn't opening the door either.

Variam took out a keycard and inserted it into the door's

slot. A light flashed green, and he turned the handle, but the door opened only an inch before coming to a halt with a *clunk*. 'Oh, for—' Variam muttered, then raised his voice. 'Take the chain off!'

Silence.

Where is she? I mouthed at Anne.

Other side, Anne mouthed back.

'I'm not in the mood for this shit, all right?' Variam called through the door.

'Go away!' Luna shouted back.

I raised my eyebrows. It was Luna's voice all right, but I'd been hoping for a slightly happier reception.

'Anne and Alex are back, you dumbass!' Variam called.

'I know!'

'Then open the bloody door!'

Silence.

'Screw this,' Variam said. Fire mages tend to have short tempers, and Vari is not an exception. 'How about I just burn a hole and we'll see if—'

'Vari?' I touched Variam lightly on the shoulder. 'Maybe let me try?'

Variam glowered but moved aside. I stepped up to the door. 'Luna?' I said. The door had opened just a crack before the latch had caught it, and through the gap I could see a sliver of wall.

There was no answer, but I could feel Luna listening. 'Are you okay?' I said. I kept my voice gentle.

A pause. 'Yes,' Luna said in a small voice.

'You got out of your flat? You weren't chased?'

'No.'

'Good.' I paused. 'Can we come in?'

Silence.

'You know, it's not that comfortable out here,' I said.

'I don't want to talk to anyone,' Luna said. She sounded miserable.

'Okay . . .' I said. 'Is there a reason?'

'No, it's just—' Luna's voice broke. 'Just go away. Please.'

I looked back at Anne and Variam. Variam lifted his hands with a shrug.

All of a sudden, I wasn't sure what to do. Maybe I'd been naïve, but I'd been expecting Luna to be happy to see me. Okay, the *way* in which I'd made my return hadn't been the best, but I'm used to Luna wanting me around. Having her tell me to go away hurt in an unexpected way.

And the fact that she was doing it at all was confusing as hell. Luna is *tough*, and I've seen her jump into full-on battles without hesitating. I really wasn't used to her acting like this. 'All right,' I said. 'If you change your mind, call us, okay?'

No answer. I walked back to the others. 'Told you,' Variam said.

'You have any clue what's going on?' I asked Variam.

'I might have an idea,' Anne said quietly. 'Give me some time alone with her?'

'You think she'll talk to you?'

'Most people do.'

I thought briefly. I still wasn't sure what was going on, but if anyone could get Luna to talk, Anne could. 'All right,' I said. 'We won't go far.'

With all the chaos of the last few days, I hadn't had much chance to eat. There was a Pizza Express a few minutes' walk from the hotel and Vari and I took shelter inside from the cold winter air.

'So,' I said once we'd ordered. 'What have we missed?'

'A lot,' Variam said gloomily. 'After you and Anne were chased away, the Keepers tore your flats apart trying to figure out where you'd gone, and then they posted sentries waiting for you to come back. Took them weeks to figure out you weren't, and by then all this shit with the Dark mages had started up again. Basically, the White Rose thing – you remember that?'

'I was right in the *middle* of that, Vari.'

'Yeah, well, turns out that big raid didn't get all of them. There was a guy who used to be third in command or something who got away, and after Marannis died he laid low for a bit, then tried to start the whole thing up again. People find out about it, everyone wants to go in and take him out, but the Council tell us to wait. So we're waiting, and everyone's getting pissed off, but the Council keep telling us we're not authorised. Then Morden takes a bunch of Dark mages, goes in and cleans it all up. Frees the kids, seizes the base, everything. So the Council try to prosecute him for it, and we're like, what, we're going to bring a charge against the guy for *breaking* a slavery ring? And the prosecution falls apart and now everyone's listening to Morden even more than before.'

'Mm,' I said. If what Variam was saying was accurate, it was a mix of good news and bad. White Rose had been a particularly nasty organisation and I was glad to hear it wasn't going to be reborn from the ashes any time soon, and from the sound of it Levistus might have taken a hit too, which made it that much less likely that he'd be in a position to come after me. On the other hand, it sounded as though what Levistus had lost, Morden had gained. Apparently Morden had been busy.

It also occurred to me that Variam would never have been able to summarise political developments this well when I'd first known him. Maybe fire magic wasn't the only thing that Landis had been teaching.

'And just so you know,' Variam added, 'you and Anne got appointed right *after* that, when Morden was still in the news. So now everyone's convinced you were the ones who helped him set it up.'

That brought me back to earth with a bump. 'Are you serious?'

Variam nodded.

'We were getting chased around half the countries in the world! How the hell would we be helping Morden? We literally didn't have *time*!'

'Yeah, well, far as everyone knows, you just disappeared,' Variam said. 'So now they're bringing up all the rumours about you from before, and saying how they always knew you were bad news, and how you must have been working for Morden and Richard all along and this is him paying you off.'

'Jesus,' I muttered. This was just going from bad to worse. 'They giving you any trouble for being connected to me?'

Variam gave me a look. 'Think you should be worrying about yourself.'

'Wouldn't do much good,' I said. It came out more bleakly than I intended. The Council hated me, Richard's faction was using me and I couldn't see a way to get away from either of them.

A shift in the futures made me look up to see Anne threading her way between the tables towards us. 'So?' Variam demanded as Anne reached us.

'Luna's . . . not doing so well,' Anne said, sitting down.

'Is this shell shock from what happened at her flat?' I asked.

'Not directly,' Anne said. She looked at Variam. 'Have you two talked since Christmas?'

Variam shrugged. 'Not much.'

'Why not?'

'I dunno.'

'Vari . . .'

'What?' Variam said. 'Look, ever since her journeyman test, she's been moody. I tried calling but she was just really weird. After a while I figured I might as well leave her alone.'

Anne gave Variam an exasperated look. 'What did you mean, "not directly"?' I asked.

'It's nothing to do with that attack of Barrayar's,' Anne said. 'Luna's just had problems.'

'With what?'

'She didn't go into detail,' Anne said. 'I think it's to do with her graduation and what happened afterwards. Most especially, it's to do with you.' Anne looked at me. 'I think you're the one she really needs to talk to.'

I thought about it for a second, and decided it sounded more believable than my earlier theory. Luna's very good at handling physical dangers – she thinks that they won't touch her, and she's usually right – but she's not so good with emotional ones. All the times that I'd seen her really off-balance, it had been because of something along those lines. 'What if I went there now?'

Anne hesitated. 'I don't think that's a good idea.'

'Why?'

'I promised her I'd give her space.' Anne thought for a

second. 'I think she'll come around in a day or two. I'll come back and try again.'

'Okay,' I said slowly. As I looked at her, I was struck by how sure of herself Anne looked. Dealing with these sorts of problems seemed to be natural to her, and I wondered just how many of Anne's skills had been ones she'd learned because she was forced to, not because she wanted to. Anne's a skilled healer and combat mage, but maybe given a choice, she would have ended up spending her life dealing with things like this . . .

But Variam had other things on his mind. 'Okay, fine, she's got issues,' he said. 'You two have got bigger problems. What are you going to do?'

'There isn't much we *can* do,' I said.

'So what, you're going to do what Morden says?'

There was a challenging note to Variam's question. It pissed me off a little. 'We don't exactly have much choice.'

'I thought the idea was to work against Richard,' Variam said. 'Not for him.'

'I'm not on Richard's side,' I snapped. 'But we can't turn on him unless we're damn sure we can make it stick.'

'And until then?' Variam said. 'You're going to work for a Dark mage?'

'We worked for Jagadev,' Anne said.

'That was different.'

'How?'

'He wasn't the Dark representative on the bloody British Council, was he? Anyway, we didn't have a choice.'

'Neither do we,' Anne said quietly.

I was silent. Jagadev (or Lord Jagadev, as he likes to be known) is a rakshasa, and one of the more influential magical creatures currently operating in the British Isles. After Anne and Variam broke away from the Dark mage who'd been holding them prisoner, they'd been alone, with no allies and few relatives, and Jagadev had taken them in. Although I'd never been able to prove it, I had circumstantial evidence that Jagadev was the *reason* that they had so few relatives. I hadn't told Anne or Vari that particular detail, mostly because I was sure that if I did, Variam would immediately try to hunt Jagadev down and kill him, which would in all probability end in Vari's death. When you're a diviner, you have to face up to the fact that if you give out information, you're responsible for the consequences.

But all that had been a long time ago, and no matter how I tried to justify it, I couldn't help feeling uncomfortable about the fact that I still hadn't told Anne and Vari what I knew. The awkward truth was that I'd been putting off dealing with it. I didn't know what would happen when I opened that particular can of worms and it was always easier to kick the can down the road.

While I'd been lost in my thoughts, Anne and Variam had been arguing. 'Turning Morden down isn't an option,' I said, interrupting Variam. 'First, he's made it clear that if we do, he'll kill all our friends and family. Second, that appointment of Morden's is the only thing keeping Levistus's death sentence off our necks. So even if we took him on and somehow won – which we wouldn't – then it'd just put us right back on the Council's hit list.'

'Then what are you going to do?' Variam said.

Neither Anne nor I had an answer, and as the seconds ticked away, I felt the pressure of just how hopeless our situation was. The pizzas arrived, but Variam's last question had killed the conversation and we ate in silence. Once we were done, we paid the bill and left. Vari headed back to

Landis's house in Edinburgh, and Anne and I headed back to Wales.

Both Anne and I had lost our old homes. Mine had been gutted by fire just before Christmas, while Anne's had been repossessed when the Keepers had shown up to arrest her. For now I was staying in my safe house in Wales, and with nowhere else to go, Anne had stuck with me. My bank accounts were getting low – weeks on the run will do that to you – but I knew I could build them up again with a little time. Anne, on the other hand, was almost flat broke. Life mages have their own ways of making money, but they can't do it as easily as diviners, particularly if they have scruples. For now, the house in Wales was the best we had, and if the Keepers knew we'd returned, they weren't raiding it. At least, not yet.

Later that evening, I shut the front door behind me and walked out into the darkness. My little house in Wales is at the end of a deserted valley, and it's far enough away from any towns that it's the next thing to pitch-black. Only the tiniest trace of light filtered down from the overcast sky, leaving the valley a mass of shadows. The nearby river rushed and splashed, steady and reassuring, its babble drowning out the sound of my footsteps and those of the local wildlife. Anne was back inside making dinner, but I was alone in the cold and the dark.

I walked absently, hands in my pockets, picking my way along the path in the darkness. Variam's question kept going through my head. What *could* we do? I took a breath and let it out, trying to let the silence of the empty landscape calm my thoughts. I needed to figure out an answer.

There are four basic responses to a threat. Fight, flee,

deceive, submit. Fleeing was out. Anne and I had tried that, and Levistus and Barrayar had dragged us back. Morden had made it clear that he'd do the same thing. Anne and I could escape eventually – maybe Luna as well – but the price would be the lives of everyone we cared about. I wasn't willing to make that trade.

Submitting was out as well. I'd decided a long time ago that I wasn't going to become like Richard. Surrendering to him, letting him decide who I was and what I was going to be, would just be an uglier and slower form of dying. I still wouldn't be *me*, at least not any of the parts of me that I really cared about. I could tell that Anne was still holding out the hope that working for Richard and Morden wouldn't be so bad, but I didn't believe it. Whatever they wanted us to do, I knew it was eventually going to lead to something horrible. The only question was when.

Fighting was, if not hopeless, then pretty close. Both Richard and Morden had enough power to crush me in any straight-up contest without breaking a sweat. But that assumed it *was* a straight-up contest. Like a lot of kids, I grew up with stories of heroes in shining armour who ride up to the bad guy and challenge him to a duel. I'm nothing like the heroes in the stories – I'd rather hide than go into battle, and most of my time in fights has been spent running away. But when it comes to combat, stealth and surprise are the great equalisers. Richard might be powerful, but Anne had already confirmed that he was still human. A knife through the ribs would see him dead enough. The trouble would be getting it there.

The final choice – deceive – seemed at first glance to be the best. Pretend to follow Morden and Richard's orders, then bring them down from within. It was an obvious plan . . . and that was the problem. If it was obvious to me, then it had to be obvious to them as well. Morden and Richard knew we had absolutely no reason to be loyal. They had to have anticipated that we'd betray them, and while I didn't know what they'd done to prepare for that, I knew that there'd be something.

So while flight and submission were out, fighting and deception were almost as bad, and I still didn't have a plan. I remembered that last conversation I'd had with Arachne, back in December. Maybe I needed to look further afield.

I sighed. My feet had taken me far down the path, away from Anne, and I turned back towards the house, its windows the only light in the darkness. Tomorrow we would face Morden.

3

The War Rooms are the nerve centre of the Council, and the heart of Light power in Britain. They're a vast tunnel network beneath London, rooms and hallways spider-webbing outward for miles, bored through the clay and rock. There's enough space for every British Light mage of Britain to live down there, and from time to time I think they actually have, but nowadays it's famous not as a fortress but as the Light Council's seat of government. The Senior and Junior Councils are based there, and so is the great bureaucracy that administers all mage business in the country. Back when I was working with Caldera as a Keeper auxiliary, I'd visit the place maybe once a month. Now I was a full Keeper, and Morden's affiliate. I wondered what kind of reception I'd get.

Anne and I arrived a few minutes early and waited out in the street. Pigeons pecked on the pavement. Every now and then a black cab would drive down the road, turning off onto the one-way system at the end, but for some reason they never seemed to stop.

Morden arrived exactly on the stroke of nine o'clock. 'Anne. Verus,' he said as he walked up. 'I'm glad to see you're on time.'

Morden is a Dark mage, one of Richard's oldest allies, and – as of last year – the first Dark mage ever to sit upon the Light Council of Britain. He's dark-haired and dark-eyed, with smooth features, and he looks a lot younger than he is. He smiles a lot, as though at some joke that only he can see.

Even without his political power, Morden is in the top ten of the most deadly mages I know. Part of what makes him so dangerous is that he usually doesn't reveal what he's capable of. The last time I'd met him had been two days ago, when he'd told me that we were working for him. I'd told him 'no' and he'd beaten me to a pulp. I'd got the message.

'You're here on your own,' I said. Morden passed us without slowing and I followed, falling into step beside him. Anne stayed a couple of paces behind.

'You seem surprised,' Morden said.

'I was expecting an entourage.'

Morden smiled. 'That would be you.'

We passed through the surface building which held the shaft down to the War Rooms. There were two Council security men on the door; they said nothing as we walked into the lift.

'Why are we here?' Anne asked once the doors had closed and we'd begun descending.

'To take up your duties,' Morden said. 'You, for instance, are meeting Hieronymus from the healer corps.'

'And what about me?' I said. I couldn't help noticing that Anne was only two steps from Morden. If she went for him, he'd have very little time to react. I could sense spells layered within Morden's body, and if there's any other magic type that can withstand the touch of a life mage, it's death magic, but Anne is very good at what she does . . .

Anne's eyes met mine, and I knew she was thinking the same thing. I glanced up at the corner of the lift to see the half-sphere of a security camera. *Later.*

'You'll be working as my personal aide,' Morden said. 'When you aren't otherwise occupied with your new duties as a Keeper.'

The doors opened and we stepped out into a large rectangular chamber. There was no indication of how far down we were, but I knew it was a long way. The walls were made of grey stone, flecked with tiny white sparks which gleamed in the light, and on the far side were more lifts; one had just opened, and people were filing out. There were a set of security gates to the left, with a small queue and a team of Council security questioning them one at a time, but Morden walked straight past and a gate swung open at his approach. The security men gave us flat looks but didn't get in our way. The gate swung shut behind Morden, and Anne had to hop forward to avoid being caught.

'So I'm your PA now?' I asked Morden.

'So to speak,' Morden said. Another mage in formal robes passed us in the hall, and Morden gave him a nod and a smile. The other mage nodded cautiously back, then swivelled to stare once he thought we weren't watching.

I looked sideways at Morden. I don't know much about Light Council politics, but I do know that the position of personal aide to a Council member is high status. One of my old acquaintances, Lyle, is the aide to a Senior Council member called Undaaris, and getting there had taken him fifteen years. 'That seems like a very senior position.'

'You're welcome.'

'As in, the kind of position that'd normally be given to someone with a little more experience.'

'I have every confidence that you will be up to the challenge.'

I decided to abandon subtlety. 'You've already got a Chosen. Why me?'

'Despite Onyx's many and varied strengths, I felt after due deliberation that this particular position might prove a poor match for someone of his particular qualifications.'

In other words, he's a violent sociopath with poor impulse control. But something didn't add up – Morden had been on the Council for nearly a year. 'Have you really gone this long without an aide?'

'As a matter of fact, I've had two,' Morden said. 'Unfortunately, they've had rather poor luck. The first disappeared in the summer and the second committed suicide.'

'Suicide?' Anne asked.

'Yes, it seems the stress of the position proved too much for him. He broke all his fingers, cut his own throat, then set himself on fire.'

Anne and I stared at Morden. Morden kept walking.

'He set himself on fire,' I said at last.

'Yes.'

'*After* cutting his own throat.'

'One has to admire his sheer dedication to avoid counselling,' Morden said. 'As a point of interest, the Crusaders had recently approached him in the hope of gaining some insight into the names and details of my supporters. The Keepers assure me that this fact is entirely unrelated to the case.'

Anne didn't answer, and neither did I. All of a sudden, those mages watching me made me feel a lot less comfortable.

We emerged from the hallway into the Belfry, the central crossroads of the War Rooms. Circular pillars ran up to buttresses and a high arched ceiling, and mages and clerks and functionaries walked across the coats of arms engraved on the grey-white floor. A mage was standing by an alcove nearby, and Morden led us towards him. 'Ah, Hieronymus,' Morden said. 'I've brought your newest recruit.'

'You're really going through with this?' the mage said in a sour voice. He was grey-haired, with a narrow, pinched face, and he wore robes with the staff-and-serpent insignia of a healer.

'I have no idea what you're talking about,' Morden said blandly.

'Waste of my bloody time,' Hieronymus muttered, then turned to Anne. 'So this is her?'

'This is Mage Anne Walker, yes,' Morden said. 'Anne, meet Mage Hieronymus, the operations manager of the healer corps. He'll be providing your orientation.'

'"Mage"?' Hieronymus said with a snort. 'Get something clear, Morden. I'm only doing this because the Council ordered me to. I might have to take her in but I'm not putting her to work.'

'Go with him please, Anne,' Morden said. 'Once you're done, you're free for the rest of the day.'

Anne hesitated, and I didn't blame her, but Hieronymus had turned and started marching away. Anne gave me a last glance, then hurried after him.

'Oh, stop looking after her as though she's going into the dragon's den, Verus,' Morden said. 'She'll be quite all right. Now come on. We'll be late.'

The doors Morden led me to were ones I'd never gone through before. From what I'd been told, the route we were following led to the Star Chamber, the meeting room where the Council actually sits. I'd never seen it, and I was curious to lay eyes on the place, but Morden stopped me. 'You'll wait here.'

I looked around to see an old and battered-looking anteroom. Worn cushions sat on wooden benches, and booths were set into the wall. Maybe half a dozen other mages were scattered around, sitting down. None turned to look at us.

'I thought I was supposed to go with you,' I said. I didn't especially want to spend the day in Morden's company, but there was no point advertising that.

'Good heavens, Verus. You can't think that non-Council members would be allowed into the Star Chamber?' Morden looked amused. 'Merely being allowed to wait in the ante-room is an honour.'

'And what am I supposed to do while I'm experiencing this honour?'

'I'm sure you'll figure something out,' Morden said. 'Good luck.' He exited through the far doors.

I was left alone. Out of the corner of my eye, I could tell that I was being watched, but as I looked back at the other mages, they turned away. I studied the room, and as I did, I noticed something odd. The booths were protected by eavesdropping wards: they were subtle but well made and I didn't think anyone would be able to overhear what was said inside without drawing attention. I walked to one of the booths and sat down to wait.

I'd barely had a chance to get settled in when the first visitor arrived.

'So you're the replacement,' the mage standing by the booth said. He was tall and thin, with curly black hair, and wore an expensive suit with a gold tie-clip.

'Something like that,' I said, and waited for the mage to introduce himself or sit.

He did neither. 'Who's Morden's pick for Shanghai?'

'I'm sorry?'

'Ao Qin's visit,' the mage said. When I didn't react he looked impatient. 'The appointment?'

'Um,' I said. 'I didn't catch your name, Mage . . . ?'

'Ictis,' the mage said. 'What about Suminai?'

'What about him?'

'My superior's willing to consider overlooking what happened in Scotland.'

'And Morden would care about this because . . . ?'

'Fine,' Ictis snapped. 'The Downs stones, then.'

I thought about it for a second. I had no idea what Ictis was talking about, but from a glance through the futures, I didn't think telling him that would be a good idea. 'I'll pass it on.'

'Good.' Ictis turned and left, and I watched him go. I had the disconcerting feeling that I'd just agreed to something.

No sooner had Ictis left than he was replaced by a woman. She had blonde hair woven into a braid that ran over the top of her head, and she would have been pretty but for the cool look in her eyes. Like Ictis, she didn't ask my name. 'I need an answer from Morden about the ID,' she told me without preamble.

'I'm sure you do,' I said, wondering what the hell the ID was. Identification? Of who?

'I assume you know it's been moved to next week?'

'I do now.'

'We aren't going to wait for ever,' the woman said. 'Which way is he going to go?'

'I'm sorry,' I said, 'but I really can't help you.'

'It's like that, is it?'

I looked back at the woman, waiting for her to explain. She gave me a flat look, turned on her heel and left.

The next arrival was another woman, this one thirty or so, with a ponytail and a black business suit which showed off the lines of her figure. Unlike the previous two, she demanded to see Morden, and wouldn't take no for an answer no matter how many times I explained that he was busy.

'Look, I don't know what else to say,' I said at last. 'You can wait if you like, but don't get your hopes up.'

The woman stared at me, then seated herself in the booth, folded her arms and looked away. I thought about trying to talk to her, but after seeing the reactions I was going to get I decided to save my breath.

Half an hour passed, then an hour. I spent the time studying the other people in the anteroom. The population stayed low – no more than eight or nine at any one time – but people kept moving in and out. They generally came to talk, always no more than two to a conversation, and they didn't look like casual conversations. I tried to eavesdrop but was frustrated by the wards. Something was going on here, and I didn't know what it was.

The woman sitting with me had been growing visibly agitated, and after an hour and a half she abruptly jumped to her feet. 'Tell him—' she began, looking down at me, then checked herself with a look of frustration and walked out. I was left alone again, and as I looked into the future I saw that more people were coming.

The pattern stayed the same throughout the day. Someone would show up and they'd want something I couldn't give.

Either they'd want to know Morden's position on an issue, or they'd want some kind of appointment or promise. I picked my answers with a mixture of divination and guess-work, trying to turn them down without giving offence, but the more mages I spoke to, the more I got the strange but definite suspicion that none of them believed a single word I was saying. Some took my refusals with annoyance, some were noncommittal, but there was a message in those silent looks. *We know you're lying*, they were saying. *You're not fooling anyone.*

'I've been waiting for this appointment,' the mage was saying. 'You understand that? Morden's supposed to be here.'

I didn't quite sigh. The mage talking to me was English, with a close-shaven head, a receding hairline, and a belligerent expression. 'Yes, I understand.'

'So where is he?'

'In the Star Chamber.'

'You trying to be funny?'

I managed to hold back a smart answer, but only just. The mage talking to me – whose name, if I'd heard him right, was Jarnaff – had been here for five minutes, and he was already my least favourite of the visitors so far. While none of the mages that I'd met today had been exactly pleased to be turned down, this was the first one who simply wasn't listening at all. According to him, he was supposed to have an appointment with Morden, and he was treating the fact that Morden wasn't here as some sort of personal insult on my part.

'I've been waiting two days,' Jarnaff said when I didn't answer. 'And now you come in here and sit around fanning yourself in your cheap shoes and tell me you can't help.'

The jibe about the shoes pissed me off. I was wearing black trainers, and okay, maybe they weren't the smartest footwear in the world, but you could run in them and fight in them, unlike Jarnaff's shiny raised-heel Oxfords. At a better time I wouldn't have let it get to me, but if there's one thing I hate it's feeling ignorant, and I'd spent the best part of the day fumbling my way through conversations I didn't understand.

'Are you listening?' Jarnaff demanded.

'Yes,' I said shortly.

'Don't "yes" me. How about you show a bit of manners?'

'Look, Jarnaff, Morden's not here. I don't know when he's coming back and frankly I don't much care. Now you can wait around, or you can leave.'

'What was that?' Jarnaff said, glaring at me. 'What did you say?'

'You heard.'

Jarnaff stared at me for a second. 'You think I don't know who you are?'

I didn't answer and Jarnaff smiled at me unpleasantly. 'I know how you got your job, Verus.'

'What's that supposed to mean?'

'Oh yeah, I know all about you. That little deal you got with Morden? He gives you this job and all of a sudden you get to pretend to be a Light mage.' Jarnaff gave me a contemptuous look. 'Except you're not.'

I was silent.

'You're still under sentence, aren't you?' Jarnaff said. 'All it takes to put you back is one vote by the Senior Council. And guess who I'm aide to?' Jarnaff looked at me with eyebrows raised and when I still didn't answer, he went on. 'Sal Sarque. He wanted you gone, he could have you packed off – ' Jarnaff snapped his fingers. ' – like that. Now, I wasn't going to bring it up, being as I'm a pretty reasonable guy. But when people like you act disrespectful, then I start getting unhappy.'

'And what'll it take to make you happy?'

Jarnaff frowned. 'I'm not done.'

I looked at him.

'Here's how this is going to work,' Jarnaff said. 'You're going to be helpful. And polite. Because if you don't, then I put a word in Sarque's ear, and you'll have the same thing happen to you as Morden's last two servants.' Jarnaff leant towards me. 'We understanding each other?'

I briefly considered how to answer. It didn't take me very long. 'Get lost.'

'Excuse me?'

'Is there something wrong with your ears?' I asked. 'Because I'm noticing that whenever I say something you don't like, you don't seem to hear very well.'

'I think maybe you don't understand—'

'I heard. You want to blackmail me.'

Jarnaff narrowed his eyes. 'You don't want to piss me off.'

'Or you'll do what?' I leant forward suddenly and had the satisfaction of seeing Jarnaff flinch. It was a small movement but I'd been watching for it, and as I looked into Jarnaff's eyes I knew he wasn't as confident as he was acting. 'Go running to Sal Sarque? Tell him that the big bad Verus is being mean to you? Here's a little detail that he apparently didn't think you needed to know, Jarnaff: your boss and his friends tried to kill me less than a week ago. Little hint for you: if you're trying to threaten someone, make sure it's not with something you've already *failed* at.

And just so you know, this last month? While you were strutting around the War Rooms in your expensive shoes, I was being chased by assassins. So unless you think you can be more intimidating than they were, I think it's time you left.'

'You don't—' Jarnaff began.

I cut him off. 'You can go now.'

Jarnaff stared at me with an expression like thunder, but I simply took out my phone, crossed one leg over the other and started checking my emails. I didn't look up, and after a moment Jarnaff abruptly stood and left. I watched him through the futures just to make sure he wouldn't try anything.

The Council meeting ended half an hour later. There was a growing swell of voices, then the doors opened and people began to filter through. I recognised one member of the Junior Council, and then Morden was there, creating a bubble of empty space with his passing as Light mages tried to edge away. He beckoned and reluctantly I fell in by his side. I could feel the eyes on us as we walked away.

'Well then,' Morden said once we were out of earshot. He kept his pace slow and I had to shorten my stride not to pull ahead of him. 'Did you have an educational day?'

'From a certain point of view.'

'Let's hear the details.'

'Okay,' I said. 'Your first would-be caller was some guy called Ictis. He wants to know who you're picking for Shanghai.'

'He already knows,' Morden said. 'The more important question is what he offered.'

'For what?'

'The undersecretary Ao Qin will be visiting Britain next

month as an envoy from the Light Council of China,' Morden said. 'They'll be choosing the next ambassador. Who did Ictis want? Mala or Suminai?'

'The only name he used was Suminai.'

'Did he try to promise amnesty for the raid in Scotland?'

'He said he'd consider it.'

'I hope you turned him down.'

'And then he said something about the Downs stones.'

'Ah.' Morden looked pleased. 'Who was next?'

'A woman. Fortyish, braided blonde hair, brown eyes. She wanted to know which way you were going to go on the ID.'

'And when you didn't give her an answer?'

'She marched out.'

Morden questioned me about each visitor in turn. Some he dismissed, while for others he probed for details. I told him what I could remember, trying to hold back my annoyance. 'Look,' I said at last. 'It'd be a lot easier for me to pick out the relevant information if I knew what was going on here.'

'What would you like to know?' Morden asked agreeably.

I was surprised but didn't show it. 'Well, what was the deal with Ictis?'

'One of the matters that will be decided during Ao Qin's visit is the identity of the next mage the Light Council will send to China as their ambassadorial representative,' Morden said. 'It's a five-year term and offers enormous opportunities for corruption, so naturally all of the Light factions want their man for the job. Ictis works for the Isolationists, and apparently they've decided on Suminai for their candidate. The real question was what they were willing to give for my support. They've been trying to pressure me over that raid in Scotland for a while – you're familiar with that? No? In any case, it seems that they've realised that I know it's a bluff, and instead they're willing to cede the rights of the Downs stones, which is a much more serious offer. When he comes back, you can tell him I'll accept.'

'What about the ID thing?'

'Identification Database. The Directors have been trying to put together a centralised registry of all the magic-users in Britain. Alma wants my co-operation in bringing the Dark mages around. When you didn't give that woman an answer – her name is Julia, incidentally – she interpreted that as a refusal.'

'And you're okay with that?'

'Of course I am,' Morden said. 'It's a ridiculous idea. The Directors have been trying to push it through for thirty years, and it's failed every time. Now they'll take it to the Guardians, and the Guardians will turn them down, and that'll kill it once again, though I expect it'll take another month or two for that to sink in.'

I was silent. We turned a corner and started down the hall that would take us back to the Belfry. 'Is something bothering you?' Morden asked.

'Maybe I'm missing something here,' I said. 'But these decisions they're asking me for don't feel like small ones.'

'What were you expecting to be doing?'

'Scheduling your appointments?'

'Honestly, Verus,' Morden said. 'Did you think I went to all this trouble simply for a secretary?'

'Actually, yes.'

Morden looked amused. 'Are you aware that somewhere

between eighty and ninety per cent of the agreements between Council members are concluded by their aides?'

I looked at Morden, and my scepticism must have shown on my face. 'Let us say that Alma wishes to make an arrangement with me,' Morden said. 'Clearly she can't have it in an open Council meeting, and equally clearly she can't be seen going to me. Instead she gives the message to her aide Julia. Julia relays the message to you, you discuss it with me, and balance is maintained in the universe.'

'All of the important business gets funnelled through aides?'

'Essentially.'

'Then what the hell do you talk about in Council?'

Morden shrugged. 'Mostly we listen to reports. It's rather tedious, really.'

We'd come out onto the Belfry floor and I stopped, turning to face Morden. 'Okay. Assuming I'm understanding all this right, one thing I'd like to know. I can't talk to you while you're in Council. So what happens if I make a decision for you, and then when you come out I find out that it *wasn't* the one you wanted me to make?'

'Then I expect I'll be looking for a new aide,' Morden said. 'Though I'd be remiss not to remind you that should you lose your position, you'll also lose your status as a Light mage, meaning that your previous death sentence will become immediately applicable.'

I stared at Morden, and he patted me on the shoulder with a smile. 'I'm sure you'll do an excellent job.' He walked away into the crowd.

I hung around the War Rooms for a little longer, waiting for Anne, but after a while I got a message from her saying that she'd be staying late. She didn't sound happy, but at least she wasn't in danger. In the meantime, I'd received another message, a slip of paper hand-delivered by a young man who disappeared before I could ask for details. I found a quiet place to read the contents.

From where you first met the Silent, take the way that runs north of west, straight as an arrow. After five minutes, a turnoff will descend on the left. I'll be waiting at six o'clock at the water's edge.

– The one who gave you your communicator.

I sighed. There was no signature, but I knew who'd sent it.

The work at Pudding Mill Lane had made some progress since the last time I was there, but the place was still fenced in by construction barriers. Up to the left, the station was a wide, low-slung box over the raised train tracks of the Docklands Light Railway, the lights of the platform visible in the darkness. I glanced up at it as I walked, remembering that encounter with Chamois the Silent. If the Dark mage's air blade had been a few inches closer I never would have left that station, but I didn't really hold a grudge towards the guy. I'd much rather deal with assassins than the Light Council. At least with assassins you know where you stand.

The road led me under the railway tracks and up to the Greenway, a long foot and cycle path that runs in a perfectly straight line across the Olympic Park. To the right, the stadium was a vast shadow in the darkness. A cyclist came up behind me, the whirr of the bike breaking the quiet as he buzzed past, a feeble red light blinking on-off-on-off as it faded into the gloom. I kept walking until I found a footpath descending to the left.

The footpath led down to the River Lea, a long stretch of dark water with concrete banks. Barges were moored on either side, silent and still, and to the right and left was a towpath, lined with grass. There were no lamp posts, and the only light came from the buildings across the river, yellow-white reflections off rippling water. A man was standing in the shadow of the fence.

'Were you followed?' the man said as I approached.

'Were the cryptic clues really necessary?'

'Better not to take avoidable risks.'

I looked around at the empty riverbank. It was cold, lonely and deserted. 'I remember when you used to take me out to dinner in Holborn.'

'Times have changed.'

'Yeah,' I said. 'I suppose they have.'

I couldn't really see Talisid in the shadows, but then I didn't need to. He always looks the same: middle-aged, receding hair, composed expression. 'How are things?' he asked.

'They suck,' I said. 'But I'm sure you know that already, and I'm also sure you didn't call me out to a riverbank in the middle of nowhere for a social catch-up.'

'No, I didn't,' Talisid said. 'I imagine you have some idea of why I *did* call you.'

'I've a pretty good notion.'

Talisid works for the Guardians. The Guardians and the Crusaders are the two main anti-Dark political groups within the Council, and the Guardians are the more pleasant of the two by a fair bit. I've done quite a few jobs for

Talisid over the years, and for the most part, they'd gone well. Unfortunately, there was one big problem. Ever since Richard's return, Talisid had been trying to get me to rejoin Richard and spy on him.

The 'rejoin' part had just happened. I knew what was coming next.

I started walking south along the towpath and Talisid matched my pace. 'I understand that your current situation is less than ideal,' he offered when I didn't speak.

'That's something of an understatement.'

'We'd be willing to offer compensation.'

'Do you know what Richard would do if he found out that I was spying on him?'

'No.'

'Nothing,' I said. 'Not personally. He'd give me to Morden instead. Or if he was feeling really sadistic, to Vihaela. Do you know what *they* would do?'

Talisid shook his head.

'Take a guess.'

'I imagine you believe they would kill you.'

'Killing me is the *least* of what they would do,' I said. 'And by the time they were done, there's a good chance I'd be wanting them to. What could you possibly offer that could be worth that?'

'If you do what they say, will the end result really be so much better?'

Barges passed by on our right, riding low in the water. On the other side of the river, a halogen lamp made a bright splash of light against a building. A man was silhouetted in it, chopping wood, his shape throwing a monstrous shadow on the brick wall. Each time the shadow swung down, the *tchunk* of the axe echoed across the water.

'I understand how large a request I'm making,' Talisid said. 'I'm willing to do whatever I can.'

'Okay,' I said. 'There is one thing you can help me out with.'

'Go ahead.'

'Get that death sentence lifted.'

Talisid was silent for a few seconds. 'That will be difficult.'

'How difficult?'

'Unfortunately, Morden appointing you as his liaison has convinced many Light mages that you and he are working together.'

'Yeah, I noticed. Why is this relevant?'

'Tensions between Light and Dark mages are high,' Talisid said. 'Many Light mages believe that we are in the lead-up to another war. Convincing them to expend political capital on someone they see as a Dark mage will be . . . problematic.'

We walked for a little way in silence. 'Is that the only reason?' I said.

'How do you mean?'

'It seems to me that the main reason you're approaching me again is that Richard and Morden have forced me to work for them,' I said. 'If I'm not working for Richard – and as Morden's aide – then I'm a lot less valuable as an agent. So I have to wonder: exactly *how* invested are your bosses in breaking me free?'

'I can see how it would appear that way.'

'Are you going to tell me it's not true?'

'Look at it another way,' Talisid said. 'You've told me in the past that your biggest reason for refusing to take the job was that you did not want to be in proximity to

Richard. As things stand, you're forced to do that whether you want to or not. Doesn't it make sense to get some kind of benefit?'

We'd passed under another bridge and had come to an empty stretch of water. There were no more barges, and up ahead I could see the orange glow and rushing traffic of a big A road. 'The answer's a maybe,' I said. 'I'm not turning you down. But I'm not putting myself at risk and I'm not working for free. If you want any intel, it'll be favour for favour.'

Talisid nodded as though it was what he'd expected. 'Here.' He handed me a small item. It looked like a disc, grey-black in the darkness.

I took it and could feel the latent magic inside. Very little stored energy, but a strong resonance. A focus item, then. 'New communicator?'

'You should find it an upgrade from the old model,' Talisid said. 'Synchronous, as before, but much better range than the Keeper issue.'

I turned it over in one hand. 'Doesn't seem to have a visual display.'

'No,' Talisid said. 'It also contains a signature lock. Once you activate it for the first time, it will be permanently keyed to your magical fingerprint.'

'Taking security seriously, aren't you?'

'As you said,' Talisid said. 'The consequences of being discovered are significant.' He nodded to me. 'Have a safe trip.'

'You too, I suppose. And by the way, I'd very much appreciate it if you didn't tell anyone else on the Council about this meeting.'

'Yes,' Talisid said. 'I believe that would be best. Good luck, Verus.' He walked away into the darkness.

I watched Talisid go, then after he'd disappeared into the shadows, I turned and carried on along the towpath. I liked Talisid, up to a point. But I had no illusions about his ultimate priorities. He was serving the Guardians and the Council. He'd keep me alive if he could, but if it came down to a choice between me and the mission, I knew which he'd pick.

I headed south towards the Bow Road overpass, looking for a place to use my gate stone. Things weren't getting any easier.

4

February

January turned into February, and while things didn't get better, they didn't immediately get any worse.

I went back to the War Rooms the next day, and again the day after that. The pattern was irregular – sometimes Morden wouldn't visit for several days in a row – but every time he did I'd be summoned, and every time things would turn out the same way. The Council would meet in the Star Chamber, I'd be left outside in the anteroom and I'd barely have the chance to sit before someone was walking up to the booth. The procession was endless, from Council aides to Keepers to file clerks, and every single one of them wanted something. At first, I was completely out of my depth. I'd spent more than enough time dealing with the Light Council from the outside, but I'd never before had to handle things from the inside, and it wasn't the same at all. It felt like being thrown into the middle of some insanely complicated game which had been running for years, with rules no one would explain, played by people who'd known each other their entire lives. Everything had a meaning, and not always the one you'd expect.

I quickly learned who to watch out for. Most of the aides proved to have pretty similar attitudes to Ictis and Julia, the mages who'd approached me on the first day. They didn't like me and they didn't trust me, but they weren't going to pick a fight. Jarnaff, on the other hand, was going to be trouble. He'd been telling the truth about being aide to Sal Sarque, and after a little digging, I was pretty sure that he'd been telling the truth about the other part too. Morden's last two aides *had* been made to disappear, and although no one said it out loud, there was a consensus that the Crusaders, or some other people with ties to Jarnaff or Sarque, had abducted them, interrogated them, then disposed of what was left. And since Morden was a Dark mage, the protests were muted at best.

I saw some familiar faces too. Lyle showed up on the second day and we had a short, awkward conversation. I saw Lyle's boss as well, Undaaris, and stared daggers at him while Undaaris pretended not to see. But that was nothing compared to what I felt for Levistus's aide, Barrayar. I saw him just once, and this time it was my turn to pretend not to notice. I doubt he was fooled. Barrayar knew I had to hold a grudge, but I was pretty sure he didn't know just how deeply I hated him. Just a glimpse of his face was enough to throw me into a cold fury, and I had to control myself to stop my muscles from clenching. *You'll pay for this*, I promised myself. *Your master won't live for ever. Neither will you.*

Oddly enough, it was the uglier sides of the Light world that most helped to accustom me to it. I'd spent my apprenticeship surrounded by Dark mages and the promise of violence, and as days turned into weeks I began to realise that the Council wasn't really so different. The weapons might be more indirect, but the stakes were the same. Everyone wanted to be king of the hill.

On the positive side, Anne seemed to be doing okay. The Light mages in the healer corps didn't like her any more than the Council aides liked me, but that kind of treatment's nothing new to Anne, and at least there were no signs that she was in immediate danger. Each evening after we both got home, we'd catch each other up on our days. Sometimes Variam would come too, but usually it was just the two of us, alone in Wales in the long dark winter evening.

Luna didn't contact me at all. I called and messaged but received no answer.

My position at the War Rooms might be hard, but at least I was making headway. The Keepers were another story.

I went to Keeper HQ the day after my meeting with Talisid. I'd half expected to be arrested, but apparently the message had been passed down that I was off the wanted list. The man on security at the front desk seemed to take a long time checking my authorisation, but at last he let me in.

I climbed the stairs to the corridor with the office I'd shared with Caldera, but the door was locked. I rattled the handle, then let it drop.

'It's not being used,' a voice said from behind me.

I turned to see Rain, a captain in the Order of the Star and Caldera's boss. 'News travels fast,' I said. I'd been about to ask how Rain had known I'd arrived, before remembering that delay at the front desk. Apparently it hadn't just been because my card was out of date.

'Could say that,' Rain said. He's tall and straight-backed with very dark skin, and one of the few Keepers I halfway trust. 'Your signet.'

I looked down. The object in Rain's hand was a small plaque, metal on leather with coloured gold and silver. The image showed a pair of eagles, wings and talons raised, flanking a tall flame. Above the flame was a single star.

'It's not going to bite,' Rain said.

'Sorry,' I said. It was strange. I've spent so long with the Council as my enemy. Now I was one of their agents, a Keeper of the Flame. I took the signet and felt a faint tingle of magic from the metal.

'Normally there'd be a little more ceremony,' Rain said. 'But, well, nothing about this has exactly been normal. Welcome to the Order of the Star.'

'Thanks,' I said. I felt awkward and didn't know why.

'Go down to the quartermaster's as soon as you have the chance and have it registered,' Rain said. He handed me a key. 'Here.'

'For the office?'

'You'll be on your own for now.'

'Where's Caldera?'

'She's got a new partner.'

'Oh,' I said. I suppose it shouldn't have been a surprise.

'Usually when a new Keeper's brought in, we assign them someone more experienced to show them the ropes. Unfortunately this whole thing's caught us a bit off guard. I don't have anyone to give you just yet.'

'Okay.'

'That's about it,' Rain said. 'Any questions?'

'Yeah,' I said. 'What do you want me working on?'

'That hasn't been settled.'

'What do you mean?'

Rain hesitated, and I had the sudden impression that he was uncomfortable. 'Haven't really fit you into the duty roster yet. Bit sudden. When we have an assignment, we'll call you.'

'Okay.'

Rain started to leave, then paused. 'Glad to have you back.' He walked away.

I watched Rain go, then tried the key in the door. Inside was the same office in which I'd spent a good part of last year. The big desk in the centre of the room which Caldera had used was empty, dust and old coffee stains marking the wood. My desk was up against the wall, and that was empty too. I wondered briefly where my stuff had gone, until I realised that it must have been taken as evidence.

I walked around the room. Two windows at the back looked down onto the London street, and I stood for a moment looking at the traffic crawl across the road below. I started to sit before realising that the chair had been taken too, so I sat on Caldera's desk and looked around. *So now I'm a Keeper.*

It didn't feel like an achievement. It just felt lonely. I went looking for my stuff.

Back when Anne and Variam lived in my flat in Camden, Luna used to come over a lot, and one of the things they'd do was watch videos on my old laptop. Variam always wanted action movies, but since Luna and Anne outnumbered him they usually ended up watching animated shows about girls in Japanese high schools. The shows Luna picked tended to be upbeat with a lot of romance, but the ones Anne chose weren't so cheerful, and more than once I remembered watching episodes where the other girls would bully the main character. They wouldn't beat her up or confront her, but they'd do things like ignore her when she talked, spread rumours behind her back and hide her stuff.

After I'd been a Keeper for a week, I knew exactly how the main characters in those shows had felt.

The first hint of how things were going to go came with Caldera. I spotted her on the second day, down at the end of a corridor, and she immediately turned the other way. Coatl, her new partner, was with her, and he looked at me and hesitated, but Caldera said something and he turned away as well with an apologetic look. By the time I caught up to where they'd been, they were gone.

Okay, I thought. *I guess that answers the question about whether she's still angry.* I decided to give her some more time.

Except it wasn't just Caldera. I'd never exactly been popular with the rest of the Order of the Star, but then I'd never expected to be. Keepers are cops, and cops tend to have an attitude of default suspicion towards outsiders. Still, I'd worked at it, and by last autumn I'd reached the point where I was accepted, if not liked.

I wasn't accepted any more. It had been Morden who'd appointed me as a Keeper, and now the rest of the Keepers hated my guts. Conversations would stop as I came near, and the Keepers would watch me in silence until I was out of earshot, at which point the conversations would start up again. When I tried talking to them, they'd tell me in so many words to go away. The emails I sent went unanswered, or I'd receive 'out of office' replies from mages whom I'd seen in the building less than an hour ago.

It wasn't even just the Keepers. The Council employs a whole bureaucracy of adepts and clued-in sensitives who work under the Light mages to do the lower-level work. I was a Keeper now, which meant that the admin personnel at HQ were supposed to do as I told them . . . in theory.

In practice, every time I asked for something, there was some reason why it couldn't be done. Getting my signet bonded took me the best part of a day. The quartermaster didn't answer my calls: when I tried to call him he was out to lunch, when I came back after lunch he referred me to the issue desk, when I went to the issue desk they told me I'd have to get it authorised at the War Rooms, and so on. When I tried to get the contents of my old desk back I was told they'd been sent to the evidence processing facility at Southampton. I gated there to be told that the records weren't on file and they couldn't help me. What if I went in and found it myself? No, you aren't authorised to do that. The warden? He's in a meeting. No, we don't know when he'll be back. Everyone I wanted to see was busy, and every question got the same blank-faced response. Even the post took two days to reach my desk.

When I'd joined the Keepers as an auxiliary, the way I'd made headway had been with work. It's a lot harder to ignore someone if you're doing a job with them, and so I waited for Rain to hand me some cases. I was a little nervous about handling an investigation without Caldera, but I'd been watching her work for more than a year, and I figured I'd give it my best shot. I waited to see what Rain would send me.

And waited.

When the call didn't come, I went to Rain. He told me that before I could be assigned to a detail and put on the duty roster, it'd have to be cleared by one of the directors. I asked how long that would take and was told that he didn't know. I asked if he could just set me some cases anyway, and he told me that he wasn't authorised to do that. He told me he'd call me as soon as he heard anything.

I went back to my desk and stared at the phone. Rain didn't call.

Variam walked into the office on a cold, rainy afternoon in February. 'Jeez,' he said, looking at me. 'You look like your dog just died.'

I looked up from the computer screen in surprise. 'What are you doing here?'

'Landis has a meeting.' Variam came around and peered down at the computer screen. 'Is that the procedure manual?'

'Procedure and tactics,' I said. It was the Order of the Star's operations manual, containing their official doctrine for all possible situations.

'Any good?'

'Not really.'

'Then why are you reading it?'

'Because I've got nothing else to do and the Order of the Star is too paranoid to allow an internet connection.'

Variam sat down on the desk. He didn't need to clear himself a space; it was nearly bare. 'I thought you guys were supposed to be busy.'

In answer, I turned my monitor towards Variam. 'This is my email.' I clicked a couple of filters. 'These are all the emails this week personally addressed to me.'

Variam squinted at the blank white box on the screen. 'Why isn't it showing?'

'Because there isn't anything to show.'

'Why not?'

'Because no one wants to bloody talk to me. Every single Keeper on the Order of the Star's duty roster is overloaded with case work. They're just apparently not overloaded *enough* to be willing to bring me in on it. I've asked them right to their faces if they need help, but they tell me no, they're fine.'

'Why?'

I lifted my hands in the air. 'Bloody-mindedness? Morden forced them to put me on the team, so now they're going out of their way to keep me on the bench just to show him that he can't tell them what to do?' I shook my head. 'Back when I was younger, I thought it'd be great to be a Keeper. I didn't think it'd be like this.'

Variam shrugged. 'You get used to it.'

I looked curiously at Variam. 'Was it like this when you joined?'

'Pretty much,' Variam said. 'You know Light mages, they're all about pedigree. Who you trained under, which school, how many years with the Council. They weren't that impressed with mine.'

'What changed their mind?'

'Landis doesn't care, and he's the one who matters. And the Order of the Shield's more easy-going that way. As long as you can pull your weight, they're okay with it.'

'Maybe I should have tried to get a job there,' I muttered.

Variam frowned. 'What's up with you?'

'You mean apart from everything else?'

'Not that,' Variam said. 'Back last year, you were always working on something. Now you're just sitting around.'

'I suppose.'

'Well, stop it,' Variam said. He sounded annoyed. 'You and Anne have got this shit with Richard, Luna's a basket case and Morden's planning God knows what. We need you doing something useful, not sitting on your arse.'

I looked at Variam, startled. Variam seemed about to

say more, then paused, touched a hand to his ear and said
'On my way' to the empty air before looking back at me.
'Landis wants me. Look, I'll see if he can do anything. But
come up with something, okay?'

'. . . Okay.'

Variam left. I stared after him, still a little nonplussed.
I really wasn't used to *Variam* telling me to get my shit
together. He'd never acted like this back when he was
living above my shop . . .

My shop, I thought. *That's it, isn't it?* Up until a month
and a half ago, I'd spent the best part of each week running
the Arcana Emporium, my little magic shop in Camden.
It hadn't been a big business and it didn't make much
money, but it had been one of the few places in Britain
and Ireland where people who didn't know much about
the magical world could come to buy materials, get an
item identified, or simply talk to someone who didn't think
they were crazy. For some of my customers, I might have
been the first person they'd ever met who could hear their
story and *not* think they were crazy. I'd taught newbies
about magical society, introduced novices to potential
teachers and warned adepts of the people and places that
they should stay away from. It hadn't been glamorous, but
it had meant something, and no matter how exasperating
my customers had sometimes been, I knew I was making
a difference.

Here with the Keepers, I *wasn't* making a difference. I
was an inconvenient and rather embarrassing addition to
the roster, to be stuck on a shelf and forgotten about.

But Variam was right: I was wasting time. I got up and
headed for the door. Time to visit an old friend.

*   *   *

I'd made it to Hampstead Heath and all the way to the little ravine, and was just about to call Arachne when I stopped. The entrance to Arachne's lair is hidden in the roots of an oak tree, the tree stretching up above the earthen wall. I'd visited the spot so many times that I hardly noticed it, but something was different this time, and as I looked more closely I saw that the entrance had been damaged. Some of the roots had been cut, and others were missing. I stepped closer and traced a finger along where one of the roots ended abruptly. It had scarred over, but even so, the cut felt unnaturally smooth. *Force blade?*

I looked ahead and saw that Arachne was going to answer. Still, it gave me an uneasy feeling. I pressed the spot on the roots and leant in to talk.

'So what happened to your front door?' I asked Arachne.

'Some mages and I had a difference of opinion,' Arachne said. We'd spent a long time saying our hellos, and now I was settled comfortably on one of the sofas, with Arachne crouched in front of me, her front legs on either side of me so that she could look down at me with her eight eyes from only a few feet away. Just like smaller spiders, Arachne's short-sighted, and for lengthy conversations she likes to be close enough to feel the vibrations of my movement and voice.

'What kind of difference of opinion?'

'They wanted to come in,' Arachne said. 'I preferred that they stayed outside. I eventually brought them around to my point of view.'

'In other words, they tried to blast their way in and couldn't?'

'More or less.'

I frowned. 'Are you okay?'

'Perfectly,' Arachne said. 'Oh, and I'm sorry about not answering the last time you called. I had to take a few security measures.'

'I'm just glad they worked,' I said. I'd tried to visit Arachne several times after getting back and received no answer. It wasn't the first time that Arachne had disappeared, but it had still left me worried. It had been a relief when I'd looked ahead today and found she'd be home. 'Were they from the Council?'

'They claimed to be,' Arachne said. It's a little hard to tell with Arachne's voice, but I thought I could detect a dry tone. 'I declined to open the front door and view their identification.'

'Wait. Were they looking for me?' Over Christmas, I'd had a few people try an ambush here on the heath. I'd seen it off without too much trouble, but it had bothered me. If people could connect me to Arachne . . .

'That may have been part of their motivations.'

'Arachne!' I sat up. 'Why didn't you tell me?'

'Well, for one thing, you weren't in the best position to help.'

I stared at Arachne, and my expression must have been obvious, because she touched a foreleg gently to my shoulder. 'It wasn't because of you, Alex. Remember, I have a history too. A much longer one than yours.'

I made an unhappy noise. I *really* didn't like the idea that Arachne might be in danger because of me.

'If they hadn't come on that pretext, they would have come on another,' Arachne said firmly. 'Now. Why don't you tell me what's on your mind?'

I looked around at the chamber we were sitting in.

Arachne's cavern is huge and it's a riot of colour, dresses and furniture and cloth blending together into a giant chaotic rainbow. I'd had a lot of conversations with Arachne here over the years, some of them small ones and some of them big ones. This was going to be a big one.

'I need to decide what to do,' I said.

'Concerning the Keepers?'

'No,' I said slowly. I tried to figure out how to say it. 'I mean, yes, I'll have to deal with that. And Luna, and Rachel, and everything else. It's just . . . Those are all important, but they're reactive. I deal with them, but once I've dealt with them, then all that does is make the problem go away. It doesn't make things any better.'

'And what would make things better?'

'That's what I need to find out.' I looked up at Arachne. 'Right now I'm fighting Levistus and Richard, and I'm losing. Part of it's because they've got better cards than me, but that's not all of it. It's that they've got a plan. They're always playing the long game, looking to next month, next year. Meanwhile I just wait around until some sort of crisis happens, then I scramble to fix it. It's like they're shooting holes in a boat, and I'm running up and down trying to plug the leaks. Sooner or later there'll be too many holes, or one of the bullets will hit me, and that'll be it.'

'So what do you need?'

'I need a win condition,' I said. 'Something that'll put me in a position where *they* have to react to *me*. You remember what you told me back at Christmas? You said I had three options.'

'Align yourself with a greater power,' Arachne said. 'Become a greater power. Or die.'

I nodded.

'So?'

'Right now I'm being forced to align,' I said. 'There are two factions who care enough to recruit me. Richard, and the Council. They both want me playing for their team.'

'Are you going to?'

'No.'

'Why?'

'Because both choices suck,' I said. 'I already learnt my lesson about working for Richard. And long-term, the Council are almost as bad. They're letting me stay there for now, but it's just a matter of time before they have another try at sticking the knife in.'

'And Talisid?'

'He wants me as an agent, but he's not going to be able to do much when things go wrong.'

'You have some allies,' Arachne said.

'And I'll keep finding more. But it's not going to be enough.'

'So what conclusion have you reached?'

'I'm not going to lie down and die,' I said quietly. 'That only leaves one choice. Make myself powerful enough to be on a level with people like Morden and Vihaela. But there's a problem.'

'How to do it?'

'How to do it. *Every* mage in Britain wants more power, whether they're Light or Dark. Hell, half the problems I've had over the last five years come down to some asshole wanting a bigger stick than the next guy. Levistus and Morden and Belthas and who knows who else. They all want it, and so do all the others, and that means that all the low-hanging fruit was picked a really long time ago. But if

I don't try to get the same thing that they want – and succeed at it, where they failed – then I'm screwed. And that's bad news, because I don't see how I *can* succeed. I know what I need, and I don't think I can get it.' I leant back against the sofa, staring at the bolts of cloth.

'I think,' Arachne said after a pause, 'you may be selling yourself short.'

I looked at Arachne curiously. 'How?'

'Your reasoning is correct,' Arachne said. 'You do need more personal power. But I think you have more channels available than you realise.'

'Just because I'm a Keeper and Morden's aide, that doesn't mean . . .'

'I don't mean exploiting your position,' Arachne said. 'Yes, yes, that's how the Council do it. And some Dark mages too. But as you said, you're stepping in late. Influence and politics are the Council's game, and they're better at it than you are. You should be looking at your own advantages.'

'Like what?'

'Three that I believe you should focus on,' Arachne said. 'First, your allies. You may not have many friends in high places, but what you do have is breadth. You are one of the few mages in this country who can count Dark mages, Light mages, independents, adepts and magical creatures among their friends. Make use of it. Don't be afraid to ask for their help, and don't wait too long.'

I thought about it. 'Second is your skill with items,' Arachne said. 'You probably have as much proficiency with magical items of all varieties as any mage in Britain.'

'Yeah, but if I could use the same spells as other mages I wouldn't *need* to rely on items.'

'Don't underestimate the power that imbued items can bring.'

My spirits had been starting to lift, but at Arachne's last words they sank again. 'Oh, come on,' I said. 'There isn't an apprentice in Britain who hasn't dreamed of getting his hands on an imbued item and lucking into huge unearned rewards just from picking it up. It's like winning the lottery: it happens just often enough to make clueless people keep on playing it. All the useful imbued items are either claimed or they've got some horrible curse or agenda just waiting for someone dumb enough to pick them up. Usually both.'

'You may have the potential to circumvent those problems.'

'Yeah, I've kind of tried that already,' I said. 'Didn't go too well.' I had access to at least two imbued items of the kind Arachne was talking about. There was the fateweaver, able to guide and shape destiny, and the monkey's paw, able to grant wishes. One was in a locked bubble realm to which Luna held the key; the other was hidden away where I'd stowed it. I could get my hands on either of the two in less than three hours, and both had the power to make all of my problems go away with a snap of my fingers.

Except that the power was the item's power, not mine. That's the thing with imbued items which most mages don't get. Imbued items don't do what *you* want; they do what *they* want. Both of those items had a history of taking bearers who'd made the mistake of trying to use them, and eating them alive. Maybe literally, in the case of the monkey's paw – I still didn't know exactly what had happened to Martin. 'All the ones I can think of that could do anything like that, using them'd be a death sentence.' A thought struck me. 'Unless you could make one? Like my armour, or . . . ?'

'No,' Arachne said. 'Oh, I could make you a weapon, but it wouldn't be enough. And any protective item I made would have its own problems. Imbued items can be possessive; you learnt that lesson, I think. And I could direct you to other items, but I doubt they'd be any more powerful than the ones you're familiar with. No, what I had in mind was something different, and to do with your third advantage. Your knowledge of Elsewhere.'

I looked at Arachne in surprise. 'But everyone knows about Elsewhere.'

'Your Light mages are *taught* about Elsewhere,' Arachne said dryly.

'Don't most of them use it?'

'If I had to make a personal estimate,' Arachne said, 'I would guess that less than half of Light mages visit it even once. And less than half of those return for a second try. The number who use it frequently enough to build up any real proficiency? Perhaps one in twenty. Light mages like environments that are controlled and predictable, and that is something that Elsewhere is most definitely not.'

I thought about it. Now that I actually tried to remember, it occurred to me that I'd hardly ever heard Light mages talk about going to Elsewhere. Lots of warnings; not many eyewitness accounts. Nearly everything I'd learnt about the place had come from first-hand experience or from books.

But I still didn't see what Arachne was getting at. 'What's that got to do with items?'

'How do you think imbued items influence their bearers?'

'I don't—' I looked at Arachne sharply. 'It's something to do with that?'

'Did you ever wonder how you were able to survive wielding that fateweaver four years ago?' Arachne answered. 'Abithriax had been subverting and possessing mages before you were even born. You used the fateweaver, let him in – and yet you were able to drive him away. Oh, you had help, but even so, he should have been able to overcome you easily. Then the next year, when you drew too deeply on the mist cloak, the same thing happened. It took hold of you, but again you survived. You retained enough of yourself to come here, to me. Did you think about how you did that?'

'Honestly?' I admitted. 'No.'

Arachne watched me, waiting for an answer. 'So you're saying . . . what?' I said. 'I can handle items that other people can't?'

'Travelling Elsewhere and making use of imbued items require similar qualities,' Arachne said. 'First and foremost is self-knowledge. Understanding who you are and what you can do. Recognising when you are being influenced. Knowing when to walk away.'

'Doesn't seem like that much.'

'You'd be surprised.'

I shrugged. 'I can buy that it helps, but it doesn't seem like it's enough either. I mean, yeah, I survived going up against Abithriax, but that was all. As soon as he started losing, he just pulled back into the fateweaver.'

'Yes,' Arachne said. 'If you picked up the fateweaver now, you would be able to fight off Abithriax easily. But as you say, you would *only* be able to fight him off. He couldn't defeat you, but nor could you defeat him. And training wouldn't help. It's a matter of the tools available to you.'

'I know, but that's what I've got,' I said. 'I'm a diviner, not a mind mage.'

'Which is why I think you should look to better tools.'

I looked at Arachne. 'You sound like you've got something in mind.'

'There is a type of magical item known as a dreamstone,' Arachne said. 'It allows a bearer to touch Elsewhere more directly, and more deeply. In Elsewhere, you can reach someone else's dreams, but with a dreamstone you can make that connection while awake.'

'Someone else's dreams,' I said. 'Or to an imbued item? Link to it the same way it links to me?'

'It wouldn't make the item serve you,' Arachne said. 'But it would put you on an even footing.'

I frowned. It could open up opportunities, but I had the feeling there was a problem. 'What's the catch?'

'Dreamstones are very rare,' Arachne said. 'They form only in certain shadow realms in extremely unusual conditions, and once formed, they must be shaped. The process takes decades, and those who own such an item tend not to advertise. Finding one will be difficult.'

'But I'm guessing that you wouldn't be suggesting this if you had any easier plans.'

'Easier, yes,' Arachne said. 'Better, no.'

I thought about it, but only briefly. I trust Arachne, and if she thought this was the best plan, then I was willing to give it a try. 'So any idea where I could find one of these things?'

'No,' Arachne said. 'As you know, items like this come onto the market very rarely. Keep your eyes open, and I'll do the same. In the meantime, I suggest you do what you can on other fronts. And be ready. If an opportunity does develop, you may have to move fast.'

I was still thinking about Arachne's words when I left. I walked out through the tunnel, then turned and watched the roots and earth fold back together with a rustling sound. Now that I knew what to look for, it was easy to make out the marks where the attack had failed.

I started walking south, climbing up out of the ravine and in a direction that would take me towards the ponds at the feet of the hills, and as I did I thought about what to do next. Technically, I was supposed to be back in Keeper HQ, but right now I didn't feel like wasting any more time sitting behind an empty desk. I needed to be expanding, developing my options. Arachne's suggestion of a dreamstone was a new long-term avenue to work on. I had something in mind involving Anne for another. For the third . . .

Suddenly I knew where I needed to go. I changed course, heading towards the road.

5

The hotel at Great Portland Street was busy with the coming evening. I signed in with the receptionist and had just started walking towards the lifts when I heard a voice calling behind me. 'Mr Verus! Excuse me! Mr Verus!'

I turned to see a man hurrying towards me. He looked to be in his forties, with a receding hairline and one of those ring-shaped beards around the mouth and chin. A metal badge on the breast of his suit read FRONT DESK TEAM LEADER. 'Mr Verus,' he called again as he reached me, slowing to a walk.

I looked at the man and raised my eyebrows. 'Ah,' he said. 'You're visiting room 638, is that right? A Miss Luna Mancuso?'

'And?'

'Well, there's a bit of a problem,' the man said. 'I mean, when she was first signed in, there was a young man who said he worked for the police. He told me that Miss Mancuso was under witness protection and wasn't to be disturbed.'

'That sounds like good advice.'

'Well, um, of course we fully understand the situation and on behalf of our company we'd be more than happy to offer all available help—'

'I'm afraid I'm in a hurry.'

'It's just that, um, the room's in arrears,' the man said. 'The advance payment was only for a week.'

'It'll be settled when she leaves.'

'We do have a strict policy of not extending credit . . .'

I looked at the man thoughtfully. There was sweat on his forehead. 'Did you try to force your way in?'

'Well, I mean, we do have the authority to enter the premises at all times. Particularly when the visitor is in violations of the terms and conditions of their stay. I mean, it's company policy. All in the terms of service.'

'And what happened when you tried to execute your terms of service?'

The man's eyes shifted away. 'There were . . . some problems.'

'Yeah,' I said. 'I'll bet there were.'

'So if you're visiting . . . would you mind asking her to leave?'

'Thought you said you wanted her to settle the bill?'

'Well, that too,' the man said. 'It's just . . . very busy . . . the season, you know . . . company policy.'

I looked inquiringly back at the man, watching him sweat. 'I'll see what I can do,' I said and turned towards the lift.

I reached Luna's room and studied the door. There was a discoloured patch next to the card reader, brownish-black against the plaster, rather like the kind of mark you'd get from an electrical fire. I swiped my keycard but the LED didn't light up. I raised my voice. 'Luna?'

Silence.

'Luna!'

More silence.

I put a snap into my voice. I knew she was listening. 'Open this door, right now.'

Luna's voice sounded muffled. 'I don't want to talk to anyone.'

'I didn't ask what you wanted.'

'It's late.'

'Luna, you have exactly ten seconds to open this door,' I said. 'After which I am going to blow it off its hinges and drag you out by your hair. Ten. Nine.'

No answer. I was pretty sure I'd shocked Luna into silence. 'Eight,' I said. 'Seven.'

'Wait!'

'Six.'

'I can't get it—'

'Five. Four.'

'All right! All right!' There was a rattle of metal, and the door swung open.

The hotel room was cramped and messy. Curtains and blinds had been pulled across the window so that the only light came from the overhead bulb, and the floor looked like someone had been using it as a rubbish bin. Food wrappers, water bottles, clothes, bags and shoes were scattered all over the carpet, and the bed was just as bad. The room had an odd musky smell, and the air felt close, as though it hadn't been ventilated in a long while.

If the room looked bad, Luna looked worse. Her skin was pale to an unhealthy degree, there were bags under her eyes and she moved without any of her usual vigour. Her hair was a crazy mess with loose strands sticking upwards – I couldn't remember the last time I'd seen it out of its usual ponytail. She was wearing tracksuit bottoms and a cardigan, and she stared at me mutely.

I didn't know what to do, but my instincts told me not

to let that show. I sniffed at the room. 'When was the last time you showered?'

Luna hesitated.

'Go take one,' I said. 'I'll wait.'

Possibilities flickered where Luna argued with me, but as she kept looking at me they winked out. Luna turned, disappeared into the bathroom, reappeared, grabbed up some clothes with a sidelong glance, then went back in. I heard the click of the bolt, then after a few minutes, the hiss of water.

Movement in the futures made me turn. There was someone else in the room, and it was . . . *Oh. That's what that smell is.* I moved towards the far side of the room, trying to pick my way through the piles of mess and mostly ending up just walking on it. Luna's never been the tidiest of people, but this was a bit much even for her. Around the other side of the bed, wedged into the corner of the room, was a pile of dirty clothes. I reached down and pulled a sweater off the top.

A head appeared, with a reddish furred muzzle, two pointed ears and a pair of bright amber eyes looking up at me. 'So this is where you ended up,' I said.

Hermes yawned, showing lines of sharp white teeth before his mouth closed with a snap. Hermes is a blink fox that I met a couple of years back, and ever since then he's sort of adopted me. I'd lost track of him after the fire that destroyed my shop, and even though my common sense had told me that few creatures had *less* to fear from a house fire, I'd worried that something had happened to him. It was good to see him again. 'Glad you're all right.'

Hermes sniffed at me.

'Let me guess,' I said. 'You came back to mine and found

it burnt down, found your way to Luna's flat instead, then followed her here?'

Hermes blinked once.

'Been looking after her?'

Hermes seemed to consider that, then blinked again.

'She okay?'

Blink blink.

I sighed. 'That's about what I figured.'

While Luna stayed in the shower, I looked around the room. It looked as though she'd been in here for a while . . . a *long* while. Anne had been back to visit, but now that I thought about it, she'd never told me where they'd gone. Had Luna been holed up in this room for two weeks straight?

When the bathroom door finally opened and Luna reappeared, she looked in better shape. Her skin had more colour, her hair had been brushed into some sort of order and her clothes were clean. She also seemed to have recovered some of her defiance. 'Anne said you were going to let me be.'

'Yeah, well, giving you space wasn't working,' I said. 'So I decided to hurry things up.'

'I don't need any help!'

I looked deliberately around the trash-covered room. To my side, Hermes yawned, got up, then began digging in one of the piles of clothes, apparently scenting food.

Luna got the message and she didn't like it. 'You know what?' she said with a flush. 'I'm not your apprentice any more. You can't just barge in.'

'That's funny, you're *acting* like an apprentice.'

'How?'

'In case you haven't noticed, the rest of us are not exactly having a fun time,' I said. 'I've got two crappy jobs working for Morden and for the Keepers, Anne's having an equally bad time in the healer corps and Vari's trying to watch out for us from the Order of the Shield. Everyone has a lot on their plate, and it's not likely to get easier. Meanwhile you, one of the *extremely* few people we can count on, are sitting around in a hotel room expecting someone else to foot the bill. It would be very helpful if you could start pulling your weight.'

'Oh, screw you,' Luna snapped. 'You are *such* a jerk.'

I was starting to get pissed off now. 'Are you going to help, or not?'

'Well, it's not like I ever have before!'

That brought me up short. 'What?'

Luna started to answer and stopped. The look on her face was the look of someone suddenly wishing they could take back what they'd said. 'Nothing.'

'What do you mean, you've never helped before?'

'I said it's nothing.'

'You've been a ton of help, and we could use some more of it.'

'Yeah,' Luna said. 'Because all of you mages *really* need an adept around.'

I frowned. 'What's got into you?'

Luna looked away. 'I don't want to talk about it.'

'What do you mean, "you mages"? You never used to say that to me.'

'Yeah, well, maybe it's finally getting to me,' Luna said. 'You think it's fun having everyone in the apprentice programme thinking you shouldn't be there?'

'You just *left* the apprentice programme. You graduated; you're officially recognised as a mage. This is literally the most ridiculous time possible to start complaining about being treated as an adept.'

Luna didn't answer.

I paused. I wanted to keep arguing, but something was telling me that the adept/mage thing was a diversion. Luna was still upset, but that wasn't what was really bothering her. The only time that she had looked really off-balance had been when she'd said . . . 'You think you're useless?'

Luna didn't meet my eyes.

'Don't seem very useless to me,' I said. 'I mean, you've saved my life how many times now?'

'Most of those times I was the reason it *needed* saving,' Luna said bitterly.

'Is that what this is all about?' I said. 'You're feeling sorry for yourself? Look, I'm sorry, but we really do not have the time. Anne and I are in deep shit and if you don't—'

'I'm the *reason* you and Anne are in deep shit!' Luna shouted. 'It didn't just happen – it was *because* of someone! Me! You two were safe, you were off running around Africa and Argentina and none of Levistus's men could catch you until they went after me, to threaten me and bring you back. And it worked! Anne told me what you were about to do, okay? You were about to commit *suicide* to stop them blowing me up! So don't tell me how much you need my help because it's *bullshit*!'

I looked at Luna, slightly shocked. 'They trapped your house while you were sleeping,' I said. 'It can happen to everyone—'

'No, it doesn't! It *doesn't* happen to everyone! Back when everyone was after the fateweaver, the whole reason you got pulled in was because of me! And then right after that I screwed things up with Martin, and you had to come rescue me again! Over and over again, and I thought okay, maybe it's time to start listening. And you told me that if I trained and worked hard then I could get better, I'd master my curse and things would be okay. And I believed you. And then when I finally passed my journeyman test you weren't there, but I still believed you'd come back. And it was all for nothing! You're stuck with Richard and Morden and Anne is too, and it's all because of me. If you'd never taken me on you'd be fine!'

Oh. I opened my mouth to give Luna an answer and nothing came to mind. She was exaggerating, but . . .

. . . but she was right. Not a hundred per cent right, but enough that I couldn't just deny it. It had been the threat against Luna that had drawn me back, and it had been to save her life that I'd been ready to fight that last stand in Bow. I tried to think how I'd have felt if that had been me, and realised I didn't have to imagine very hard. Only a couple of hours ago I'd been listening to Arachne tell me about the attack on her lair, and believing that it had been because of me.

I remembered exactly how that felt. It had felt shitty.

'Say they hadn't been able to catch you,' I said. 'You think they'd have had an attack of conscience and just stopped? They'd have worked their way down the list until they found someone else I cared about.'

'Great,' Luna said bitterly. 'So I'm in the same category as helpless acquaintances now.'

I frowned at Luna. 'That's not fair.'

'Why didn't you take me with you?'

'Where?'

'With you and Anne,' Luna said. 'At least then I might have been good for something.'

'The whole reason we went through that crash course of throwing you into the journeyman tests was so that you *wouldn't* have to run away with us,' I said. 'Anne and I spent that month running between hotel rooms and spending every spare second looking over our shoulders wondering when the next assassination attempt would come along.'

'Yeah, well, that sounds a lot more fun than how I spent this January.'

'How?' I demanded. 'You had a place to stay. I left you some money, enough to get you on your feet. And you were a recognised mage.'

'Great, so I get to call myself a mage while I'm sitting alone in my room.'

'What do you mean, alone? We weren't there, but you could find someone else and—'

'There isn't anyone else.'

I looked at Luna in surprise. 'What?'

'I don't have any other friends,' Luna said. 'There's you, there's Anne and there's Vari.'

'What about the others at your duelling class?'

'You think I could talk to them about *this*?'

'But there has to be someone else,' I said. 'Friends or family. Someone you're honest with, tell them what's on your mind . . . ?'

I trailed off. Luna was shaking her head. 'Wait,' I said. 'We're the *only* ones you talk to?'

'I'm not like you guys, okay?' Luna said. 'Vari can walk up to anyone and he'll be rude and insult them and somehow they'll like him for it. Anne might be a life mage, but she's beautiful and kids love her. And you . . .'

'You think I'm some kind of social butterfly?'

'You're better at it than I am.'

'Only after I spent a really long time behind a shop counter learning to field questions. Is that what this is about? You feeling lonely?'

'No.' Luna ran a hand through her hair. 'I mean, yes. It's that . . . Look. You know why I came to your shop? That first time?'

'You told me that you woke up one morning and couldn't think of any reason to get out of bed,' I said. 'And you decided that you needed to find someone who could help. Because if you didn't change something, then one day you'd just stop getting out of bed altogether.'

Luna looked at me in surprise.

'I've got a pretty good memory for things I care about,' I told her.

'Yeah, well, it's not that bad any more, but . . . ever since I joined up with you, it feels kind of like I've been running, running, running. You know how sharks have to keep swimming or they drown? Like that. Like I'm always running from something. From Dark mages who'd go after me, from Light mages who wanted to prove I couldn't make it in the programme, from myself . . . I dunno. It just felt like I had to keep moving, you know? Prove something. And then there were the journeyman tests, and then . . . I just stopped. There wasn't anywhere to go.'

I was silent. 'And then you came back,' Luna said. 'And it was like it was all for nothing. No, *worse*. If I'd never been here at all then you'd have been fine. But I spent all those years working and learning and fighting and in the end I was just another liability. You know how Anne complains about all those people who expect her to take care of them? She says I'm different, but I'm not, am I? I'm just another victim.'

I sighed. 'I'm . . . not sure what to tell you.'

'Tell me it gets better,' Luna said. 'Or that there's something I can do. Just please don't tell me this is it. You know what it's like, realising you're a living bad luck charm? That everyone else's lives would be better if you just gave up and died? Please don't tell me I'm back there again. I won't be able to stand it.'

I looked at Luna. She had a pleading expression, and I knew she wasn't kidding. Luna's curse is an inherited one, and usually the bearers don't die of natural causes. They die from misery or suicide, and each time the curse jumps to the next youngest daughter of that original victim, so many generations ago. The curse protects the bearer, in its way, but it can also kill, and it might still be just as deadly to Luna as Barrayar's explosives could have been.

It suddenly occurred to me that maybe this was why Luna had done so well as a duellist. She had been introduced to duelling around our visit to Fountain Reach, not long after she'd first met Anne and Variam, and she'd taken to it with a will, practising alone and with partners for hours and hours until she could beat every other apprentice in her class. She'd placed in tournaments, beating initiate mages with far more power and experience, and that skill had been one of the reasons she'd been able to pass her journeyman test so convincingly. I'd never really thought about *why* she'd practised so hard. Maybe it hadn't been just because she liked it. Maybe it had been to prove something – prove to the Light mages that she was as good as they were, prove to herself that she could be a help to her friends instead of a millstone around their necks.

But if that were true, she'd never been working towards

something: she'd been running *away* from something. That might be why she was at such a loss now. 'Did you ever think about what you wanted to do after passing your journeyman test?'

Luna shook her head.

'Why?'

'I didn't really like any of the choices,' Luna said. 'I mean, some of the Light mages were saying I should go study in America – they're supposed to have some good chance mages there. But I'm not sure I want to. And I don't want to be a Keeper.'

'Then what *do* you want to do?'

Luna shrugged helplessly.

'Okay,' I said. 'Then the first thing you're going to have to do is answer that question.'

'How?'

'Look, maybe if times were easier, we could sit down together and spend a few weeks coming up with ideas,' I said. 'But I'm stretched to my limit right now, and so's everyone else. You said you weren't my apprentice any more? Well, this is what not being an apprentice means. We need you to be a mage, and long-term, you're the only one who can figure out how to do that.'

Luna was silent. 'But if you want a place to start,' I said, gesturing to the hotel room, 'then sort out all of this. Find a place to live, get back into shape, make yourself self-sufficient. Are you going to need any help getting on your feet?'

Luna hesitated, then shook her head. 'No,' she said. 'I'll be okay.'

'Good.' I straightened. 'You ready to settle things with the management?'

Luna looked unenthusiastic, but with a visible effort got to her feet. 'Let's go.'

I kept an eye on Luna, but in the end she managed to pull herself together without any extra help from me. Within a few days, she was settled in a new flat and in the process of looking for somewhere better.

For my part, I started putting out feelers for the item Arachne had told me about. Unfortunately, before I could make much progress, I got the visit I'd been afraid of.

It was the last week of February, and I was in my house in Wales. Anne had a late shift and I was alone for the evening, and I was sitting in the kitchen with a set of tools spread out on the table, along with what looked like coils of grey plastic rope. The rope was a material known as detcord. Jarnaff had been particularly threatening at the War Rooms today, and I was starting to get the feeling that it might not be too long before he decided to scale things up. I wasn't sure what form that was going to take, so I was trying to cover all my bases.

I sensed my visitor a way off. I was already paying close attention to the short-term futures – when working with explosives, it's highly important to know exactly what will and won't make them go bang – and he wasn't making any effort to hide. I sat up, studying the interactions. No immediate threat, but I didn't think I was going to be happy with anything he had to say. I got to my feet, stepped out into the night, then shut the front door and waited.

The Welsh valley was quiet. Wind blew in the trees and to my right came the sound of the flowing river, but as far as people went, I could have been the only person alive.

The night was overcast, and the sky and hills all around were pitch-dark. The only light was the glow through the kitchen windows behind, throwing splashes of bright yellow across the grass and to the edge of the garden wall.

Footsteps sounded. A figure emerged from the shadow, walking through the garden gate to face me.

'I assume you're here for a reason,' I told him. I knew that my position, leaning against the door with the lit windows on either side, would make me hard to see.

'I have a message for Mage Verus,' the figure said. The voice was mechanical, artificial-sounding.

'Okay.'

The figure stepped forward into the light. He – at least I thought it was a he – was clothed from head to toe in black body armour, with thick gloves and boots and a full-face helmet with an opaque visor. Not an inch of skin was visible. 'Your presence is required.'

It sounded as though the guy was using a voice distorter. It's not unknown among really paranoid Dark mages. 'And you are?'

'You may call me Archon. I represent Richard Drakh.'

It was exactly what I'd known he'd say, and what I'd been desperately hoping not to hear. 'Anyone can use a name,' I told him. It was a weak retort, but I was grasping at straws.

'If you doubt that I am who I say,' Archon said, 'then perhaps you should contact him directly.'

I stood there for a moment, studying Archon. 'You know what, I think I will,' I said. 'Don't go anywhere.'

Archon stood unmoving as I withdrew back through the door. Once I was out of sight, I studied the futures in which I waited. Archon wasn't going to move, and that, more than anything, killed any hopes I had that he was bluffing.

But I might as well play things out. I picked up my phone and dialled the number Morden had given me. He had claimed that it would put me in touch with Richard, and that it was only to be used when strictly necessary. The line rang, clicked and paused, rang again. Maybe no one would answer and I'd have an excuse to turn Archon away . . .

Click. 'Hello, Alex,' the old, familiar voice said.

My heart sank. 'There's some guy called Archon at my front door.'

'Yes, I know. You may treat him as my representative in these matters. That includes following his orders. Is that understood?'

I let out a breath. 'Yes.'

Richard hung up. I looked out the window. Archon was still waiting.

'I assume you're satisfied with my credentials,' Archon said when I finally stepped outside.

'Let's get on with it,' I said curtly. I'd taken the time to change into my armour, and I was carrying several items on my belt that were not the kind you'd take for a meeting with someone you trusted.

If Archon noticed, he gave no sign. He lifted a hand and a black disc appeared in front of him, the air darkening and shifting to become a portal. 'This way,' he said, and stepped through.

I stared at the portal, frowning. That had looked like a gate spell, but the magic hadn't been anything that I'd recognised. Archon hadn't used a gate stone, but it hadn't been the standard space-derived effect either. How had he . . . ?

Archon's mechanical voice floated through the portal. 'Today, please, Verus.'

The gate led into a small alleyway, smelling of dust and old brickwork. The sky was lit up in faint orange, and the sounds of a city were all around. Usually mages will gate through several staging points before forming the one that leads to their destination; it's rare to do it in a single jump. Archon led his way out of the alley, and I followed.

We'd entered an old industrial district, tall warehouses with darkened windows reaching up into an overcast sky. Trains rumbled past nearby, and from somewhere over the rooftops I could hear the mournful hoot of a boat's horn. I'd already figured out that we were in Manchester, but I didn't know much more than that. Instead, as we walked, I took the opportunity to study Archon. I'd never heard of or met anyone by that name before, and that on its own wouldn't have been a cause for concern – there are lots of Dark mages who keep to themselves – but if he really was Richard's new enforcer, then I wanted to know everything about him I could. I looked into all the futures of my possible interactions with him, fishing for anything I could find. He was willing to talk, but not at length, and while he wasn't going to attack me unprovoked, he'd react swiftly to aggression. The main thing that struck me as unusual was the magic he commanded. Visually it took the form of thin black strands, not especially powerful but quick and precise. I couldn't figure out what type it was – it felt as though it should be universal, but it wasn't anything like the darkness or radiation magic I'd seen. If anything, it seemed closest to the general multi-family spells that apprentices learn, but that didn't make sense . . .

I didn't have long to speculate before Archon halted in front of a warehouse complex, several differently sized buildings overtopping each other. 'We are here for a negotiation,' Archon told me. 'You may respond if questioned, but do not draw undue attention. I expect that the bulk of the meeting will take place between myself and two or three others. During this time, you will wait outside.'

'And do what?' I asked. 'Bodyguard you?'

'That will not be necessary.'

'Then if you don't want me as a guard and you don't want me to talk or go into the meeting, what am I here for?'

'I believe Richard Drakh instructed you to follow my orders.'

In other words, don't ask questions. I rolled my eyes and followed Archon in.

The inside of the warehouse held metal crates stacked on top of one another, with stairs running up to a catwalk and windows high on the walls. Six people were clustered around the far end, five men and one woman. They watched us warily as we approached.

Archon came to a stop some distance from the group. 'Good evening.'

'Who are you?' one of the men said.

'We know who he is,' another man said. Something about his stance and the way he spoke made me peg him as the leader. He was thin and balding, with glasses and a hooked nose, and he watched the two of us closely. 'Where's Morden?'

'Councillor Morden is unable to attend.'

'That's bullshit,' the first man said.

The leader flicked his eyes at the first man but kept his voice level. 'We want to talk to Morden.'

'As I have told you, that is not practical,' Archon said. 'Councillor Morden has sent his personal aide. That is the best you are going to get.'

The men looked at each other, and I saw one lean in to mutter something. I'd had long enough to study the group now to peg them as adepts, or something close. Magic, but not much. They were also carrying weapons, concealed but not concealed enough, and there were other adepts nearby too, hiding behind one of the doors and ready to rush in at the first sign of trouble. Whoever these people were, they didn't trust us much.

The leader looked at me. 'You're Verus?'

'Yes,' I told him. There had been an odd inflection to his words, as though he was purposely not giving me a title and inviting me to make an issue of it.

The leader looked sideways. 'It's him,' the woman said.

'You sure?'

She nodded.

The leader turned to Archon. 'All right, Archon, or whoever you are,' he said. 'We're listening.'

Archon nodded. 'Wait here,' he told me, and walked forward. Most of the group fell in around him, keeping an uneasy distance from the Dark mage. One of them opened the door, leading Archon in, and three others trailed him inside. I had a brief glimpse of a lit room with a table and chairs before the door closed with a clang.

'Don't get any funny ideas,' one of the two remaining men told me.

I looked back at him silently and saw him take an

involuntary step back before steadying himself. *They really are scared of me.* I suppose it made sense; I'd have been scared of anyone acting as Morden's emissary too. I turned and headed for the door.

'Hey,' the man called. 'Where are you going?'

'Out,' I said over my shoulder. 'Call me when they're done.'

'You're supposed to . . .' the man began, then tailed off when he saw that I wasn't stopping. I opened the warehouse door and stepped through.

The instant I was outside I ran quickly and quietly to the alley that ran alongside the building. I'd already confirmed that I had a few minutes before those two men would decide to come after me, and I had no intention of wasting them. I'd scanned the building on the way in, and I'd noticed a few places where . . . *there. That should work.* This side of the warehouse was smooth brick with no windows, but a metal drainpipe ran down from the first-floor roof. I got a grip and started climbing.

It was harder than I'd expected. With my divination, I knew the pipe would support my weight, but it creaked alarmingly and pulling myself up wasn't as easy as it should have been. With the chaos of the past couple of months I hadn't had the chance to work out much. I pulled myself over the edge to see that the roof ran flat to merge into the taller warehouse ahead. Most of its windows were dark; two were lit. There was no cover. I crept forward, crouching down as I came close, then looked ahead to see what I'd see.

The window looked down into the room where Archon and the adepts were meeting. I stayed very still and focused, looking ahead to find out what I'd hear if I pressed my ear to the glass. Nothing but murmurs. The other window had a piece broken out of one of the panes, and I moved closer to the hole.

The murmurs resolved into voices. '. . . grass-roots,' someone was saying. '. . . get the word out, it would . . .'

I lost the rest of the sentence. I edged closer.

There was more talking. I recognised the flat, mechanical sound of Archon's voice, but I couldn't quite make out what he was saying. '. . . not enough,' someone replied sharply. 'Not enough identification. They have to feel *threatened*, that they're coming for *them*.'

Archon said something; I caught the word 'martyr'. *Just need to be a little closer.* I crept almost to the window.

I was near enough now that only one more step would leave me looking down into the room. Through the futures I could see that Archon was sitting at a table across from the man in glasses I'd pegged as the leader, with the other three standing behind. All seemed focused on each other. 'And Morden can arrange that, can he?' the man in glasses asked suspiciously.

'Morden can arrange a great many things,' Archon said. 'A better question is what you can bring to the table.'

'How do we know this isn't a trap?' one of the other men demanded.

'If the Keepers wanted to arrest you,' Archon said, 'they could simply arrest you. There would be no need for pretence. This is your first – and perhaps only – chance to gain the support of someone with real political power.'

'Then if Morden's on our side,' the man in glasses said, 'why's his aide out there?'

'Mage Verus is close enough,' Archon said. And turned his head slightly up towards the window.

I was already scrambling back. I kept just enough presence of mind not to let my footsteps ring out on the rooftop, but I moved as fast as I could back the way I'd come. I could hear voices from street level; the men I'd left behind had followed me out. I swung over the rooftop to the pipe, dropped to the pavement, and pulled my phone out of my pocket just as the man appeared in the mouth of the alley.

'Yeah,' I said into the switched-off phone. 'Okay.'

'Hey,' the man behind me called. It was the same one who'd told me not to get any funny ideas.

I frowned at him, then carried on talking. 'That's fine.'

'You're not supposed to be out here.'

'Okay,' I said into the phone. 'I'll talk to you then.' I lowered it and stared at the man. 'Do you mind?'

'You're not supposed to be out here,' he repeated.

I walked past without bothering to answer. He hesitated, then followed. Up ahead, the other man appeared around the corner of the building. I already knew they weren't going to let me out of their sight again.

The bits and pieces I'd overheard were only snippets, and I wished I'd been able to hear just a little more, but at least now I knew why Archon had brought me along: it had been to use my position as Morden's aide to give his words authority. Did Morden know about it? Probably. A better question was what they were trying to achieve.

Archon appeared from the warehouse fifteen minutes later. I braced myself, expecting to be questioned, but he walked past without a word. I fell in beside him. Behind us, the adepts at the warehouse watched us go.

'So?' I asked once we were a couple of streets away.

'So?'

'What happened in there?'

'Why?' Archon asked. 'Were you offering feedback?'

I shot Archon a look that he didn't seem to notice. 'I believe you can find your way home from here,' Archon said. 'I'll be in touch. Oh, and next time, I'll expect you to be ready to leave more promptly.' He walked away without a backward glance.

Sourly I watched Archon disappear into the darkness. *Next time. Great.* And it wasn't as though I was in any kind of a position to turn him down. But maybe if I could figure out what he was doing . . .

I turned away, already searching for a place to gate back to Wales. I was pretty sure Talisid would want to hear about this.

March

You know, I thought as I looked at the three men glowering at me, *with hindsight, I really should have seen this coming.*

It had seemed like such an easy job. I'd received an order from Rain's office telling me to deliver an item to the Vault, the high-security location where the Council stores all of its most dangerous and valuable items, the ones they really don't want Dark mages (or Light mages they don't like) to get their hands on. The order hadn't come directly *from* Rain – which, again with hindsight, should have been a tip-off – but it had been the first job the Keepers had given me this year and I'd been hoping that, if I made myself useful enough, they might start trusting me a little. On top of that, the person I was supposed to be doing the hand-off to was Caldera, and I still wanted to talk to her about what had happened over Christmas.

So I'd gone down to the quartermaster's, signed some papers, sat patiently through a lecture on security and finally I'd been issued a small package, about the size of a paperback book. I'd been told several times that I absolutely must not open it, or try to open it, or even *think* about trying to open it, and I'd followed my orders. I hadn't even tried looking into the futures in which I did any of those things (which in my opinion showed a really impressive degree of forbearance on my part), and now as I looked across the concrete floor at the three men waiting for me, I was quite sure that it all had been a waste of time.

We were in the tunnels beneath Old Street Roundabout. I'd taken the stairs down, watching the wide arches at the roundabout's centre disappear behind the railings to leave only a narrowing patch of cloud-covered sky, before that in turn had vanished too. I'd followed the other pedestrians along the underpass until I'd found the steel door set into the tiled wall. The door had been locked but had opened to my Keeper signet, and I'd closed it behind me and taken the spiral stairs down, hearing the rumble of the traffic overhead. The spiral stairs had led into a wide, open area with a concrete floor, a low ceiling, a rather out-of-place tiled mosaic around the walls, and three heavily muscled goons in the centre of the room. I didn't think they were here for a friendly conversation.

It wasn't like I hadn't had warning. Jarnaff had been trying for weeks to get me to tell him Morden's plans, and at our last encounter he'd as good as told me that if I didn't co-operate they were going to get the information out of me the hard way. I'd already suspected that Jarnaff knew something about what had happened to Morden's last two aides, and I wouldn't have been surprised if he'd been the one to give the orders. Oh, there'd be no direct link – Light mages are too careful for that – but it's an open secret that a lot of Keepers have Crusader sympathies, and somehow I didn't think it was a coincidence that these guys just happened to be waiting for me right after I received orders through official Keeper channels.

'Hi there, guys,' I said.

The three goons stared at me and I gave an inward sigh. 'You know,' I said, 'I'm on official Keeper business here.'

The central goon spat on the floor. 'You're no Keeper.'

'Yeah, I'm starting to figure that out,' I said. 'Do you mind?'

'Fucking Dark mages,' the goon said. 'Think you can get away with anything.'

I am getting really tired of being called that. 'I'm not a Dark mage,' I said, holding my temper.

'Bullshit,' the goon on the right said.

'You work for fucking Morden,' the central goon said. 'You murder kids. You're a piece of shit.'

I hesitated for just a second, responses going through my head. I wanted to argue, justify myself, but . . . *No.* I remembered what Arachne had once told me about my reputation. *If you have it, use it.* I walked forward, closing the distance to the central man, stopping only a few feet away to stare up into his eyes. 'Then if you really believe all that,' I said softly, 'why are you standing in my way?'

The goon hesitated. He'd been about to advance on me, and now that I'd pre-empted him, he wasn't sure what to do. But he was bigger and stronger than I am, and like a lot of big, strong, stupid people, his fall-back plan when things didn't go his way was to grab the problem and overpower it. He reached out to do just that.

I slid under the goon's arm and hit him low and viciously. His eyes bulged and he stumbled to the ground. The second one started towards me but I turned on him, staring, and he checked, looking at his friends. 'Don't even think about it,' I said, my voice hard.

'Come on!' the third goon called. 'He's only a diviner!'

I snapped my head around to stare at him, and he took an involuntary step back. 'You're right,' I said. 'I'm a diviner. Now here's a question for you: if I thought any of you was the slightest possible threat to me, would I still be here?'

Goon #3 hesitated, and I saw the futures flicker as he tried to figure out what to do. I already knew what he could do, and what his friends could do as well. I knew that he had a knuckleduster in his pocket, just as I knew that his partner was carrying a club. I also knew that all three had no combat magic, or none that would make a difference. In all practical terms, they were no stronger than mundane normals, which meant that their chances against me in any kind of fight were close to zero. It should have been reassuring, but if anything, it pissed me off. Apparently the Crusaders still weren't taking me seriously. *Well, they'll learn.*

Goon #1 struggled to his feet. His movements were awkward, and he was still clutching his groin, but his face was dark with rage. 'Come on!' he snarled. With his words, the wavering futures of Goons #2 and #3 steadied, and now every possible outcome led to violence. They spread out, surrounding me, and then Goon #1 lunged.

Divination isn't great at predicting people's movements. Even if you can pick the general course of action that someone will follow, it's still hard to know *how* they're going to do it. Looking more than a few minutes ahead into a conversation is close to impossible unless you have some kind of workaround, and a really chaotic environment like a fight is even worse. To divination magic, a battle is an impenetrable wall; anything on the other side is completely invisible. All you can see is what'll happen in the next few seconds.

But in combat, a lead of a few seconds is huge. Most people who die in battle die through being caught by surprise. Either they're looking in the wrong place, or they don't understand what they're looking at, or they make a move that they didn't know was the wrong one until too late. When you can see which futures are the bad ones, then combat is suddenly much less dangerous. It doesn't make you invincible – if your enemy is too tough or too fast then seeing his moves before he makes them isn't enough, and if they have enough numbers on their side, then they can pull you down no matter how good you are. But if you're fighting an enemy *without* those sorts of advantages, divination is pretty hard to beat.

The three goons weren't that fast, they weren't that tough and there weren't that many of them. They'd already lost; they just didn't know it yet.

I let the first man go past, sliding aside as he grasped at the empty air, and came around facing Goon #3. He'd pulled out his knuckleduster but hesitated, reluctant to attack me head-on. My movement had put Goon #2 at my back, and I could see the futures only moments away in which his club would crack across my skull. I held still, giving him a clear target, then as he started his swing, I kicked back and out. The force of his momentum drove his knee onto my foot and I heard a *snap*, followed by a scream of pain.

Goon #3 looked down behind me, his eyes wide, and by the time he looked back I was on him. He flung his hands up, which blocked his view of my hands, and I was already aiming low. Stomach and groin, then as he doubled over I caught his head and slammed my knee into his face. He went down and I turned to face the first man.

Goon #1 had recovered from his failed rush and was coming at me again. He hesitated just briefly upon seeing that the other two were down, but his blood was up and with a roar he charged straight at me, arms wide to grab and crush.

I threw glitterdust in his eyes, and that was that.

After I'd retrieved the club and used it to deal with the blinded one, I dusted myself off and looked around. Goon #1 was unconscious, #3 was stirring and moaning and #2 was trying and failing to drag himself away across the floor with his broken leg. He looked up at me with terrified eyes and I shook my head. 'You boys took the wrong job.'

'You know what they say,' a voice said from the other end of the chamber. 'You get what you pay for.'

I looked up to see that two more men had entered. They were far enough away that I couldn't get a clear look at them, but both were wearing masks that hid their upper face, which pretty much ruled out any possibility that they were here on legitimate business. 'How many of you idiots *are* there?' I said in annoyance.

The two men advanced. 'Look,' I said. 'I'm getting tired of this. How about you just walk away, and we can . . .'

And then I stopped.

I'd had a chance to look into the short-term futures. Unlike Goons #1 to #3, these two *did* have magic backing them. They were battle mages, and they were a lot stronger than me.

I'd been wrong. The Crusaders *were* taking me seriously. They'd laid a trap, one designed especially to catch a diviner: throw a weak enemy at me, one I'd be confident I could beat, and use that as a screen to hide the real threat. I felt a nasty sensation in my stomach as I realised that I'd been overconfident. Winning wasn't on the cards any more. Escaping was.

I took a step back, scanning. There were two exits from

the chamber, one ahead and one behind. Of the two men facing me, the closer one was dark-skinned and strong, and from the futures of combat, I could tell that he was some sort of light-force hybrid, able to create weapons and shields of hardened energy. The second man, the one who'd been doing the talking, was smaller, and he was a lightning mage. He was hanging back, keeping the other man between him and me.

The two of them came to a stop about forty feet away. 'Going to come quietly?' the lightning mage said. He had a London accent.

'Going to introduce yourself first?' I said. Only a little of my attention was on the conversation. If I ran straight back, the big guy would throw up a barrier to block the exit. What if I tried a sneak attack? No, they were waiting for that . . .

'We just want a chat,' the lightning mage said.

'Uh-huh,' I said. 'From what I heard, your chats with Morden's last couple of aides didn't go so well for them.'

'Dunno what you mean.'

'You have mind mages on staff,' I said quietly. 'Why use torture?'

The lightning mage shrugged. 'Fight fire with fire.'

'How many times do you think you can try this before people start noticing?' I said. 'No one is going to believe that this is just a coincidence.'

'No, no, Verus,' the lightning mage said. 'You've got it all wrong. You see, you're about to be abducted by some Dark mages who're after that package you're carrying.'

'Abducted by Dark mages who just happened to be inside the Vault?'

'The Vault?' The lightning mage smiled. 'Who said

anything about the Vault? When they check the records, they'll find your signet was never used on the door.'

I felt a chill. If they had connections in the Keepers, it wouldn't be hard for them to falsify the records. For that matter, if I suddenly disappeared, would anyone in the Keepers even think it was an abduction at all? Or would they assume I'd run off with the package I was carrying? The only reason anyone had known about what had happened to Morden's last aide was that he'd been allowed to be found. I remembered the condition of his body – broken fingers and burned alive – and felt a flicker of fear. Both the mages were staring at me, and I recognised the expression in their eyes. As far as they were concerned, I was just another Dark mage.

'Time's up, Verus,' the lightning mage said. 'You going to make this easy?'

'Fuck you,' I said quietly.

The lightning mage's smile didn't change. 'I was hoping you'd say that.'

Light flared, crisp and sharp. I was already dodging right, and the ball flashed past with a smell of sulphur. My hand came out of my pocket holding a small marble, and I flung it at my attacker.

The other man put out a hand and a glowing shield appeared in mid-air. The marble struck the shield and shattered, and mist rushed out, hiding both the mages in a sphere of fog. I sprinted back, aiming for the exit, but I only made it halfway before the air in the tunnel mouth shimmered and another force barrier appeared, blocking my path. A second ball of lightning arrowed in and I swerved and turned on my attackers as the dark-skinned man came striding out of the fog.

I went for him, my knife in one hand and my stun focus in the other. Swords of light appeared in the man's hands; the blade of each was a plane of glowing force, each sharp enough to take off my arm, and I twisted and weaved, trying to find a way past the flashing blades. I fought not just in the present but in the future, trying every weapon I could think of to get past the big man's defence. Glitterdust and stuns and dispels all struck at him, ghostly and unrealised, and all failed.

Ball lightning slashed at me and I had to jump back. The force mage lowered his blades and advanced, light glowing from the swords. The lightning mage was behind him, still keeping his distance. They were watching me, careful but not cautious, and I knew that they were confident that they were winning. I backed up, giving ground.

Energy crackled around the lightning mage's hands, pulsed from the force swords. I kept moving backwards. The exit was behind me, but without looking I knew that the barrier was still there; the force mage was holding the spell as he fought me. *Can't outfight these guys.* I needed an edge, but what? The chamber was bare, concrete and empty. There were pillars scattered around, but hiding behind them wouldn't help. The force mage would just trap me with walls and I'd be cornered.

Pain flashed in my futures and I jumped left, placing the force mage between me and the spell. The lightning mage aborted his attack, letting the energy crackle away, and the two of them kept advancing. The lightning blast would have stunned and paralysed me . . .

. . . but it wouldn't have killed me, and suddenly I was paying very close attention. *They want me alive.* The force mage had never tried to cut me in half with those swords, only hold me off. I needed to be in one piece for interrogation – but how were they going to do that? A memory jumped out at me: back when I'd been talking, I'd looked very briefly at the futures in which I'd agreed to go quietly, and I'd caught a fleeting image of a syringe . . .

It fit, and all of a sudden I had a plan. I broke right, sprinting for the pillar.

The lightning mage tracked me, and in the futures I saw the ball lightning leap out to intersect my path. I could see a future in which I dodged it cleanly, but I rejected it, looked for a future of a grazing hit. I saw the flash reflected from the tiles as the spell was loosed behind me and I tried to pick out just the right moment to drop. *Got to make it look good.* It was going to be close—

The spell hit just as I was starting my roll, spidering across my back and shoulder. Pain shot through my body and my limbs twitched and jerked. The roll turned into a fall and I slammed into the concrete, tumbling. I hit the pillar and lay still.

'Better not have killed him,' the force mage said, speaking for the first time. He had a deep, rumbling voice.

'He's fine,' the lightning mage said dismissively. 'Go check.'

Footsteps drew closer. I kept my eyes closed, breathing slowly, steadily. I still felt sick, the electric shock filling me with nausea and numbing my muscles, and the stink of sulphur filled my nostrils. I heard the force mage step to within arm's reach and I could feel the presence of the blades, only inches away, and every instinct urged me to block, to defend myself. I held absolutely still, blind and helpless.

Something hard and narrow poked my arm roughly. It

didn't pierce the flesh; the force mage must have blunted the tip. 'Still breathing,' the deep voice said.

'All right,' the lightning mage said. 'Let's hurry this up.'

I felt the spell dissipate and heard the rustle of clothing as the force mage reached into a pocket. The big man was standing right over me, holding a syringe in his right hand, and as I watched he slid the cap off the needle, tapped the side of the glass, then bent down.

As soon as I'd glimpsed that syringe, I'd guessed that it held some sort of knockout drug. Electricity can't render someone unconscious, not reliably, but there are plenty of anaesthetics that'll put someone under pretty fast if you inject them in the right place. Shock spells to take the target down, then a drug to make them unconscious for transport. The force mage took hold of my wrist, turning it so that the inside was facing up, and brought the syringe in for the injection. For a brief second, all of his attention was focused on getting that needle into the vein.

My hand closed over his. The force mage jerked back, but I'd been ready and used the movement to stab the needle into his wrist. My thumb came down on the plunger, and I saw his eyes widen as he felt the contents of the syringe go in.

'Surprise,' I told him.

He lashed out, but I was already rolling away and the force blade cut the concrete where I'd been lying. I ducked behind the pillar, letting another lightning blast soak into the stone, and circled around to face them.

The force mage was still up, but he was starting to stagger and I knew that the stress of combat would be making his blood pump faster, carrying the drug to his heart and brain. His eyes slipped as they tried to focus on me, and the sword in his hand blurred and steadied. 'Block it!' the lightning mage snapped at him. 'Block it!'

I turned and sprinted for the tunnel, but even drugged and dazed, the force mage wasn't out of the fight. A wall of opaque light appeared; in a flash I saw the future in which I tried to smash through fail, and instead I broke right, feeling another lightning ball scorch past my head, and as I turned I was drawing the hidden knife from under my coat. I flipped it to hold the blade between finger and thumb, took a second to aim, then hurled it at the force mage as hard as I could.

Throwing a knife at someone with the aim of killing them is a complete waste of time. Just throwing a blade into a stationary target is hard enough – doing the same thing against someone who's fighting back is basically impossible. I'm one of the best combat throwers I know, and even I can't do it consistently. If you really insist on using a thrown weapon, you're better off with a dart or a javelin, or you could just take a hint from military history and use a gun like everybody else.

There's one thing that knife throwing is good for though. It's *really* distracting for the guy on the receiving end.

The force mage flinched and reflexively threw up a shield. If he'd been at full strength he could have done that while holding up the barrier at the same time, but he wasn't. The knife hit the shield and clattered to the floor, the barrier behind me vanished, and before either mage could react I was gone.

I sprinted up the stairs, out through the locked door and back out into the tunnels beneath the roundabout. Someone, probably the lightning mage, was trying to gate out to cut me off, but he'd picked the tunnels to my north and I ran south instead. It took about three minutes for the mage to gate in and search the area, and by the time he figured out that he was looking in the wrong place I was long gone.

I stopped running after about half a mile and settled into a fast walk, scanning ahead through every future that I could find. Nothing showed and I kept walking south until I reached Liverpool Street, losing myself in the crowd of Londoners. I bought myself a bottle of water from a coffee shop and sat down, feeling the blood rushing in my veins. I looked down at my hands and watched them tremble. It took them a long time to stop shaking.

Once I was sure I was safe, I retraced my steps back to Old Street. I found a vantage point near the roundabout and thoroughly explored all the possible futures in which I went back down into the tunnels. There was no sign of either mage, but then I hadn't expected there to be. Now that the attack had failed, they'd withdrawn and cut their losses, waiting for the next time.

And so, once I was absolutely sure that they were gone, I went back.

'You took your sweet time,' Caldera said.

'I suppose I did,' I said.

The entrance to the Vault had none of the beauty of the Belfry. It was a big, rectangular room, with metal walls and fluorescent lights. A thick sheet of armoured glass ran across the middle, with airlock-style doors and security booths from which guards could watch people as they entered and left. Caldera and I were in one of the booths, standing on opposite sides of a table.

'You got it?' Caldera asked.

I held up the package.

Caldera took it and turned it over in her hands with a frown. Caldera is an earth mage with thick arms and legs, broad and heavy and tough. We'd been fairly close until three months ago. 'You sit on it, or what?'

'Something like that.'

Caldera looked sharply at me. 'You open it?'

'No.'

'You sure?'

'Christ. Yes, I'm sure.'

Caldera grunted and slid a form across the table. 'Fill in the box and sign.'

I scribbled with the pen. Caldera took the form back and started filling it in with a look of concentration.

I was left standing. A couple of security guards were talking thirty feet away, but I couldn't hear them through the armoured glass. The only noise was the scratch of pen on paper.

'You want to talk about it?' I asked.

Caldera didn't look up. 'About what?'

'You know what.'

Caldera got to the bottom of the page, flipped it over and kept writing. She didn't answer.

'The last time we talked?' I said. 'You know, on Boxing Day?'

'I don't really have time for this, all right?' Caldera said. She spun the form around and handed me the pen. 'Sign and date.'

I did. Caldera took the form back and started towards the door at the other end of the booth. I followed, only for Caldera to turn and block me. 'Where are you going?'

'Uh, with you.'

'No, you're not.'

'I'm supposed to put this in the Vault.'

'Your orders are to deliver it *to* the Vault,' Caldera said. 'You can go now.'

'Oh, come on,' I said in exasperation.

'What did you expect?' Caldera said. 'A guided tour?'

'Would have been nice,' I said. The Vault is supposed to be the highest-security facility that the Council has, next to the War Rooms themselves, and I was curious about the defences. According to rumour, they're guarded by everything from laser tripwires to bound elementals. I have no idea what's behind that security, but it's supposed to contain everything that the Council absolutely can't afford to lose. According to rumour, there are whole rooms of magical items in there, numbered and sealed away and gathering dust. The fateweaver is there too, or at least the statue that's the door to its resting place, or so I'd been told. I didn't really have any legitimate reason to look at the place, but quite frankly, I felt that I'd earned it. 'Isn't guarding the Vault supposed to be a Keeper duty?'

'And here I am guarding it.'

I reached into my pocket and held up my own Keeper signet.

'Funny thing,' Caldera said. 'The Council don't seem too keen on you poking around inside their top-end security.' She looked at me. 'Almost like they don't trust you.'

'Seem to remember you telling me not too long ago that you *did* trust me.'

'Yeah, well,' Caldera said. 'Things change.'

'Look, I'm sorry about Boxing Day, okay? I was on the run and I was scared. I was just trying to stay alive.'

'Sure,' Caldera said. Her eyes were flint. *Apology not accepted.*

I felt a flash of anger. I could understand Caldera holding a grudge – last Boxing Day I'd hit her with insults, several punches and a Sainsbury's truck, in that order – but only because she'd been trying to arrest me at the time. If I'd gone along quietly, then I would have been dead within the week, but she thought *she* was the one with a reason to hold a grudge? I took a breath and let it out, forcing myself to calm. 'Can you do one thing for me?' I said once I could make my voice level. 'Check the entry records for the Old Street entrance.'

'For when?'

'Say an hour ago.'

Caldera frowned at me, then left the security booth, heading towards the far end. She opened a steel door and disappeared inside. She was gone a long time, and when she reappeared and walked back across to open the door her frown had deepened. 'What's going on?'

'Was hoping you could tell me.'

'There's no record of your signet being used to access the top door,' Caldera said. 'And when I tried to check the video feed, there's a problem with the cameras. What are you playing at?'

'Nothing.'

'Is this another one of your stunts where you break into somewhere to show off?'

'No.'

'I'm serious, okay? If you've been tampering with the security systems then you need to tell me right the hell now. No one is in a mood to screw around and—'

'I said no,' I said in annoyance. 'Go check up on it, since I know that's what you're going to do anyway. I only just got in the damn facility.'

Caldera stared at me. 'Fine,' she said at last.

I left. The guards buzzed me out, and when I was almost at the exit I turned to look back. Caldera was still staring at me, and as I looked back at her I felt a sudden flash of unease. Those two mages who'd tried to abduct me had as good as admitted that they'd had Keeper help. Just for a moment, I imagined Caldera standing in a security room, arms folded, watching the fight on a TV screen.

I pushed the image away. Caldera might hold a grudge, but she'd always been straight. She wouldn't betray me like that.

Would she?

I turned and walked into the tunnel, but the unease didn't go away.

'So what are you going to do?' Anne asked.

It was the next day, and Anne and I were out on the slope of a hill in Wales. Cold winds blew across the hilltop above, but the valley we were in gave us shelter from the worst of the gusts. White clouds were scattered across a blue sky, and from our vantage point we could see the clouds' shadows below, the high winds sending them gliding across fields and hedges faster than a man could run.

'I spoke to Talisid last night,' I said. 'He's pretty sure that they're a pair of mages called Lightbringer and Zilean. Officially, they're aligned with the Guardian and Crusader factions and work as Keeper auxiliaries. Unofficially, they're part of the Crusaders' black ops squad. He didn't know whether they were involved in what happened to Morden's last couple of aides, but after yesterday, I think it's a safe bet that the answer's yes.'

'But Talisid's with the Guardians,' Anne said. 'Can't he stop them?'

I shrugged. 'I'm not optimistic.'

'But you're working for him!'

'Which is a secret,' I said. 'And if Talisid tells everyone in the Guardians about that, then Morden and Richard will find out about fifteen minutes later, and then what do you think'll happen?'

We were sitting on a flat-topped granite rock halfway up the hillside. I was wearing a T-shirt, my jumper lying on the grass and sweat cooling on my skin. Anne sat cross-legged on the rock itself. The wind still carried the bite of the Welsh winter, but Anne didn't seem to feel the cold.

'Are you going to report it to Rain?' Anne asked.

'What's the point?' I said. 'I can't even get a new desk delivered without the order getting lost in the files. Lightbringer and Zilean will just deny it, the investigation will get bogged down in paperwork, and by the time it finally starts they'll have had more than long enough to scrub any evidence. And all the time that's going on, the Crusaders will be busy spinning it as another example of the evil, manipulative Dark mages taking advantage of their position in the Council to make false accusations against honourable Keepers who are just doing their job.'

'So what are you going to do? Just wait for them to try again?'

'That, and keep a better lookout next time.'

Anne let out an angry breath and looked away.

I leant back against the rock. 'So how's your job as a Council healer?'

'You've got to be joking,' Anne said. 'They won't let me treat so much as a papercut.'

'I thought they'd authorised you.'

'Turns out they only certified me for *emergency* healing, and only if I'm on duty. Except that they're never short of emergency healers except in a war, so they never have to put me on duty, so they don't. Ninety-five per cent of what they do is physiology adjustments and treatments for basic stuff, and they won't let me touch that. And do you know the worst part? They won't let me do anything else either. I tried to start up my clinic again and they told me I wasn't allowed! I'm not allowed to do any kind of healing without a licence, which you need to jump through so many hoops to get that it'll take me a year at least, and that's if they sign off on it at all. So I just go in every day, and I sit at my desk and do nothing, waiting for someone to call. I was more useful working in the supermarket.'

'Sounds familiar,' I said, and stood. 'Okay, I'm ready to go again.'

I used to think of myself as pretty fit. My magic type means I have to rely on my body more than most mages, and so I've got a motive to stay in shape and strong. But when you've got a tool as useful as divination, it's easy to fall into the trap of over-relying on it, and that climb last month had come as a wake-up call.

It all came down to that conversation with Arachne. I needed to be stronger, and while being in shape probably wouldn't make all that big a difference in the grand scheme of things, it was a good place to start. I was never going to be as strong as Caldera or as tough as Morden, and no reflexes can match the speed of a time mage or an air mage. But I could narrow the edge, and that was what I was trying to do.

With a little help.

I ran a circuit around the hill, following a sheep track through the grass. One third of the way around the hillside the grass broke up into a field of boulders, great hulks of granite half buried in the ground, and I ran up the side of one and started jumping from one to the other, trying not to let my feet touch the grass. The second-last jump was a little further than I could safely reach and I felt a twinge of pain as my feet slammed into it. I hopped off the last boulder and kept going.

Two thirds of the way around was a ruined stone cottage. Its tiny front porch was the only flat piece of ground on the hillside and I dropped down to do calisthenics. Push-ups, sit-ups, squats, pull-ups using what was left of the roof, then I went down into a plank, resting on my forearms and toes, keeping my body straight. I held the position as long as I could, my muscles trembling, until at last my arms and abdominals gave out and I collapsed gasping to the ground. I stayed down for a few seconds, catching my breath, then pulled myself up.

My lungs were burning by the time I made it back to Anne. 'Thirty seconds faster,' she said, checking her watch. 'Did you do fewer sets?'

'No,' I managed to get out, sucking in deep breaths. The cold air felt like an ice pack. 'Same.'

Anne hopped off the rock and laid a hand on my chest. Green light glowed, and I felt warmth flowing through me, taking away the pain. The burning in my lungs faded first, followed by the soreness in my muscles, and then all of it was gone and I felt fresh and active and full of energy, as though I could run for miles. I was also *starving*.

'Looks good,' Anne said. 'You had a slight sprain in your knee, by the way.'

'Should I go again?'

'You could, but I think that's enough for the day.'

'Good,' I said. 'Then I'm going to eat everything in that pack.'

I'd brought along a packed lunch, and given my experience with the effects of Anne's spells, I'd made it big enough for about four people. One chicken wrap, two beef sandwiches, an apple, three bananas, a couple of cereal bars, a mini-cheese and a salami later, I was feeling human again. 'Is this what you feel like all the time?' I asked Anne.

'Only when I'm doing heavy work,' Anne said. Anne might be thin, but she eats enough for two or three normal people. It's one of the side effects of life magic – life spells, especially healing, use a lot of energy, and the easiest way to supply it is from the body's natural energy reserves.

Right now, though, I was thinking less about food and more about Anne. She was leaning back on the rock, gazing down over the valley as she ate, and I found myself noticing how the wind ruffled her hair, remembering the feel of her hands on my chest. It wasn't the first time either, and since we'd started training, it had become harder and harder to ignore. A part of me didn't *want* to ignore it, and I felt a flash of guilt. Right now Anne was in almost as much danger as me, and it was mostly my fault. Taking advantage of the fact that we'd been thrown together felt wrong . . .

I cast about for something to distract me. 'Something I was wondering,' I said. 'When I was in that fight yesterday, I took a hit from a lightning spell. The reason electricity has the effect that it does on the body is that it's running along the parts that conduct electricity anyway, right? Like the nerves?'

Anne hesitated. 'Partly.'

'So could you do something so that electrical shocks wouldn't affect me?' I said. 'Changing the layout of my body so that it grounds safely, or . . .'

I trailed off; Anne was shaking her head. 'That's not how it works.'

'I've heard of weirder alterations than that.'

Anne sighed. 'Okay, rephrase: there are other mages who'd do it. It's not how *I* work.'

'Why not?'

'Because that's not what I do,' Anne said. 'I heal bodies and I help them. I don't *modify* them. I know it seems like my spells do a lot, but they don't, not really. I don't do anything that your body can't do on its own.'

'I don't think saving someone from death really counts.'

'Yes, it does,' Anne said. 'Your body can recover from almost anything. The reason people die from injury isn't because their bodies can't fix it; it's because they get overloaded. When I heal someone, all I do is apply a little first aid, then I channel extra energy to their body's regeneration and guide it to make sure it heals cleanly. Your body knows how to fix itself. All it needs is a little help.'

'Okay, but what about what you've been doing with me? I mean, we've only been at this a few weeks, and already I went through two fights yesterday without getting out of breath. Even when I was training every day, I wasn't this fit.'

'Do you know why exercise makes you fitter?'

'Uh . . . not exactly.'

'When you stress your muscles, you create micro-tears in the tissue,' Anne said. 'Your body reads that and overcompensates, building the muscle back so that it'll be stronger next time. Cardiorespiratory is the same. You strain the system and your heart enlarges; your arteries spread out and develop so that they can pump more blood and oxygen. Normally you have to take a day or two off to let your body rebuild, but if I'm here I can give your body a boost so that you're ready to go again right away. So you can do one workout with me and get five times as much effect as you would from doing it on your own.'

'And five times as much muscle pain.'

Anne smiled. 'No such thing as something for nothing. But the point is, I'm not actually doing anything that your body couldn't do already. You could get this strong and this fit on your own, the way athletes do. It would just take you longer.'

I thought about it. 'So what about the major modifications, then? Electrical shielding, bone claws . . .'

'That's *completely* different. You've got a blueprint in your body that's the working model for your cells – that's how your body knows what to build and replace. To make those kind of changes, you have to actually redraw the blueprint. I've seen much worse things than claws. Gills, extra organs, extra limbs . . . They're a really bad idea.'

'Why?'

'Because they're working against your body's design,' Anne said. 'Say you want claws. Okay, so you grow some out of keratin and set them in the fingers, that's easy enough. Then to make them retractable, you need a muscle to flex them. Except that your finger doesn't have enough space for those muscles, so you're going to need to enlarge it. You're going to have to put in new nerves too, and the person is going to have to learn to use them from scratch, the way a baby does. Then on top of that, now the nerves and blood vessels to the fingers are being overstressed, because they're having to support twice as much activity as they were designed to, and so you'll have to modify them too, and that modification means you have to do more modifications, and so on. It's never just one thing. Everything in your body is connected, and everything has a knock-on effect on everything else. And that's just for a small change. The really big changes, the person has to keep coming back to get more treatments and check-ups, over and over again to make sure that nothing's going wrong. That's why shapeshifters can't really transform anyone except themselves. It takes so much maintenance to keep everything working right that if they did it to someone else, they'd have to stay with them twenty-four hours a day. And you don't want to know about the side effects.'

'So, I'm guessing you don't like the idea.'

'I don't like the idea of modifications at all,' Anne said. 'I mean, if someone's seriously disabled, that's one thing, but people who are perfectly healthy? Your body is fine the way it is. Why do you want to change it so badly?'

I made a noncommittal noise and Anne flashed me an apologetic smile. 'Sorry. I didn't mean to complain. I just don't feel as though I'm doing enough.'

'You're helping me.'

Anne paused. 'Can I ask you something?'

'Sure.'

'What makes someone effective in a fight?'

I looked at Anne in surprise. 'As in, what qualities?'

'More or less.'

'If we're just working off what makes someone more dangerous . . .' I stopped and thought for a second, then shrugged. 'Most important is aggression and willingness to hurt the other person. Second most important is willingness to be hurt yourself. Third would be skill and knowledge, fourth would be strength and power.'

'Only fourth?'

'Who's scarier?' I said. 'A tough, six-foot, two-hundred-pound man who's trying to steal your phone, feels guilty about it and doesn't want anyone to actually get hurt? Or a five-foot-nothing, one-hundred-pound woman who's never been in a fight in her life but who honestly believes that you stole her baby?'

Anne nodded. 'Why is skill above it?'

'That's more of a judgement call,' I said. 'If you're outclassed enough in terms of power then it doesn't matter how much skill you have. But most of the time knowing what to do's more important than brute strength. The dumb muscle types usually end up getting into fights they can't win.' I looked at Anne curiously. 'Why are you asking?'

'Well,' Anne said. 'If I'm going to be your physical trainer, do you think you could teach me how to fight?'

'Seriously?'

'I've never actually learned,' Anne said. 'I can run fast, but I don't really know how to hit people or use weapons.'

'Uh . . .'

'Is there something wrong?'

'Well, I could do it,' I said. 'It's just . . . isn't it kind of pointless? You picking up a weapon is like a soldier using a machine gun to bash someone over the head.'

'Only if the machine gun works,' Anne said. 'What if I'm fighting a construct, or someone with a life shield? Anyway, you have a bunch of guns and *you* still end up hitting people.'

'My guns are a lot less versatile than your magic, but I get your point. Okay. Figure out the two or three things that you most want to focus on, and we'll work from there. What made you start thinking about this now?'

'I suppose I just don't like feeling useless.'

I laughed. 'You think *you're* useless? You've got more raw power than any of us, except maybe Vari.'

'Do you really think so?'

'Haven't you noticed how every time we get into a fight, anyone who knows you're there and knows what you can do goes for you first? It's not me or Luna or Vari they're scared of, it's you. You're the most dangerous out of us by a long way.'

'Oh,' Anne said. 'Okay.' She paused. 'Then why did you trick me and leave me behind when you went back to London to fight Levistus's men two months ago?'

Oh. That went very quickly from good to bad. 'Ah . . .' I said. 'I was sort of hoping you'd forgotten about that.'

Anne just looked at me.

'Right.' I tried to think of an argument and couldn't. For being a diviner, I'd sure managed to walk into a lot of traps in the past twenty-four hours.

'Well?'

'Um,' I said. 'I was trying to keep you safe.'

'You were going into a fight.'

'Yes.'

'Didn't you just say that I was the most dangerous out of us?'

I felt cornered. 'Yes . . .'

'Then why?'

I let out a breath. 'Because I wasn't going in there expecting to win.'

'I would have come,' Anne said. 'Vari would have come. Maybe with us both—'

'No,' I said. 'This was Levistus's A-team we were going up against. He could have kept throwing in bodies until he buried us under them. We've always known this, right from the start. If we go up against the Council directly, there's only one way it's going to end.'

'But you didn't say any of that,' Anne said. 'You lied to me.'

'Technically I didn't actually . . .'

Anne looked at me.

'Okay, fine,' I said. 'Yes, I did, because I knew you wouldn't let me go if you knew. I didn't want you to die and I didn't want Luna to die and that was the only way I could think of to keep you both alive.'

'Why does that matter to you so much?'

'Why wouldn't it?'

'I'm not saying it shouldn't,' Anne said. 'But there's trust, and then there's "take a bullet for someone".'

'You've all put yourself in danger for me more than once.'

'Yes,' Anne said. 'Because we're a team. We protect each *other*.'

'I know, but . . .' I ran a hand through my hair. 'Look, all of this stuff with Richard and Levistus, it all comes back to me. If it hadn't been for me, none of you would have ever heard of them, and if you had, it'd be as names in the paper that you never expected to meet. I'm the reason that all this crap is happening.'

'We know about you and Richard,' Anne said. 'We're on board with it.'

'Seem to remember you were a little later about doing that than the others.'

Anne gave me a look.

'Okay, okay,' I said. 'Sorry.'

'Did you think about what would happen afterwards?' Anne said.

'You mean after I was . . . ?'

'Yes.'

'Not very much,' I admitted. 'I guess I figured I was

allowed to slack off a little on that one seeing as how I wasn't going to be around to do anything about it.'

'Luna and Vari and I would still have had enemies,' Anne said. 'Except that you wouldn't have been around to help.'

'I think you could have made it.'

'I didn't mean the physical side.'

'Then what did you mean?'

'You saw how Luna was last month,' Anne said. 'That was just because she thought you'd been forced into being Morden's aide. How do you think she would have dealt with it if she found out you'd *died* because of her?'

I stopped. 'Oh.'

Anne looked at me, waiting for an answer.

'I don't know,' I admitted.

'And what about me?'

'What do you mean?'

'Do you know how many people I've known over my life who've had something happen to them?' Anne said. 'Dead, or worse? Luna's got a curse on her. But before I met her, I was starting to think that maybe *I* was the one with the curse. Literally everything good that's happened in my and Vari's lives over the past three years has been connected to you and Luna. Do you know what it'd feel like if it ended with you committing suicide?'

'At least you'd be alive.'

'But it wouldn't have been our choice,' Anne said. 'If you'd gone through with your plan, you'd have taken that away.'

I sighed. 'I know.'

'Then why did you do it?'

I sat in silence for a few seconds before answering that

one. The wind blew across the hillside, and it was cold on my bare arms, but I didn't reach for my jumper. 'Because everyone's got their limits,' I said at last. 'The one thing they just won't do.'

'So what's yours?'

I shrugged. 'Loyalty, I suppose. I don't have many friends. I won't do anything that feels like betraying that.'

'No matter what?'

I nodded.

Anne sat there, looking at me. 'So . . . what if the same thing happens again?' she asked. 'To me, or Luna, or Vari? Would you do the same?'

I thought briefly about dodging the question. But there was no point, not really, and the last time I'd made a promise to Anne that I couldn't keep, it hadn't turned out well. 'Yes,' I said. 'I know that's not what you want to hear. But . . .' I shrugged again. 'Sorry.'

Anne was quiet. I thought for a moment she was going to say more, but she didn't. We sat there for a while, watching the sun and the shadows, until at last we rose to pick up our things and turn for home.

We'd just crested the hillside up above my house, about to go down the slope to the bridge, when something in the futures caught my eye. I signalled to Anne and she stopped, instantly on guard. 'What's wrong?' she said, her eyes flicking across the valley.

'Hold still.'

Anne stood still and silent. I looked ahead, following the future in which I walked down the slope, over the bridge, along the path and through the gate towards the—

A green flash, one moment of searing pain, then darkness.

I snapped back to the present, shuddering slightly. Feeling yourself die is an experience you never get completely used to. 'We've got trouble.'

'Someone's waiting for us?'

I nodded. 'They're not going to be firing warning shots either.'

'Let me guess,' Anne said. 'Those two Light mages?'

'I wish,' I said. Light mages are bad, but at least they're predictable. 'Rachel.'

Anne frowned. 'But you haven't seen her—'

'For months, yeah. Apparently she missed me.' I raised my eyebrows. 'Suppose I should count my blessings. It's a lot easier to spot her out here.'

'Wonderful,' Anne sighed. 'Are we running?'

I hesitated. It was definitely the sensible choice. Rachel is both fast and deadly, and even with Anne at my side, I didn't like our chances if it came to a fight. Anne can heal a lot of things, but being turned into a pile of dust isn't one of them.

But I also remembered what Shireen had told me. If I needed to get Rachel on my side, then sooner or later I was going to have to talk to her, and this was the best chance I'd had in a long time. Gating away might keep us safe, but not for ever . . . and one of the things I'd been learning the hard way this year was that running away wasn't always enough. Besides, it wasn't just Shireen. There was also the deal I'd struck with Cinder.

Cinder . . .

I looked at Anne. 'I'm going to make a call.'

Anne was still with me when I came down the slope and over the bridge. We'd argued and I'd tried to convince her to stay behind, but Anne had told me that she was coming with my agreement or without it. I'd given in, on the condition that she stay in cover. Though I was pretty sure she wouldn't be the primary target in any case.

I got to the garden wall and stopped. The stone was only three feet high, but enough to block a disintegrate spell if worst came to worst. My front door was closed, and Rachel was inside. If I kept going up the path, she'd fling the door open and attack.

A minute passed, two. The futures didn't change. I glanced sideways at Anne and saw her slight nod; Rachel was still there. Four minutes.

The door opened.

Rachel is around the same height as Luna, or maybe a little taller. She has blonde hair which she'd let grow out since the last time I'd seen her, and she was dressed in black. Something about her clothes looked a little dishevelled, as though she'd been in the middle of something else and run out without getting ready, but what really worried me was the black domino mask on her face. That mask seems to have some kind of effect on Rachel's personalities, and it's rarely good news for anyone else.

'You know,' I said, 'this used to be a private house.'

Rachel stared at me.

'I mean, it's one thing to invite someone over,' I said. 'But since Christmas I've had the Keepers, then Morden and now you. I'm starting to think that repairing that lock was a complete waste of time.'

'You shouldn't be here,' Rachel said.

'Yeah, well, tell that to the people who burned down my shop.'

'How stupid are you?'

I didn't answer. 'You shouldn't have come back,' Rachel said. 'You should have stayed in that shop selling crystal balls.'

'You know what?' I said. 'I was happy doing exactly that. Guess who made sure I couldn't? The same guy you're taking orders from right now. So if you want to know why Morden brought me back, why don't you ask him?'

Rachel stiffened at that, and I knew that shot had got through. Rachel is Richard's Chosen, and that meant she was supposed to be one short step below Richard himself. Now, as far as I could tell, it was Morden and Vihaela who were closest to Richard. Rachel had been pushed down in the hierarchy, and she didn't like it.

'I was the one who waited for him,' Rachel said. Her voice was starting to rise, and I could sense the futures of violence drawing nearer. 'Me! Year after year after year, and what did you do? Nothing.' Rachel was ignoring Anne completely; her eyes were locked onto me. 'Then he calls you in, and he doesn't even talk to me. He doesn't even talk to me! Were you planning it?'

'Planning what?'

'You were always his favourite.' Rachel stared at me. 'I do all the work, then you take the credit. That was what was really going on with those adepts, wasn't it? You wanted my place as Chosen.'

'Jesus.' I shook my head. 'You really are insane.'

'Tell me!'

'Of course I didn't!' I snapped. 'You seriously think I wanted to go back to Richard? Stay as his fucking Chosen. It's not worth what you paid for it.'

It didn't work. The futures in which Rachel attacked

were coming closer and closer. With one finger I pressed a button on my phone.

'You want to be Chosen,' Rachel said. It was as though she hadn't even heard what I'd said. 'That's what this is for.'

And the futures shifted in the way I'd been hoping. I breathed a silent sigh of relief. 'Yeah, well, it's not me you should be trying to convince,' I said. 'It's him.' And I nodded to the side of the house.

Rachel stared back at me, then the sound of a heavy footfall made her blink and break her concentration. She turned to look just as Cinder stepped into view.

'Wait,' Rachel said. She looked at Cinder, then at me, then back at Cinder again, blinking. 'Wait.'

'Del,' Cinder said in his rumbling voice. He was wearing a windbreaker, his big hands stuffed into the pockets, and the breeze was blowing his hair.

'You shouldn't be—' Rachel began, then stopped. 'Wait. She's not here. That's why she's not here. You're here, so—'

'Del,' Cinder said.

'What?'

'Take it off.'

Rachel blinked. 'Why?'

'Take it off,' Cinder repeated.

'I don't want to,' Rachel said. All of a sudden she sounded like a child.

'Take it off, Del.'

'He deserves it,' Rachel pleaded. 'It'd make everything so much easier.'

'You know what Richard said.'

Slowly, unwillingly, Rachel reached up. Her fingers worked at the ties of her mask, hesitated, then undid them.

The silk mask slid from her face and she looked up at us, blinking in the light.

Next to me, I could feel Anne looking at Rachel in fascination. Rachel is quite beautiful without her mask, in a diamond-like way: finely carved, but hard. Rachel looked from me to Cinder. All the futures in which she attacked had vanished. She didn't seem to know what to do.

Cinder shifted slightly. It was only a small movement, but it made me realise that he'd been ready for a fight. He glanced at me. 'We're okay,' I told him.

Cinder nodded. 'We need to talk.'

I glanced at Rachel. 'With her,' Cinder said.

'Got anywhere in mind?' I asked.

'Not here.'

I looked at Anne, then back at Cinder. 'Well,' I said. 'I don't know about you, but I'm still hungry.'

'Seriously?' Anne said.

I shrugged. 'He picked it.'

'You didn't exactly complain.'

'Problem?' Cinder asked.

'I'm fine with it,' I said.

We were sitting at a four-person table, Anne and me on one side and Cinder and Rachel on the other. The restaurant was a McDonald's, a drive-through next to the intersection of two A roads in some town I'd never been to before. Cinder had brought us here through a gate to a nearby wood, whereupon we'd walked five minutes, tapped our orders into the machines and sat down.

'There has *got* to be somewhere better to eat,' Anne said.

'You're the one saying I need to eat enough to keep my strength up.'

'If you want to go to a hamburger restaurant, why not pick a decent one?'

'Some of the food here isn't bad,' I said.

'Like what?'

'Fries,' Cinder said.

I pointed at Cinder. 'What he said.'

'They're just oil-fried potatoes doused in about ten different chemicals.'

'Yes, but they're *thin* oil-fried potatoes. Do you know how hard it is to find decent-quality thin fries in the UK?'

'These are not decent-quality.'

Cinder snorted and Anne looked at him. 'What?'

Cinder nodded at Rachel. 'You sound like her.'

There was something surreal about sitting here with the two Dark mages. So far, no one had paid us any particular attention. Fast food restaurants get a pretty wide mix of customers, and compared to the men in workmen's clothing by the far window, the bunch of construction workers in their hi-vis jackets at the counter and the two women with a pram sitting a few tables over, we didn't look especially out of place. We obviously weren't locals, but someone taking a casual glance would probably have pegged us as tourists or travellers.

Rachel hadn't said a word since our conversation outside the house, and she didn't react to our looks now, staring out of the window at the cars flashing past on the road. Without her mask she was a very different person: less forceful, more withdrawn. There was no more violence in the futures, and the deadly menace to her manner was gone. I could tell that Anne sensed it too, or she wouldn't have been talking as she was.

'Where does she like to go to eat?' Anne asked once it was clear that Rachel wasn't going to answer.

'Fancy places,' Cinder said.

'Like where?' I asked.

Rachel spoke without looking at me. 'How long are you idiots going to keep talking about food?'

I looked at Cinder and raised my eyebrows. Cinder looked back at me without expression.

I was saved from having to answer the question by the waitress, who came with our trays, set them down on the tables with a clatter and walked away. It's unusual for a McDonald's to have table service. Maybe that was why Cinder liked this one in particular.

I'd been hoping Cinder would break the ice and give me something to work with, but it seemed as though he was expecting me to do it myself. 'So,' I said to Rachel. 'I'm getting the impression you're not happy.'

Rachel gave me a look which I'd become quite familiar with from the times over the past few years where we'd had a peaceful conversation, which come to think of it could probably be counted on the fingers of one hand. The look said that if I was going to say something this stupid, she wasn't going to bother answering.

'Want to talk about it?' I asked.

'No.'

'Going to be kind of hard to work this out if you're just going to stare at me.'

Rachel raised her eyes to meet mine, and there was a flat, emotionless look to them. 'You want to work this out?' she said. 'Fine. I kill you. I get to shut you up, and you get your way out. That was what you wanted, wasn't it?'

'That's not really my ideal solution.'

'I don't care.' Rachel looked at Cinder. 'This is a waste of time.'

I paused. Anne was staying quiet, presumably figuring that anything she said to Rachel would only make things worse. She was probably right, and right now, what I was doing wasn't working either. I remembered a conversation I'd had with Morden long ago. 'What do you want?'

'What's that supposed to mean?' Rachel said.

'You work for Richard,' I said. 'And now, apparently, for Morden. I'm guessing it's not because you don't have anything better to do with your time.'

Rachel looked coldly at me.

'So why do you do it?'

Rachel turned to Cinder. Cinder shrugged, as if to say it was a fair question. 'I mean, with us, it's not exactly complicated,' I said. 'We're under duress. Given the choice, we'd be as far away from all of you as we possibly could.'

'Sounds perfect.'

'Thanks,' I said. 'You, on the other hand? You're a volunteer. I mean, how long did you guard that mansion for? Maintaining the alarms, watching to see when they were triggered. Then when they pinged, you'd gate over to kill every living thing you could find. You kept that up for how long, nine years?'

'Ten.'

'Ten,' I said. 'That's serious dedication.'

Rachel stared at me.

'Seems to me you'd need some pretty powerful motivation to stick it out that long.'

'So?'

'So why'd you do it?'

'Because I'm Richard's Chosen,' Rachel said. 'Something you wouldn't understand.'

'For how long?'

'What?'

'How long are you going to stay his Chosen?'

'None of your business.'

'Most new Dark mages leave their masters within three, maybe four years,' I said. 'Some leave as soon as they have their name. But you? You've been Richard's Chosen for twelve and a half years. There are mages out there who'd train three Chosen in that time. So I have to wonder. What is it you're getting that's worth so much that you're willing to spend your entire adult life doing nothing else?'

Rachel was silent. 'I mean, there's power,' I said. 'Influence. Respect. You get all that from Richard, no question there. But here's the thing. It seems to me that you're pretty powerful on your own.'

'You have no idea what you're talking about.'

'Let me guess,' I said. 'You think Richard's going to be running the country in a few years, and he'll reward you for your loyalty. That about right?'

Rachel looked at me, sharp and suspicious. 'It's not exactly a secret,' I said.

'And who's going to stop them?' Rachel said. 'You?'

'I doubt it,' I said. 'But let's say he does win. Let's say he becomes the new dark lord of Britain, with the power of life and death over everyone in the country, and he has to choose someone to stand one step below him and rule in his name. Why would he choose you?'

'I'm his Chosen,' Rachel said, a little too quickly.

'Except when he came back, the one he chose for his partner was *Morden*.'

'That's different,' Rachel said. 'Anyway, Morden has influence on the Council. It's politics.'

'And Vihaela?' I said.

Rachel had no answer to that. While Rachel, Morden and I had all known Richard for a very long time, Vihaela, relatively speaking, was the new kid on the block. I didn't know much about Vihaela's relationship with Richard and I didn't know how he'd convinced her to work for him, but I did know that it had been Vihaela who'd been brought into Richard's inner circle while Rachel had stayed where she was. 'And now there's us,' I continued. 'Anne and me, working for Morden, just like you. Kind of sounds like we're on the same level, doesn't it?'

'For now.'

'Until what?' I said harshly. 'Until you kill me? For once in your life, stop trying to murder your way out of problems and *think*. If you'd managed to get me today, what do you think would have happened next? Richard wasn't happy with that shot you took at me back in January, was he? He made it pretty clear that his plans involved us alive. How do you think he's going to react when he finds out that the diviner he went to all the trouble to press-gang is a pile of dust?'

'He doesn't need you!' Rachel snapped.

'And you think he couldn't find a dozen Dark mages to take your place?'

'I was the one who waited for him,' Rachel said. 'I was the one he trusted to guard the mansion.'

'Great, so you're his housekeeper.'

Rachel's eyes flared and for a moment I was afraid I'd pushed her too far, but I finally had her listening to me and I couldn't afford to play it safe. 'You want to know why Richard picked Morden and Vihaela and not you?' I said. 'Because they've got self-control. Richard's playing in the big leagues now. He needs people he can trust *not* to do stupid shit like assassinating someone he's explicitly ordered to be kept alive. You think killing me will make your problems go away?'

'Maybe it'd be worth it.' Rachel's voice was savage. 'Just to not have to look at your smirking face.'

I could sense violence very close now, and I tensed. Rachel was only a few feet away, staring at me over the table and her untouched meal. If she struck, I'd have to react very fast. I could sense Anne at my side, sitting very still, and I knew she'd read Rachel's body language.

Then Cinder's big hand closed over Rachel's. 'Del,' Cinder said. He'd been silent while Rachel and I had talked, but now he was turned towards her.

Rachel jerked at Cinder's hand. 'Let go of me!'

'You know what he said,' Cinder said in his rumbling voice.

Rachel pulled again and this time Cinder let her go. Rachel rubbed her right hand with her left, glaring at Cinder, but the moment was gone. 'That hurt.'

Cinder didn't answer and Rachel got to her feet. 'I'm done talking to you,' she said, then paused and made herself a liar. 'You're wrong. He can't replace me.'

'Maybe he can't,' I said. 'But you might want to think about what that means. If you can't be replaced, you can't be promoted.'

Rachel turned and walked out. I watched her go, checking the futures to make sure she wouldn't turn and blow up the whole restaurant. I wouldn't have put it past her.

Beside me, I felt Anne let out a breath. 'That was . . . not a fun experience.' She looked at Cinder. 'Is she usually like this?'

'No,' Cinder said curtly, and stood. 'We're done. Verus.' He walked out, following Rachel.

I kept checking until I was certain they were both gone, then gave a long sigh and leant my head back, closing my eyes. 'Jesus.' I felt as though I'd just gone through a fight.

'You told me she was crazy, but I didn't think . . .' Anne shook her head. 'Do you think she listened?'

'Maybe,' I said. Rachel had given away more than she realised. She might still be Richard's Chosen, but she wasn't bound to him so tightly any more. There were cracks in the wall now, and I had the feeling that there might be a way to split them open, if I could only find it. But that was a problem for another day. I shook my head and rose. 'Let's get out of here.'

8

April and May

The cold winter turned into a cold spring. Down in London, the days grew warmer, but every morning in the Welsh valleys still dawned icy and sharp.

Rachel didn't come back. I put out some feelers, trying to talk to her again, but she didn't respond, which frankly was pretty much what I'd expected. I still remembered what Shireen had told me, but I couldn't really track her down against her will, and short of some order from Richard bringing us together, we had a stalemate. In any case, I didn't have time to sit around waiting: between training with Anne and my duties at the War Rooms with Morden, I was busy all spring. What spare time I did have I put into following Arachne's advice and searching for a dream-stone. It was slow and frustrating work. Arachne hadn't been exaggerating about how rare they were, and the few rumours I could find suggested that the only dreamstones anyone knew about were in the private collections of master mages, where they were most definitely not for sale. Trying to steal one from said master mages seemed like a bad idea for a variety of reasons, but as the weeks crept by I started to wonder if I was getting desperate enough to try.

In the meantime, life went on. Luna found a new flat to live in, but this time she kept the location a secret from everyone but us, arriving and departing via gate stone. As the spring wore on, she started disappearing, working on some project that she didn't tell us about. Her spare time she mostly spent with Variam, who'd started training for his journeyman tests; Landis had started the negotiations for a testing date, and Variam was clearly determined to pass first try. As for Anne, when the healer corps continued to refuse to give her shift work, she put in a request to be allowed to treat normals in her own time. The Council said no. Anne ignored them and did it anyway. Given our position, we really couldn't afford to get caught breaking the rules, but Anne was adamant and I gave in and worked to help her keep it a secret.

The Crusaders stayed quiet for April, then took another shot at me in May, trying to catch me while I was sleeping. The attack was well planned, but I'd been expecting it this time, and managed to give them the slip without having to fight. Unfortunately, the attack also showed up the weaknesses of the Welsh farmhouse. The location just wasn't defensible, and I'd never had the chance to set up the protections that I'd had at my shop in Camden. It had been meant as a place to hide, but I'd been using it for too long and now too many people knew how to find it. Reluctantly I left the house empty and switched to hotels and temporary accommodation, staying on the move. It threw off the Crusaders, but as the weeks went by it started to wear me down. It's depressing being a nomad.

Morden kept playing his political games, but more defensively. Rather than pursue active plans, he simply waited, occupying himself by blocking the Crusaders' and Guardians' schemes. Instead of taking it at face value, this apparent inactivity seemed to convince his enemies among the Light mages that Morden must be up to something even *more* secret and nefarious, and they drove themselves crazy trying to figure out what it was. It wouldn't have been my problem, except that one of the first people they'd go calling upon to find that out was me. By the beginning of the summer, it felt as though everyone on the Council was trying to pump me for information.

One Light mage in particular was especially persistent.

June

'For the fourth time,' I told Talisid, 'I don't know.'

'What about the apprentice committee?' Talisid asked. 'What's going on with that?'

'Morden's still trying to get a Dark mage on there.'

'Which one?'

'No names yet.'

'Then what's his objective?'

'That *is* his objective.'

'Then what about the debate on South America?' Talisid asked. 'Morden's been siding with the Isolationists.'

'Yes.'

'Why?'

I was staying at a hotel near Leicester Square. The room was pretty nice, with draped windows and a big comfortable bed on which I was currently lying, my head propped up against the headboard. In my left hand I held Talisid's communicator, while in my right hand I held a knife. Right at the moment, I was a lot more interested in playing with the knife. 'Why not?' I asked.

'Come on, Verus,' Talisid said. The audio quality was

good enough that I could pick up the undertone of annoyance in his voice.

I balanced the knife hilt-first on one finger, then flipped it into the air and caught it by the blade. 'Don't know what to tell you.'

'What's he pushing for?' Talisid asked. 'What's the long game?'

'Make people owe him favours? Foster acceptance of a Dark mage on the Council?'

'That can't be all of it.'

I sighed. 'Look. Ever since Morden was raised, he's built political capital and increased his influence on the Council. Has it occurred to you that maybe the reason he's doing that is because that's what he wants? That the reason it looks like he's playing nice with the Council and building political influence is because that really is exactly what he's doing?'

'But to what end?'

I swung the knife – still hilt-first – onto the bed and watched it bounce. 'Why do any of the Council mages want what they want? In case it's escaped your notice, Morden's acting exactly like any other Light mage. Scramble and manoeuvre until you're on top of the heap. He's just somewhat better at it than average.'

'Don't fall into the trap of assuming that there's no difference between him and his rivals,' Talisid said sharply. 'You have no idea of the things Morden did to get where he is now.'

I rolled my eyes. I like Talisid, more or less, but he's definitely a Light mage. Council good, Dark mages bad, and anything that doesn't fit with that is just an individual exception to the rule. 'Sure.'

'So what are his plans?'

'What exactly are you expecting me to do here?' I said. 'Break into Morden's office and grab a PowerPoint presentation lying on his desk titled "World Domination in Six Easy Steps"? Here's an idea for you. Has it occurred to you that Morden might know perfectly well that I'm giving you these reports?'

Talisid's voice was suddenly alert. 'Has he hinted at that?'

'No,' I said. 'And no, I wasn't traced to where I am right now, and yes, I've taken precautions. The point I'm making is that it doesn't matter. I could be the perfect employee and do everything Morden possibly wants, and he still isn't going to trust me with anything top secret, because he's *not fucking stupid.*'

'But do you think he suspects anything?'

I closed my eyes and banged my head against the headboard. 'Jesus Christ.'

'All right,' Talisid said, his voice soothing. 'I hear what you're saying.'

'Right from the start, you knew that Morden was the face of Richard's operation,' I said. 'He can't exactly do that if he's breaking the Concord every five minutes, can he? If you want my advice, you'd spent less time looking at Morden and more time at whatever the hell Archon's doing.'

'Has there been another meeting?'

I'd seen Archon twice more since our first encounter in February. He'd returned in late March, and again in April. One of the meetings had been in Birmingham, and one in London, but other than the location, things had gone pretty much the same way. We'd been met by a bunch of adepts, who'd questioned me to make sure I was really Morden's aide, then they'd all disappeared into a private room. There had been no more opportunities to eavesdrop, but if Archon knew I'd been spying on him that first time, he hadn't given any hint of it. 'Not since April,' I said.

'Hm.'

'I don't understand why you haven't moved on this,' I said. 'The whole reason you wanted me as a spy was to know Richard's plans. Now that I'm reporting on them, you don't seem to care.'

'We care very much,' Talisid said. 'But it's Morden who's the priority now.'

'And the whole reason that Archon's bringing me along to these meetings is so that I can represent Morden.'

'But not officially,' Talisid said. 'He's being too careful for that. Even if we could prove that this Archon is involved in something illegal with these adepts – which is by no means certain – there's no direct link to Morden. Without that, there's no case.'

And that's what you really care about, I thought. The Guardians and Crusaders *hated* having a Dark mage on the Council. 'What about the adepts Archon's been talking to?'

'We've done some follow-up,' Talisid said. 'Several of them have links to political groups – agitating for changes to the Concord, that sort of thing. Nothing serious.'

'You haven't found out anything more?'

'We don't want to tip our hand just yet.'

I was silent. What Talisid had told me didn't seem like much to have turned up in all this time, and I had a feeling I knew why. Adepts just aren't taken seriously by the Council, and Talisid probably had standing orders not to report further on the subject unless something changed.

And that worried me. Yes, adepts are less powerful than mages, and they don't have anything like the organisation of the Council, but there are a *lot* of them. By most estimates, there aren't much more than five thousand mages in all of Britain. The exact number of adepts is hard to pin down, but I've heard guesses ranging between five and twenty times that. The idea of Richard having dealings with them made me uneasy, but I didn't see what I could do about it. Talisid had no more news, and after a few more exchanges he hung up.

The summons came two days later.

'And if Tarantis comes asking about Columbia, tell him that I'm willing to meet him privately to discuss the matter,' Morden said. 'Give him the usual number, but be sure to make it clear that none of his Guardian associates will be welcome.'

'Sure,' I said. We were just leaving the War Rooms, walking out from the entrance hall. It was a warm summer's day, but the high buildings all around blocked out the sunlight. 'What about the War Rooms security?'

'Tell them whatever you like.'

'They're still convinced that you might know something about any possible attacks,' I said. Recently a rumour had been going around that Dark mages were planning some kind of assault on Council headquarters. The Keepers hadn't been able to turn up any evidence for the claim, but it had still provoked a flurry of activity.

'I really have no interest in enabling their paranoia,' Morden said. 'But if they insist on an official response, then tell them that it is my personal opinion that their fears are exaggerated and that the War Rooms will be equally safe whether they enact new security measures or not.'

Probably my biggest surprise in the five months I'd spent working for Morden had been coming to realise that he wasn't actually a bad boss. He was ruthless with any challenges to his authority, but as long as I didn't do that, he was fairly easy-going. He didn't threaten or bully or give me pointless tasks just for the sake of it. Oddest of all, he actually seemed willing to listen. He'd rarely change his plans based on my input, but he did pay attention, and if I didn't understand what he was doing, then he'd take the time to fill me in.

I suppose it sounds weird for me to talk like that about someone who'd threatened to murder my entire family, and I have to admit, it's a bit hard to explain. I suppose the best way to put it is that Dark mages are a known quantity to me. Morden had never pretended to be anything other than what he was. As far as he was concerned, authority derived from power. He had power over me; therefore I was under his authority. A equals B equals C. I might not like it, but I could live with it.

Then again, it might also have been because all the Light mages kept treating me as a Dark mage. When you're surrounded week in week out by people constantly lumping you in with a particular group, it's hard not to start thinking of that group as 'your side' and the others as 'their side'. I'd caught myself falling into that trap over the past month, and each time I'd had to remind myself that I wasn't doing this by choice.

'Oh,' Morden said. 'One more thing.'

I paused, having just turned to go. 'Richard has a job for you,' Morden said. He tossed me a small pouch and

I caught it reflexively. 'Report to that address tomorrow morning.'

'What?'

'Address in the pouch, tomorrow before noon,' Morden said. 'Don't be late.' He started to turn away.

'Wait.'

Morden looked back at me. 'Is there a problem?'

'What is it?' I said. It wasn't the most coherent of questions, but I was off guard.

'A gate stone.'

'I've got a gate stone for the mansion,' I said.

'You're not going to Richard's mansion.' Morden smiled. 'That stone is for Vihaela's shadow realm. You'll be reporting to her for instructions. Good luck.' He turned and walked away.

With hindsight, I wonder whether Morden went out of his way to tell me the day before just to make me sweat. If he did, it worked. I did not have a good night's sleep.

The next morning found me in Plymouth, standing on a narrow, sloping street near the city centre. A fresh breeze was blowing from the south, carrying the smell of salt air, and the sky was cloudless and blue. I was standing outside a tall building made of grey stone blocks with high windows. Carved into the stone were the words STOKEDAMEREL HIGH SCHOOL FOR GIRLS. According to the directions Morden had given me, the access point to Vihaela's shadow realm was somewhere inside. I couldn't see a door.

Like many British people, I know a lot about the city I grew up in, but I've got only a hazy grasp of the rest of the country. London is my home, and here, in England's far south-west, I felt as uneasy as an animal outside its native territory. I found myself wishing that the gate stone wouldn't work and that I'd be able to go back to Morden, but somehow I didn't think that was going to happen. There were no doors on the street side of the school, and I circled around.

The front of the building didn't look so well-preserved. Some of the lower windows had been knocked out, green mould was creeping up one of the inside corners and I could see black scorch marks around the outbuildings which suggested a fire. The gates were locked, but they weren't tall, and I vaulted over to see that the main doors were boarded up. Graffiti covered every surface and I could see security cameras watching the doors and windows. A brief glance through the futures confirmed that they weren't just for show: if I got spotted, the police would be here within thirty minutes. I wondered why they were so determined to chase people away.

Of course, Vihaela wouldn't care if the police were guarding the outside. She could just gate straight in. I could have done the same, if I were an elemental mage.

I sighed and pulled out my burglary tools. Sometimes being a diviner feels a lot like being a small-time criminal.

The inside of the school hadn't aged as well as the outside. Paint was flaking onto the floor, cracks were showing through the walls, and broken building supplies and children's toys were scattered on filthy tables; the only light was the gleams of sunlight through the dirty windows, and the air smelt of rot and damp. I checked whether I was close enough for the gate stone to work and then took it out, a long splinter of petrified wood. I've become a lot better with gate stones than I used to be. The air shimmered and coalesced into a black vertical oval, and I stepped through, letting the portal close behind me.

I was standing on a floor of black stone. Dim lights shone from crevices, illuminating a bare and starkly furnished room. The air tasted different, and there was one person standing in front of me, a child. One other thing I noticed: the sounds of the city were gone. I was in Vihaela's shadow realm, and all around me was silence.

The child was a boy, maybe twelve or thirteen, thin and black-haired, with darting, nervous eyes. 'Welcome, Mage Verus,' he said in a high voice. 'Is there anything you need?'

'You can drop the "Mage Verus" stuff,' I said. I tried to make my voice reassuring; I'd already seen the boy wasn't a threat. 'I'm guessing you're here to take me to Vihaela?'

The boy bobbed his head but didn't meet my eyes. 'What's your name?' I asked.

'Luke.'

'Okay, Luke,' I said. 'Lead on.'

Luke didn't move. He glanced behind me, then down at the floor.

'What's wrong?'

'Mage— Is anyone else coming?'

'Just me.'

Luke flinched and I looked at him. 'Is there a problem?'

Luke licked his lips. 'Mistress Vihaela said to expect two.'

'Mistress Vihaela was mistaken.'

Luke darted a glance up at my face, then looked behind me again as if hoping that the second guest might appear if he waited long enough.

'We probably shouldn't keep her waiting,' I said.

Luke jumped and gave me a frightened glance. I'd expected that to get a response, but not one so strong. 'It's this way. Please.' He didn't quite say *hurry*.

Luke led me out of the room and onto a widely curving spiral staircase. Our shoes rang on the stone as we climbed, echoing up and down. A window cut into the wall provided the first natural light, giving a view of decaying sandstone ruins. I wondered what the outside would be like. Shadow realms are shaped from the location they reflect in the real world, but they can grow apart given time. If this was an old one, it could have very little in common with the school.

As I climbed, I studied the back of Luke's head, wondering who he was. He definitely wasn't Vihaela's Chosen or her apprentice. I hadn't seen any futures in which he used magic, which pointed to him being a normal or a sensitive. Normally, Dark mages only allow mages or adepts into their shadow realms, but Vihaela was apparently an exception, and I had a nasty feeling that I knew why. When I'd first heard of Vihaela, she'd been a member of White Rose, an organisation that specialised in supplying sex slaves to Light mages and independents. Vihaela had been the one in charge of training new acquisitions, and her methods inspired so much fear that the Keepers had never been able to get any clear reports because her victims were too terrified of her to report anything. I wondered whether Luke was a leftover or a new acquisition, and whether there was anything I could do about it.

Another window passed by, this one showing branches and leaves. The spiral stairs kept going; apparently we were ascending the outside of a tower. From time to time, an archway to the left would lead off into a corridor. I looked into the futures in which I tried to talk to Luke and didn't get much. He was afraid of displeasing me, but he was far more afraid of Vihaela, and he clearly didn't dare breathe a word against her. We passed a third window, this one looking out onto a snow-swept tundra, and I wondered if I could—

I stopped short. *What the hell?*

The view from the window seemed to go on for miles, brown rocks poking out of patches of white snow, fading away into distant hills that rose up into mountains. Except that the *last* window had looked out onto a forest. What was going on?

I looked to the left, where an archway led off into a corridor. There was no trace of gate magic or dimensional warping, but . . . *wait*. If I moved a little further down, I'd hear someone crying out. It was faint, but it was definitely there and it sounded like they were calling for—

'Mage Verus?'

The future splintered and turned to smoke. I looked up to see Luke giving me a nervous look. 'This way, please?'

I took a last look at the archway, then turned away.

The top of the staircase opened out onto grass. Tall trees rose up all around, their trunks dark and shadowed, and beyond them I could see ornate walls and arches. Beams of light filtered down from far above, giving glimpses of sky. A faint wind blew, stirring the leaves on the trees, but although I could sense birds and animals around us, all was quiet. This place was alive, but almost as silent as the tower beneath. Something about the whole shadow realm – the black stone and the tower and the trees – nagged at my memory, reminding me of something, but I pushed the thought away, focusing on the person waiting for us.

Vihaela was sitting at a small table and chairs beneath the trees, and I walked towards her without waiting to be told. She'd been smiling, about to make some pleasantry, but as she saw that I was alone, the smile faded. 'Where's the other?' she asked Luke.

Luke quailed. I had the feeling he was about to be the scapegoat, and I took a step forward before he could answer. 'There is no other.'

Vihaela frowned. 'Anne was supposed to be here.'

'She's not.'

Vihaela looked me up and down, and there was a slow, calculating look in her eyes. 'Morden promised me both of you.'

I felt a chill go through me. Here in her shadow realm, Vihaela held all the cards. If she decided to stop being civilised, things could get very nasty, very fast . . . but the number one rule for dealing with Dark mages is that you don't show fear. 'Did he?'

'Yes.'

'Did he really?' I said. 'Or did he just *imply* that she'd be coming, and let you hear what you wanted to hear?'

Vihaela kept frowning. I wanted to hold my breath, but didn't. Then suddenly Vihaela's brow cleared and a smile flashed across her face. 'Oh well,' she said. 'I'll just have to make do with you.'

I sat. 'So did he behave himself?' Vihaela asked.

For a moment, I didn't understand what Vihaela was asking, then she nodded behind me at where Luke was standing. 'Sure,' I said.

'Really? Nothing you'd like to add?'

'Not really.'

Vihaela looked at Luke. The boy had been very still throughout the conversation, stiff and tense. 'Well, Luke?' Her voice was suddenly kindly. 'Anything you'd like to tell me?'

Luke hesitated. 'Go on,' Vihaela said.

Luke opened his mouth, licked his lips. 'No, Mistress Vihaela.' His voice wobbled.

Vihaela kept looking at him. Luke hunched over. 'That's odd,' Vihaela said. Her eyes lingered on Luke. 'It seems to me you took a very long time getting here.'

Luke froze and Vihaela leant back in her chair, studying him. 'Do you have a reason?'

I could already tell that Luke wasn't going to answer. I didn't know exactly what was going on, but I didn't like it. 'The reason was that I was doing some sightseeing,' I said.

Vihaela's attention switched back to me. 'You went off the stairs?'

'I went straight from the entry room to here, with some pauses at the windows,' I said. 'You have some interesting views.'

Vihaela stared at me. I tried very hard not to tense up. 'I suppose that does explain it,' she said at last. She sounded disappointed.

I let out a breath.

'However . . .' Vihaela looked at Luke. 'Do you remember my instructions? I told you to bring Verus up here *promptly*. You can go. We'll discuss this later.'

I saw Luke's face go white. He swayed, then turned and scuttled away. Vihaela watched him disappear down the stairs.

'Was that necessary?' I asked Vihaela tightly.

'You seem angry.' Vihaela cocked her head. 'You're not one of those white-knight types, are you?'

'I have a problem with seeing people hurt for no reason,' I said. I *was* angry, and all of a sudden I didn't care very much about offending her. 'Did you set that up just to have a reason to punish him? As a demonstration?'

'Morden told me you had tendencies that way,' Vihaela said. 'Ruthless but sentimental. I wasn't sure if he was telling the truth, but come to think of it, that was when you first crossed my path, wasn't it? When the Council went after White Rose. I thought you were just a contractor, but maybe you took it personally?' Vihaela smiled suddenly. 'So is it anyone you don't like seeing hurt? Or only children?'

'You didn't answer my question.'

'Whether it was necessary?' Vihaela shrugged. 'Not really.'

'Then why?'

'Because he's getting boring,' Vihaela said. 'They always do, once they stop putting up a fight.'

A bolt of anger spiked through me. Vihaela saw it and smiled. 'Well, well. Maybe Morden was telling the truth after all. Tell me, if I brought him up here and tortured him in front of you, would you try to rescue him?'

I looked at Vihaela, sitting in her garden chair with her chin resting in one hand, relaxed and interested, and felt an instant of pure hatred. The threat was bad enough, but that she could be so casual about it made it worse. I've met a lot of Dark mages in my life, and a lot of the time I think Light mages exaggerate how bad they are, but there's a minority of Dark mages that are exactly as evil as the stories make them out to be, and Vihaela is one of them. All of a sudden I wanted to hurt her, to have her suffer the same way as her victims did . . .

. . . except that there was nothing I could do. I couldn't match Vihaela in a fight. If I tried, I'd lose. I wasn't willing to fight when I knew I couldn't beat her, and a part of me was ashamed at that.

'I think you actually would,' Vihaela said. She'd sensed my anger, but not my thoughts. 'How on earth did you manage as Richard's apprentice? Actually, don't bother answering; I can guess.' Vihaela studied me. 'It wouldn't work, by the way.'

'What?'

Vihaela crossed her legs, leaning back. 'If I brought that boy up here and offered him the opportunity to leave with you, right now, do you know what he'd do? He'd refuse. And if I asked, he would tell me that it's my right to hurt him or to reward him, whenever I please, for no other reason than that it's what I desire. He'd mean it too.'

I looked back at Vihaela. I would have liked to believe she was bluffing, but I had an ugly feeling she wasn't. 'Part of it is his age, obviously,' Vihaela went on. From her tone, she might have been discussing the weather. 'But I've found that boys are more easily broken than girls. Girls will bend, but it's very hard to stamp out that last little spark. Boys are more like eggs. Once you break the shell . . .' She shrugged. 'Someone at White Rose once brought me a boy who'd tried to escape. He was quite popular and one of their higher earners, but he'd managed to injure a guard, and so Marannis insisted I make an example of him. So I made him beg for me to amputate his body parts, one at a time. Toes first, then fingers. Then his left foot, then his right, then what was left of his hands, then his genitals. Once there wasn't anything left of the arms or legs I started on the face. It's really quite a challenge keeping a body alive when the mind wants so desperately to die. I made him plead quite creatively before agreeing to remove the eyes. I saved the tongue for last, but he didn't really have much to say by then in any case. Once I was done, they brought the other children out to watch and had what was left thrown to the sniffers. You wouldn't believe the sounds it made.'

I looked at Vihaela. She met my gaze, her eyes calm. 'I don't understand you,' I said. 'Why do you do this?'

'Why not?' Vihaela said. 'I decide how I live. Not the Council, not any other mages. Just me. I can do whatever I like, and this –' She opened her hands out, palms up. '– is what I like.' She smiled. 'Would you be surprised to know that a good number of Light mages envy me? Especially the girls. They're given a taste of all that power, then they have to spend their time bowing and scraping to that old boys' club above. Then they see me walk into a room and they see the Light mages flinch, and a part of them wishes that that could be them. They don't have the courage to actually *do* it, of course, or they wouldn't be Light mages in the first place, but they *want* it, even if they're too scared to say it out loud. I can always tell when someone's afraid of me.' Vihaela looked at me and the smile stayed on her face. 'Always.'

I let out a breath, feeling a chill go through me. Inside me, anger was fighting with fear and losing. I wanted to put up a fight, to do *something*, but I've fought enough battles to know when I'm losing. 'What do you want?'

'Maybe I'm just enjoying talking to you.'

'I don't get the impression that you care about me that much.'

'Well, that's true enough.' Vihaela stretched and rose to her feet. She walked to my right, towards a tree, so that I had to turn my head to keep her in view. 'I would have much preferred Anne. Just as I would have rather pursued my own projects than made that little example for Marannis. But one has to make the best of what one gets.'

'So?'

Vihaela stroked the bark of the tree, not looking at me. 'So?'

'What are you going to do?'

'Well, Richard has a job he wants done, and he asked me to brief you. I could do that.' And then Vihaela turned towards me, and all of a sudden she wasn't smiling any more. 'Or then again, I could paralyse you, strip you of your clothes and those pathetic weapons you're carrying, take you down to my dungeons and torture you to death.'

I held very still, watching the Dark mage. Vihaela walked towards me, her movements graceful and sinuous, and she didn't take her eyes off mine. 'I've never broken a diviner before. As I understand it, you'd be able to see what I was going to do in advance. Which would mean I'd lose the element of surprise, but then, couldn't that be its own form of punishment? To know exactly what's going to happen to you, and not be able to do a thing to stop it?' Vihaela leant forward onto the chair, forcing me to turn my head further to keep her in view. 'What do you think?'

I didn't move. Vihaela was leaning forward, her hands clasped flat over the back of the chair. Dark brown eyes in a dark brown face stared at me from only inches away. She was within touching distance, but I didn't reach for any of the weapons in my clothes. I knew I wouldn't be fast enough. 'I think Richard might have a problem with that.'

'Richard doesn't always get what he wants,' Vihaela said calmly.

The futures spread out before me, twisting and changing, and the patterns they made sent a spike of fear through me. Vihaela wasn't definitely going to attack . . . but she wasn't definitely *not* going to attack either, and if she decided she wanted it badly enough, Richard's name wouldn't stop her. She reached out with one finger and traced it along my cheekbone, her eyes dark and enigmatic, and I stopped myself from flinching. Vihaela is a hybrid rather than a pure life mage, and unlike Anne, she doesn't need to touch you to kill you. Range wouldn't be any defence against her. But the touch was a threat all the same, and this close I could sense the spells inside her, complex and powerful, ready to lash out to bind or cripple.

I looked Vihaela straight in the eyes. 'How much is Richard paying you?'

Vihaela threw her head back and laughed. She stood up, smiling again, and just that fast, the futures of violence were gone. 'I do like you, Verus.' She made it sound as though I were a stray cat. 'The answer is: more than you can match. But don't worry, I'm not going to hurt you. At least, not right now.' She sat back down in her chair, her manner suddenly businesslike. 'Let's get to work.'

I nodded, not showing my relief. 'What's the job?'

'Richard wants you to retrieve an item currently located in a deep shadow realm,' Vihaela said. 'It's called a dream-stone. Ah, I see that rings a bell.'

I'd tried to hide my reaction, but Vihaela had caught it anyway. 'I've heard the name.'

'Good. Now, shut up and listen.'

I shut up and listened. Vihaela gave me the details about the deep shadow realm, her descriptions quick and efficient, and it didn't take me long to realise that she was an expert on the subject. It's not hard to see why Richard chose Vihaela for his inner circle. What she does, she does very well.

Only at the very end did she revert to form. 'Any questions?'

'Just one,' I said. 'How soon does Richard want this?'

'As long as it arrives, he's not picky.'

I nodded and rose to my feet.

'Oh, Verus?'

I paused.

'Do bear in mind that you're not working for the Keepers this time. The Council is quite happy to send mages out on missions and have them come back empty-handed. Richard is . . . less tolerant, shall we say, of people who fail to carry out instructions? I wouldn't think he's as likely as Marannis to demand I make an example. But then again, maybe he would.'

I looked back at Vihaela. 'You can tell Richard,' I said, 'that the message has been received.'

'Good.' Vihaela waved. 'Have fun.'

9

It was later the same day.

'So it's definitely going to be in August?' I asked.

'They said August, but it's the Council,' Variam said. 'I'll count myself lucky if it's done by autumn.'

'Funny coincidence that you start prepping for your journeyman tests within a few months of Luna doing hers.'

Variam gave me a suspicious look. 'What's that supposed to mean?'

'Just wondering if she's trying to give you orders,' I said. 'You know, seeing as she's a journeyman and you aren't.'

Variam tried to look expressionless, and did it so badly that I burst out laughing. Variam held the stone-faced look for a few seconds more, then reluctantly cracked a smile. 'She told you?'

'You think I couldn't guess?'

We were sitting in Arachne's cave, warm lights shining down onto cloth and sofas and rolls of thread. Arachne herself was crouched over a table just a little way away, working on some new creation, her front legs deft and quick as she wove. 'You getting any more shit from the Keepers?' Variam asked.

'About what happened at the Vault?' I said. 'No, but that's probably because they don't want the embarrassment of admitting that, one, they sent me on a suicide mission, and two, they failed at it.'

Variam grunted. 'Landis said he talked to Rain. He thinks he can probably ask enough awkward questions to stop that pair from trying any more abductions.'

'Probably means they'll just find another way, but every little helps.'

The sound of voices made us look up as Luna and Anne walked in. Anne was in the middle of telling Luna some story or other, but it was Luna I looked at most keenly, and to my eyes she looked better. I still didn't know what she was doing when she wasn't with us, but whatever it was, she seemed to have recovered her confidence.

'Hello, Anne,' Arachne said warmly. 'Luna, you're looking well. It's been a while.'

'Oh,' Luna said, looking embarrassed. 'Sorry, I've been meaning to stop by, but . . .'

'It's no trouble.' Arachne gestured to me. 'Alex, are you ready?'

'Yeah,' I said. 'Let's get started.'

Anne and Luna sat on a sofa. With Variam, they formed a semicircle, and all of them looked expectantly at me. I looked between the three of their faces, young and alert and trusting, and for a moment I felt a pang. Should I be involving them in this?

But they were here willingly; all three had made that clear. And out of all the mages in Britain, while there might be plenty who were stronger, there were none I'd rather have with me. I just hoped I wasn't leading them somewhere I shouldn't.

'I met Vihaela this morning,' I began. 'The good news, as you can see, is that I'm in one piece. The bad news is that Anne and I now have a mission. It's going to be difficult and dangerous, and part of the reason that it's dangerous is that we don't know exactly *how* it'll be dangerous.' I took a breath. 'If you're willing, I could really use your help.'

The three of them looked at me, then Luna and Variam looked at each other. 'Wow,' Luna said.

'Wow?'

'You're actually asking us for help.'

'Well . . . yes.'

'Normally you don't do that until you've been stabbed or something,' Luna said. 'Or unless you're so blatantly outmatched that even you can't think of any way to get out of it.'

'No, I don't,' I said in annoyance.

'Actually, you kind of do,' Variam said.

'This isn't either one of those situations, all right?'

'I know, that's what makes it so weird,' Luna said. 'You're asking us *before* everything's gone completely to hell.'

I threw up my hands. 'Do you guys want to hear the details or not?'

'We do,' Anne said. 'What does Richard want?'

'He wants a very rare item called a dreamstone.'

'Wait,' Variam said. 'Isn't that the same thing—?'

'Yes.'

Variam thought about it, then shrugged. 'No wonder you weren't having any luck, if even Richard needs help to get one. But what's so special about these things? From what Arachne said, they just sounded like a mind magic focus.'

'That is an oversimplification,' Arachne said. 'Yes, a dreamstone can achieve the same results as some mind or charm spells, but the method by which it does so is very different. And there are some effects that a dreamstone can produce which are outside the realm of living magic altogether.'

'Like what?' Luna asked in interest.

'Like stepping physically into Elsewhere.'

'You can do that?' Anne asked, and she looked surprised. 'I didn't think . . .'

'In theory,' Arachne said. 'There is, however, a catch. Dreamstones are closer to imbued items than to focuses, and they can be unpredictable in the hands of new bearers. The most reliable dreamstones are those that have been in the possession of mages for many years. Newly formed dreamstones are another matter altogether. They are powerful but not easy to use.'

'What do you mean "newly formed"?' Luna asked.

'Well, that brings us to problem number one,' I said. 'The place we're supposed to find this dreamstone is inside a deep shadow realm.'

'A what?'

'You know that shadow realms are formed by taking a reflection of a location in our world,' I said. 'Deep shadow realms are ones where they took a reflection of another shadow realm, like a copy of a copy. They're supposed to be more fluid than our reality, and they can be pretty weird. Natural laws don't work consistently. They're not as closely tethered as shadow realms, and they can drift out of phase for years or centuries.'

'It's believed that this process, where deep shadow realms become distant from our reality, is what provides the conditions that allow the growth of dreamstones,' Arachne added. 'To the best of my knowledge, they've never been found anywhere else.'

'Okay,' Variam said. 'So we gate to this deep shadow place, grab your dream thingy and get out. Right?'

'That brings us to problem two,' I said. 'First, you can only access deep shadow realms from another shadow realm which connects to them. Think of it as like links in a chain.' I shrugged. 'Some mages claim that if you know what to look for, you can keep going from one deep shadow realm to another until you find yourself in another world completely. Point is, we're going to have to go through a regular shadow realm first.'

'Which one?' Luna asked.

'That would be problem number three,' I said. 'It's a shadow realm called the Hollow. And it's occupied.' I nodded at Arachne.

'The Hollow is a shadow realm of moderate age, grown from a location here in England,' Arachne said. 'It was first created by Karyos, a hamadryad, and she withdrew into it ninety or a hundred years ago.'

Luna frowned. 'I think I've heard of those. Aren't hamadryads the ones who are . . . ?'

'Bonded to a tree, yes.'

'Do you think she'd allow us passage?' Anne asked quietly.

'Once upon a time, perhaps,' Arachne said. 'Karyos was cool to humans, but had no hatred of them. Unfortunately, during your First World War, a group of people affiliated with the Council saw fit to cut her tree down.'

Luna grimaced. 'Oh.'

'So I'm guessing mages aren't her favourite people,' I said. It's depressing how often I've heard this kind of story.

'I visited her once, some years after,' Arachne said. 'Apparently she survived by transferring her spirit to a tree within the shadow realm. The process had . . . side effects. She recognised me, I think, but little more. When I next attempted to visit, she refused me entry.'

'Do you think she'll let us pass through?' Anne asked.

'I do not know,' Arachne said. 'What I do know is that on at least one occasion, mages have entered the Hollow for their own reasons. They did not come out.'

'And unfortunately, it doesn't seem as though there's any other way in,' I said. 'We go through the Hollow, or we don't go at all.'

'What if she says no?' Anne asked.

I sighed. 'Then it's going to come down to a fight.'

'Isn't there anywhere else we could go?'

'No,' Arachne said. 'And if there were, the dangers would be just as great.'

'Come on,' Luna said to Anne. She looked more cheerful now. 'We've handled a lot worse than this.'

'I just don't like the idea of forcing our way in.'

'It's not like we're asking much,' Variam said. 'All we want is to go through.'

Anne looked unhappy but didn't answer. I didn't say anything, but I had some of the same uneasiness as Anne. Isolating yourself in a shadow realm tends to be a bad sign. Anne's first master, Sagash, had been one of those shadow realm recluses. By the time I'd met him, he'd been holed up for maybe twenty years, and talking to him had given me the uneasy feeling that while he might not be actually insane, it wouldn't take much of a push. If Arachne was right, Karyos had been doing the same thing for a full century. I wasn't sure that boded well for negotiations.

'So,' Variam said. 'We either talk our way or fight our way past this Karyos, find a way through into the deep shadow realm, grab the dreamstone and get out.' He frowned. 'What does Richard even want with a dreamstone, anyway?'

'Yeah, I was wondering that too,' Luna said. 'I mean, once we get the thing, what's the plan? Are you thinking of pulling some kind of switch? Giving him a fake, or . . . ?'

I couldn't help but be amused that it didn't even seem to occur to Luna that we'd fail to get it. 'I'd like to, but I don't dare,' I said. 'Vihaela made it pretty clear what the consequences would be for me and for Anne if we failed. I don't like handing something this dangerous over to Richard, but it's not a hill I'm willing to die on.'

'But then even if we succeed, we'll be right back where we started,' Anne said. 'Actually, worse.'

'Not quite,' I said. 'Richard ordered me to fetch a dreamstone. He didn't say anything about taking more than one. Arachne thinks there's a good chance that if two of us go in there, we'll be able to bring two dreamstones out.'

'Just two?' Variam said.

'For one person to attempt to carry two newly formed dreamstones would be too dangerous,' Arachne said. 'As I said, they have some of the characteristics of imbued items. And deep shadow realms are unstable. Sending in more than two people at once carries its own risks.'

'So, it's going to be a four-person job,' I said. 'Two to go into the deep shadow realm, and two to stay in the Hollow and guard our way out.' I looked between the three of them. 'Are you in?'

'Does Richard know you're bringing us in on this?' Variam asked.

I shrugged. 'Vihaela and Morden didn't mention it, and as far as I'm concerned, it's none of their business.'

The three of them looked at each other. 'I'm in,' Variam said.

Luna smiled. 'I think you know what I'm going to say.'

'When do you want to go?' Anne asked in her soft voice.

'If Richard knows about this deep shadow realm, others could too,' I said. 'So I don't see any reason to wait around . . .'

The next morning found us in the Chilterns.

I sat on bumpy ground, my back resting against a tree. It was a type I didn't recognise, with serrated leaves and a narrow dividing trunk which spread out into branches almost as soon as it left the ground. The tree and a dozen like it formed a hangar, and the hangar was on top of a hill, green grass falling off into hedges and fields. A few scattered houses were tucked in between the trees in the valleys below, but for whatever reason, this particular spot had never been chosen as a site for buildings or paths, and here up on the hilltop, we were alone. Despite the morning sun, the air was cool, and a steady breeze blew from the west, ruffling the grass and the leaves on the trees. Above us, a kestrel hovered in a blue sky.

It was a beautiful view, exactly the kind that people picture when they think of the English countryside in the summer, and the sight of it had raised my spirits when we'd arrived. Shadow realms tend to have associations with the locations they reflect in the real world, and I'd optimistically hoped that no shadow realm tied to a spot like this could be too bad. Now that I'd had the chance to reconnoitre, I wasn't so sure.

Variam was sprawled on the grass a little way away, a

tiny spark of fire jumping between his fingers. He knew not to interrupt me, but he was obviously impatient for the action to start. Behind him, I could hear the murmur of Luna and Anne's voices; I couldn't make out the words, but I knew they were arguing over who was going into the deep shadow realm and who was staying in the Hollow.

Of course, before we could reach the deep shadow realm, we had to *survive* the Hollow.

I sighed and rose to my feet. Variam looked up alertly. 'We ready?'

'We're ready.'

There were two big sports bags next to Variam's resting place. 'Black bag or blue bag?' he asked.

'Black.'

Variam grinned. 'Thought so.'

I unzipped the black bag and took out my body armour, then started putting it on. 'But we'll take the seed as well.'

'Why?' Variam said, donning his own armour. My armour is an integrated set of mesh and plate, an imbued item that's alive in its own way, and I could feel its presence as I sealed the jacket, alert and watchful. The pieces Variam was putting on were just regular body armour, but then Variam can shield.

I buckled my sword belt onto my waist at its usual hole. It slid down my hips and I tightened it a couple of notches. I'd lost a fair bit of weight since I started training with Anne. 'Arachne put a lot of work into that thing.'

'So when are you going to use it?' Variam asked. 'Before this haberdasher thing starts trying to kill us, or after?'

'Hamadryad. And she's still got free will. That means she's got a choice.'

Variam rolled his eyes. 'If you say so.'

Anne and Luna walked in just as I lifted a gun from the black bag. It was a H&K MP7, a compact, nasty little assault weapon that I'd taken off a guy who tried to kill me a few years back. 'So much for the diplomatic approach, huh?' Luna said with a glance at my weapons.

'I thought we were trying to talk to her?' Anne said.

'Let's just say that the odds aren't good.'

'And you think walking in like that is going to help?'

'I'm going to have my shield up too,' Variam put in.

'Not helping.'

'Maybe I should get some armour like that,' Luna said. She reached into a case strapped to her belt and produced a slim white wand, which she held like the handle of a whip. 'Could take the pressure off my curse.'

'It's dicey against bullets,' Variam said. 'Anything fast enough will just go straight through.'

'Alex?' Anne asked.

'This isn't for Karyos,' I said. 'I don't want to kill her if there's any possible way to avoid it, but I don't think we're getting through without a fight. Now.' I looked around. 'Here's what we're going to face.'

Briefing and final preparations took a little longer, then at last, the four of us were ready. I looked at Anne and Luna. 'You decided who's going in?'

Anne and Luna looked at each other. 'If you two still can't make up your minds—' Variam began.

'No,' Anne and Luna said at exactly the same time.

'Come on, guys,' I said. 'We already agreed on this part. Two people to guard the gate, and one to go in with me.'

'This place is supposed to be kind of like Elsewhere,'

Luna said. The tone of her voice sounded as though she'd made the argument before. 'I've had more practice.'

'I'm the one whose job it is,' Anne said.

Variam threw up his hands. 'Can you just flip a coin or something?'

'You know what, that's as good a way as any,' I said. I dug into my bag and pulled out a 50p piece. 'Who's calling?'

'Heads,' Luna said.

'No!' Anne said.

Luna looked at Anne. 'What?'

'You're not calling it.'

'Why not?'

'Because,' Anne said, 'whatever face you call is going to be the one it lands on.'

Variam laughed and Luna rolled her eyes. 'Well, I'm not letting Alex do it,' Luna said. 'He'll know what face it is right *after* it lands.'

'Oh, for crying out loud,' I said. These are the kinds of ridiculous arguments you get when you've got a chance mage and a probability mage in the same group. 'Vari flips, Anne calls.' I tossed the coin to Variam. 'Okay?'

'Okay,' Anne said.

Luna looked reluctant. 'Fine.'

'Do I get a say in this?' Variam asked.

'No,' both girls said in unison.

Variam rolled his eyes. The coin flashed silver in the air as he flipped it, then caught it mid-fall and slapped it onto the back of his wrist. He looked at Anne. 'Call it.'

Anne stared at his hand for a long moment. 'Tails,' she said at last.

Variam took his hand away to see the coin. 'Tails it is.'

'That's not fair,' Luna objected.

Variam rolled his eyes. 'What, you think I rigged it?' He strode away towards the centre of the hangar. With an annoyed glance back at Anne, Luna followed.

Anne was about to go after them, but a small movement from me stopped her. 'I saw you looking at Vari's hand,' I said.

Anne looked back at me.

'I'm curious,' I said. 'How accurate *is* that lifesight of yours? Enough to see impressions in skin?'

'You're not the only one who doesn't want to put other people in danger,' Anne said quietly.

'Hey!' Variam called back at us. 'You coming or what?'

Getting into a shadow realm can be very hard or very easy. This one was somewhere in between. None of us had visited the Hollow before, meaning that we had to make a bunch of educated guesses rather than simply opening up a gate and stepping straight through. On the plus side, the place didn't have wards. When mages move into a shadow realm, typically the first thing they do is set up a bunch of restrictions on gating into the place, kind of the magical equivalent of changing the locks. Common methods include password systems, requiring a keystone, or simply barring all gates that aren't made from a specific location. That was why I'd had to go to that school in Plymouth yesterday to reach Vihaela's shadow realm – if I'd tried to gate there from anywhere else then the gate simply wouldn't have worked, and I was willing to bet that there were a bunch of nasty security measures waiting for someone to try to force it.

In this case, we hadn't needed to travel to the hilltop in the Chilterns to make the gate, but since we were gating to an unknown location, it helped. Variam ended up doing most of the heavy lifting – out of the four of us, he's the best with gate magic by a long way – while I gave advice. 'All right,' Variam said at last. 'Ready?'

I drew my sword an inch from its scabbard, testing that it could be drawn easily, then let it drop back. 'Ready.'

Variam opened the gate, and we stepped through into a scene out of fantasy.

I don't know what I'd expected the Hollow to be like. When we'd been sitting in Arachne's cave, the name and her description of its owner had given me a mental image of twisted trees, dark and close. My divinations had given me a more accurate picture, but I'd been concentrating on dangers and paths, not stopping to look at the view. I hadn't been prepared for how beautiful it was.

We'd stepped out onto a grassy clearing in the middle of light woodland. Most of the trees were the same green, thicket-like ones we'd seen on the hilltop on the Chilterns, but they seemed bigger and stronger, more *real* somehow, their leaves more bright, the branches more thick. Pathways of packed dirt wound through the trees, roots showing through the earth, and flowered bushes formed clumps on the grass.

To our right was blue sky. And to the left was orange sky, and ahead was green sky, and behind was violet sky, but that wasn't what made Anne and Luna widen their eyes and instinctively take a step closer together. There was sky *under* us too. Our feet were resting on grass, but only a dozen yards away, the ground dropped away into nothingness and we could see more sky to the left and right. We were on a floating island.

'Wow,' Luna said, her eyes wide.

'Okay,' Variam said. 'That's impressive.'

I couldn't help myself. I walked towards the edge.

'Alex!' Anne called warningly.

I stopped a foot or two from the lip, watching the futures carefully for any sign of it crumbling, and peered over. There was nothing there. Sky and clouds, going on for ever, both above and below, and I felt a moment of dizziness as my brain tried to make sense of it. The sky wasn't supposed to be on *every* side—

A hand closed around my arm and I snapped back to reality. The grass and earth seemed to sway for a second, then steadied. 'I think maybe,' Anne said, 'you shouldn't stand so close.'

'Maybe you're right,' I said, stepping back. Anne didn't let go until I was well away.

'How does it stay up?' Luna asked in fascination.

'I'm not sure it *is* staying up,' I said. The island had little peninsulas sticking off into space, and I could see the earth on the underside of them. Tree roots stuck out below, branching into empty air. 'I think it's staying in the middle.'

'What happens if you fall?' Variam asked.

'Let's not find out.'

We walked deeper into the shadow realm. Birds sang from the trees, and red and orange roses grew in clumps. There was a faint breeze, just warm enough to be pleasant. Despite how it had looked, I was realising that this was quite a small shadow realm; the boundary had probably been no more than a hundred feet from where the ground ended. Up ahead, a much larger tree loomed up above the canopy, gnarled branches spreading wide to shade the grass beneath. 'That's where we need to go,' Variam said.

We'd walked into a clearing, and as we did I held up a hand. Luna, Anne and Variam halted instantly and I looked from left to right. Dense trees formed a half circle around us, with more of the rosebushes clustered at their trunks. The grass was a bright green, with vivid crimson flowers scattered in patches here and there, and at the far end the ground rose up slightly into piles of moss-covered rocks.

'She here?' Variam asked.

I nodded, not taking my eyes off the trees.

'Alex,' Anne said warningly. 'Those plants . . .'

'I know.'

'So you still planning to talk?' Variam said. 'Or are we skipping to the part where we burn things?'

I took a step forward. '*Despoina* Karyos,' I said, clearly and loudly. I hoped I'd got the pronunciation right. 'We seek audience.'

The leaves rustled in the breeze.

'We ask for safe passage through your territory,' I said. 'We intend only to travel and return. We will undertake to commit no harm against you, nor any damage to your home.'

'Only if she doesn't pick a fight first,' Luna said under her breath.

'Shh,' Anne said.

'In exchange for the right of passage,' I said, ignoring Luna, 'we offer a gift.' I brought out a small, inlaid wooden box. 'A regeneration seed, made by Arachne, the weaver. She offers it freely to you with her regards, and in the hope that you and she might meet again, as you once did.'

The item in the box was our best card in these negotiations, and Arachne had explained to me in detail what it meant. Hamadryads can live for ever, but only as long as their tree does. When it dies, hamadryads quickly waste away unless they can find a new tree to bond to; it has to be of the right species and it has to be a new sapling, and the hamadryad goes into a cocoon to regenerate, emerging years later with a new, young body. The seed in the box was supposed to be a necessary part of that process. According to Arachne, when Karyos's last tree had been killed, she'd survived by jumping to a grown tree as an emergency measure. For whatever reason, she hadn't followed that up by completing the ritual normally. Arachne's guess was that she'd been injured in the process and no longer had the strength to grow a seed of her own.

There was another possible explanation. According to Arachne, jumping to an adult tree could have damaged Karyos mentally as well as physically, and being sealed away in a shadow realm for a century probably wouldn't have helped. If so, Karyos could very well be completely insane, which given that we were standing in her territory – territory that she'd had had years to cultivate – was not a pleasant thought.

The four of us stood in the clearing. For all the response, I might have been speaking to the empty air. The flowers stirred in the wind, red petals bright against the grass.

'She's not going for it,' Variam said under his breath.

'*Shh*,' Anne said.

'Well, she's not.'

'She's still deciding,' I said. The futures were mostly of violence – actually, nearly all of them were of violence – but there were a tentative few in which nothing happened. I could even catch a few glimpses of ones in which something came out to talk. Unfortunately it was someone else's choice, not mine, and I'd already played all of my cards.

'We could still go with the burn-things plan,' Variam said. 'I like that plan.'

'Will you shut *up*?' Anne whispered.

'If she wanted to be nice, she'd have come out by now,' Variam said.

I took a breath. I still didn't like the look of the futures, but I didn't think sitting and waiting would help. '*Despoina* Karyos,' I began again, taking a step forward.

The attack came from three sides.

The flowers seemed to ripple, as though in a strong breeze, then rise. For a moment, it looked as though they were flowing along the grass, then my eyes focused and I saw that they were flying, petals flapping like wings, wheeling and twisting like a flock of starlings. Three, four, five of the flocks lifted off, each flying towards us, and now I could see that the stalks ended in sharp points.

At the same time, creatures burst seemingly from nowhere. They were humanoids, small and twisted, and there was only time for a blurred impression of thorns and stick-thin limbs before they were on us. They'd been camouflaged so perfectly that our eyes had slid right over without seeing them, and now they dashed straight for us. The multiple angles were confusing; an unprepared group would have been overwhelmed in those first few seconds.

Luckily, if there's one thing diviners are good at, it's being prepared.

I'd briefed the others thoroughly before gating into the shadow realm. I hadn't been able to see past the first few seconds of the fight, but I'd been able to see where and how the attack would come, and Luna, Anne and Variam reacted instantly. I felt a flash of heat to my left and knew Variam was casting, but I didn't turn to look. The front arc was Variam's responsibility, but the right arc was mine, and three of the creatures were racing in. I'd trust Variam and the girls to watch my back, just as they trusted me to cover theirs.

The gun came up smoothly to my shoulder, kicked back with a stuttering *ba-ba-bang!* and I had a fraction of a second to see the creature framed clearly in my sights, an elfin humanoid with blackened teeth and thorned spindly limbs, before its head disappeared in a spray of green liquid. It dropped and I was already swinging to aim for the next one but it swerved just as I fired and I missed and corrected and fired again, sending it tumbling to the ground.

The moment's delay had given the last one the chance to close, and as I started to wheel I realised I wouldn't get the gun around in time. I turned the movement into a twist and a blow jarred my arm, spikes digging in, but my armour held and the thing's momentum took it past. It came around, slashing at my eyes, but I'd had just long enough to sight and with a *ba-ba-bang!* the MP7 tore a hole through its body. It staggered, took another volley and fell to the grass.

All of that happened in less than five seconds, yet it felt like ten times that long and when I turned back the battle was raging. Variam held the front alone, sheets of flame walling us off from the clearing, and through the fire I could see the flowers shying away: those that touched the flame crisped and burned, falling to join the others on the blackening grass. Luna and Anne were facing twice their number of the thorned humanoids, yet two more were lying on the grass and as I watched Anne caught one jumping in and the thing dropped like a puppet with its strings cut. The thornling behind shied away and soaked up a lash of silver mist from Luna's whip. It tried to slide around to flank her, tripped and fell into Variam's wall of fire and was gone with a single piercing scream.

I sighted and fired, saw one more of the thornlings stagger, then my precognition sent me jumping back as two of the flowers zipped through the space where my face had been. Now that I was close, I could see that the points at the end of their stalks were long and barbed with a reddish tinge, and they flew like birds, reversing and darting at me. The gun was useless against such small targets; I dropped it in its sling and tried to draw my sword, fumbling at the hilt as more of the flowers gathered, thorns stabbing. The air tasted sweet, foggy, and I coughed, managed to drag the sword out, split one of the flowers with a clumsy slash, but there were more and more of them and thorns stabbed into me, bouncing off the armour on my arms, my back. I kept slashing but my movements were slower now; it was harder to lift my arms and I managed to cut down one more of the flowers but there were more than a dozen and they were swarming all over me. One caught my neck and I stumbled, going to one knee—

Then Anne was there, her hands quick and sure. As her fingers brushed each flower they stiffened and went limp, falling to the grass, and she touched my neck. Warmth seemed to flow through me, the pain from the wound vanished and I could move freely again. I pulled myself up but Anne was already gone, running back to cover Luna.

Airborne toxin. I'd seen from my divination that we'd face venom, but I hadn't been able to see how, and I'd assumed that it was going to be delivered on claws or teeth. Instead it had been carried in the air. Anne had promised that she'd be able to immunise us as soon as she saw it working, and she'd been as good as her word.

I cut down one more flower and suddenly the battle was over. Variam had scattered the swarms and now only a few stragglers remained; occasionally one would swoop in and Variam would burn it to ash. All the thornlings were down, dead or both. 'Anyone poisoned?' I called to Anne.

'You're all clear,' Anne called back.

Another flower came winging towards Luna. Variam flicked a hand at it and a small burst of fire engulfed it, there and gone in a second. A blackened stalk dropped to the earth. 'Nice work,' I said to Variam. Vari's never been short of power, but control's another story. Obviously he'd improved.

'Guys,' Luna said, pointing. 'Look.'

I followed the direction of Luna's finger and shivered. Where the red flowers had been planted, the grass was thinner, and now that the flowers were gone I could see silhouettes of flesh and bone. The wind shifted slightly, blowing towards us, and just for a second I caught the aroma of rotting meat. From the shapes there were at least three bodies, maybe more.

'You know,' Variam said, 'I can't quite put my finger on it, but something's telling me we're not welcome here.'

'Look how desiccated they are,' Anne said, staring. Her lifesight had shown her the flowers, but not the dead bodies beneath. 'I think something drained their blood.'

'Guess those flowers get hungry,' Luna said.

'And I guess we're not the only ones trying to get through,' I said. 'Those bodies can't be more than a week old.' Apparently they'd tried to get past Karyos too, and lost the argument. Might explain why she hadn't bothered to talk.

'Heads up,' Variam said. 'We've got company.'

There was movement above the treetops, small objects flitting between the branches. From a distance they looked like birds, but I knew they weren't. 'Anne?' I asked. 'Any more of those thorn things?'

'No . . . yes,' Anne said. 'They're staying behind the trees.'

'Guess they saw what happened to the last lot,' Luna said.

I shook my head. 'No. You saw how they just charged in? These things are pretty much mindless. They're being directed.'

'Karyos,' Luna said. 'We take her out, they stop, right?'

'Then you better hurry,' Variam said, 'because they brought friends.'

Looking into the futures, I saw that Variam was right. In only a few minutes we'd be attacked again, and this time there'd be almost three times as many. I didn't know how many reserves Karyos had, and I didn't like the idea of waiting around to find out. 'Anne, can you see her?' I asked.

Anne shook her head. 'Not in my range.'

I thought quickly. Karyos must be relying on her minions, keeping herself away from the fight. Which meant that the surest way to bait out a response would be to threaten her directly . . .

I looked ahead again, but this time I searched the futures in which we advanced, scanning the different directions. In most of them, the creatures fell back before us, content to wait while they gathered their forces. But in one cluster, if we went ahead and a little to the left, it'd provoke a furious attack.

'I think I've found her,' I said. 'Head straight forward and angle left around the big tree. And get ready. Once they realise where we're going, they're not going to be happy.'

'You want to take point?' Variam asked.

'You and me together,' I said. 'Luna, you're rearguard. Anne, stay at the centre where you can reach everyone. Got it?'

Three faces nodded at me. 'Okay,' I said. 'Keep to a walk until I say.'

We advanced. The charred remains of flowers crunched under my feet, leaving soot on my shoes, and I pulled out the half-empty magazine from the MP7 and replaced it with a new one, snapping it into the pistol grip with a click. The woods were silent, waiting. From behind, I could hear Luna's breathing. There was a clatter and Variam swore as he stumbled over one of the skeletons; a skull went bouncing away.

The futures of violence were getting closer and I knew Karyos wouldn't wait much longer. 'Get ready,' I said. 'When I say run, head for that tree. Stay close.' It was in view now: a huge thing with a thick trunk, visible through the rest of the wood. I counted as I walked. *Three . . . two . . . one . . .* 'Now!' I called, and broke into a trot.

For a few seconds the only sound was our running feet, then the woods seemed to come alive, thornlings and flowers closing in on all sides. I fired, saw a thornling explode in a bloom of flame, knelt and fired again. A flower swarm was engulfed in searing heat, then I heard Variam yell and the flow of fire magic winked out.

I spun. Variam had come too close to a knot of rose bushes and they'd seized him, stalks and branches binding around his limbs. He thrashed, trying to burn them off, and I changed direction and sprinted for him; I was halfway through drawing my sword when my precognition warned me of danger to the right and I twisted my head to see more of the thornlings on top of us. One was just about to hit Vari from behind and as it drew back its arm, long thorns aiming for Variam's neck, my bullets took it in the head. Another was intercepted by Luna; the other two jumped on me.

Suddenly I didn't have time to worry about Variam or Luna; the futures had narrowed to a whirl of combat where one wrong move could get me impaled. The thornlings threw themselves at me, slashing and stabbing; my armour took the worst of the hits but it didn't cover everywhere, and pain flared in my cheek and hand. I hit one with the gun's stock, but the MP7's polymer didn't have enough weight and the thing leapt on me. I fell back with one leg up, let my foot sink into its body, then heaved to send it flying over me. Before the thing could rise, I rolled over onto my elbows and shot it through the chest.

I scrambled to my feet to see that Variam was free, staggering back; Anne had reached him and the rose bushes that had ensnared him were dead. There was blood on Variam's legs but Anne was dragging him back, and as Luna stood over them to cover them both Anne put her hands on Variam; green light surged into him and he gasped and shuddered but a second later he was pulling himself to his feet just as another pair of flowers were snapped out of the air by Luna's whip.

All of a sudden, our enemies were gone again. The four

of us crouched in a defensive ring, shielded by the dead rosebushes and a tree. Thornling bodies were scattered all around us but the remaining ones had disappeared. 'They've backed off,' Luna said.

'They'll be back as soon as we start moving,' I said.

'Shit,' Luna said. 'You see how many of those things there are?'

The path towards the centre of the shadow realm was littered with those rosebushes. They looked innocuous, their blooms red and pink and orange, but I knew that as soon as we got close enough they'd lash out. 'Screw this,' Variam said. His armour had been punctured and I could see blood through the holes, but he mostly just looked pissed off. 'I'm going to burn a way through.'

'No,' Luna said sharply. 'We need you taking out the swarms.'

'So I'll do both.'

'Luna's right,' I said. 'We're going to get bogged down.'

A scream sounded from ahead of us, and at the sound of it, all of us froze. There was something inhuman about it, wild and frenzied, a woman's voice but one that spoke of madness and death. It sounded again and this time there were words in it, a shrieked challenge in some language I didn't understand. It died away and all of us crouched motionless, waiting.

'I'm guessing that's Karyos,' Luna said at last.

'No shit, Sherlock,' Variam said.

'Shut up,' I said tersely. 'Listen.'

The scream came again, but this time I could make out the words. 'Trespassers!' it shrieked. 'Despoilers!'

'Go fuck yourself!' Luna shouted back.

'Slayers of the wood, burners of the groves!' The voice

was coming from somewhere off ahead and to the left. 'Die and be forgotten!'

The echoes faded away and there was silence. I stood very still, listening, but Karyos didn't speak again.

'Hey, maybe you should try asking her nicely some more,' Variam said. 'I'm sure this time it'll work.'

I gave Variam a look. 'She's not far,' Luna said.

'I don't think it's her,' Anne said.

I looked at Anne. 'Can you see?'

'Maybe,' Anne was frowning. 'Everything is connected here . . . But she wouldn't give her position away unless she had to, would she? If she can make thornlings, she can make something with vocal cords.'

My hopes fell. 'Shit.'

'They're moving,' Luna warned. 'More thornlings.'

Variam swore. 'How many of those things does she *have*?'

'She's been in here a hundred years with nothing else to do,' I said. 'I'm guessing a lot.' More and more my instincts were telling me that we were outmatched here. We had to come up with something different, and fast.

'Alex, check something for me,' Anne said. 'I'm going to run straight at those rose bushes. Tell me what'll happen.'

I frowned, not understanding, but there was a note of urgency in Anne's voice and I didn't argue. I seized the future just seconds away in which she went sprinting forward, coming within range of the roses' grasping thorns, and . . . I blinked. 'Huh?'

'Well?' Anne asked.

'They're not going to attack,' I said. It had been only a brief glimpse, but I was sure. 'They'll go for us, but not for you. What are you doing?'

'Trying something,' Anne said. She took a breath. 'Okay. I'm going after Karyos. Can you get her attention?'

'Wait,' I said. 'Take someone—'

'We don't have time,' Anne said. 'Just trust me.'

I hesitated for an instant. Luna and Variam were looking at Anne and Variam was frowning, about to argue, and I made a snap decision. 'All right. Vari, you're not going to force a way through, but make it *look* like you're trying to force a way through. Burn a path through the bushes, but at the first sign of a counterattack go back to focusing on the flowers. Luna, you and I'll cover him. Anne, do what you've got to do, but if you get into trouble, you yell for help and we'll come get you. And if this doesn't work then we're pulling out, because we're not going to get another shot. Understand?'

All three of them nodded and I took a breath. 'Go!'

Variam cut loose. Fire erupted, leaves blackening and flaring in the heat, and thick smoke rolled up into the sky. Bark charred as Variam spread the flame outwards, burning a path.

The wood's defenders recoiled, then struck back. Anne was gone; I'd had a brief glimpse of her running left before she'd disappeared into the trees. I sighted and fired, dropping one thornling, then two. The MP7 clicked empty and I ejected the magazine and slapped in a new one. Luna was fighting by my side, one hand lashing out with her whip, the other throwing hexes.

We made it maybe twenty feet before we were halted again. There were just too many, and now they had us surrounded. With only three of us, we each had to watch too wide a sector, and the thornlings weren't presenting such easy targets any more. Their attacks were just as furious but they were using the trees as cover, forcing me to take longer to line up a shot. Variam burnt a swarm of the flowers to ash, but all of his attention was on the sky and he didn't have time to burn us a new path through the roses. As if sensing that they'd stopped us, the creatures pulled away, leaving us standing back to back.

'You okay?' I said without turning my head.

'Got scratched,' Luna said. 'It's not bad.'

'This is like fighting fucking army ants,' Variam said.

Movement to the right caught my eye. I brought the gun up, but the thornling ducked behind a tree and I lost the shot. 'The way you beat swarms,' I said, 'is to take out the queen.'

'You see Anne?' Luna asked.

'No.'

'Defilers!' the voice screamed again. 'Barbarians!'

'Okay, that's definitely closer,' Luna said.

'Yeah, and it's definitely a trap.'

'Your flesh will feed the leaves and bark!' the voice screamed. It actually sounded more unhinged, if possible. 'Your blood will be drunk by the hawthorn roots! Your bones will be nests and chattel!'

'I'm really getting tired of listening to her,' I said.

'More thornlings,' Luna said. 'Behind the forked tree, my two o'clock.'

'I see them,' I said. 'Vari, get ready to blast them.'

'Got it.'

'Wait,' I said. 'Cancel that.'

'What?'

'Just . . .' I looked ahead, concentrating. *Yes.* All we had to do was not screw anything up. 'Don't do anything. Hold steady.'

Seconds ticked away. 'Alex?' Luna said.

'Steady.'

'They're getting ready for a rush,' Luna said. There was an urgent note in her voice.

'Ten more seconds.'

I could see the thornlings now, creeping forward in a wide arc centred on Luna. I kept my gun up but didn't level it, counting down in my head. *Three . . . two . . . one . . .*

A piercing scream echoed through the trees, cut off abruptly.

Luna twisted her head. 'Wait. That was from the other side—'

I pointed. 'Look.'

First one by one, then in a shower, the vampire flowers were dropping from the sky, spiralling down to plant their stalks in the ground. 'The bushes are stopping too,' I said, checking the futures. 'We can go near them safely.'

'The thornlings aren't,' Variam said. 'Get ready.'

The thornlings came again, rushing from cover, but oddly hesitant. Their single-minded ferocity was gone, and when Variam incinerated the first pair, the two behind checked their advance and ran. Luna's whip took out a third, I shot down two more, and suddenly the remaining thornlings were running. This time they didn't retreat to shelter, ready for a new attack; they just kept going, dodging between trees until they'd disappeared from sight. It was over in seconds. None of us had taken so much as a scratch.

'Guys!' Anne called from somewhere off to our right. It was the same direction the scream had come from.

'You okay?' I shouted back.

'I'm fine! Come over.'

We shared a glance and walked across the clearing, stepping over scorched flowers and dead thornlings. I was still scanning the futures, but I couldn't see any more combat. The battle was over.

Anne was in the midst of a small thicket. The entrance was cunningly camouflaged, and we walked all the way around it twice before figuring out where to look; if we'd still been fighting, we would have skirted it without a second glance. Slipping between the branches, we found Anne in a tiny enclosed space at the centre.

Lying at Anne's feet was a woman . . . or what could have been one, if you didn't look too closely. Twigs sprouted from ash-blond hair, and lichen and moss grew over skin. The fingers ended in curved wooden claws. Below the waist, the skin transitioned to bark, and in place of legs the lower half was a mass of branching roots, making her look like some strange, leafy, wooden octopus. The hamadryad's eyes were closed.

'Huh,' Luna said, looking down at Karyos. 'That was easy.'

'How did you figure it out?' I asked Anne.

We'd carried Karyos to the centre of the shadow realm. It had been harder work than I'd expected; it turns out roots are heavy. Thornlings were still lurking around, but they hadn't made any move to rescue their mistress, and now Variam was working on opening the gate while Luna, Anne and I kept watch.

'You saw how those flowers and the roses went for us?' Anne said. 'Like they knew exactly where we were?'

I nodded.

'But they didn't have eyes,' Anne said. 'So I wondered how they could know where to go, and I looked and I thought I could pick up some kind of life magic. That made me think of lifesight, and that made me wonder if I could use the same shrouding spell that I figured out all those years back to stop Sagash from tracking me. That was why I asked you to check. Once you told me it would, then I just ran straight past.'

'How'd you know where to find Karyos?'

'The plants and the thornlings all had . . . ripples,' Anne said. 'Like a fish leaves in the water. I traced them back and once I got close enough I could see her with my lifesight. Then I just circled behind her. She was so focused on you that she didn't see me, even when I slipped through the branches.' Anne shrugged. 'That was that.'

'Okay,' Variam said, walking back to us. 'Gate's clear and we're ready to go. What do we do with her?'

The tree at the centre of the shadow realm was huge, gnarled branches spreading out from a thick, ancient trunk. The four of us gathered under the branches, looking down at Karyos's unconscious form.

'She won't wake up for a day or so,' Anne said.

'Yeah, but what if she does?'

'I do know what I'm doing,' Anne said.

Variam shrugged. 'Not saying you don't, but why take the chance?'

'Is there something you're hinting at?' I asked.

'Wouldn't it be easier to just kill her?'

'No!' Anne said before I could speak.

'Not to get all school playground here,' Variam said, 'but she started it.'

'We're the ones who broke into her home,' Anne said.

'Yeah, and she tried to kill us on sight.'

'Anne's kind of got a point though,' I said. 'We did break in without an invitation, and I'm not sure if she was really in a fit enough mental state to notice much else.'

'Isn't that kind of a reason *not* to leave her around?' Luna asked. 'I mean, if we leave her here, then isn't she going to go right back to murdering everyone who walks in?'

'It's not as if random innocents are going to come walking in.'

'Yeah, well,' Variam said. 'All I'm saying is that she seems to be pretty much exactly the kind of thing the Order of the Shield were formed to fight in the first place.'

'I didn't knock her out so that you could burn her to death,' Anne said flatly.

Variam got a stubborn look on his face. I knew he was about to argue, and I also knew that Anne wasn't going to back down. 'I think Anne's right,' I said before Variam could speak.

'Oh, come on,' Variam said. 'You saw those bodies.'

'Yes, but I think it's worth remembering that we got an awful lot of help from Arachne in getting here. Now she didn't actually make us promise to keep Karyos alive, but it was pretty clear what outcome she was hoping for. Fighting in self-defence is one thing. Executing someone while they're helpless . . .' I shrugged. 'Besides, Karyos might be the last hamadryad still on Earth. I don't want to kill her if I can avoid it.'

'If they're like this, then I don't think they'd be missed much,' Variam muttered, then held up a hand before Anne or I could speak. 'Fine, whatever. I won't burn the bitch to death while she's sleeping. But you'd better hurry, because if she wakes up while you're gone, I'm not making any promises.'

'We'll make sure it's clear for when you come out,' Luna added.

I nodded, then glanced at Anne. 'Ready?'

'Let's do it.'

We stood together in front of the great tree. 'Here we go,' Variam said. 'Don't think I can keep this open for more than a few seconds, so don't hang around.'

I felt the spell start to form and took a deep breath, then as the rent in the air formed in front of us I darted through, Anne at my side.

The Hollow had been otherworldly and beautiful. The hill on the Chilterns from which we'd gated had been ordinary, but still beautiful. The deep shadow realm was neither.

We came down in a wide, tall chamber. Pillars ran from the floor to the ceiling, and platforms linked by spiralling ramps jutted from the walls. Everything was coloured in different shades of purple, mauve to lavender to violet, and a thick haze hung in the air. From somewhere above, white light filtered down through the mist. The air smelt dry and clean, almost antiseptic, but there was no sound.

Anne and I scanned left and right, reflexively taking positions back to back. 'Anything?' Anne asked.

'Nothing in the futures,' I said. 'You?'

'Nothing alive.'

There was something alien-looking about this place. Maybe it was the architecture – too many rounded corners, not enough straight lines – but then again, maybe it was something else. The Hollow had been deadly, but that had been the creatures inside it. Here, it felt as though the whole environment was watching us, and I didn't think we were welcome.

'So how are we supposed to be finding these dreamstones again?' Anne asked.

'Still working on that part,' I said, frowning. There was something strange about this place. I was looking through the futures of us searching, and while some of them were what you'd expect, there were flashes of possibilities that just didn't fit. Strange creatures, natural hazards, even glimpses of what looked like combat . . . but when I looked again, they weren't there.

'Something about this place feels like Elsewhere,' Anne said. 'I don't know why, but . . .'

'The futures do too,' I said. 'Too fluid.' I pointed. 'Okay,

I'm pretty sure that this direction has *something*. Can't promise what. But let's check in first.' I touched the communicator in my ear. 'Vari, come in.'

Silence.

'Vari, it's Alex. Come in.'

'Why is it,' Anne said, 'that these communicators always seem to fail whenever we really need them?'

I bit back a couple of swear-words. It wouldn't have helped Anne's morale. 'Okay, so calling for extraction is out. Good news is that it looks like the gate stone'll work.'

The gate stone was the backup plan. Variam was holding its mirror, meaning that it should gate us straight back to where he was. 'Except that we won't be able to call for help,' Anne pointed out.

'There is that.'

Anne shrugged. 'Nothing new then.'

We set off, walking in the direction I'd marked. 'So,' Anne said, 'what exactly do dreamstones look like?'

'According to Arachne, it's a case of "you'll know it when you see it".'

'Do you think there's some way we could make sure Richard has a weaker one?'

'I got the impression that . . .' I trailed off. 'Heads up.'

Ahead of us, the corridor opened up into a tunnel. The features were the same, weirdly curved purple lines, with strange objects hanging from the ceiling that looked like a cross between stalactites and giant frozen bats, but straight ahead was a sphere of pure black, edged in violet.

I walked forward cautiously. I couldn't see any immediate danger, but there was the same weird fluidity to the futures, half-glimpsed possibilities of horror and surprise blinking in and out. 'It's a portal,' I said.

'To where?' Anne said.

'I don't know,' I said. 'But there's something . . .'

'There's something inside,' Anne said.

I nodded slowly. I couldn't get a clear vision, but I could get a sense of *something* within the darkness, an impression of silent power. Stepping through would take me into a maze of narrower corridors, but I wasn't sure I'd be able to get back out. 'There's a problem,' I said. 'It's not stable.'

Anne didn't take her eyes off the sphere. 'Hmm?'

'If I step through, I think it'll collapse,' I said. 'Or redirect, maybe. Wherever it'll take me, I can't see you there too.' I frowned. 'Maybe there's some way to stabilise it . . .'

'I don't think it wants you,' Anne said absently.

I started to ask what she meant, then spun. Just for an instant I had an impression of something behind us, huge and looming, then it was gone. The corridor behind was empty. 'Anne,' I said. '*Anne!*'

'Hmm?'

'Was there something there?'

'It's okay,' Anne said. 'I'll be back.'

I should have realised what Anne was about to do, but the phantoms were distracting me and I put it together just a second too late. I grabbed for her just as Anne stepped forward and touched the sphere. There was a moment where she seemed to twist and warp, then she was gone. I swore, hesitated an instant, jumped after her—

—and stumbled through into an empty corridor. The sphere was gone. The corridor was empty both ahead and behind. 'Anne!' I shouted.

My voice echoed from the walls, fading into silence. I couldn't see Anne. Except that it felt as though I *should* be able to see her – there was a future where she was right ahead of me, walking slowly down the corridor – then as I reached for it, it was gone. 'Damn it,' I muttered. Anne was usually more careful than this.

I thought I could see a possibility in which I found Anne. Just like the others, it blinked in and out, there and gone again, but it was the best lead I had and I went running down the corridor. I could gate out at any time I wanted, but Anne wasn't holding the gate stone and if I couldn't find her then she would be in real trouble. I turned a corner to find a black wall blocking my path, sheer and lightless and straight as a razor, but a glance at the futures told me that it wasn't dangerous and I stepped through.

And stopped. Right in front of me was a boy, maybe twelve years old, light-skinned with a shock of black hair and dark watchful eyes. He was sitting upon a curved shelf, his legs swinging underneath him, and he was looking at me. 'What are you doing here?' I said.

'You aren't ready,' the boy said.

Something about the boy's face and the way he was watching me seemed weirdly familiar, but I didn't have time to think about it. 'I'm looking for a girl,' I said. 'Have you seen her?'

'She's not looking for you.'

I advanced cautiously. I didn't think the boy was hostile, but something about him made me uneasy. He didn't move, looking up at me with those big dark eyes. 'Where's Anne?'

'You're going to lose more than you think.'

I stared at the boy. 'Who are you?'

The boy hopped off from where he was sitting, his shoes thumping onto the floor. 'I won't stop you,' he said. 'Just don't forget.'

'What are you—?'

The boy knelt down, sinking into a ball, and then he was gone. The curving, chair-like rest that he'd been sitting on was gone as well. In its place was a jagged, mound-like crystalline formation, amethyst-coloured and rising to a blunted point.

I stared down at the stone, trying to make sense of what I was seeing. There were veins running through the crystal, converging towards its tip, and the centre had a hollow like that of a very small volcano. Resting in the hollow was a shard of the same crystal, but brighter, clearer. Somehow, I knew that it would come away if I reached for it.

A voice in my mind spoke up. *Pretty sure that's what we're looking for.*

Screw that! the other half of my mind said. *Where the hell did he go? And what* was *he?*

Which were two very good questions that I had absolutely no clue how to answer, so I scanned the futures for what would happen if I picked up the shard. Once I was reasonably sure that it wasn't going to poison, burn, electrocute or otherwise inconvenience me, I leant forward and clasped my hand around the crystal. It resisted slightly, then came away. The veins running through the mound pulsed once, then went dark.

I looked at the shard. It was small enough for my fingers to wrap around, but it was heavy. I had no idea what it was made of, but I was pretty sure this was what we were looking for. I'd need to get it back to Arachne to check, but before I could do that I needed to find—

'Alex,' Anne's voice said from behind me.

I jumped, spinning around with my heart pounding in

my chest. I *never* get surprised like that, and more times than I can count that's been the only thing that's kept me alive, yet here in this place I apparently couldn't even walk around a corner without missing something crucial. It was starting to really scare me now. What would happen when I met something actually dangerous? 'Jesus,' I said. 'You scared the shit out of me.'

'Sorry,' Anne said, but she sounded distracted. She nodded towards my hand. 'Did you find one too?'

'Yeah – wait. What do you mean, "too"?'

In answer, Anne lifted something in her hand. It was a dark purplish-black, gleaming in the light, similar to the crystal I was carrying but slightly smaller. 'I think it wanted to be found,' Anne said.

'Never mind that,' I said. Now that the initial rush of relief had worn off, I was angry. 'What were you thinking, running off like that? You could have been lost here.'

'I don't think it would have wanted that.'

I threw up my hands in frustration. 'You know what? Let's just get out of here.'

'Is there anything you want to tell me?'

I looked at Anne, puzzled. 'What?'

'Anything you want to tell me,' Anne said. Her reddish eyes were dark as she watched me.

'What kind of thing?'

Anne stared at me for a long moment. 'Okay,' she said at last.

I shook my head. 'Look, let's just open the gate. I don't like this place.'

Anne crossed to my side and I took out the gate stone, turning it around in my hand. 'Did you see anything when you picked it up?' Anne asked.

'Yeah,' I said. 'Did you?'

'Yes,' Anne said. There was something distant in her voice.

I kept focusing on the gate, starting to weave the spell. 'What did you see?'

There was a moment's pause before Anne answered, and when she did her voice was suddenly cold. 'Something about you.'

Agony shot through me, spiking through my limbs. The gate stone dropped from my hand as I collapsed, shuddering; the floor was cold and smooth against my cheek. I couldn't move or think. My muscles were burning.

A hand grabbed me, dragging me onto my back. Through hazy eyes, I could see Anne bending over me, her face contorted with rage. 'Why didn't you tell me?'

I stared at Anne in shock. I couldn't understand it. Anne would never hurt me; this had to be some kind of mistake—

'I trusted you!' Anne's face twisted into a snarl. 'And you did this! *This!*' Her fingers touched my chest, and I felt a spell weaving.

A terrible pain flashed through me, a ripping, tearing sensation that made me convulse, followed by a horrible silence. I couldn't hear anything and my limbs felt still, leaden, with a terrible sense of pressure. My heart wasn't beating. I tried to open my mouth, tried to speak, but my muscles wouldn't obey me. A grey veil was falling over my eyes.

'I trusted you,' Anne said again. She was staring down at me, and the light was fading from all around, the room going from purple to grey to black. As it slipped away, my last sight was of those furious eyes—

* * *

I jerked upright with a gasp. I was lying on the floor next to the crystal mound and I looked around wildly. There was no sign of the boy, or of Anne. Clutched in my hand was a shard of amethyst, small but heavy. My fingers were wrapped around it, and when with an effort I made them release, I could see white and red lines where the crystal's edges had sunk into my hands. The floor was smooth and cold.

Movement in the futures. Someone was coming and I twisted around, staring at the corridor from which I'd entered. I saw who it was going to be and sudden fear spiked through me.

A figure appeared, tall and slender, with shoulder-length hair. 'Alex?' Anne said. Her eyes went down to the shard of crystal in my hand. 'Did you find one too?'

I opened my mouth to speak, but no words came out.

Anne looked down at me, frowning. 'Alex?'

I took a breath, then another. I looked at the futures, searching for any sign of danger, and found nothing. But then, I hadn't seen any danger *before* either, and my divination wasn't working the way it should be—

'What's wrong?'

I tried to speak, failed, cleared my throat and tried again. 'Nothing. I'm fine.'

'You don't look fine,' Anne said doubtfully. She walked towards me, reaching out a hand.

I flinched. It was only a small movement, but Anne stopped dead. I scrambled to my feet. 'I'm all right.'

'I could check—' Anne began.

'No,' I said quickly. All of a sudden I didn't want Anne touching me. 'It's okay.'

Anne was looking at me. She didn't come any closer and

there was a puzzled, hurt look in her eyes. I dragged my gaze away. 'What did you find?' I said.

'This,' Anne said, and I knew what she was going to show me before she held it up. A shard of crystal, a dark purplish-black, smaller than the one I was holding but similar in its design . . .

'Alex?' Anne asked when I didn't speak.

I didn't want to look; just a glimpse of the dreamstone brought the memory back. 'Yeah.'

'Don't you want to check?'

'It's what we're looking for,' I said. I didn't meet her gaze. 'Good job.'

'I know you said to stay together,' Anne said. 'But it felt as though something was calling me, and I knew it'd be . . .' She frowned, paused. 'Did something . . . happen when you found that?'

I opened my mouth, began to answer, then found myself looking into Anne's eyes. Reddish-brown, just as they had been before, and a shiver went through me and suddenly the thought of telling her about it was more than I could face. 'It's fine,' I said. 'Let's get out of here.'

Anne gave a dubious nod, stepping closer. She was watching me closely and I managed not to pull away this time, but I could feel her eyes on me.

We stepped through into bright, peaceful light. The multi-coloured sky of the Hollow was all around us and the branches of the great tree hung overhead. As I looked through the futures, I could see that they were solid once more and I closed my eyes and sagged in relief. I did *not* want to do that again.

A girl with light brown hair was carrying a handful of

sticks across the grass. As she saw us, she stopped and stared, then dropped the bundle of wood with a clatter and shouted. 'Vari, Vari!' Then she ran towards me.

'Hey, Luna,' I began. 'We— oof!'

Luna crashed into me, hugging me tight. I staggered back and immediately Luna was backing off, apologetic. 'Sorry, sorry. I know I shouldn't— wait a sec.' She held out a hand and the threads of half-seen silver mist which had clung to me from the touch slid away, sinking down into the earth. 'Vari!' she shouted over her shoulder, then turned to Anne. 'You're okay? You're both okay?'

'We're fine,' Anne said. 'And we got what we came for.'

'Screw what you came for! I thought you were never coming out!'

'Luna, relax,' I said. I'd been enjoying the attention – it was kind of touching – but it was still a funny overreaction. 'We said we'd be back.'

Luna laughed. 'Yeah, I guess you did.'

Variam came running into view through the trees. As he saw us, he slowed to a walk, but his eyes flicked sharply over Anne. 'You're all right?' he demanded.

'We're all right,' Anne said.

'Wow,' I said, looking around. 'You guys have been busy.' When we'd left, the clearing had been scattered with the remains of the thornlings and those flowers. All of them were gone now: a blackened heap marked where the bodies had been burned in a pyre, and off to the right was what looked like a makeshift camp-site, with the supplies we'd left back on the hilltop. Both Luna and Vari must have worked like crazy to get all that done so fast.

'What's that?' Anne asked.

I turned to see that Anne was staring at something to

the right of the clearing. It looked like a small fallen tree with a sapling growing nearby. 'What's what?' I asked, then when she continued to stare, I looked at Variam and Luna. 'Guys?'

Luna and Variam looked at me, then Luna turned to look at Variam. 'I told you,' Variam said.

'Um,' Luna said. 'So. There was a slight problem.'

'A problem with . . . ?' Anne started to ask, then her eyes went wide. She started to walk towards the tree.

Luna fell in beside her. 'Okay,' Luna said as she walked. 'First of all, I'd like to point out that this was not remotely our fault.'

My heart sank. I recognised that tone of voice. 'Luna, what have you done?'

'I *said*, it wasn't our fault.'

'What did . . . ?' I started to say, then tailed off. Looking around the clearing, I could see the remains of the pyre, and Luna and Variam's camp-site. But there was something I wasn't seeing that I should have been seeing. 'Luna?' I said, and this time there was a warning note to my voice. 'Where's Karyos?'

Luna and Variam looked at each other. 'You said you'd tell him,' Variam said.

'I'm trying, okay?'

I started to answer, then shot a sharp look at the remains of the fire. A big fire. Too big to have been fuelled only by the thornlings we'd killed. '*Vari!*'

'What?'

'Did you burn Karyos on that?'

'No!' Variam said indignantly.

'Of course we didn't!' Luna said, then hesitated. 'Well, not most of her.'

'Not *most* of her?'

'Let me explain,' Luna began.

'Wait,' Anne said. She'd been crouched over the fallen tree, studying it, and now she turned to Luna and Variam. 'Is this what I think it is?'

'Pretty much,' Variam said.

Luna rounded on Vari. 'Will you shut up and let me explain?'

'Because you're doing such a great job.'

'Anne?' I said. 'Can you explain what's going on here?'

Anne pointed down at the tree. 'That's a cocoon.'

I frowned. 'You mean—?'

'A regeneration cocoon?' Anne said. 'Yes.'

I stared at it for a second. Now that I looked more closely at the thing, I could see that it wasn't a tree. It was too round, without enough of a trunk, and the only branches came from the sapling whose roots were twined into it. 'You guys used the seed?'

'Actually, that was her,' Variam put in.

'Shut *up*, Vari!' Luna snapped.

I put a hand to my forehead. 'Christ.'

'Well, she's alive,' Anne said. She knelt down, one hand on the cocoon, frowning. 'Or something is.'

I glared at Luna. 'The idea was to offer the thing to Karyos. Not use it on her against her will!'

'If you'd let me finish,' Variam said, 'the reason I told you that it was Luna was to make the point that you really should be thanking her. If it had been up to me, I just would have fried her.'

'Jesus,' I said. 'What's wrong with you?'

'Okay, you know what?' Luna said. 'I've about had enough of this. What did you expect us to do?'

'Leave her unconscious until we got back!'

'Uh, yeah, slight problem with that,' Variam said. 'She woke up.'

'She— Wait, what?'

'Or started to,' Variam said. 'And given how the last conversation went, I think it's safe to say that her mood would not have been improved by finding out what we'd done with her pets, right? So we had a choice between letting her *finish* waking up, and getting a fun and exciting lesson about weaponised dryad magic, or cutting things off early. We voted for option number two. Only question was how.'

'That doesn't make sense,' Anne said, frowning. 'That spell should have kept her sleeping for at *least* eighteen hours. More like twenty-four.'

Luna and Variam stared at Anne. Luna opened her mouth to speak, and then an odd expression crossed her face. 'How long did you spend in that other shadow realm?' she asked me.

Anne and I looked at each other. 'Forty minutes?' Anne guessed.

'Less,' I said.

Variam and Luna looked at each other.

'What?' I said.

'Alex,' Luna said slowly. 'You've been gone for three days.'

I blinked. 'No we haven't.'

'Two days, twenty-one hours and thirty minutes,' Variam put in. 'Give or take half an hour.'

The four of us stared at each other.

Putting the pieces together took a while.

From Anne's and my perspectives, we'd been gone for

slightly over half an hour. Anne assured me that we hadn't burned enough body energy for it to be more, and the clocks on our phones agreed with her. But while we'd been in that deep shadow realm, the sun had set and risen again three times on Earth and in the Hollow that mirrored it.

Once I'd finally accepted that yes, Luna and Variam were telling the truth, and no, this wasn't a practical joke, the full creepy implications set in. I remembered passing through those black screens, the feelings of dislocation, and wondered just how much time we'd lost in those moments. Or did time simply flow faster inside the shadow realm than outside? If we'd taken our time with the exploration, stayed in those corridors for hours, then how much time would have passed outside? Weeks? More?

Of course, while we'd been gone, Luna and Variam had had more immediate problems. They couldn't go back to Earth out of fear that we'd try to use the gate stone while they were gone, so they'd been stuck in a shadow realm full of hostile monsters. And it turned out that while the vampire flowers and the bushes weren't a threat with Karyos gone, the same was not true for the thornlings.

'They didn't do any more coordinated rushes,' Luna explained. 'But they didn't give up either. They just kept stalking us, and with you and Anne gone it was really hard to spot the bloody things.'

'What did you do?' Anne asked.

'Wiped them out, what do you think?' Variam said. 'And don't you even start giving us grief about that. Those things were *not* willing to sit down and talk.'

'Did Karyos wake up in the middle of one of those attacks?' I asked.

'How'd you guess?' Variam said. 'Let's just say it got a

little exciting. Just as well Luna had been playing around with the regeneration thing.'

I looked at Luna. 'Well, you weren't coming back,' she said with a shrug. 'I'd been thinking about what to do if we needed it.'

'And you figured out a way to get it working?' I asked.

'Pretty much.'

I was actually impressed. When Arachne had given me that seed, she'd implied that it had been meant to be used by Karyos, not by someone else, particularly not under that kind of time pressure. 'Well, it worked,' Anne said. 'Karyos is in there, or her new body is.' She nodded towards the cocoon. 'And as far as I can tell, it took. She's bonded to that sapling now.'

'So what does that mean?' Luna asked.

'Means in another few years, that thing'll open and a baby hamadryad'll come out.'

'With the freaky roots-for-legs or without?' Luna asked.

I shrugged. 'I'm not exactly an expert on this stuff.'

'So is the whole kill-crazy murder-all-humans thing going to carry over as well?' Variam asked. 'Because if it does, I'm not sure if Luna did anyone any favours.'

'It shouldn't,' I said. 'That was the whole point of the thing. But now we've got another problem.'

'What?'

'I think I know,' Anne said. 'This shadow realm's accessible from the outside, isn't it?'

I nodded. 'And those bodies prove that people know about it.'

Luna looked between the two of us.

'Shadow realms are valuable,' I explained to Luna. 'You know how some mages live in their own shadow realm?

And how they make sure everyone knows it? It's a status symbol.'

'I thought they just grew their own.'

'Yes, but it takes years and years, and from what I've heard, the only way to find out whether it's somewhere you want to live or a little pocket hellhole is to wait and see. It's much easier to find an existing shadow realm that someone else has done the work of making. A place like this?' I nodded at the multicoloured sky, the trees, the warm air. 'This is prime real estate. The only reason some mage hasn't planted their flag here already is that Karyos was defending it.'

'Huh,' Luna said. 'So now that she's gone . . .'

'Now this place is like a three-storey house with a garden in central London. *Someone* is going to grab it.'

'And the first thing they'll do is destroy that,' Anne said, nodding to the cocoon. 'Or use it for experiments.'

'What if you moved it?' Luna asked.

'It's too fragile. In six months, maybe, but now . . .'

'Okay, I know I'm sounding like a broken record here,' Variam said, 'but I don't see how any of this is our problem. We wanted dreamstones, we've got dreamstones. I say we call the mission a success and bail while the going's good.'

'And leave her to die?' Anne asked.

'Did you miss the part where she was about to kill us?'

Anne threw up her hands and looked at me. 'Can you think of any mage who'd be willing to help?'

'I've been trying,' I admitted. 'But the only mages I can think of who might be sympathetic don't really have the resources to take on something like this. Maybe Landis . . .'

Variam shook his head. 'He's got *way* too much on his plate right now.'

'What about us?' Luna asked.

All three of us looked at her. 'I'm not saying we should move in,' Luna said. 'But we could set up gate wards and all that stuff, right?'

'None of us knows how to set up gate wards,' Variam said.

Luna pointed at me. 'Alex knows people who do.'

'Yeah, but they don't work for free,' I said.

Luna shrugged. 'You're the one who's always storing up favours.'

'Come on,' Variam said. 'I can't believe you're thinking seriously about this. Yes, this place is pretty, but it's a frigging death-trap. Hanging out in a place where a crazy dryad's spent the last fifty years magically modifying every single plant to either poison you or eat you is not my idea of fun!'

'We could clear it out,' Luna said. 'The only reason we were having so much trouble was that neither of us had any senses that could tell us what to watch out for. With Anne's lifesight and your precognition, we could sweep the place.'

'That'll take days,' I said. 'Maybe weeks. And that's not even the part I'm worried about. What happens when the next bunch of mages comes along? We'd have to set up gate wards and a security system, and the mages who specialise in that kind of stuff don't work cheap.'

'It'd also give us a base,' Luna pointed out.

That made me pause. Ever since my house in Camden had been burnt down, it had been difficult for the four of us to find places to meet or train. The house in Wales had been a stopgap, but now that I'd abandoned that too, we'd had to fall back upon Arachne's lair. Which was a good place – a very good place – but it required Arachne to be comfortable with us planning our operations from what was, basically, her living room. She hadn't complained, but I was uncomfortably aware that we were presuming on her hospitality, and ever since that conversation we'd had in February there'd been the nasty thought at the back of my mind that I could be storing up trouble for the future. Arachne's position with the Council is precarious, and I'm not a popular person these days. By using her home as a base I could be putting her in danger. Of course, trying to use an unsecured shadow realm as a base would be almost as bad . . .

I paused. Except that I *did* know someone with the influence to get a shadow realm properly secured, who also owed me favours. Talisid. Was my spying on Richard worth enough to get him to do this?

Maybe I should find out.

'. . . really don't want to deal with this,' Variam was saying. 'Can't we just—?'

'Okay,' I said.

The others looked at me. 'Really?' Variam said.

'No promises, but I've got an idea that might be able to help,' I said. 'But I only want you guys in on this if you want to be. Vari's right: it's going to be a lot of work.'

'I'm up for it,' Luna said. 'I kind of like this place, and it's not like I don't have the time. Besides, there's something I've been having trouble with that a shadow realm would be handy for. I'll tell you about it later.'

I looked at Anne, who nodded. 'I'd like to,' she said in her soft voice. 'I'm the reason Karyos can't defend herself now. I'm not comfortable leaving her like this.'

Luna turned to Variam with a grin. 'Looks like you're outvoted.'

Variam threw up his hands. 'Luna,' I said, and Luna rolled her eyes but didn't answer. 'It's okay, Vari, you've done plenty already. We can handle the clean-up.'

'Yeah, unless you run into another nest of those vampire flowers. What are you going to do, pick them out of the air?' Variam scowled. 'Fine. But just so you know, this is a stupid plan.'

'Oh, come on,' Luna said. 'How many new journeyman get to say they're part owner of their own shadow realm?'

'We're splitting it into parts now?'

I got to my feet. 'Come on, guys. Time to go.'

Walking back into Arachne's cave felt like coming home after a long, long day. Luna and Variam were exhausted from three days of watching for danger, and I wasn't much better – the vision or dream or whatever it was in the deep shadow realm had shaken me more than I'd been willing to admit. Only Anne seemed in good shape.

We told the story to Arachne. She didn't make a big demonstration upon hearing what we'd decided to do with Karyos and the Hollow – that's not her style – but I could tell she was pleased. She thanked us, and thanked me again later in private.

We'd meant to have a party to celebrate our success, but it didn't last very long. Within an hour Luna and Variam were asleep, sprawled on sofas, and only Anne and I were left awake, talking to Arachne. She promised to help with the work on the Hollow, and curled up in an armchair surrounded by silks, I felt warm and safe.

Eventually the conversation turned to the dreamstones,

and Anne and I laid our prizes out on one of the tables. Arachne crouched over them on her eight legs and studied them. 'What do you think?' I said when I couldn't take the suspense any longer.

'About which you should give to Richard?' Arachne asked.

'Yeah.'

'Preferably neither.'

'That's not really helpful.'

'The mages of your Council would be extremely uncomfortable about placing either of these into the hands of a Dark mage,' Arachne said. 'I think I would agree with them.'

'Are they alive?' I asked curiously. I hadn't sensed anything from either crystal since returning to the Hollow, but I still couldn't make sense of that boy I'd met. Had it been the crystal, or . . . ?

Arachne gave the spider equivalent of a shrug. 'If you write down someone's life, do they live for ever?'

I wasn't sure how to answer that one. 'These are powerful items,' Arachne said. 'Whatever Richard intends to use them for, I doubt it will be anything good.'

'Yeah, well, if we keep them, then I'm pretty sure what's going to happen to us will be a lot *less* good,' I said. 'So given that we're going with the least bad option, which one do you recommend?'

Arachne tapped one of the crystals with one tapering foreleg. 'This.'

I looked at it. The one Arachne had tapped was the one Anne had brought, slightly slimmer and darker than the other. If mine was amethyst, hers was a deep violet. 'Why that one?'

'The darker of the two crystals is more suited for compulsion,' Arachne said. 'To use it to its full potential, the wielder must want to impose their will upon another. Not out of necessity, but out of desire. It would be a poor match for you, I think.' She tapped the other crystal. 'This could have a similar use, but its focus is slightly different. More of a tool for linking.'

I nodded slowly, then looked at Anne. 'What do you think?'

Anne looked down at the crystal she'd carried out of the shadow realm. 'Get rid of it,' she said at last.

Much later, after Luna and Variam had yawned themselves awake and we were preparing to leave, I spoke quietly to Anne while the other two were putting on their coats. 'Are you okay?'

'I'm okay,' Anne said after a moment. 'Just thinking.'

'About what?'

Anne shook her head.

I met her eyes. 'What did you see when you picked up that thing?'

Anne hesitated and I knew she was thinking about dodging the question, but I held her gaze and the moment passed. 'If I were in danger,' she said slowly, 'real danger, would you come to help?'

I frowned. 'Of course.'

'What if you couldn't do anything?' Anne said bluntly. 'You're not as powerful as any of us. Would you still try?'

That stung. But still . . . 'Probably.'

'Why?'

I shrugged. I could have said that I had few enough friends and that I didn't want to lose the ones I had. I could have just said that that was the sort of thing I do. There was another reason, a truer one perhaps, but I shied away from admitting that, even to myself. But something in Anne's eyes made me uncomfortable, and I fell back on a less naked answer. 'We all have things we don't want to give up.'

Anne stood looking back at me for a long moment, then a burst of laughter came from Luna and Variam behind us, and the moment was gone. She turned away.

I looked at Anne, frowning. Somehow I had the uneasy feeling that I'd said the wrong thing. But then Luna and Variam came to rejoin us, and we fell in together for the walk out.

11

July and August

The handover took place without incident. Morden contacted me a couple of days after our return, giving me instructions to deliver the dreamstone to Onyx. I prepared for the worst, but to my mild surprise, when the day came, Onyx showed up at the meeting point, gave me one poisonous look, took the package and left without a word. Either Morden had drilled into his Chosen's head what the consequences of picking a fight would be, or Onyx was just biding his time.

With that done, things went back to normal, or as normal as they got these days. I tried asking Morden what Richard wanted the dreamstone for, but I hadn't really been expecting an answer and I didn't get one. I wasn't comfortable with Richard having the thing, and Arachne and I spent a couple of evenings talking over what his intentions might be, but all we could come up with was speculation.

The deep shadow realm fell out of alignment with the Hollow about two weeks after we left it. Variam tested it thoroughly and confirmed the next day that it was gone – gating from the Hollow to the deep shadow realm didn't work any more, and that strange place would stay inaccessible in some distant reality for years, if not for ever. I couldn't help but feel relieved. That vision had shaken me badly, and it was a long time before I could look Anne in the eyes without feeling a twinge of fear. But Anne acted just the same as she always had, and as the weeks passed, my uneasiness faded away.

Clearing out the Hollow turned out to be even harder than Variam had predicted. Karyos had spent decades turning the shadow realm into her personal fortress, and the place was littered with traps and guardian plants. Most had been failures – based on what we found, Karyos's creations had tended towards the imaginative rather than the practical – but they definitely made life interesting, and we learned to be extremely grateful for Anne's healing.

'You know,' Luna said after one particularly memorable encounter, picking the last of the venomous thorns out of her leg, 'I'm really starting to go off plants.' But she persisted, and by the end of the third week we were no longer nervous about walking the grounds.

Troublesome as the plants were, they weren't our biggest worry. An expedition led by a pair of independent mages tried to penetrate the Hollow, hoping to access the same deep shadow realm, and they weren't terribly happy when we told them we'd looted it already. For a change, we were able to resolve things diplomatically, but only two days later a Dark mage called Blackout arrived. He'd heard about Karyos, had decided that with the dryad gone the Hollow would be a great place to set up shop, and unlike the last pair, he wasn't willing to take no for an answer. Convincing him otherwise took some work.

But one thing did go our way. Talisid was initially less than enthusiastic about helping out with our new project, but once I made it politely but firmly clear to him that no help for us meant no more intelligence reports for him, he changed his mind. Within an astonishingly short space of time a group of gate magic specialists arrived, and by the time they were done, gating into the Hollow was all but impossible without the access keys – a set of six focuses carved from the wood of one of the Hollow's trees, allowing their wielder to step through the wards. As an added bonus, they doubled as regular gate stones, meaning that Anne, Luna and I could use them to gate to the Hollow whenever we wanted. We took one each, hid the last two and met up for a celebration in our new shadow realm, where we ate and drank and told stories under the spreading branches.

Clearing the Hollow might have been hard work, but it was satisfying. All of us except Vari had lost our homes over the past year – several times, in my case – and with the Hollow, we had a sense that at last we might have a place from which we couldn't be driven away. Morden's demands on my time eased, and the continuing refusal of the Keepers to put me on the duty roster became a plus instead of a minus. On top of that, the Crusaders stayed quiet. I hadn't really expected Landis's efforts to make any difference, but to my surprise his prediction proved accurate, and neither Lightbringer and Zilean nor any other Crusader hit team came hunting for me during those long summer days.

There was only one catch. The Hollow might be turning into a prize, but the item we'd brought out of it was exactly the opposite.

'Are you ready?' Arachne said at last.

'Just one question,' I said. 'What am I supposed to be ready *for*?'

Luna and I were in Arachne's lair, standing in a space that we'd cleared of furniture. Luna was dressed in jeans and a T-shirt, and looked relaxed. Of course, she wasn't the one expected to perform.

I was standing facing Luna, holding the dreamstone that I'd brought out of the deep shadow realm. Arachne had set it into a lattice of silver wire, and beneath the wire the facets gleamed amethyst in the light. I could sense power from it, but no more so than from any other focus. It didn't look dangerous. It looked like a pretty piece of rock.

'For trying to bond with the dreamstone,' Arachne said.

'Haven't we been doing that already?'

'Yes,' Arachne said. 'And as you've no doubt noticed, it hasn't been working especially well. Today we're going to try a more direct approach.'

'You mean activating it?'

'Hence the lattice. The material has some ability to conduct thoughts.'

'I thought you said I wouldn't need to touch this thing.'

'*Once* you bond with it, physical touch should no longer be necessary,' Arachne said. 'For now, I think you need all the help you can get.'

'You know, I might not need so much help if you could tell me exactly what this thing's supposed to do.'

'As I've told you repeatedly, it isn't so simple,' Arachne said. 'All dreamstones have a connection to Elsewhere, but their exact properties depend on the bond they forge with their bearers. Until you practise with it . . .'

'I *have* practised with it. I've tried channelling through it, I've tried meditating on it, I've even tried talking to it. About the only things I haven't tried are hitting someone over the head with it or sitting it down with biscuits and a cup of tea, and I'd be about ready to try those too if I thought they'd work.'

'I think we'll leave that for later.'

I gave Arachne an exasperated look.

'This is an exploration, Alex,' Arachne said. 'Not an instruction manual. The best analogy I can give you is that so far, your voyages into Elsewhere have been like diving into a very great ocean. You can explore widely, but not deeply.'

'So this focus would be – what?' I said. 'Scuba gear?'

'More like turning into a fish,' Arachne said. 'But only if you can make it accept you.'

I sighed. 'What do you want me to do?'

'Through Elsewhere, one can find another person and speak to them through their dreams,' Arachne said. 'It's not a use of Elsewhere that most mages would expect, nor one they would recommend, but it can be done, and it's something you've practised with Luna.' Arachne nodded to her. 'You can find her dreams faster and more effectively than you can anyone else's, and most importantly, the two of you trust each other. I want you to try to do that here.'

'While I'm awake?'

'While you're awake. Mental connection is, I believe, this dreamstone's most basic use. Any other abilities will require you to master this first.'

'I'll give it a try,' I said. Luna stood there expectantly. I held up the dreamstone and concentrated.

Using a new focus takes a bit of trial and error, but it's not usually all that hard. Focuses all work in basically the same way – the wielder channels power through them and the item shapes it, in the same way that a hammer or a saw directs kinetic energy. The trick is to get the channel going in the first place.

I looked through the futures, searching for the ones in which I got a reaction. Nothing jumped out at me, and I kept looking. Ten minutes passed.

'Anything happening?' Luna asked.

'No,' I said. I wasn't sure what was going on. Normally, channelling your power into a focus gives you *some* sort of result, even if it's not the one you're looking for. But the futures in which I did that didn't seem to hold anything at all. Admittedly I was looking for a future with a mental connection, but still . . .

I gave up on divination and tried just focusing my power into the thing. For a second, it seemed as though I almost had it – I could feel something, a sense of the focus coming alive – but then I tried to direct it and it slipped away. I tried again, and the same thing happened. It was like trying to pick up water between my fingers. I looked into the futures in which I tried other things: command words, invoking, shouting at it, hitting it, every possible action that might or might not produce a reaction from a focus item. The crystal just sat there.

After I'd run out of ideas to do it solo, we tried alternatives. A capacitor focus to overcharge the crystal, linking directly with a mind magic focus, special invocation rituals that Arachne knows.

'Is this going to take much longer?' Luna asked at last.

'I don't know,' I said.

'Because my arm is starting to ache.' Luna was holding the dreamstone to her forehead. Arachne had suggested that having her touching the thing instead of me might work. It hadn't.

'Just wait, okay?' I said. It sounded more impatient than I'd meant it to, but we'd been at this for two hours and I was getting frustrated.

Apparently I wasn't the only one. 'Look,' Luna said, letting her hand drop. 'I've been standing here like a shop dummy. I don't mind lessons where I've got something to do, but this is getting ridiculous.'

'If you've got any better ideas, feel free.'

'How about I try?' Luna said. 'I mean, if you just want a link, it shouldn't matter who initiates it, right?'

'I don't think that's the—'

'Actually,' Arachne said unexpectedly, 'that could be worth a try. Go ahead, Luna.'

I started to object, then waited in a bad temper. Luna took a breath, closed her eyes, then clasped her fingers around the lattice and concentrated.

For a moment nothing happened. 'Anything?' I asked.

'Give me a minute,' Luna said.

I waited. 'Now?'

'Just wait! You took way longer than . . .' Luna trailed off, staring down at the crystal.

'Luna?'

Luna didn't answer. She was looking down at the focus with an odd expression, as though she were looking through it to see something far away. And as I looked at her I noticed something else. In my magesight, I usually see Luna's curse as a cloud of silver mist swirling around her. It was doing that now, but some of it was seeping into the dreamstone, soaking into the crystal without trace.

'Luna?' I asked, then my eyes went wide. Arachne's cave is one of the few places I feel comfortable enough to relax my precognition, and I hadn't been looking ahead until it was too late. 'Arachne!'

Arachne is much faster than she looks. As Luna collapsed, Arachne's legs blurred in motion, and she caught Luna an instant before her head could hit the stone. The dreamstone fell to the floor with a clink.

'Is she all right?' I asked anxiously. Luna looked perfectly healthy, but she was unconscious, breathing steadily in and out. The silver mist of her curse tried to soak into Arachne's forelegs and was turned aside, blown away like smoke in a wind.

'No spells harming her,' Arachne said after a moment. 'At least, none that I can see.'

'What happened?' I asked. I itched to get closer to Luna, put a hand to her forehead, but I don't have Arachne's abilities. The curse had been repelled from Arachne's body; it wouldn't be repelled from mine.

'I believe she's sleeping,' Arachne said. 'Check when she'll wake.'

I looked ahead into the futures. I saw future after future of Luna lying silent and still and my heart jumped, then I looked further and felt a surge of relief. 'She's going to wake up. Four minutes, maybe five.'

Arachne looked down at Luna. 'Hmm.'

'Did you expect this?' I demanded.

'No, but as far as I can tell she's perfectly healthy. Wait.'

I waited, pacing up and down. At last Luna stirred and looked up at me, her eyes unfocused and clouded. 'Alex?'

'Are you okay?'

'I think so.' Luna blinked, sitting up and running a hand through her hair. 'Man. That was weird.'

'Okay,' I said. I walked to pick up the dreamstone, then

set it firmly down on a table. 'I think we've had enough experiments for one day.'

'I agree,' Arachne said. 'Luna, rest. When you're ready, tell us what you saw.'

'That was *really* strange,' Luna said fifteen minutes later.

'You just dropped,' I said. 'It was like you went to sleep standing up.'

'Wasn't how it felt. I was in Elsewhere, I think. I was in . . .'

'In?'

'My great-aunt's village,' Luna said quietly.

'Where's that?'

Luna glanced around. Arachne was off a little way away, giving us space. 'You haven't been there,' Luna said. 'At least not . . . you remember when we got caught by Belthas, and you went looking for me? You remember the place we saw, right at the end?'

'A village in the mountains,' I said. It had been a memorable experience, though I hadn't spent much time looking at the scenery. 'Not in Britain, I think. It looked deserted.'

Luna looked at me in surprise. 'You never said anything.'

I shrugged. 'Figured you'd tell me when you were ready.'

'Huh. Well, it's in Sicily, up in the hills.'

'When did you go?'

'A long time ago.' Luna's voice was normal, but her eyes were distant. 'After the accident. My dad had told me something about his family, the ones who never went to the mainland. I thought if I could find them, they could tell me what I was.' Luna was silent for a second. 'She was my great-aunt, I think. I only saw her that one time. A little old woman, sitting in an armchair in the corner. And then I left . . .'

Luna trailed off and I didn't ask her what had happened next. I knew that she was remembering the bad time in her life, her teenage years when her curse had reached its full power. Luna hadn't had any way of understanding what was happening to her – all she knew was that everyone who got close to her was hurt, often badly, and she had no idea why. The 'accident' had been when her parents had gone to fetch a psychologist, and their car had been hit by a truck. They'd survived, but that had been the last time Luna had ever seen her parents. She'd run out of the house and never come back.

'So you saw it again?' I asked. 'That was where it took you?'

'What?' Luna started, then shook herself as though she'd been asleep. 'Yes. I think.'

'What did you see?'

Luna looked up at me, and there was still that distant look in her eyes. 'The same thing we saw the last time we went there in Elsewhere.'

'Oh.'

'Not my parents this time. Just . . . that.'

I knew what she was talking about. I'd only had one look at that creature, and it had been enough. 'What happened?'

Luna shrugged. 'We talked. Not in words. More like . . . you know when you have a dream, and you dream that someone's talking to you? And you know what they're saying, even though you don't actually hear?'

I leant back, frowning.

Luna sat waiting for a while. 'So was I in Elsewhere?' she said at last.

'Makes as much sense as anything else,' I said. 'I wonder . . .'

'Wonder what?'

'The first time I picked up that crystal, I saw something,' I said slowly. 'I thought it was something to do with the deep shadow realm, but maybe it was the dreamstone doing . . .'

'Doing what?' Luna asked. I shrugged and she tilted her head, thinking. 'Do you think it was some sort of test?'

'For what?'

Luna shrugged. 'Beats me.'

I looked across at the dreamstone, where it lay on the table. I wasn't sure if Luna's guess was right or wrong, but if it really had been a test, I had the unpleasant feeling that I'd failed. 'I don't know,' I said. 'We'll try again tomorrow.'

Luna was quiet for a few days, then spoke up about a week later. We were in the Hollow, midway through setting up a perimeter security system, and the two of us were alone – Anne was off at her clinic and Variam was training for his journeyman test. 'Alex?' Luna asked. 'How did you pick your mage name?'

I looked at her in surprise. We were sitting under a tree, soaking up the warm air. A stack of rods were piled untidily on the grass – the idea was to plant them around the border of the island to detect any space magic effects. In theory, gate wards are supposed to stop that sort of thing, but it's always good to have a backup. 'That's what you were thinking about?' I said. 'I thought it was to do with your curse.'

'That's not really something I worry about any more.'

'Huh,' I said. 'Well, I didn't pick it so much as I was told it.'

'Told it? By . . . ?'

I shook my head. 'Not by Richard. He had a hand in it though. He sent us all to Elsewhere and told us that that was where we'd find our names.'

'That was how you found out about Elsewhere?'

I nodded. 'I always wondered how Richard knew it would work, because in all the times that I've been back there, the same thing's never happened since. Not exactly, anyway. Maybe he did something. Or maybe it was just as simple as telling us, and our minds did the rest.'

'For all of you?'

'Well, Tobruk was bragging afterwards that now he had his name,' I said. 'So I'm guessing it worked for him. He was going to announce it once he became Richard's Chosen. Or he would have.' I looked at Luna. 'Thinking about your own?'

'I've been back to the apprentice programme a few times,' Luna said. 'For duelling, or picking stuff up, or things like that. And I noticed that . . . I don't know. I'm supposed to be a mage, but it doesn't *feel* like I'm a mage. They don't really treat me like one.'

'And you think the name's got something to do with it?'

'Does it?'

'Yes,' I said. 'You know that Light and Dark mages are more similar than they like to admit. The naming ceremony means a lot to them. They're not just picking how they'll be addressed; they're leaving their old lives behind. The way they see it, humans are in the normal world, mages are in the magical world, apprentices are somewhere in between. Becoming a journeyman and taking a new name is the sign that they're choosing the magical world.'

'I'm not sure that's what I want.'

'I know,' I said. 'Thing is, so do they.'

'Can I be a mage *without* giving up on the normal world?'

'You're asking the wrong question,' I said. 'You *are* a mage. You're the one who decides what that means.'

Luna was silent for a couple of minutes. 'Why did you run the shop?' she asked eventually.

'This is your day for out-of-left-field questions, isn't it?'

'I know how you got the Arcana Emporium,' Luna said. 'You told me the story. But you never told me why you kept at it. I mean, you ran it for how long, six years?'

'Seven.'

'So why didn't you sell up and go do something else?' Luna said. 'I mean, you could have made more money somewhere else.'

'Pretty much anywhere else.'

'So why?'

I've been asked that question a lot over the years, and usually I throw off some pat reply. This time I told the truth. 'Because of the one in a thousand.'

'The what?'

'You did enough shifts at the shop,' I said. 'Out of every thousand people who walked through that door, about nine hundred are tourists or cranks. Another ninety are hobbyists or small-timers. That leaves ten. About nine out of those ten are there for business. They want information, or they're buying, or selling, or they're looking for something that's not on the shelves. Sometimes it's trouble, but usually it's not. You add all those together, that's nine hundred and ninety-nine. The thousandth person . . . that's the one who needs help. I don't mean they *want* help, like all those idiots who come in asking for love potions or a way to win the lottery; I mean they *need* help. A new mage who's just started to wake up to their power, and who doesn't understand what's happening to them. An adept who's being hunted by a Dark mage. Someone who's in danger from an item or a creature or a spell, who doesn't have anywhere else to go.'

'Like me,' Luna said.

'Like you,' I said. 'The other nine hundred and ninety-nine? They don't really need me. The tourists and the hobbyists can all buy their stuff from some other shop. The mages and the adepts have other places they can go. But what about the ones who *don't* have anywhere else to go?'

'The one in a thousand,' Luna said. 'Wait. Was that why you put me in charge of the emails?'

I laughed. A while back I'd given Luna the job of running the Arcana Emporium's email account, which mostly had meant writing answers to a seemingly endless stream of questions. She'd complained for months, but somewhat to my surprise, she'd stuck with it.

'It was, wasn't it?' Luna said. 'I thought it was just a way to make me study.'

'Well, that too,' I said. 'But it was the same deal. For nearly every one of those emails, whether you answered them or ignored them didn't make any real difference. But every now and then . . .'

'Yeah,' Luna said. She paused. 'They still keep emailing, you know.'

'Would have thought they'd have stopped by now.'

'Actually, there are more than there used to be,' Luna

said. 'Mostly, they want to know when you're going to reopen the shop.'

I was silent. I'd thought about it from time to time. I could do it. I'd lost my stock in the fire that had gutted the building, but I could build that back up. I could rent or buy a new place, or even rebuild the old one. Then I could fit it out, spread the word that I was back in business . . .

. . . and someone else would probably blow the place up again. And maybe me with it. A shop is too visible, a shopkeeper too vulnerable. I'd been able to get away with it when I was a little fish and beneath everyone's notice, but not now.

Or maybe ever. Somewhere at the back of my mind over the past six months, I'd had the vague idea that once this was all over and things were back to normal, I could start the Arcana Emporium up again. But were things *ever* going to get back to normal? The number of enemies I had was going up, not down, and the number of attempts on my life was doing the same. Even if Morden replaced me as his aide, even if I walked away from the Keepers, there'd still be Richard to deal with, and Levistus, and the Crusaders, and all of the other mages and mercenaries and monsters that I'd pissed off over the years. They'd come hunting me, and if I was standing behind a counter, it'd be that much harder for me to get away. And no matter whether they succeeded or failed, my shop wouldn't be a safe place to visit. Now that I looked back on it, I was lucky the Arcana Emporium had lasted as long as it had. I didn't think I'd be so lucky twice.

It was a depressing thought. For years, my shop had been part of my identity. Now I had to face the fact that

I wasn't going to be able to go back to it for a very long time, if ever. Maybe it wasn't just Luna who needed to figure out who she was going to be.

'I don't think it's going to happen any time soon,' I said at last.

Luna nodded. She looked sad, but not surprised. We sat together, listening to the birds singing in the trees.

There was one last thing which happened that August.

I was still going in to Keeper HQ, and for several days running I saw references in the department bulletins to 'the Barnes inquiry'. It felt as though something was going on, and the next time I managed to catch Coatl alone, I asked him about it.

'Oh, that clusterfuck,' Coatl said. Coatl is a fat, cheerful mind mage from South America who arrived in London on an exchange programme a few years ago. He was one of the few Keepers I was on speaking terms with, though we were still talking alone with the door closed. 'You heard about the raid in Pimlico?'

I shook my head.

'Met were doing a drugs bust. There were adepts, we got called in and it got messy.'

'So why the inquiry?'

'When the whole thing was done, there were a few injured normals and some fire adept called Goldman was dead. Keeper at the scene was Reyes; he claimed the burns were from fires that Goldman started.'

'Isn't Reyes a heat mage?' I said sceptically. I'd met the Keeper a few times, and didn't like him much. Back when I'd still been talking to Caldera, she hadn't liked Reyes either; apparently he had a reputation for excessive force.

'Yep.' Coatl shrugged. 'On the other hand, Goldman was a violent little shit. Only reason he was there was that he was trying to rip off those drug dealers so he could sell the stuff himself.'

'So what really happened?'

'God knows,' Coatl said. 'Probably both were dirty. But people have been making noise, so the Council are holding an inquiry.'

I snorted. 'Which means either they're going to clear Reyes of everything, or they'll find some minor fault and give him a slap on the wrist.'

'Probably.'

I checked things out for myself the next day, but everything I could find matched with what I'd heard from Coatl. I kept hearing rumblings about the case, both in the Keeper news and from my adept contacts, but I had more immediate things to worry about, and as the days went by, it became background noise.

Now that I look back on the whole thing, I wonder if there was anything I could have done. Maybe there was, but it's a lot easier to see warning signs in hindsight. In any case, in the first week of September, something happened that drove everything to do with the Keepers out of my thoughts.

12

I was down in Arachne's lair when I heard the news.

Pretty much the only downside to Arachne's lair as a home base is that it gets terrible reception. The wards screw up magical callers, and radio signals can't make it through the tons of earth and rock. Which means that if you want to get a message to someone there and you want to do it fast, then you have to go there in person.

This particular day was a Friday, and we were planning a birthday party for Anne. She was turning twenty-five on Monday, but we'd decided to have the party at the weekend instead, partly to make it more of a surprise, and partly because that way I wouldn't have to worry about being called away to the War Rooms. Luna and Variam had been supposed to be doing the arrangements, but they were having a fight about something or other. I wasn't sure of the details and didn't really want to get involved: Luna and Vari have a complicated relationship that regularly hits rough patches and I've learned that when that happens, the best thing to do is to give them space. Instead, I'd gone back to Arachne's for yet another try with the dreamstone. It was going about as well as usual (i.e. badly) and so I wasn't really listening when I heard Arachne talking to Variam through her message focus. I did vaguely notice that Variam sounded more urgent than usual, but all of my attention was on the futures of me interacting with the dreamstone, and I kept focusing on that right up until I heard running footsteps from the tunnel and Variam's shout of 'Alex!'

I looked up. 'What?'

Variam skidded to a halt at the tunnel entrance, one hand resting on the wall as though he were poised to turn and run back. 'They've taken Anne.'

'What? Who?'

'Don't know. Come on.'

I stared at Variam for about one second, then dropped the dreamstone onto a table. 'Arachne—'

'Go,' Arachne said. 'I'll clean up here.'

I grabbed my coat and ran after Variam up the tunnel.

Variam filled me in on the way. Luna had been due to meet up with Anne in the evening, and when Anne hadn't shown up, Luna had called and had no answer. At this point, a normal person would have assumed that Anne had forgotten to charge their phone, or left it switched off, or had no signal. Luna had treated it as a potential emergency and gone straight to red alert. It was just as well she had.

'How did they get her?' I asked.

'Looks like by surprise.'

'How?' I demanded. Anne had a flat which we'd set her up with in the spring. 'The wards should have bought her enough time . . .'

'She wasn't at her flat,' Variam said. 'She was at her clinic.'

I swore. 'So they just walked straight in pretending to be patients. Who's "they"?'

'Dunno,' Variam said. 'You got any ideas?'

I tried to think of the most likely suspects. It wasn't easy – Anne's list of enemies is almost as long as mine. 'Crystal?'

'She's been lying low for years.'

'Didn't stop her last time.'

Variam grimaced. 'Maybe someone got a description.'

But we didn't need to look for a description. After Luna had sent Variam to find me, she'd done some thinking and quite sensibly realised that while we might be able to figure out what had happened to Anne, there was someone else who could do it a lot faster. So she called him instead.

Sonder was waiting next to Luna when we found her, a young man with curly black hair and a scholarly look, his clothes a little nicer since the last time we'd met and his stomach a little rounder. It was a measure of how serious things were that neither of us mentioned last Christmas. I'd worked with Sonder back then, and things had happened, and at some point we'd have to talk about it, but right now we had bigger problems. I looked at Sonder, and he looked back at me, and somehow all of that was communicated and agreed upon in less than a second. 'What did you find?' I asked.

'Two mages,' Sonder said. We were out in the street, and there were houses around, enough to make it possible that someone could overhear, but we didn't have the time to worry about that. 'They managed to knock Anne out and take her through a gateway.'

'That sounds way too— Wait.' My mind made the connection with what Sonder had just said. 'Was one of them big and dark-skinned, and the other one white and skinny?'

'It wasn't Sagash's apprentices this time.'

I shook my head. 'Not them. The Crusaders have a black-ops team who've been coming after me. Lightbringer and Zilean.'

Sonder frowned. 'The Crusaders? Why?'

'I don't know . . .' I trailed off. Over the last couple of months, the Council had been fortifying the War Rooms, but the rumours of an impending Dark attack hadn't gone away. And everyone still seemed to believe that it was linked to Richard and Morden.

Anne didn't know anything about Morden's activities. Ever since that first day in January, she hadn't even seen him. But on that day, she'd been seen *with* him. And the Crusaders didn't know that Anne wasn't secretly still in touch with him. All they'd know was that Anne was still officially Morden's appointee . . .

'Oh, shit,' I said.

'What?'

'I've got a bad feeling.' I looked at Sonder. 'Where did they go?'

'They gated, but it was masked,' Sonder said. 'I can try to trace it.'

I nodded. 'I'm going to try and track her directly. Tell me if you find anything that might help.'

Sonder left, hurrying across the road. 'Track her how?' Variam asked.

'Here, this is for Anne's flat,' I said, handing Variam a gate stone as we started running the other way. 'Remember that seeker focus?'

'I thought you lost that at Christmas?' Luna asked as we ran.

'We got a replacement,' I said. Two years ago, Anne had

been attacked by a pair of Dark apprentices; their master was Anne's old enemy, Sagash, but they'd been working for a renegade Light mage called Crystal. We'd won the battle but Crystal had escaped, and she still wanted Anne as an ingredient for a particularly nasty ritual that she'd shown no sign of giving up on, so once we'd made it back to London, we'd set things up so that if she had another try at kidnapping Anne and actually succeeded, the rest of us would be able to do something about it.

It's probably not obvious, but this sort of thing is one of the main reasons that all the members of our little group are still alive. When we get attacked or ambushed, one of the first things we do as soon as we have the chance is figure out some kind of defence against the same thing happening again. We have contingency plans for anything from night attacks on our homes to getting outlawed by the Council in the middle of the workday. They aren't foolproof, but Variam, Luna, Anne and I are all much more difficult targets than we look.

We reached the park and Variam ducked behind a tree. Quickly he created a gate through into Anne's flat, a small one-bedroom in Ealing, and we jumped through into the warm air. Light was streaming through the windows and past the plants on the sill, and it all looked very pretty, but I wasn't here to sightsee. I pulled away a chair in the living room, took off a small ventilation grate that would have looked solid to a casual glance and pulled out a box. 'Now we pray she's kept it up to date.'

'It needs updates?' Variam said, peering down at the thing inside. It looked like a glass rod with a thread of dark red running through the centre.

'More like blood,' I said. The hard part of setting this

up hadn't been figuring out a way to track Anne: it had been figuring out a way to track Anne that would stick. The standard trick of planting a subcutaneous tracer was hopeless; the simplest magical scans pick up that kind of thing. Tracking spells are better, but they're easy to block with wards. But wards aren't foolproof either. If you have a piece of someone's body to set up a sympathetic link, you can put together a tracking spell with enough power to punch through most things. Hair or nail clippings are decent; saliva is better; blood is best of all. But it has to be fresh.

Luna and Variam fell silent as I closed my eyes and concentrated, channelling into the focus. My heart was in my mouth: if this didn't work, it would be very bad. For a moment, as I scanned the futures, I could see nothing but myself standing there; then my heart leapt as I saw movement. An instant later, I could feel it: a mental direction. It was fuzzy, as though the signal was struggling to get through, but it was there.

I snapped back to the present and pulled a map from where it had been folded in the box. 'Got something?' Variam asked.

'Yeah.' I dug around until I found a ruler and a pencil, pulled out the compass on my phone, checked again with the rod, then drew a line on the map. It ran a little south of north-east. 'Okay,' I said. 'Vari, gate us to . . .' I traced the pencil right, and made a wide circle below the line. 'There. Anywhere between Barking and Greenwich.' From there we could get another reference point to triangulate. If we were lucky, that would be enough.

Variam nodded and we gated out.

* * *

We were lucky. The mages who'd taken Anne could have gated her to Scotland or Sweden or Australia or anywhere else in the world where they had a roof and enough time to ward up a safe house. They could even have taken her to a shadow realm, and any of those things would have made it far more difficult for the tracer to work. But they were Light mages, and like so many other Light mages, they didn't want to get too far away from the Council's centre of power. They couldn't take her to the War Rooms or to Keeper HQ and so instead they'd taken her here, to a small, nondescript end-of-terrace house in Walthamstow, with few windows and high walls.

'No,' I said over the phone. Variam, Luna and I were on the other side of a set of railings and a small car park, using a block of flats to shield us from the house. 'It's E17, not N17. House number one.'

'All right,' Sonder said. In the background I could hear the clicking of keys. 'One sec.'

'You think they've got cameras?' Luna asked quietly.

'They're bloody idiots if they don't,' Variam said. Evening was turning to night, and the autumn sky was fading to black.

'Alex?' Sonder said. 'I've got it. It's Council-owned, but the records show it as mothballed. It should be empty.'

'It's not,' I said. The curtains on the windows were thick, and only a faint glow of light showed from behind them, but the tracer focus was pointing straight there.

'It could be squatters . . .'

'And they're having Anne inside for a cup of tea?'

I heard Sonder sigh. 'Okay, it's not squatters. What do you want to do?'

'What do you think I'm going to do?'

'You don't have any authorisation . . .'

'I'm a Keeper, blah blah, emergency situation, necessary use of force,' I said. 'But honestly, I really don't give a fuck. Acting now, rationalising later.'

'All right,' Sonder said. 'But, Alex? None of the Keepers I've talked to seem to have any idea what's going on. Be careful.'

'Yeah, I'm pretty sure I know why. We'll keep you posted.' I hung up.

'Think I see a camera over the porch,' Variam said.

I looked into the futures in which I ran closer, branching them so that my future images searched the outside of the house from all three sides. 'Two cameras,' I said. 'One front, one back.' I looked at Luna. 'Remember that spell Chalice taught you?'

'You point me at them and I'll turn them into junk.'

We moved forward to the corner of the flats and Luna and Variam waited as I concentrated, looking ahead. Sometimes I have to make an effort to get into the mental state to do something dangerous, but not this time. Anne was in there, and I was going to get her. The only question was how.

'Well?' Variam demanded. He was shifting from one foot to the other, clearly itching to go.

'Tricking our way in isn't going to work,' I said. Ringing the doorbell would result in being ignored at best and outright attacked at worst. 'We're going to have to blow the doors.'

'Good,' Variam said. 'What's the count?'

'I'm not seeing many,' I said with a frown. Normally Council mages have servants – guards, security, cannon fodder, whatever you call them – but in all the futures where we blasted the door down, the house was barely occupied. It didn't occur to me at the time that there might be a reason for that. There are some kinds of work for which people don't want witnesses. 'One or two, maybe. But at least one's a mage.'

'What kind?'

'Light and force. I'm guessing it's Lightbringer.' Which meant it was a good bet that we could also expect Zilean.

'So we clear to go?'

I hesitated, feeling the coin of fate spin. I couldn't get a clear read on what would happen after we forced our way inside. There might be traps, hidden deeper where my divination couldn't so easily see, or the enemy could be there in greater numbers. If I waited, and kept path-walking, I could narrow the odds. But that would take time, and every extra minute increased the chances that they'd get reinforcements or move Anne . . . or worse. I remembered what had happened to Morden's last two aides, and what Lightbringer and Zilean had been planning to do to me, and all of a sudden waiting wasn't an option. 'I'll take the front,' I said. 'You two take the back. Luna fries the cameras, then you go in first. I'll follow a second later, try to split their focus. Fight your way upstairs the first chance you get. Remember, our best guess is that Anne's on the first floor, so don't get caught up. We want to punch through to where she is. All clear?'

Luna and Variam nodded.

'Do it,' I said to Luna.

Luna stood up, reaching out a hand towards the front of the house, and to my eyes a tendril of silver mist seemed to extend from her fingers, crossing the street to soak into the small dark shape of the camera. When Luna's curse touches something, then whatever can go wrong, will, which in the case of computers means bugs, crashes and hardware failure. With the amount of power Luna had just put into that camera, the only thing it would ever be useful for again was scrap metal.

I broke cover, running for the front door, while Variam and Luna split off towards the garden. I was dimly aware of Luna working the spell a second time, but I didn't stop to analyse. At any second the mages inside might notice something, and our best defence was speed. I dropped my bag beside the front door, pulled out one of a handful of things that looked to a casual glance like bundles of thick cord wrapped in electrical tape, ripped off the backing, stuck it to the door around the keyhole, unwrapped the wire leading to the activator, let the wire unspool as I backed off around the corner, pulled out my 1911 from the bag, took the gun in my right hand and the activator in my left and spoke into the communicator in my ear. 'Vari. I'm ready at the front.'

There was a moment's pause, then Variam's voice spoke into my ear. 'Ready at the back.'

'Ready at the back,' Luna said.

I took a breath, let it out. 'Go.'

Fire magic flared behind the house. The walls around flashed red and I felt the vibration as the spell went off with an echoing *boom*. I counted one heartbeat, two, four, then there was the scuffle of footsteps and I heard movement from inside and I covered one ear with my gun, pushed the other down into my shoulder, closed my eyes and pressed the button.

There was a roaring *whoom* which seemed to go all the way through my body. Something bounced off my shoulder;

the door was still attached to the hinges but there was a ragged hole where the middle had been and I clambered through. There was smoke everywhere and my ears were ringing, but my divination told me where the stairs were and I ran for them, taking them two at a time. My foot had just hit the first-floor landing when a door opened and Zilean came out.

I'd seen him coming and I was already bringing my gun up, but everything seemed to be going very slowly and I had what felt like all the time in the world to study the Crusader mage. I saw his hair, brown and combed back but with a few strands out of place – that stuck in my mind for some reason – and the downward lines to either side of his mouth, and I saw his eyes widen as he recognised me, and then something made me glance down and I saw that he was holding a surgical knife in one hand, and the blade was red, and then everything else I might have noticed vanished in a rush of fury and I fired.

Zilean was quick, but not quite quick enough. He twisted and a wall of crackling energy came up between us, but the shot had been on target and I heard a gasp. I steadied on the landing and kept firing. I couldn't see through the barrier and so I spaced the shots out to cover the hallway, but as I did I felt the surge of another spell and there was a blinding flash, then the wall was gone and the hallway was empty.

I could hear the *whoompf* of fire magic down below, and racing footsteps from above. Bright spots were dancing before my eyes, but there was red blood on the plaster and I knew at least one of my shots had found its mark. I sprinted upwards.

I didn't think about going down to help Variam and

Luna, and I didn't give any thought for a possible ambush. I could say that I was counting on my precognition to keep me safe, and maybe it would have; I could say that I thought that Variam and Luna could handle themselves, and maybe that was true too. But the truth is, none of those things made it into my mind at all. The one glimpse I'd had of that knife had filled me with bloodlust and I wanted Zilean dead. Zilean could have turned on me and maybe it would have gone badly if he had, but my instincts told me that Zilean was afraid. I chased him up to the attic; the door was locked, but I ran at it without breaking stride and kicked with all of the strength that my training with Anne had given me, and the wood splintered and broke.

Zilean was at the far end of the room. He'd managed to get the window open and stood clutching his shoulder with his other hand and he looked back at me in panic and I sighted on him but as I fired he cast his spell and his body seemed to turn white and distort, and with a flash he turned into a bolt of lightning that zipped through the window and out into the night and my shot kicked splinters from the window frame.

I swore and darted to the window, but as I reached it I saw the flash as Zilean cast his lightning jump again, and as my vision returned I saw nothing but rooftops. Another flash reflected from the next street over, and I knew that the Crusader was gone.

I realised that I couldn't sense any more spells below. 'Vari, come in,' I said, turning and heading back down the stairs. 'Report.'

'He's gone!' Variam shouted back at me.

'Who?'

'The other mage, Lightbringer, whatever his name is. There's a gate portal – he's gone through!'

I ran down the stairs. 'It's still open?'

'Yeah, but it's masked. You want us to chase?'

I hesitated, but for only an instant. 'No. Burn it.'

I saw the red flash from all the way up the stairwell, and felt a surge of gate magic as the spell in the portal collapsed. 'Clear,' Variam said.

'Ground floor is clear,' Luna said. 'We're moving up.'

It was only much later that I got the full story from Luna and Variam, about how they'd run into Lightbringer down in the kitchen. There had been a brief, furious battle, Variam's orange fire and the trailing mist of Luna's curse meeting Lightbringer's flashing blades, and now that I think back on it, I cringe at the risk we took. Zilean and Lightbringer were both individually stronger than us, and they had God only knows how many reinforcements just a phone call away, but they'd been caught by surprise and in the end that had been enough. I think if they'd realised that there were only three of us, they would have stood and fought, but the speed and fury of the attack had caught them off guard and they never had the chance to learn just how few of us there were.

But all that was still in the future; for now, the house was ours and we went through the rooms one by one looking for Anne. It took only seconds to figure out where we needed to go. The room that Zilean had come out of had a metal door, with a complicated lock which had sealed when the door had swung shut behind him. Variam melted it to slag. Rivulets of molten metal trickled down, burning black streaks into the door-frame and floor, and Variam shoved the door open with the palm of his hand.

I don't have a very visual memory, at least not for most things. It's not that my memory's bad; it just works best on connections and patterns. If I spend an hour with a group of people, then I'll remember what they talked about, who was in charge and who interacted with whom, but ask me what one of them was wearing or what colour their hair was and I'll come up blank. My mind just doesn't work that way; I can remember things that happened, but not exactly what they looked like.

But every now and again you see a sight which burns into your memory and never goes away.

The inside of the room was thickly lined with brown padding. A small, wheeled trolley was pushed up against the wall, and on it were two trays holding what looked like surgical instruments: forceps and hooks and scalpels. The centre of the room was dominated by a long, wide table, and on it was something that was hard to identify. For a second, my eyes told me that I was looking at some kind of crude doll, coloured red with scraps hanging off, then I noticed that it was the size and shape of a person, then the doll took a breath and with a sense of dawning nightmare I realised that it *was* a person; my eyes just hadn't made the connection because I'd never seen someone without their skin before.

My stomach clenched and I wanted to vomit. It would have been horrible enough if it were a stranger: that it was Anne made it a thousand times worse. Luna stared, her face going pale, then she clapped a hand over her mouth and stumbled back out onto the landing. Variam didn't quite join her, but I could see the muscles in his jaw working. I felt bile rising up in my throat and choked it back. One by one I was noticing all the things that I'd missed, and each one made me desperately wish that I could stop thinking about what they meant. Small metal scaffolds were set up on the table, with thin wires running down to where they were attached to flaps of skin. Around the chest someone had started to cut through the muscle, revealing bone, and the torn flesh pulsed rhythmically. A soldering iron was resting on the table, a tiny wisp of smoke rising up from its tip.

'What . . .' Variam paused, swallowed. 'What do we do?'

I tried to think of something to say and failed. I felt paralysed.

Luna came back in, wiping her mouth. 'Oh God,' she said, staring at Anne. 'How do we help her?'

I tried to figure out how to go about curing Anne or stabilising her, and just the thought of it overwhelmed me. I was out of my depth, but both Luna and Variam were looking at me, and I grasped at straws. 'We have to get her out of here.'

'Maybe a hospital . . .' Variam started to say, then trailed off. The Crusaders had contacts with the Keepers, the Keepers had contacts with the emergency services, and if we brought Anne into an emergency room, then they'd know within an hour.

But it made me realise what we had to do. 'Not a hospital,' I said. 'Somewhere safe.'

'The Hollow,' Luna said instantly.

'If we carry . . .' I started to say, then stopped as I realised what that would mean. First, we'd have to untangle Anne from the net of wires and hooks sunk into her skin . . . and then what? I imagined picking her up and had a horrific vision of her screaming and thrashing and crashing to the floor.

'Carry the table,' Variam said. 'I'll burn the legs off if we have to. Luna opens a gate, we get it through.'

I turned to Luna. 'The gate wards on the house must have a keystone. Hurry.'

I don't remember much of the rest of that visit. I remember that Luna managed to disable the wards, and I think Variam did manage to sort out the table, but I don't recall him doing it. The sight of Anne's mutilated body made everything else hazy. I remember talking to her, telling her that we were here, that she was going to be okay, but she didn't speak and I couldn't tell if she heard.

But it worked. Luna got a gate open to the Hollow and managed to hold it open long enough for Variam to lift the tabletop and carry it through. I remember being terrified that we'd drop it, but we didn't, and Luna followed us through to leave us alone in the Hollow, the three of us standing over Anne's body while the night sky of the shadow realm glowed above.

Variam and I stayed to watch over Anne and we cut away the wires and hooks, one by one. It took a long time, and Anne didn't flinch or wince, but we did. Meanwhile, Luna went to find Arachne, and Arachne came. She doesn't like to leave her lair, but she has her ways out in case of emergency, and this was an emergency. Arachne looked over Anne and worked what magic she could, but she warned us that Anne had been so badly maimed that any attempt to cure her would likely make things worse. We'd taken out the foreign objects and now Anne's body was working to heal itself, and the best thing we could do for her was guard her and make sure she was undisturbed. So we did.

It was a long night.

* * *

It was some time in the early hours of the morning. We had tents set up, but they were small three- and four-person affairs, and none of us had wanted to try moving Anne inside one or setting it up around her. In the end, we'd just set up windbreaks, and taken turns keeping watch. It was my shift and I was lying half-awake, dozing. Above, the stars were shining, brilliant and bright. The Hollow's sunset and sunrise matches its mirror in England, but for some reason, instead of the stars of Earth, the view you see when you look up is some impossible sky out of a fairy tale, clusters of blue and purple and red glowing from between multicoloured nebulae. I could just hear the sound of Anne's breathing, and listening to it kept me on edge. I think at some level I was afraid that if I didn't keep listening to it, then it might stop.

When I heard my name, I thought at first it was just another dream. I'd been drifting in and out of them, imagining that Anne would wake up and talk to me, and I kept waiting for it to fade, then I realised that I'd opened my eyes and I was looking up at the stars and I heard Anne's voice again.

I sat bolt upright. 'I'm here. Can you hear me?'

I heard Anne take a laboured breath. 'Yes.'

I scrambled to Anne's side. In the starlight, she was only a shape in the darkness, but my divination told me she was there and moving. 'Don't move. You were hurt, badly. We've taken you to the Hollow and you're safe, but you have to stay where you are. Okay?'

'I know.'

'What do you need?'

Another breath. 'Water.'

I helped Anne drink. She couldn't hold the bottle, but

we'd brought straws. 'What else?' I said when she was done.

'Time.'

I hesitated. It was a stupid question, but I needed to ask. 'Are you okay?'

Anne was silent for a second. 'No.'

I didn't know what to say.

'I'm not going to die,' Anne said. Her voice was a little stronger, but it still sounded as though it was an effort for her to talk. 'But . . . no. I'm not.'

'Which one of them was it?' I said quietly.

'The white one,' Anne said. 'Zilean.' She paused, and when she spoke again her voice was empty. 'They wanted to know about Morden's plans. I kept telling them I didn't know. They didn't listen . . .'

I felt a wash of emotions go through me – sorrow and pain and guilt, but mostly rage. I wanted to see someone dead for this. My list of enemies was already too long, but Zilean had just made it to the top. I took long, steady breaths until I could speak calmly again. 'Is there anything I can do?'

'Stay and talk,' Anne said. She was sounding drowsy now. 'Have to sleep. But . . . be nice to hear your voice. Just for a little while . . .'

'Talk to you about what?'

'Anything,' Anne said sleepily.

'Anything? Well . . . okay. I never did tell you about how I met Luna, did I?' I settled back slightly on the mat. 'It would have been about five years ago. I was in my shop, same as I usually was, and I remember hearing the bell go as someone walked in. I didn't really notice her until she came up to the counter . . .'

The stars glowed down from above.

* * *

It was two days before Anne was well enough to get up and walk around, and two more before she was strong enough to work a gate stone to leave the Hollow. Not long by medical standards, but it was the longest I'd ever seen Anne out of action, and I kept a close eye on her. Physically she was back to perfect health in less than a week, but she was quieter, more withdrawn. I was worried about her, but when I tried probing, Anne made it clear that she didn't want to talk.

I tried to get Lightbringer and Zilean indicted for breaking the Concord. Anne was officially a mage now, after all, and that meant she had the same rights as any other Light mage . . . in theory. An investigation was started, but I wasn't surprised when it began to drag. What *really* made me flip my lid was the news Rain gave me afterwards.

'They're doing *what?*' I nearly shouted.

'Don't jump to conclusions,' Rain said. I'd come into Keeper HQ, and we were in my office. A little paper had accumulated on the desk since the spring, but not much. 'It's still at preliminaries.'

'They're investigating Anne for running that *clinic?*'

'According to the records, it wasn't authorised . . .'

'Let me see if I've got this straight,' I said. 'Lightbringer and Zilean just literally *flayed Anne alive* and as far as I can tell, the investigation team's response has been to have one interview and then let the two of them go. But they're willing to prosecute Anne for *fucking healing people for free?*'

'They're not connected, Verus.' Rain looked weary, but I was too angry to care. 'One is the Order of the Star; the other is the regulatory staff at—'

'Jesus Christ.' I stalked to the window and stared down

over the street. Right at that moment, if Morden had given me the opportunity to burn the whole Council, I'd have said yes. Why was I working for these people?

'I might have a different job for you,' Rain said.

I didn't answer.

'The Council are still worried about the possibility of an attack on the War Rooms,' Rain said. 'They've set up some new security systems, but they're in the preliminary phase. A diviner would be useful.'

I didn't turn around.

'Verus?'

'The last time I checked, the Council thought that the one who was supposed to be behind this attack on the War Rooms was Morden,' I said. 'So why would they want me of all people messing with their security systems?'

'Not everyone thinks that way.'

'This isn't their idea, is it? It's yours.'

'I don't think you're a traitor,' Rain said. 'No, the Council didn't ask for you, not specifically. But they assigned me the job, and you're the person I'd pick for it. You've been wanting to get on the duty roster – well, this is a way to do it.'

I still didn't answer. 'Well?' Rain asked.

'Morden isn't going to attack the War Rooms,' I said.

'How do you know?'

'It's not because he tells me his plans,' I said. 'I just know he won't. You know why?'

Rain shook his head.

'Because he doesn't need to,' I said. 'If Morden really does want to bring the Council down, then attacking them directly would be the worst thing he could do. It'd unify them, give them an external threat. You know the real reason the Council are so weak nowadays? It's shit like this. Lightbringer and Zilean just kidnapped Anne in broad daylight and tortured her for information, and everyone *knows* they tortured her for information, and you know what's going to happen to them? Nothing. We'll give evidence, and there'll be interviews and reports. And then something will go wrong. The paperwork will get held up, or your superior won't authorise it, and a year from now Lightbringer and Zilean will still be around. Maybe their freedom to act will be curtailed a bit, but that's all. What message do you think that sends? All the other mages who aren't in tight with the Council look at this, and they think: that could be me; that could happen to me. Every time that happens, it chips a little bit away at the Council's base of support. Out of all the mages in Britain – Light, Dark and independent – how many are really loyal to the Council any more? One in ten? The only reason the Council works at all is because of mages like you. And there are fewer of you than there used to be.' I shook my head. 'Morden doesn't need to destroy the Council. He just needs to wait for it to destroy itself.'

Rain was silent for a moment. 'Do you want the job?'

'No,' I told him, and walked out.

13

'So what have you got for me?' I asked.

I was sitting in a small café on Upper Street, Islington. The table was round, a waiter had just brought over two cups of tea and the air was filled with the buzz of conversation. Outside, buses and cars crept up and down the road.

The woman sitting opposite me stirring her masala chai was Indian, with small, neat features and wearing a coat and skirt which blended in with the people around us. Her name was Chalice, and she was a Dark chance mage and one of Luna's teachers. Since Luna's graduation, Chalice had stopped giving her regular lessons, although I knew Luna still went back to her from time to time for help with something difficult. But that wasn't why I was meeting her today.

'Straight to business?' Chalice said with a smile. She tapped her spoon on the side of her cup, then laid it in the saucer. 'I'd thought you might want to catch up.'

'I've been busy.'

'So I've heard.'

My relationship with Chalice was originally a business one, favour for favour. She'd provide Luna with lessons, and I'd provide her with information. This time, though, I was the one looking for information. Chalice is still a Dark mage and I still wouldn't exactly call us friends, but she'd dealt fairly with me so far and there were very good reasons that I didn't want to approach someone on the Light side of the fence for this one.

'So, with regards to the two individuals in question, I've managed to pick up some bits and pieces,' Chalice said. 'It turns out they have something of a reputation among Dark mages over here. However, most of what's available is personal information and history.'

'I'll take what I can get.'

Chalice withdrew a small red folder from her bag and laid it on the table. Some mages, like Talisid, are paranoid to the extreme about being seen with me in public, but that's not Chalice's way. Every time we've met, it's been openly. 'Lightbringer and Zilean,' Chalice murmured. 'Light mages do like their poetic names, don't they?' She glanced at me. 'I understand they're currently under investigation for an attack on another mage.'

I met Chalice's gaze, my expression neutral. 'Like you said, we all have our reasons.'

'True.' Chalice slid the folder across the table. 'There you go. I suspect it won't be what you're looking for.'

I opened the folder. It contained four typed sheets of paper, and I scanned them one at a time. 'And what would I be looking for?'

'Most of the information there is historical,' Chalice said. 'Their masters, events they've been involved in, details on their capabilities and allies. I suspect you were looking for something more geographical.'

I turned a page. 'By geographical, you mean where they can be found.'

'Which is somewhat more difficult,' Chalice said. 'Both Lightbringer and Zilean own London town houses, but they don't live in them for most of the year. I rather suspect they don't live in them at all. Their activities have not made them terribly popular in the Dark community, and they haven't lived this long by presenting easy targets. They most likely sleep in some fortified base. A little inconvenient if you're planning a . . . shall we say, surprise visit?'

'I have no idea what you mean.'

'Of course,' Chalice said. 'In any case, your suspicion that they report directly to Jarnaff may be correct. Whenever they're deployed, it seems to be reactively.'

'Reactively?'

'If you really want to find them, your best bet seems to be to hang around something or someone that the Crusaders care about. They'll show up soon enough.'

I looked up to see that Chalice was studying me. 'Might I make a suggestion?' Chalice said.

'Go ahead.'

'Lightbringer and Zilean report to Jarnaff,' Chalice said. 'Jarnaff is aide to Councilman Sal Sarque. One of the two Guardians on the Council, and according to most opinions, the de facto head of the Crusaders. A very short chain.'

'Your point?'

'These are heavy hitters,' Chalice said. 'I'd advise caution.'

They didn't do so well against us, I wanted to say, but I knew better. It was probably years since the Crusaders had had a safe house attacked, and they'd grown complacent. Next time wouldn't be so easy. 'I'll bear it in mind. Anything else?'

'As a matter of fact, yes,' Chalice said. 'What can you tell me about Richard Drakh's magic type?'

'Why are you asking about *that* of all things?'

'Our deal still applies, yes?'

'I'm not arguing. It's just . . . why do you want to know?'

'As you said, we all have our reasons.'

I sat back, frowning. The question Chalice was asking was one that we'd spent plenty of time batting around ourselves, so it wasn't as though I didn't have an answer, but it wasn't something I'd expected from her. Still, a deal was a deal. 'Conventional wisdom is that he's from the mental branch of the living family,' I said. 'Either an enchanter or a mind mage.'

'So I've heard,' Chalice said. 'But no one seems to give substance to the rumours.'

'That's because Richard keeps it that way,' I said. 'He's a grey.'

Chalice looked blank.

'Someone who keeps their magic type hidden,' I explained. 'He won't cast spells where anyone can see: he'll use items as substitutes; he'll rely on creatures and other mages . . .'

Chalice nodded. 'So what's your personal opinion?'

'Okay, so I can't deny that the mind or charm thing is a possibility. He's very good at manipulating people, and he always seems to know exactly what their motivations are. The other possibility I've wondered about is that he might be a diviner.'

'Why?'

'It's the only magic type that can rival enchantment for undetectability,' I said. 'So if you *have* managed to keep your magic type secret for that long, that's evidence for it. Besides . . . back when I was with him, he had three other apprentices. Know their types?'

Chalice shook her head.

'All elementalists,' I said. 'Two fire, one water. By itself, that doesn't mean much. Fire mages are everywhere and water mages are pretty common too. But three elementalists and one diviner?' I shrugged. 'It's a strange mix. If Richard were a diviner, that would be one way to explain it.'

'Are there any arguments against?'

'Yes,' I said. 'I've never actually seen Richard fight, but I don't think there's any real doubt that he's killed a lot of mages in single combat. Right before he disappeared, the Council sent a battle mage after him leading an entire strike team and Richard killed them all. And that does *not* fit with him being a diviner.'

'Given your reputation, that seems rather odd for you to say.'

'Because I'm a diviner too?' I snorted. 'Half the fights I've survived have been by the skin of my teeth and the other half have been because I've had help. Besides, the attitude's different. It's hard to explain, but the times I've met Richard since he came back, he doesn't *act* like a diviner. All the diviners I've met, they're on guard, always watching. Richard doesn't seem like he's on guard. He seems relaxed. Like he knows nothing around could possibly be a threat.'

'Could it be a bluff?' Chalice said. 'He won his victories by trickery, and now he's trading off his reputation?'

I shrugged. 'Maybe, but I'm not picking a fight with him to check.'

Chalice nodded. 'One last thing. I assume you know that Morden's Chosen, Onyx, has something of a grudge against you?'

'I'd noticed,' I said dryly. 'I think Morden's keeping him off my back for now.'

'Well, a little bird told me that Onyx is rather resentful of your new position as Morden's aide,' Chalice said. 'To the point where he was taking active steps to do something about it. He was warned off, but not by Morden. By Drakh.'

I frowned. 'Are you sure?'

Chalice shrugged. 'It's only second-hand.' She lifted her cup and drank the last of her tea. 'But it sounds to me as though your old master still has plans for you. Be wary.'

I didn't need to be reminded that Richard wasn't done with me. Archon was proof of that.

'Were there any problems?' Archon asked. It was the evening of the same day, and Archon was standing where I'd first met him, in the front garden of my house in Wales. I didn't use the house as a base any more, but it still worked as a meeting point and I sure as hell wasn't letting Archon see where I slept.

'Nothing serious,' I said. 'Though it would have been helpful to know that the guy leaving your message was wanted by the authorities.'

My jobs for Archon had continued to prove frustratingly obscure. Over the summer, he'd had me digging up rumours of some Indian relic, and in September, he'd had me out in South America. Both had proven to be dead ends, but if it had bothered Archon, he hadn't shown any signs of it. Instead, just yesterday, he'd sent me to China to retrieve a message drop in Xinjiang.

It hadn't been a dead end this time. The message had been exactly where Archon had told me it would be. Of course, Archon hadn't mentioned the team of Chinese mages and adepts staking the place out. I'd managed to retrieve the thing without a fight, but it had been close.

Archon held out a gloved hand and I handed over the message cylinder. It was a small inlaid tube, pale yellow in colour. 'Did you open it?' Archon asked.

I looked back at Archon, my gaze steady. 'No.'

Archon looked back at me for just a second — at least I assumed he was looking back at me; with that full-face helmet, it wasn't as though I could really tell — then nodded. 'I'll be in touch.' He turned and disappeared into the darkness.

I waited until I was sure that Archon was gone, then went back into the house. The item I'd handed over was a one-shot message cylinder, just big enough to contain a single rolled-up sheet of paper. The items were developed by the magical government of China some time back, and while they're outdated nowadays, they're quite secure. They're designed to be opened only by a single intended recipient, and if anyone else tries to break or interfere with one in any way, a small charge goes off which incinerates the contents. Bypassing the security to read the contents is very difficult.

Of course, *difficult* doesn't mean *impossible*.

I took out my phone and studied the picture on the screen. Archon's timetable had been tight, and by the time I'd managed to figure out how to get the cylinder open, I'd only barely had time to snap a picture before I'd had to reseal the item and gate to Wales to make the handover. The cylinder had contained only a slip of paper, with a few lines of Chinese characters. I can't read Chinese, but I know someone who can.

'Interesting,' Arachne said, studying the image.

'Can you read it?'

'Oh, that's simple enough,' Arachne said. 'The gist of the message is that the writer is reporting a lack of success. He says that the matter has been studied, and that similar attempts have been made, but that all substitutes for the traditional approach are believed to have failed due to a lack of a specific quality.'

'What quality?'

'*That* is the interesting part,' Arachne said. We were in her lair and she was leaning over the sofa, the phone held delicately in her legs right below her two rows of eyes. I was sitting in her shadow, close enough to brush her lower legs. It probably would have looked really bizarre to someone walking in. 'The word he uses is "tóngqíng", which literally means "alike feeling", but given the context, I think the most accurate translation would be empathy.'

I frowned. 'Substitutes for the traditional approach are believed to have failed due to a lack of empathy?'

'Yes.'

'Well, I have absolutely no idea what they're talking about.'

'Really?' Arachne said. There was a thoughtful sound to her voice. 'I think it's quite suggestive.'

'Then maybe you can explain it to me.'

'What do you think Richard wants with you, Alex?'

The question caught me off guard. 'I still don't know,' I admitted. 'I mean, we asked him back in January. He gave us some vague bullshit about the Council undervaluing us.'

'Not untrue, but not the whole truth, either,' Arachne said. 'Perhaps a better question would be why Richard would take the risk of trusting you. You've made no secret of the fact that you're working for him only under duress.

Which, from his point of view, rather limits your usefulness. No matter how competent you may be, it would probably be possible for Richard to find an equally competent person who is *not* profoundly opposed to everything he stands for. Which brings us back to the first question: why you?'

'So what's your answer?'

'I can think of two,' Arachne said. 'It could be personal. As you've said, Richard is a persuasive and manipulative man. He's used to people doing what he wants, and for the most part, they do. You, however, rejected and fled from him. It's very possible that he resents that. With all of his power and charisma, Richard still failed to keep your loyalty. Perhaps he won't be truly satisfied until you return to him of your own free will.'

I had to stop and think about that one. 'I . . . guess?' I said slowly. I was so used to seeing Richard as my old master that it was difficult for me to think of him as a human being. 'It seems kind of petty.'

'The powerful and the great can be as petty as anyone else,' Arachne said. 'I only suggest it as something to keep in mind.'

'All right. What's the second answer?'

'The second answer is simpler,' Arachne said. 'Richard has made such an effort to recruit you because you have something he *can't* easily obtain somewhere else.'

'That seems to fit better with what I know of him,' I said, 'but I don't get what that something is. Okay, Anne and I are good at what we do, but he could probably find a Dark diviner or life mage who could do the same thing. Actually, with Vihaela, he kind of already did.'

'A Dark mage, yes,' Arachne said. 'But think of all the

people you know who work for Richard and have worked for Richard over the years. Morden, Vihaela, Rachel, Tobruk, Onyx and all those other Dark mages you've heard of or gathered information on. What do they have that you and Anne don't?'

'Better salaries?'

'A lack of conscience,' Arachne said. 'All of them chose to serve Richard willingly.'

'Okay, but I don't exactly think that's a selling point on our part.'

'Which brings us to this message,' Arachne said. 'And to the jinn.'

I looked at Arachne curiously.

'Last Christmas, when Richard sent Morden and those other mages into that bubble realm in Syria, he did it to recover a storage box,' Arachne said. 'Our best guess was that the box contained a bound jinn.'

I nodded. 'You said you'd tell me that story another time.'

'That time is now,' Arachne said. 'Listen, and attend. The jinn are magical creatures, but thousands of years ago, they were not so very different from humans. They had a physical form, and they ate, slept, lived and died much as other creatures did. They were divided into orders – the weakest were the jann, followed by the jinn, then the shaitan, the ifrit and finally the marid. All had abilities that you would consider magical, though their strength varied by their order – the jann would barely qualify as adepts by the standards of mages today. Rising through the ranks, though, their powers increased greatly. They could take the shape of animals, fly or levitate, or read thoughts, but what truly set them apart was something else. The greater jinn – the marid and ifrit, primarily – could grant wishes.'

'I remember now,' I said. 'You said they were the only creatures in the world that could use true wish magic.'

Arachne nodded. 'It was their greatest secret, and their greatest power. It was also their downfall. Other creatures coveted the power of the jinn. Humans more than anyone else, and mages most of all.'

'I thought mages didn't trust wish magic.'

'With very good reason,' Arachne said dryly. 'But in those times, things were different. Gaining the favour of the jinn was difficult – they were capricious – but for the lucky few who succeeded, the rewards were enormous. Power and glory and treasure beyond dreams. Men were raised up as lords or kings, and were thrown down as well. Wish magic has no inherent limitations. It has the potential for anything.'

I frowned. 'What's the catch?'

'The catch,' Arachne said, 'was that the outcome of the wish would depend on the interaction between the human and jinn. The jinn could not use their wish magic for themselves – another creature had to shape it, give it will and desire. Humans, with their ambitious souls, seemed best, but even then, the results were unpredictable. Sometimes it would grant the wisher their dream, sometimes their nightmare, and for the most part, the jinn cared nothing either way. When humans raged against them, they would laugh.' Arachne was silent for a moment. 'They should have been more cautious.'

'What happened?'

'Humans grew angry,' Arachne said. 'They came to resent the jinn for their interference, and so the mages of the

Council went to the leaders among the marids and ordered them to grant wishes only as the Council decreed. The jinn refused, and so it came to war. At first, the battles were even, but the tide of the war was turned by the master mage Suleiman. He invented a way of subjugating jinn, stripping them of their physical form and binding their spirits to items so that they were compelled to serve. They could still grant wishes, but now they could do so only at the command of their bearer.'

'That sounds kind of like slavery.'

'That's because it *is* slavery,' Arachne said. 'Oh, and additionally, the ritual that stripped away the jinn's bodies also granted them immortality. So they could look forward to an eternity of servitude at the hands of their bearer.'

I sighed. 'I'm guessing this is why I haven't heard about any jinn wandering around.'

'To the best of my knowledge, the last embodied jinn was bound and sealed away more than a thousand years before you were born.'

Like I said, it's depressing how often you hear some version of this story. I guess it's not hard to understand why creatures like Karyos react to mages on their territory by trying to kill them on sight. 'Okay, so what went wrong? Because I'm sure there's a reason every master mage doesn't carry around a jinn in a bottle, and I doubt it's because of ethics.'

'It all comes back to the nature of the jinn,' Arachne said. 'The Council hated how unpredictable wishes were. They wanted the process to be ordered, and they did everything in their power to make it that way. In the early days, they would investigate every case of a successful wish; later, once the war had begun, they tested hundreds of jinn to destruction in an attempt to take the ability for themselves. But the only answer they could ever find was one that they couldn't accept.'

'What answer?'

'Empathy,' Arachne said. 'The humans who had their wishes granted were the ones who were able to share the feelings of others. Those who made wishes for purely selfish ends tended to receive nothing, or a result that worked against them. Those who made wishes to help another, or wishes that helped the jinn as well, did not. It was to do with the bond between the wisher and the jinn. You can imagine how maddening that was for the Council. They were looking for something they could *do*, to make jinn operate like machines – commands go in; wishes come out. But if it was based on what they *were* . . .'

'Couldn't they just be a bit more considerate with their wishes?'

'Haven't you been listening to what I've been saying?' Arachne said. 'It wasn't enough to put on a show. They would have had to genuinely care for the jinn they were dealing with. Inner nature isn't so malleable.' Arachne looked at me. 'How many high-ranking mages do you know – Light *or* Dark – who deeply care for the magical creatures of this world?'

I paused. 'Oh.'

'That was the purpose of Suleiman's binding,' Arachne said. 'It was intended to force jinn to grant their wishes to whoever held the item by creating an artificial bond. And it worked. After a fashion.'

'Let me guess,' I said. 'For some strange reason, the jinn bound to these items didn't have very much motivation to make sure the wishes turned out well.'

'Funnily enough, yes,' Arachne said. 'The binding process did great harm to the jinn. Weaker ones were driven to madness, while the stronger ones were filled with hatred and the desire for vengeance, first against the mages who bound them, and eventually against all humans. They couldn't disobey their masters – not at first – but they could twist and corrupt the wishes they were forced to carry out. And the more their master relied upon them, the more influence they gained over their bearer in turn. Eventually they could strike their bearer down, or carry them away to torment at their leisure.'

I started to answer, then stopped dead, my eyes going wide. 'Wait. The monkey's paw—'

'Yes,' Arachne said. 'When you first told me about it, I suspected. After I heard what happened to Martin, I was sure. You remember I told you never to use it.'

'Holy shit,' I muttered. I remembered that time I'd come home to find it lying on my pillow, and felt a chill. What would have happened if I hadn't listened to Arachne? Or if Luna hadn't listened to me? 'There's a jinn inside?'

'And a powerful one. An ifrit if not a marid.'

I thought about it for a second. I wondered how long the creature had been trapped there. 'Could I just free it?'

Arachne looked at me, then quite unexpectedly reached out with one foreleg and patted me on the head, and when she spoke her voice was warm. 'You're a good person, Alex.'

'Hey,' I protested.

'It wouldn't help, I'm afraid,' Arachne said. 'That jinn's body was destroyed millennia ago. There's nowhere for you to free it *to*.'

'Oh.'

'In any case,' Arachne said, 'mages eventually came to

accept that their bound jinn were more harm than help. So they destroyed the items, or sealed them away, or left them forgotten in treasure hoards until they themselves died, whereupon the items would be passed on until they found their way into the hands of normal humans. And over time, knowledge of the jinn faded into folktale and myth. But underneath it, the essence remained. A human who called up the jinn according to the old rituals, with the jinn as a willing partner, could still unlock their full power.'

'But according to you, that'd only work if the human actually cared about the jinn in the first place.'

'Yes.'

'So for Morden and Richard to carry out their secret plan and get a jinn as a superweapon, they need someone who empathises with magical creatures?' I laughed. 'Good bloody luck. The average empathy level of that band of psychos has got to be lower than even the Light Council. They're going to have serious trouble finding anyone who . . .'

I trailed off.

Arachne looked at me.

'Oh, shit,' I said.

'Figured it out yet?' Arachne said.

'Wait,' I said. 'That can't be it. It doesn't . . .'

'You've said in the past that you were never quite sure why Richard chose you,' Arachne said. 'Perhaps he was hedging his bets. He chose his first three apprentices in the classical Dark mould, but he understood that came with limitations. So when it came to choosing his fourth and last apprentice, he selected someone different. Someone with the potential for other things.'

'No,' I said. 'He has to know I'd never agree. Not to that. Okay, working as Morden's aide is one thing, but . . .'

'And you remember how that came about?' Arachne said. 'What if Richard and Morden simply tell you: bond with the jinn, use it as we order, or we'll kill Luna? Or Anne, or Variam, or everyone else you care about?'

I opened my mouth to give an answer and couldn't think of one.

'Richard isn't stupid, Alex,' Arachne said. 'He has little enough empathy himself, but he understands how to exploit it in others.'

'How long have you been suspecting this?'

'I've *suspected* ever since your trip to Syria. This –' She tapped the phone. '– makes it more than a suspicion.'

'But Richard didn't get that box from Syria,' I said. 'The Council did. If there really was a jinn inside, he missed his chance.'

'There are other jinn,' Arachne said. 'So for the meantime, I would strongly suggest that you do all you can to make a breakthrough with the dreamstone.'

I'd already been feeling uneasy, and the mention of the dreamstone made my mood worse. 'What kind of breakthrough?' I demanded. I gestured over to the right, where the dreamstone sat on a small table on its stand. 'We've been working on that thing for months now. We've tried command words, we've tried spells, we've tried fifty different channelling methods, and all for what? So the damn thing can sit there and do an imitation of a chunk of rock, which is apparently a really *good* imitation since it hasn't broken character once! I've explored every single possible thing I could do with this focus and nothing works!'

Arachne was silent for a moment. 'I am starting to suspect,' she said at last, 'that the stone may be testing you.'

'But I've tried to pass its tests,' I said. 'I've tried every possible interaction with this stone that I can imagine.'

'With your divination.'

'Well, yeah.'

'Perhaps the issue is one of commitment,' Arachne said. 'Many imbued items require some kind of sacrifice before they will accept a bearer. Blood, possessions, oaths.'

'I already tried the bleeding-on-it plan,' I said. It said something that I'd been willing to even consider that future in the first place.

'You didn't actually *try* it,' Arachne said. 'You looked at what the consequences would be if you did.'

'What's your point?'

'This item may be more intelligent than you give it credit for.'

'So what are you saying I should do?' I asked. 'Start cutting myself?'

'No,' Arachne said. 'Doing that on my say-so would work no better, I think. The impetus must come from you. But whatever you try, I think you should do it soon. We may be running out of time.'

I didn't sleep well that night. I kept thinking about what would happen if Arachne was right, and I remembered that prophecy I'd been told last Christmas, about how the Council believed that Richard's rise to power would be done through me. The two blended together into a series of worst-case scenarios that just got more and more horrible, and at some point I fell asleep and they turned into a muddle of frightening dreams where I was a monstrous beast roaming an abandoned London.

I woke tired, with grit in my eyes and a sore throat. Morden didn't need me in at the War Rooms until tomorrow, but there was a message on my phone from Luna asking for me to come meet her. I might have been tempted to put her off, but the place she named caught my attention.

Luna was waiting for me at the end of the street. 'Okay, I have to ask,' I said as I walked up. 'Why did you want to meet *here*?'

Luna grinned. She was dressed in white and green, with a ribbon in her hair, and somehow she looked different from usual. Luna's never been classically beautiful, but she's got vitality, and today there was a particular sparkle to her eye. I could see passers-by giving her second looks. 'You'll find out. Come on.'

Luna had brought me back to Camden, to the same street that the Arcana Emporium had been on. It had been months since I'd been here, and it felt strange to recognise the old sights and smells: tourists in the streets, cafés and restaurants with their doors open, the scent of the canal. This place had been my home for so long that going back felt weirdly dislocating, like stepping back in time. 'Look, I like the place too, but I've kind of seen the sights already,' I said as we walked up the street. 'So unless you've got somewhere new to show me . . .'

Luna pointed. 'Funny you should say that.'

I followed the direction of Luna's finger and stopped. 'What the hell?'

Luna was pointing at the wreck of the old Arcana

Emporium . . . except that it wasn't a wreck any more. When I'd last seen it, it had been a burnt-out ruin. Now it was a construction site. The building was up to two storeys already, and the height of the scaffolding and some steel I-beams rising up over the first floor suggested that another one would be added in time. Tarpaulins covered the area where the shop-front had been, and a skip was parked outside.

I turned to Luna. 'Is some property developer doing this?'

Luna shrugged. 'You're looking at her.'

I stared. 'Come on,' Luna said, taking out a key and unlocking the door. 'Take a look inside.'

The ground floor smelt of concrete and paint. What had once been the main shop was just a bare box, but the rubble had been cleared away and the room was empty and clean. The walls were whitewashed and a new wall had been placed in roughly the spot where the old one had been, a little heavier and thicker. The tarpaulins made the room gloomy, but I could see that the street-facing side had been designed for tall windows running nearly to the ceiling. 'What do you think?' Luna said. 'The first firm I talked to said the whole building was a write-off, but then I found some Polish guys who thought they could salvage the structure for the ground floor. Needed a bit of reinforcing, but I figured that was a good idea anyway, right?'

'How exactly did you pay for this?' I asked. I give Luna a stipend and I'd left her some money during the dust-up over Christmas, but this kind of work is not cheap.

'Remember back when you were taking me to casinos trying to figure out if I could use my curse that way?'

'Yeah, and the answer we came up with was that it probably didn't.'

'That was before I started studying with Chalice,' Luna said. 'A few months ago, I decided to give it another try. It didn't work at first, but I finally figured out that that was because I was doing it the wrong way. Turns out my curse might not be all that good at making me win, but it's *great* at making everyone else lose.'

'And that paid for a new building,' I said. For some reason, seeing the place rebuilt made my spirits lift. 'Arcana Emporium, mark two?'

'I thought I'd just keep the old name,' Luna said. 'More consistency.'

I thought about going back to my old life as a shopkeeper, and just for a moment I could see myself behind the counter again, selling to Wiccans in dresses and kids in T-shirts. It was tempting, maybe not so much for what it was as for what it meant. I'd been happy working as a shopkeeper, I think, though I hadn't known it at the time.

But then reality set in. I sighed and let the image fade. 'Luna, I appreciate it, I really do. But . . . I don't think I can go back to running a shop any more. Maybe some day in the future, a long, long time off, when things have quietened down. But it won't be any time soon. If I did it now, I'd just be putting myself and everyone else in danger.'

'I know,' Luna said. 'That's why I thought I could do it instead.'

I looked at her.

'I've been doing some thinking,' Luna said. 'Back when I first started learning to duel and learning to fight, I loved it. I thought I could use it to protect myself, not be useless. Only . . . I guess I started to notice after a while that it didn't actually *help* all that much. Don't get me wrong, I'd rather know how to fight than not, but when we *do* get into fights, it doesn't usually make anything better. It's just sort of a bad outcome that we only take because it's a choice between that and an even *worse* outcome.'

'If you're competent, then violence is your first option and last resort.'

'Yeah, Landis said something like that once,' Luna said. 'I think it was the White Rose fight that made me really think. I mean, there was so much Council power there, and what did it accomplish? White Rose was broken, but that was almost by accident. If things had turned out a little differently then just as many people would have died, but nothing would have changed. And that made me think back and count up the number of times that me being able to fight actually made a positive difference. And there were a few, but . . . not many.'

I nodded. Every now and then you wind up in a situation that calls for violence, and when that happens, you need to know what you're doing. But even if you live an especially dangerous life – which, to be fair, Luna and I do – all of those times put together are going to average to less than twenty-four hours per year. The other ninety-nine point something per cent of the time you're going to spend doing something else. And if you try to solve problems with violence when you *don't* need to, it really doesn't take long before you turn into the kind of person other people are worried about protecting *against*.

'So I started thinking about what else I should be doing,' Luna said. 'And you know what? The thing that made the biggest difference in my life wasn't anything to do with duelling or fighting. It was what you did for me. And I wouldn't have found you without your shop.' Luna shrugged. 'I think it should still be here.'

I looked at Luna. She looked back at me steadily, and there was something in her eyes that made me think she was serious. But I wanted to be sure. 'What if I told you it was too dangerous?'

'You said that people would be coming after you,' Luna said. 'Not me.'

'That hasn't stopped you from becoming collateral damage before.'

'Yeah, well, I've got a few ideas,' Luna said. 'For one thing, no offence, but I think that habit of yours of sleeping right above your shop was kind of dumb. Once the building's done, I'm going to set up the top floor as a flat, put in a bed and a wardrobe and everything, and then every night I'll go up there and then I'll gate somewhere else and make very sure not to sleep there, ever.'

'And what if I told you not to do it at all?'

Luna frowned. 'Why?'

'Because I said so.'

'But why?'

'Because I said so.'

Luna looked at me strangely. 'I thought you'd be okay with . . .'

I didn't answer. Luna wavered, then her expression set. 'No. This is important. *Someone* should do it. And okay, this is still your shop, but if you won't let me do it here? Then I can find somewhere else.'

I looked at Luna, and she looked at me, then I relaxed. 'I think it's a good idea.'

'That's— wait.' Luna looked suspicious. 'Were you testing me?'

'You'll need one thing more,' I said. 'Mages won't take you seriously until you've taken a name.'

'Vesta,' Luna said.

'Vesta?'

'Vesta.'

I looked at Luna curiously. Vesta is the Roman goddess of hearth and home, and I've never heard of a mage taking her name. Most who choose mythological names pick ones associated with magic or war or rulership. 'You don't want something grander or more imposing?'

'I've met plenty of mages who want to be grand and imposing,' Luna said. 'I didn't like them much. I'm sticking with Vesta.'

'Sounds good to me.' I held out my hand with a smile. 'Congratulations, Journeyman Vesta.'

Luna laughed and took my hand, pulling the curse back along her arm so that we could shake hands without the silver mist touching my skin. Then she opened the door and I followed behind her to take a look at the rest of what would one day become the new Arcana Emporium.

14

Everything changes. Pick any constant about your life and wait long enough, and it'll be different. We all know that, but for some reason, it's a hard lesson to remember. I suppose it's because to do anything, we have to assume that things *won't* change – you can't make plans without assuming a certain degree of permanence. And for the most part, that assumption turns out to be true. Until it isn't.

But one of the things I've noticed as I've grown older is that while everything changes, the change usually isn't obvious. Sometimes that's because the change is so slow and gradual. A pair of shoes wears out, a person ages, the tree outside your window grows; every day it's different, but in such tiny increments that you never notice. But sometimes you don't notice not because the change is slow, but because it's invisible. All too often, the really big changes – the kind that go through our lives like a tornado and throw everything upside down – happen where we can't see them. Somewhere far out in the ocean, the sea breezes meet, and the breezes turn into eddies, and the eddies into gusts, and the gusts build into a storm that whirls faster and faster into a roaring hurricane. The satellites watching from space see it and piece it together, but to the people on the ground living under a blue and cloudless sky, it seems like nothing's happening. Until it's too late.

Now that I look back on it, that had been what had happened over Christmas. The seeds had been sown when

I'd rejected Levistus's threat during the business with White Rose the winter before. After that battle was over I'd gone home, and in time I'd forgotten about it, but Levistus hadn't forgotten. He'd planned and waited and finally later that year, when the time was right, he'd made his move and had me sentenced to death. To me, it had seemed as though nothing was happening, but things *were* happening, just not where I could see. And so I'd gone about my business in blissful ignorance, until one Saturday evening Talisid called me and everything fell apart.

As it turned out, the same thing had been happening this year as well. Now that I look back on the whole thing, I can see the clues I missed, but that's how it works with hindsight. When you know what's relevant and what you can ignore, then everything is obvious, but it's not so obvious when you're caught up in surviving from day to day. At least until life reaches out and smacks you over the head.

'But that's a matter for another time,' Morden said, 'For now, a different task.'

I looked at Morden, instantly wary. It was late October, only a week after my conversation with Luna. Luna was still working away on the shop, Variam was still training for his journeyman tests, Anne was still avoiding everyone and spending too much time alone in the Hollow and I was still working for Morden. We were at the end of a workday and my mind immediately flashed back to how he'd given me the last 'job'. It had been in a similar manner to this. 'What kind of job?'

'Tomorrow night, you and Anne Walker will be accompanying some of my associates on a little expedition,'

Morden said. 'I'd suggest you come prepared. There'll be opposition.'

'What kind of opposition?'

'The kind you get at the Council War Rooms.'

I stopped dead. We were walking along the street away from one of the War Rooms' entrances, and Morden slowed slightly, giving me an inquiring look. 'Wait,' I said, hurrying to catch up. 'What was that?'

'We're going to launch an attack on the Council,' Morden said. 'Or you will, at any rate. I'm afraid I won't be personally accompanying you, but I have every confidence in your success.'

I stared at Morden, trying to figure out what to say. The Dark mage navigated around a pedestrian, nodding to the man as he was given space. 'I don't understand,' I said once we were out of earshot again.

'It's not complicated,' Morden said. 'We're launching an attack on the Council. The ones participating in said attack are the mages who work for me. You are a mage who works for me, therefore you will be participating. Which part of this chain of causation is giving you difficulty?'

'This is . . .'

'I hope you're not going to say that this is morally objectionable,' Morden said.

'I was going to say "insane".'

'Oh?'

'Did I hear you right?' I said. Normally I watched my words more carefully around Morden, but my guard was down. 'Did you *seriously* just tell me to attack the War Rooms?'

'Isn't it exactly what the Council have been expecting me to do?'

'Which is exactly why it's insane!'

'You worry too much, Verus.'

'You told me back in the summer that they were just paranoid!'

'Actually, what I said was that the War Rooms would be equally safe regardless of any new security measures,' Morden said. 'A subtle but important difference. And a judgement I'd still agree with. I've seen no sign that anything they've done will make any difference.'

'Not the slightest . . .' I stared at Morden, lost for words.

'Was there anything else?' Morden asked.

'Have you gone completely nuts?' I demanded. 'Has being made a Council member made you as delusional as they are? You think you can just give any order, no matter how crazy, and it'll happen?'

'I can understand that this must be something of a surprise, but please remain civil.'

I struggled to control myself. Morden watched with an expression of mild interest. 'Then do you mind telling me,' I said at last, 'exactly how you are planning to carry this out?'

'I'm afraid the details are being kept a secret for the time being,' Morden said. 'Operational security. I'm sure you understand.'

'You have to be planning to attack the place from range,' I said. 'Right? There's no way you could be mounting a manned assault—'

'Oh no, it's manned,' Morden said. 'We're doing this the old-fashioned way. And please do stop saying "you". As I explained, you'll be coming.'

'But that's insane,' I said. 'Literally insane. As in, you can't be a rational person and expect that to work. The

Council has bound elementals. Mantis golems. Devourers. Every kind of spell ward and attack ward you can think of. And those are just the things I *know* about. There'll be other kinds of guardian constructs and creatures that I've never even heard of because they keep them an absolute secret. They've been working on fortifying that place for hundreds of years. Dark mages have attacked it I don't know how many times, and they've *always* failed. The Council literally have more security and fortification measures at the War Rooms than at every other facility in Britain put together. And that's in times of peace. With all those rumours going around, they'll have made it even stronger. Attacking the War Rooms is *suicide*.'

Morden kept walking, listening patiently. 'Are you finished?'

'. . . Yes.'

'Your reservations are noted,' Morden said. 'Your orders stand. Oh, and since you and she seemed to work so well together last time, you'll be under Vihaela's orders again.'

I just stared at Morden. 'Of course,' I said at last when I could speak. 'Why not? So is Richard going to be coming along too, just to make it a party?'

'There's really no point in having subordinates if you do everything yourself,' Morden said. 'Vihaela will be in tactical command. If you have no further questions, I suggest you go prepare.'

I stopped walking again, and this time Morden didn't pause to let me catch up. He disappeared around a corner ahead, leaving me alone.

The first thing I did was to tell Luna and Vari. Anne was in the Hollow and out of contact, so Luna went to relay the news. Which left me free to figure out what the hell I was supposed to do.

I was staying in the Hollow at the moment – we were in the process of putting together a more permanent set of living arrangements, but it was taking time – but for some reason, I didn't want to go back there. The Hollow is peaceful, but I don't find it so good for thinking. I wanted to stay in London. And so I wandered, letting my feet find their own path while my mind searched for a way out.

In the end, the place my feet took me to was Suicide Bridge, the high red arch at the very peak of the hill that rises between Archway and Highgate. As you'd guess from the name, the bridge is a favourite spot for those intending to take a hands-on approach to the question of their life expectancy, and with an eighty-foot drop to the dual carriageway below, it does the job pretty well. Successive local governments have increased the height of the fence and put up anti-climbing spikes, but if there's one thing you can count on, it's that someone who's sufficiently dedicated to getting themselves killed will find a way to do it.

Looking at those railings sent my thoughts back to last January, and my own suicide attempt. Oh, I hadn't thought of it that way at the time, but if I was being honest, that was what it had been: a way to escape my problems. It hadn't worked. If anything, it had . . . well, I suppose it hadn't exactly made things *worse*, but God knows it hadn't made things any better. And now I was back in London, and back with another impossible problem to solve.

I rested my elbows on the railing, staring out over the city. The view from Suicide Bridge is impressive, particularly to the south – it's downhill all the way to the river, meaning that you can look out over all of London. The sun was sinking to the west, painting the sky in purple and violet, and its light glinted off the skyscrapers in the distance, reflecting off the windows of the towers of Liverpool Street and the cluster of Canary Wharf and the Shard. Directly below, the lights of cars shone in the dusk, red on the left side and pale white on the right, two bus lanes and four car lanes carrying a steady stream of traffic up and down the hill. Each of those cars and buses was filled with people, each with their own lives and struggles and hopes, and probably not a single one was paying the slightest attention to the tall, stooping figure leaning on the fence above. The city's a busy place, and if you wait for people to notice your problems, you'll be waiting a long time. You want to fix your life, you have to do it yourself.

What was I going to do?

A few years ago – maybe as recently as one year ago – my solution to this problem would have been to run. Get as far away from Richard and Morden and the Council as I could, and wait for things all to blow over. The events of this January had shown me the drawbacks with that plan. Running and hiding only works if you don't have anything you're willing to fight for. Or in my case, any*one*.

Obeying Morden and taking part in the attack sounded like an equally terrible idea. Everything about Morden's plan screamed 'trap'. I didn't know whether it was Morden's trap, the Council's trap or both, but if I just marched off to attack the War Rooms, I'd be a mouse between two grinding gears. The only question was which would crush me first.

So what if I turned on Morden before he could do the same to me? I had Talisid's communicator in my pocket. I could be in touch with him in five minutes. This was exactly the kind of tip-off he'd been hoping for – in fact, I wouldn't be surprised if it was the whole reason he'd cultivated a relationship with me in the first place. If I did that, what would happen?

Well, the first thing that would happen would be that Morden's attack would fail. I mean, based off all the evidence I could see, it would almost certainly fail anyway, but my intervention would push the chances from 'slim' down to 'none'. At least this way I'd get something out of it. The Dark mages would either have to abort their attack, or be killed or captured.

But Richard and Morden wouldn't be killed or captured. They wouldn't be there. And once they figured out that they'd been betrayed . . .

I shivered at the thought of what would happen then. Morden and Richard would *have* to know that it was me, and even if they didn't, the first thing they'd do would be to get the information out of me, one way or another. If I was lucky, they'd have a mind mage pull it out of my skull. If I was *unlucky* they'd just hand me over to Vihaela, in which case I was pretty sure I'd tell them everything they wanted to know in short order. I had no illusions about my ability to resist the kind of torture Vihaela could administer.

But if I *didn't* tip anyone off, then the Council would be after me instead. I could claim that I hadn't known about the attack, but the Council wouldn't care. A direct attack on the War Rooms would rouse the Council into a fury and the first thing they'd do would be to find targets to vent their rage on, which would probably mean arresting Morden and every one of his associates. After which point, the consequences for Anne and me would be pretty much the same, only with a slightly lower chance of torture and a significantly higher chance of being mentally violated, which would continue until they confirmed that yes, I'd known about the attack in advance, whereupon I'd promptly be executed for treason.

Both choices sucked. I needed a third option.

Maybe I was looking at this the wrong way. What if Morden was lying from start to finish? He hadn't made the slightest effort to reassure me – in fact, looking back on it, he'd practically dared me to resist. Maybe there *was* no attack, and the whole thing was a test. I'd go tip off Talisid, the Council would go onto high alert and tomorrow evening would come and the War Rooms would be left completely alone. I'd be discredited, the Crusaders and Guardians would be seen as overreacting to a phantom threat and the Council as a whole would be that much more likely to ignore any future warnings. Meanwhile, I'd wake up the next morning to Morden and Vihaela politely inquiring if I had any idea why the Council had suddenly gone on red alert last night.

Looked at from that angle, it all sounded horribly plausible. But was I really that important to Morden that it was worth going to so much trouble just to trap me? And why would he even *need* to trap me? Morden already knew I was working against my will; if he wanted to have me imprisoned and tortured, he didn't need an excuse.

Or then again, maybe this *was* all a test, and he was waiting to see what I was going to do. In which case there was probably someone watching me right now . . .

I hissed out a breath and paced along the bridge. The sun had set, the light was fading from the sky and as far as I could tell I was alone. I felt as though I was guessing in the dark, and if I guessed wrong then the consequences would be awful, except there was no way to know which was right and which was wrong. Maybe I could try path-walking, looking to see what would happen if I waited until tomorrow night and did nothing. But that could take hours: any information I got would be fragmentary, and it would eat into my window for tipping Talisid off. Still, it was the best plan I could think of.

Unless . . .

A dark thought swam up from the depths of my mind. The War Rooms were impregnable – everyone knew that. There was no way Morden could touch them. Except . . . what if he could? I already knew that Richard had abilities I couldn't match, maybe ones I'd never even heard of. Maybe he *did* have some secret plan that actually could take down the nerve centre of the British Council.

In which case, did I really want to stop him?

I thought about Anne, and what had been done to her by the Crusaders. About the attacks by Levistus's men on me last year, and how I'd been forced to flee the country just to survive. The winter before that, a Council Keeper had tried to assassinate me over White Rose; the year before that, they'd expelled Anne from the apprentice programme and left her to die; the year before *that*, they'd stood by and deliberately stayed their hand as the Nightstalkers had done their best to assassinate me. Most of all, I remembered what the consequences had been . . . or at least the consequences for them. Nothing. They could outlaw me and break their own treaties and even sponsor outright assassinations and kidnappings, and somehow they never paid any price.

Maybe it was time they did.

Standing up there in the twilight, looking at the lights of London as the city lit up for the coming night, I had a sudden feeling of power. For once, I knew what was coming and the Council didn't. All I had to do was stay my hand and watch them fall. I've spent so long struggling against the Council, feeling helpless and hunted. Now, for the first time, it felt as though *I* might be able to hurt *them*. And I liked it.

Maybe this is how Dark mages feel all the time.

That thought came as a jolt, and with it my castle of dark thoughts crumbled away. All of a sudden I felt foolish. I wasn't some sort of avenging angel – I was just a pawn for Morden to sacrifice. And even if his plan did have some chance of bringing down the Council, why would I want to replace them with *Richard* of all people? Hadn't I learnt anything?

No. I shook my head. If I was going to survive this, I had to think. Right now, I didn't know enough, so the first step was to learn more. I turned and walked away off the bridge without looking back.

'So what did you find?' Luna asked.

'Nothing good,' I said.

It was later that night and we were in the Hollow, sitting in a loose circle of four. I was on a packing crate; Luna and Vari were sharing our log bench, while Anne was a little further away, arms wrapped around herself and dark eyes watching. Our tents and storage were a little way back; there were plans underway for a proper building, but we were still having trouble with the logistics. The sky above was filled with brilliant stars and nebulae, and set low on the ground, three sphere lamps provided light. Electricity wasn't an option in the shadow realm and was likely to stay that way, so we'd been forced to fall back on magical illumination. I'd spent much of the evening gathering what information I could find. Now we had to decide what to do with it.

'I've looked into all the futures I can easily reach where I just sit around and wait,' I said. 'There are some variations, but generally speaking, someone working for Morden or the Council comes looking for me. It's too far away to get any details of the conversation, but it's a safe bet they aren't there to discuss the weather. Second point. I've tried contacting – or at least hypothetically contacting – all the Dark mages I know who are connected to Richard in some way. Cinder, Deleo, Onyx and all the others. Deleo and Onyx aren't going to talk to me, but I get the vibe that they're busy. The only one I could get in touch with was Cinder, and he pretty much confirmed that something was going down.'

'So it's not a bluff,' Anne said quietly.

'Not unless Morden is planning the biggest practical joke of all time.'

'So he's really going to do it?' Variam said. He was frowning. 'He's going to attack the War Rooms?'

'Slow down,' I said. 'We know he's going to do *something*. He could be attacking some other place, or going after the Council of another country, or maybe raiding somewhere that has nothing to do with the Council at all.'

'But why?' Luna asked.

'We don't even know why he'd attack the War Rooms,

much less somewhere else,' I said. 'So your guess is as good as mine. The one thing I'm willing to bet on is that he's not telling the whole truth.'

'Maybe not,' Variam said. 'Landis was telling me just a few days ago about some adepts the Keepers picked up who were telling some crazy story about how Richard was going to lead an army of them to take down the Council. Everyone was just laughing, but . . .'

'Maybe tomorrow they won't be laughing,' Luna said.

'Even an army of adepts wouldn't do it,' I said. 'The War Rooms are a fortress. Numbers aren't going to mean shit.'

'It seems weird, though,' Luna said. 'Why do it at all?'

'Because he wants to take down the Council and set himself up as Dark Lord Look-How-Scary-I-Am,' Variam said. 'Seems pretty obvious to me.'

'But that isn't what he's been doing so far,' Luna said. 'Morden's been worming his way into the Council all the years we've known him. And it's working. Why would he mess up a good thing?'

'Because this was what he was planning from the start?' Variam said.

Luna rolled her eyes. 'You sound like those Guardians. "Oh, you can't trust Dark mages; they all want to take over the world".'

'It's possible that Morden's political position is worse than we know,' I said. 'Everyone knows the Council hate him. Maybe they've managed to manoeuvre him to where this is his best option.'

'Do you really think that's true?' Anne asked.

'No,' I admitted. 'Honestly, I'm with Luna. For years now, Morden's done the softly-softly approach. He always stays at arm's length from anything that's too risky. This feels out of character.'

'Unless there's something he knows that we don't,' Luna said.

'Which I'm pretty sure there is,' I said. 'But right now, we have to decide what to do, and I can only really see two choices. Option one: we tip off the Council. Warn them that the info might be wrong, but that it's a threat. If nothing happens, well, they'll live. But if Morden *does* go through with the attack, it'll be huge.'

'Doesn't sound so bad,' Variam said.

'Yeah, except there's a catch,' I said. 'If we do that, and we don't show up to the attack, then we might as well be hanging up a big sign saying "HEY, EVERYONE, WE BETRAYED YOU." On the other hand, if we *do* show up, then when the Council comes down on Morden like a ton of bricks, we'll have the Council shooting at us from one side and Richard's lot shooting at us from the other.'

'I don't really like option one,' Anne said. 'What's option two?'

'We play along,' I said. 'We join Morden and take part in the job – whatever the hell it is – and do as we're told, on the theory that the consequences for us can't possibly be any worse than what he'll do if he catches us selling him out.'

'So we'd be hoping he succeeds,' Anne said.

'And if he doesn't,' I said, 'then we'll have to find a way to get the hell out before Morden's goons decide we're being insufficiently loyal and shoot us in the back.'

'Except you just said that if he's going after the War Rooms, then he's *not* going to succeed,' Variam said.

'Option two is counting very heavily on the assumption that it *won't* be the War Rooms.'

'And if it is?'

'Then either the Council kills us in the attack, or we get hunted down and executed for treason afterwards.'

'That sounds even worse than option one,' Luna said.

'I said I had two options,' I said. 'I didn't say they were good ones.'

'There's got to be something we can do.'

'We could hope that Morden's actually just taking us off on a treasure hunt or something and attacking the Council is just an elaborate disinformation plan,' I said. 'But I really don't think we're that lucky. As far as I can tell, tipping off the Council or going along and obeying are the only half-viable choices.'

'I can think of another,' Luna said. 'You tip off the Council and then we all go take a holiday and stop answering our phones for the next week. Morden goes ahead with his attack and gets his arse kicked. We watch from a really long way away and eat popcorn. The Council can't do anything because we warned them, and Morden can't do anything because he's too busy being dead.'

Variam tilted his head. 'That sounds pretty good.'

'Yeah, there's kind of a problem with that,' I said. 'In Luna's plan, one way or another, Morden ends up gone. Either executed by the Council or on the run. Either way, he's not going to have his Council position any more.'

'So?' Variam said.

I just waited for them to figure it out. 'The death sentence,' Anne said quietly.

'How does . . . ?' Variam began, then stopped.

'Morden attacks the War Rooms, he goes,' I said. 'Morden goes, Anne and I aren't his aides any more. Which means the death sentence on us both goes live. Which puts us right back where we were in January.'

'Well, shit,' Luna said.

We sat in silence for a minute or two.

'Okay,' Variam said at last. 'Then in that case, I guess I'm voting for the tip-off plan.'

'Sorry, Vari,' I said. 'You don't get a vote.'

'Why not?'

'Because you aren't going.'

'If you attack the War Rooms without telling the Council, they're going to rake me over the coals,' Variam said.

'True, I'll admit you do have some stake in this, but if things go wrong, you'll be facing an investigation or a reprimand. *We* are going to be facing either an execution or instant death. I kind of think our issues trump yours.'

Luna looked at Anne. 'What do you think?'

We all looked at Anne, who sat there in silence. The glow of the sphere lamps sank into the hair on either side of her face, leaving her features in shadow. 'I think . . .' she said at last, '. . . go ahead and tip them off.'

'You actually want to help the Council?' Luna asked.

'No.'

'Then why—?'

'I'm hoping Richard really *does* have some sort of secret weapon,' Anne said. 'And that he uses it, and he and the Council wipe each other out.' She looked up at me, and there was anger on her face. 'I can't do anything about the Council, but maybe Richard can.'

Both Luna and Variam just stared, taken aback. 'That's . . .' I said slowly, '. . . maybe not the best reason to be making a decision.'

'Maybe not,' Anne said. 'But it's not as though anything we do is going to make a difference.'

There was an awkward silence. I looked at Anne, and felt uneasy. She'd been in bad shape since September, and she didn't seem to be getting better. Three times in the past fortnight, I'd tried to talk to her about things, and she'd turned me away every time. She'd started finding excuses to put off our training sessions, and when I'd called her a few days ago to schedule a new one, she'd turned me down that time too. I didn't want to force the issue, but I couldn't think of any way to—

'Alex?' Luna said. 'What do you think?'

'Uh, yeah,' I said. 'I'm leaning the same way as Anne, but for different reasons. The way I see it, if we stay silent, it burns our bridges with the Council. No matter what Morden's planning, if he carries out any sort of attack and we *don't* tell them, then we can give up on any chance of ever getting rid of outlaw status.'

'You're not an outlaw now,' Variam said.

'Because of Morden,' I said. 'Which means we'll be tied to him for the rest of our lives.'

'Yeah, but if we *do* tip off the Council, then it screws things up with Morden,' Luna said.

'I'm not a hundred per cent sure it will,' I said. 'The more I think about it, the more it feels as though Morden was almost daring me to tell someone. There'll still be a price, but honestly, I think if he was going to have me tortured to death for something like this, he'd have done it already. Besides . . .'

'Besides what?' Variam asked.

'Staying quiet and doing nothing is basically the same as helping out Richard,' I said. 'Maybe tipping off the

Council is going to help in the long run, and maybe it won't, but at least this way I'll be fighting back against Richard and Morden somehow. I suppose that's not the most amazing reason either, but . . .'

'No, I'm fine with that,' Variam said with a shrug. 'Screw those guys.'

'Works for me,' Luna said.

I laughed. 'So we all end up at the same place, but for different reasons.' I looked around at the other three, and wondered suddenly how many times we'd done this by now. Talking over the latest problem, sharing ideas, trying to come up with a solution. We'd always managed until now, right?

A quiet voice spoke inside my head. *Or maybe this time, not all of you are going to come back.*

That killed my laughter. The four of us sat in silence under the stars.

It was close to midnight when I finally got in touch with Talisid. Talisid's paranoia can be annoying at times, but at least it does mean he keeps his communicator close to hand. Given what we were about to be talking about, it would have been really annoying to have to go around to his house and bang on the door.

The first half of the conversation went more or less as I'd predicted. First Talisid asked if I was sure, then he asked if I'd told anyone else, then he wanted an exhaustive recap of every single word that Morden had said. Once I was done, he wanted to go through it all again.

As I went through it for the second time though, I started to notice something odd. Talisid was clearly paying attention, but he didn't seem particularly shocked or off-balance. 'Go over again exactly how many mages he suggested he was bringing,' Talisid said.

'I told you, he didn't give numbers,' I said. 'He just said the mages who worked for him.'

'But he also said Vihaela would be leading the attack,' Talisid said. 'That implies that Richard's other subordinates would be coming as well. Do you know which ones?'

'No. Look, Talisid, don't take this the wrong way, but you really aren't acting as surprised as you should be.'

'We've been concerned about this possibility for some time.'

'Yeah, in the abstract,' I said. 'But given that I just told you it's happening tomorrow night – as in less than twenty-four hours away – you don't seem all that panicked. Shouldn't you be running to tell the Council?'

'At the moment, I'm more concerned with verification.'

I stood silently, thinking. It didn't take long to put the pieces together. 'You knew already, didn't you?'

Talisid hesitated for just an instant, which was all the answer I needed. 'You know I can't discuss—' Talisid began.

'Talisid,' I said wearily.

'We've had reports,' Talisid said. 'From various sources, but they all mention the War Rooms, and they all give the time as tomorrow night. The Senior Council is in closed session to discuss it now.'

'They didn't invite Morden? I'm shocked.'

'But you *are* the only person to have heard it from Morden directly,' Talisid said. 'Until now, we didn't have any substantive evidence against him. If you can testify to what you've heard, then it may be enough to tie Morden to the attack and bring him down once and for all.'

'Yeah, I wouldn't get too ahead of yourselves. We still don't know if it's the War Rooms he's attacking.'

'I assure you, that concern has been raised.'

'So are you going to tell them?'

'Yes,' Talisid said. 'However . . .'

'However?'

'I can't speak for them,' Talisid said. 'But I would prepare yourself for the possibility that you may be asked to join Morden's attack regardless.'

'Fuck that.'

'If you don't, it could tip him off—'

'If I *do*, I'll have the Council shooting me from one side and Morden's lot shooting me from the other. No way in hell.'

'The Council will be very grateful.'

I told Talisid exactly what the Council could do with their gratitude.

'Verus,' Talisid said. He sounded slightly shocked.

'You seriously think that after everything they've done to me, I'm going to do the Council favours?' I said. 'Answer is no.'

Talisid was silent for a second. 'What if I could offer you something in exchange?'

'Like what?'

'The lifting of your death sentence.'

That shut me up.

'I can't promise anything,' Talisid said. 'However . . . given the circumstances, I think they would be willing to consider it.'

'Are they really that scared?' I asked. 'Enough that they're willing to overrule a resolution just to have me as an inside man?'

'As I said, I can't promise anything,' Talisid said. 'But it's a realistic possibility.'

I thought fast. My first instinct was to take the deal. But another voice spoke up: *if they're willing to give this much, maybe you could get more.* 'I want the death sentence revoked,' I said. 'Both for me *and* for Anne. And I don't want it to be conditional on the accuracy of my information, either. Everything I've told you has been in good faith, but I've got no guarantee that Morden was telling the truth. Even if the attack doesn't go through, the sentence is still gone.'

'That may be difficult to sell.'

'Deal with it. Oh, and one more thing. If I'm going to be testifying against Morden, I also want a full pardon for anything I do during the attack tomorrow, as well as retroactively for all the time I've been working as Morden's aide. Take it or leave it.'

Talisid was silent. 'Well,' he said at last. 'They won't be happy, but I'll see what I can do. I'll contact the Council immediately and I'll call you back as soon as I hear anything.'

'I'll be waiting.'

15

Talisid was as good as his word. I'd expected to be left hanging all night, but he called me back barely an hour later. 'The Council have agreed to your offer,' Talisid said, 'but with conditions.'

'Okay.'

'The Council will lift the death sentence on you and Anne Walker,' Talisid said. 'In exchange you will both accompany Morden's team on whatever mission they order. You will be exempt from any criminal charges for any actions you take during this operation and during your past tenure as Morden's aide, *providing* you can demonstrate that you performed those actions under duress. In exchange, the two of you will both co-operate fully with any criminal case brought against Morden, including testifying against him. If you don't, the deal is off.'

It was more than I'd dared hope for. 'How exactly did they get Levistus to agree to that?'

'Levistus was . . . not happy,' Talisid said dryly. 'Neither was Sal Sarque. However, Bahamus and Druss voted in your favour, and Alma and Undaaris were sufficiently convinced by the urgency of the situation. The final vote was four to two.'

'In other words, they were afraid that their own necks might actually be on the line,' I said. The fear Morden had stirred up was working to my advantage. 'Undaaris voted for me?'

'Yes.'

So after being bribed by Levistus last year to betray me, Undaaris had turned around and betrayed Levistus right back. There was a certain justice to it. 'Agreed,' I said.

'All right,' Talisid said. 'You and Anne are to meet with Morden and—'

'Not so fast,' I said. 'Let's have it in writing.'

Talisid paused. 'Now?'

'No time like the present.'

'The Council are more than a little busy—'

'Talisid, maybe you don't remember, but this isn't the first time I've made a deal with a Council member,' I said. 'I'm done with working on credit. I get my payment in advance or I don't do it at all.'

'That . . . may take some time.'

I sat back, putting my hands behind my head. 'I'll wait.'

There was more negotiation, but I held firm and to my amazement, the Council actually went through with it. By the next morning, I was holding a piece of paper in my hands with the Council seal stipulating that should I follow the terms listed below, etc., etc., then the outlaw status for myself and my dependents, to whit, Anne Walker, was annulled.

'I hope you realise how rare this is,' Talisid said dryly.

I gave a short laugh. 'Realising isn't exactly top of my thoughts right now.'

'What is?'

I was silent for a moment, weighing the piece of paper in my hands. It was thick and stiff, with only a little flex. One small sheet of paper, with maybe a couple of hundred printed words. 'It was a resolution like this that got Anne and me outlawed last Christmas,' I said quietly. 'One sheet of paper. That was all it took to drive us out of Britain and have us hunted across the world.'

'Yes . . .'

'And now another sheet of paper, and it's all whisked away.' I looked at the communicator, even though I knew Talisid couldn't see me. 'You could have done this at any time.'

'The decision wasn't—'

'I know it wasn't yours,' I said. 'It was the Council's. From that chamber in the War Rooms, they make their laws, and everyone else lives or dies by them. It would have been five minutes' work for them to end our exile. They didn't. That's how much we mean to them.'

I heard Talisid shift. 'The situations have changed somewhat . . .'

'Yeah,' I said. 'This time I've got something they want. Don't worry, Talisid. I'm not going to do anything stupid. But I think I understand how Council politics work a little better now.'

Talisid didn't have an answer to that. 'Are you going to be ready?' he said at last.

'I'll be in touch.'

We finished our conversation and I sat silent for a moment. I knew I should be happy – this death mark had been hanging over my head for so long – but it was hard not to be bitter. All that pain and hardship, and the Council had wiped it away almost absent-mindedly. This was how quickly they could have done something if they'd actually cared.

Then I shook the feeling off. I might have squared things with the Council, but getting that death sentence lifted was only going to help if I survived.

* * *

'There's going to be a what?' I asked over the phone.

'A demonstration.'

'About?'

'The thing with Daniel Goldman,' Lucian said. 'You know?'

Lucian is an adept I first met a year or two ago when he wandered into my shop looking for advice. Most of the adepts I meet that way drift off, but a few stay in touch, and over the years I've picked up a pretty decent information network as a result. It's not much good for learning about what the big dogs are doing, like the Council or Richard – those guys don't really get down to street level – but it does come in useful. 'I heard about it, yeah.'

'So you heard what they did? He was just in that club for a night out. Then the Keepers burst in and they just burnt him to death. No warning, nothing.'

Just in the club for a night out? 'That's not exactly what . . .' I began, then changed my mind. 'Never mind. Since when?'

'Last few days, I guess? Ever since the Council cleared that Keeper.'

I frowned. I hadn't been keeping up with the details, but I had noticed that at some point Daniel Goldman's death had become politicised – adepts had been holding him up as a symbol of the innocent lives crushed under Council oppression. When the results of the inquiry had been released, it had criticised Reyes but had stopped short of issuing any actual punishment, which unsurprisingly hadn't pleased anyone. Still, there was something that didn't quite fit. 'Weren't those findings released about three weeks ago?'

'Yeah.'

'So why are they holding a demonstration now?'

'Took them a while to get organised, I guess.'

'So what are they going to do? Make a bunch of signs and walk up and down outside the War Rooms?'

'Dunno, but a lot of adepts are going,' Lucian said. 'Sensitives, too. Everyone's talking about it; it's supposed to start after sundown. I think it's going to be big.'

Something about this was bothering me. The idea of all those adepts just sitting around for three weeks before suddenly deciding to take action felt wrong. Why would they wait so long?

Unless someone's chosen this particular evening for a reason. 'Are you going?' I asked Lucian.

'I was thinking about it,' Lucian admitted.

'If I were you, I'd stay away.'

'Why?'

'Because right now the Council are expecting an attack,' I said. 'If you march a crowd of adepts up to the War Rooms, they are not going to respond well.'

'*We're* the ones getting attacked.'

'Just listen to me, all right? This is sounding like a really bad idea. And spread the word if you can.'

Lucian agreed, but he sounded half-hearted and I wasn't sure if I'd convinced him. I hung up with a bad feeling, and the more I thought about it, the worse it got. The idea of a crowd of angry adepts trying to do a protest march just as the Council was going to a war footing made me uneasy.

I called Variam, but Vari had his own news. 'I've been drafted,' he told me.

'To do what?'

'Defend the War Rooms, what do you think?'

'Jesus,' I said. 'They're pulling in apprentices now?'

'More like they *really* don't want to lose. The whole Order of the Shield's been mobilised, and half the Star as well. Called in reserves and everything.'

I did some quick mental arithmetic. 'So you're telling me that more than half the combat-capable Keepers in Britain are going to be at the War Rooms just waiting for someone to stick their nose in so that they can blow it off.'

'Looks like,' Variam said. 'Piece of advice: don't walk in first.'

'Yeah, no shit.'

'You know, I'm kind of hoping that Morden does go ahead with this stupid plan,' Variam said. 'I'd love to see the look on his face.'

I frowned. 'This feels wrong.'

'Seems pretty right to me.'

'No, I mean we're missing something,' I said. 'Morden isn't this stupid.'

'Maybe he actually thinks he's going to win,' Variam said. 'I mean, that's what a lot of Dark mages believe, isn't it? They think all Light mages are wimps. And yeah, plenty of them are, but when you never run into the ones who aren't . . .'

'Yes, but Morden's spent the past year and a half on the Council. He should *not* be making this sort of mistake.'

'Will you stop worrying about what Morden's going to do?'

'It's kind of important to know.'

'No,' Variam said. 'It's not. You'll find out sooner or later, and then you'll do what you have to do. You should be worrying about you and Anne.'

I sighed. *Yet another problem I don't know how to solve.* 'I *am* worried. I just don't know what to do about it. When she wouldn't talk to me, I thought that maybe she just wanted to work through it on her own, but she doesn't seem to be getting better.'

'Yeah, well, here's the thing about Anne,' Variam said. 'And this is something that most people don't get. Most people, once they learn what she can do, they think she's indestructible or something. And they're right, kind of. She can take a beating and get back up. But she's got limits . . .'

Variam trailed off. 'Limits?' I asked when he didn't go on.

'Never mind. Just stay close to her.'

'I tried talking—'

'The last thing she needs is another pep talk.'

'Fine,' I said. 'You've known her longer than I have. What do you recommend?'

'I dunno, how about you try telling her how you feel for once?'

'What do you mean?'

'You know exactly what I mean.'

I considered that idea for maybe an eighth of a second before shying away. I did *not* want to deal with that right now. 'This isn't really the time.'

Variam was silent for a moment. 'You know,' he said, 'for someone who's supposed to be so bright, you can be really dumb sometimes.'

'Vari, something useful please?'

'Just remember what I said.'

The day seemed to take for ever, and my mood got worse and worse. Finally, I called Talisid. It took me a while to get through, and when he learnt that I didn't have any new information about Richard or Morden, he didn't seem very interested in continuing the call.

'Verus, I appreciate the information about the adepts,' Talisid cut in, 'but it's something we're aware of. What we want to know about is Morden's plans.'

'I don't think he's going after the War Rooms,' I said.

'You've heard from him?'

'No.'

'You've heard from someone else in his cabal? Or from Drakh's?'

'No,' I admitted.

'Then what's changed?'

'It doesn't feel right.'

'Unless you have something solid—'

'*Listen* to me, all right? None of this feels right. You guys are setting up a trap based on the assumption that Morden is stupid. I've spent the last eight months working for him, and trust me when I say that that is one thing he is most definitely *not*.'

'Yes, Verus, I know,' Talisid said. 'What you may have failed to take into account is that neither are we. You're right: it's very possible that he's not going to go through with this attack. In fact, I'd say that it's likely. Now, consider. What will happen if he calls it off?'

I was silent, thinking. 'Everyone'll know he backed down,' I said after a moment.

'All of the successes Morden has had in the past year have come from being seen as the winning horse. If he commits his forces to an attack, he'll lose. If he backs down, he will also lose.'

'Is that what all this is about?' I said. 'Is that why you've called in so many Keepers to defend the War Rooms tonight? A show of force?'

'It's the ideal solution, don't you think?' Talisid said. 'Regardless of what happens, everyone will know that Morden attempted to overthrow the Council, and failed.'

I thought about it. Suddenly the Council's actions in calling in Vari and the rest of the apprentices made sense. They didn't want a fight – they wanted to win *without* fighting, by forcing Morden to blink. It was a very Light-mage solution, and from their perspective, it made sense.

And set against that was . . . what? Why did I feel that things were going to go so badly? Maybe because I knew Morden better than the Council did. I'd spent a lot of time with the Dark mage over the course of this year, and over the months I'd been forced into a kind of unwilling respect for him. He was clearly and unapologetically one of the bad guys, but he was also very good at what he did, and I didn't believe he'd be beaten this easily.

'Look,' I said. 'The whole reason you wanted me in this position was so that I could report on Richard and Morden's plans. Well, this is my best guess at what they are. Are you going to take it to the Council or not?'

'Yes,' Talisid said after a moment's pause. 'But I can already predict what they're going to say. They're expecting you to hold up your end of the deal.'

'Great.'

'Let me know if you hear anything more.'

I spent the last few hours before Morden's deadline in the Hollow.

'So?' I asked Luna, turning. 'How do I look?'

Luna studied me critically. 'Pretty good,' she said. 'Though I still think you should be taking that sub-machine-gun.'

I was wearing my armour, the plate and mesh that Arachne had made for me, over a set of black clothes. Thin gloves covered my hands (partly for protection, more to avoid fingerprints) and I had a webbing belt around my waist and hips with half a dozen nondescript-looking pouches holding everything from gate stones to healing salves. My feet were covered with a pair of black running shoes, and I had a mask tucked away to hide my face if it became necessary. 'Sends the wrong message,' I said. 'Assuming it really is the War Rooms, the main people we'll be running into are Council security, and I don't really want to shoot them.'

'Won't stop them from shooting you.'

'Which is why I want to be as unencumbered as possible,' I said. 'Besides, if I look unarmed, there's more chance they'll yell at me to put my hands up instead of just shooting on sight.'

'Doesn't carrying a handgun behind your back kind of invalidate the whole "unarmed" thing?'

'I said I wanted to *look* unarmed,' I said. The gun was in the small of my back, held in a holster designed for concealment. I'd have to pull back the flap before I could reach the gun, which could cost me precious seconds in combat, but you can't have everything. 'I'm not leaving my knife behind, either.'

'I don't know what's weirder,' Luna said, 'the fact that you carry a knife with the kind of people you run into, or that it actually seems to work.' She leant back against the tree and sighed. 'I wish I was coming with you.'

'No, you don't,' I said. 'Besides, our deal with the Council only gives amnesty to me and to Anne.'

'I know, I know. You'll call if you need backup?'

'I will, but I wouldn't get your hopes up. If it really is the War Rooms then there'll be gate wards, and without some way to get you in . . .'

'I'll be sitting this one out,' Luna finished. 'Great.'

I walked over to the table where I'd laid out my gear. 'So if you're attacking this place,' Luna asked, 'and Vari's been drafted to defend it, what'll happen if you come face to face?'

'Then I guess we'll be putting on an amateur dramatic performance where he shouts "Surrender, Dark villain!" while I yell that he'll never take me alive.'

Luna grinned. 'I'd like to see that. What are you staring at?'

'This,' I said, tapping the dreamstone.

'You're taking it?'

'Thinking about it.'

'Not sure it's really the time for experiments.'

'Normally I'd agree with you,' I said. 'I'd do that kind of testing in a safe, controlled environment, using divination to make it as risk-free as possible. Which is what I've been doing for three months straight. Maybe it's time I stopped being so safe and controlled.'

'Mm.' Luna watched me as I slipped the dreamstone into one of my pouches and sealed it closed. 'Alex?'

'Yeah?'

'You said that if Morden did attack, then the Crusaders were going to do something.'

'Yeah.'

'Like sending a bunch of people to stop him?' Luna said. 'Including those two mages who tortured Anne?'

'That does seem like a possibility.'

'Is that why you're doing this?'

'No.'

'Really?'

'It's more like a potential side objective.'

'Alex . . .'

'I'm not planning to take any chances I don't have to,' I said. 'But let's just say I'll be on the lookout for opportunities.' I checked my gun one last time and turned to go.

I got back to the real world to find a message from Morden giving me instructions to meet Vihaela via gate and follow her orders. I scanned through the futures, then once I'd found out what I could, I called Anne.

'All we have to do is survive,' I said once I'd finished catching her up. 'If Morden's going ahead with this attack – and it looks like he is – then the Council's going to crucify him. We just have to stay alive until then. Once we do, it's over. We'll be away from Morden and out from under that death sentence too.'

Anne was silent.

'Anne?'

'Yes.'

'You okay?'

'We're going to be meeting Vihaela,' Anne said.

'Yeah.'

'She scares me.' Anne's voice was distant. 'It feels like she wants to take something.'

I sighed inwardly. That death sentence had been hanging over us for a really long time and I'd hoped that the news that it was lifted might have made Anne happy. *So much for that.* 'Anyway, there's good news and bad news,' I said.

'The good news is that we're not going to be immediately grabbed, accused of being traitors and tortured for information the second we step through. So either Morden doesn't know that we've gone to the Council, or he's not planning to do anything about it just yet.'

'What's the bad news?'

'The bad news is that Deleo is going to be there too.'

'All right.'

I paused. 'There anything you want to talk about before we go?'

'Let's just get on with it.'

The tone of Anne's voice worried me. Fleetingly, it occurred to me that while dealing with Morden and Talisid and the Council hadn't exactly been fun, it had at least kept me busy. Anne had had nothing to do but brood, and maybe that was making things worse. But we didn't have time to talk things over. 'Okay. Let's go.'

We gated through into a small sitting room, the kind you'd find in a medium-sized house. Bright daylight was coming through the windows and the air felt warmer than the autumn chill of London – we were probably somewhere far south and either east or west, but I couldn't tell where. Anne had arrived a few seconds before, and I stepped through my own gate and let it close behind me.

The two women in the room were exactly the ones I'd expected to see and exactly the ones I didn't want to spend time with. Vihaela was standing in the centre, dressed in brown and black and red. Rachel – Deleo – was to one side. She had her mask on and was leaning against the wall with her arms folded. She didn't look happy, but then she rarely does.

'Verus,' Vihaela said. 'I'm glad you finally decided to show up. I'd hate to think we were keeping you from something important.'

I didn't rise to the bait. 'I was told you'd have orders for me.'

'I think you mean "for us",' Vihaela said. 'Oh, and it's so nice to see you again, Anne. I was almost starting to think you were avoiding me.' She gave Anne a smile. 'Still no name? You really should do something about that.'

Anne returned Vihaela's gaze silently. 'So where are we going?' I said.

'You,' Vihaela said, 'are going to wait here.'

'Wait for what?'

'Wait for my call.'

'And then you'll want us to . . . ?'

'To do what I tell you.' Vihaela's smile didn't alter. 'I think it was explained to you that you were to follow my instructions?'

I didn't reply.

'Good. Oh, we're under strict communications discipline, so no calls in or out please. I'm sure the three of you will be able to keep yourselves occupied. There's probably a pack of cards or something in the drawers.' She turned and left. I felt her opening a gate the next room over, and then she was gone.

Anne and I exchanged looks. I didn't want to show it in front of Rachel, but I was confused. I'd been expecting some kind of large-scale preparation. Why were we just being left to wait?

Well, there's one person who knows the answer. 'So where are we going?' I asked Rachel.

Rachel stayed with her arms folded, leaning against the wall. 'Where you're told.'

'I got that part.'

Rachel shrugged.

'I thought there was going to be a fight.'

'Because you're so useful in those,' Rachel said sarcastically.

'If we're fighting—'

'No, *we'll* be fighting,' Rachel said. '*You* are going to be useless as always.'

I looked at Rachel, unease nagging at me. *Something's wrong.* Rachel was talking as though there was going to be a fight and she was angry at being left out. But if there was going to be a fight, why *was* she being left out? Richard didn't have so many servants that he could afford to bench someone as powerful as Rachel without good reason, which meant that whatever she was accomplishing by staying here watching us, it was more important than being out there taking part in the attack . . .

They know. All of a sudden, I was sure. Somehow Morden and Richard knew that we'd betrayed them, and we were being held away from the location of the attack until they could deal with us properly.

Rachel spoke without looking at me. 'Don't even think about it.'

Damn it. Had I shown something? *Never mind.* I glanced sideways at Anne and saw her looking back at me, watchful; from her stance, I knew her thoughts hadn't reached the place that mine had, but if I did attack, I knew she'd back me up. On the other side of the room, Rachel shifted slightly, pushing off the wall. I studied the distance between us. Both of us could cross it in maybe one second. Rachel's shield would block my attacks but not Anne's, and if Rachel went for Anne, I could dispel it and use my gun before she could throw it up again. Except . . .

Except in that second, Rachel would have enough time for a disintegrate spell. She couldn't hit both of us; if Anne and I timed our movements correctly, then one of us would be certain to get her, but the other would just as certainly be killed.

I looked at Rachel. Behind her mask, her eyes were alight, and with a chill, I realised that she *wanted* me to go for her. Not much seems to make Rachel happy any more, but as far as I can tell, hurting me is near the top of a short list. I looked at the futures, calculating our chances.

And I found something odd. Rachel would fight, hurt me if she could, kill me if she had to . . . but only if she had to. If I just ran, she'd try to stop me, but she wouldn't try to put a disintegrate ray into my back. About the only thing I could think of that could explain it was the threat of extreme force, which meant explicit orders from Vihaela, Morden, or Richard . . . actually, probably just Richard.

You don't go out of your way to keep a known traitor alive, especially not if you're about to finish them off anyway. I hesitated.

Rachel shook her head in disgust and looked away. 'You just never change.'

I looked at Rachel. *I'm going about this the wrong way.* Rachel's always had the edge on me when it comes to brute strength; I shouldn't be trying to outfight her. 'So, have you thought about it?'

'Thought about what?'

'What I told you last time.'

'No.'

'Seems like Vihaela's settled in pretty comfortably as your boss,' I said. 'And she's giving you orders to your face now?'

Silence.

'I guess Richard and Morden must really trust her, to give her authority over a job like this,' I said. 'I mean, it's obviously really important to them. They'd want to have their best people on it.' I tilted my head. 'Kind of odd they've set you to watch us.'

Rachel's eyes snapped, but she didn't have an answer. 'You do realise you've been replaced, right?' I said. 'Back then, you were Richard's Chosen. Now you're just another mage.'

'I'm still his Chosen!'

'If he'd been going to move you up to bigger and better things, he'd have done it by now. There isn't going to be some big reward waiting at the end of the tunnel. You're not his star pupil. You're just an early experiment.'

Rage flashed in Rachel's eyes, and she took a step towards me. I watched her warily but didn't jump aside; I still couldn't see any futures in which she actually attacked. 'You,' Rachel said tightly. 'You think you're so clever. I hope Vihaela *does* take me along. It'll all be worth it if I get to see the look on your face. Whatever she's got in mind—' Rachel stopped.

'What?' All of a sudden, I was wary. 'What are you hoping?'

Rachel turned away.

I took a step towards her. 'If there's something you want to—'

'Shut up,' Rachel said. 'I might have to watch you, but

I don't have any orders about having to listen to you running your mouth. He only said I had to keep you alive. Nothing about being able to talk. So if you don't shut up right now, I'm going to break your jaw.'

I wondered if Rachel was bluffing, and I looked at the futures where I tested it. *Ouch.* Okay, she wasn't bluffing. I looked at Anne, who only gave me a tiny shrug.

Time passed. I stayed standing in the room, and to all appearances it would have looked as though I was doing nothing, but in truth I was looking into the futures in which I used my phone or communicator, trying to get in touch with Luna or Variam or Talisid. In all of them Rachel interfered, but I was able to get brief glimpses in which I was able to try completing the calls. In every case, I didn't get an answer, and that made me uneasy. The longer we stayed waiting here, the more certain I became that something was happening. I didn't know what that something was, but I didn't think it was anything good.

I looked sideways at Anne, but she didn't meet my gaze. She was staring through the window, and that bothered me too. Anne and I have been through a lot, and I'd become used to her intuitively reading my moods. Now all of a sudden we felt disconnected, as though she'd signed off. It felt ominous, as though I was on my own. I wanted to boost our chances, but I couldn't see any course of action that wouldn't make things worse.

I sensed Vihaela coming back a long time before she returned; she still wasn't coming to kill us, but she was bringing company. The futures were spidered, shifting; it seemed events were altering her plans. For a moment, it looked as though she'd be here in five minutes; then there was a shift and it was fifteen, then ten, then all of a sudden she was making the gate right now and I turned my head towards the door as I felt the portal opening in the next room.

Vihaela came striding in, and her manner had changed. She looked keyed up and alert, and there was a blackened patch on her clothes that I didn't think had been there before. Behind her was Archon, dressed in his signature head-to-toe armour and full-face helmet. My divination had seen him coming so I wasn't surprised, but the sight of him made me realise just how many people Richard was committing to this.

'We're on,' Vihaela said to Rachel. She didn't speak to Archon, but something about their stance suggested they were familiar with each other. 'Get moving.'

Rachel pointed at Archon. 'What's *he* doing here?'

'Gating you to the control room,' Vihaela said. 'Do as he says.'

'I'm not taking orders from him.'

'Do not even *think* about giving me shit on this one, Deleo.' Vihaela's voice was hard and she stared at Rachel with a raptor's gaze. 'You do as I say or I'll burst every blood vessel in your lungs and leave you to drown in your own blood. Pick one. Now.'

Rachel glared hate at Vihaela, and just for an instant I saw a flash of deadly violence, then it was gone. 'Fine,' Rachel said, biting off the word.

Vihaela was already turning to Anne. 'Come with me.'

'Where—?' Anne started to ask.

Vihaela's eyes narrowed. It was a very slight movement but it was enough to make Anne stop. Vihaela jerked her head and Anne began to follow.

A spike of dread went through me. 'Wait.'

'Verus, this is a *very* bad time to get in my way,' Vihaela said. 'So I will only say this once. If you try to argue or spin me some line about taking you instead, then I will hurt you.'

That had been exactly the approach I'd been about to try. Vihaela and Anne started towards the door and without thinking, I took a step forward, opening my mouth—

'Alex,' Anne said to me without turning. Her voice was soft but clear. 'Don't.'

I hesitated, then Anne and Vihaela disappeared and the moment was gone. I was left alone with Archon and Rachel.

'I wouldn't worry,' Archon said. 'You'll see her soon enough.'

I shot the Dark mage a look, but Rachel was already turning on Archon. 'You think we're just going to do whatever you say?'

'It would be advisable,' Archon said. I felt him starting to cast one of those strange gates that wasn't a gate.

'And what if I don't?'

'Follow, or don't,' Archon said. 'The choice is yours.' He glanced at me. 'Oh, and once you step through, duck.'

'Step through to where?' I asked. On the other side of the portal-to-be I could sense battle and danger, but I couldn't recognise the destination.

'I'm not going anywhere without—' Rachel began.

'Time,' Archon said, and a black gate flickered and formed in the air in front of him, revealing a tiled hallway. He stepped through without waiting.

I hesitated for an instant, but wherever Archon was going, our mission was there and so was Anne. I stepped through.

16

My feet came down onto smooth concrete. I was in a corridor with recessed doorways, and I could hear shouting. Footsteps sounded behind me and I turned.

Two men rounded the corner. They were carrying guns, and I reached instinctively for my holster, then hesitated as my brain registered what they were wearing. Those were Council security uniforms—

The man at the front saw me and his gun came up. I dived into one of the doorways, bullets whining past. The concrete recesses were thick, like a bunker, and the door was steel.

I looked back just in time to see Rachel step through, the gate fading out of existence behind her. Gunfire barked and there was a flare of blue-green light, bullets splashing off her shield. With an irritated glance, Rachel sent two sea-green rays flashing down the corridor, quick and precise.

There was a brief, agonised scream, and the gunfire stopped.

I poked my head out of the doorway. Where the men had been were two small, scattered piles of dust. A lone sub-machine-gun lay on the floor next to them. 'This is your idea of a staging point?' Rachel said to Archon.

Archon was standing in the middle of the corridor; somehow all the fire had missed him. 'This way,' he said, and turned down the corridor.

I gave a last glance back at the remains of the Council

security men and hurried after Archon. Now that I had the time to listen, I could hear shouting and gunfire from all around us. The rattle of sub-machine-guns mixed with the *whoompf* of fire spells, and I could sense more combat magic. We'd come right into the middle of a battle. 'Where are—?' I began.

Archon didn't break stride. 'Eyes right, Verus.'

I looked right and started. We were passing a corridor and two constructs were charging down it straight towards us, grey-black panther-like forms with glowing blue eyes. Wisps of mist trailed from their claws as they covered the ground in great bounding leaps, closing the distance shockingly fast. Sixty feet, forty feet, twenty— 'Deleo!' I shouted, and jumped out of the way.

Rachel turned and her eyes narrowed, sea-green light glowing as she began to bring her hand up, but as Archon walked past, he tossed something small and round from one hand. It hit the floor just inside the corridor and there was a flash of magic and a shimmer as a transparent barrier formed, blocking the entrance. The constructs – icecats – crashed into the barrier a half-second later. The impact would have broken any living creature's neck but they just rebounded and threw themselves at it again. Rachel frowned, the disintegrate spell hovering at her hand.

I stared at the icecats clawing at the other side of the barrier. Their eyes burned with a cold fire, and I could almost imagine that I could feel the chill in the air. The barrier was force magic, and now that I looked at it, it felt similar to the ones I used . . . *very* similar. I turned to Archon to see that he hadn't stopped walking. In fact, he was disappearing around a corner as I watched.

'Arsehole,' Rachel muttered, and followed.

I hurried after her, and as I did I scanned the futures in which I went left and right, trying to figure out where the hell the Dark mages had brought me. This had to be a Council installation, but where? It couldn't be the War Rooms – the floors were concrete, the doors looked like the kind you'd find in an industrial facility and most of all, there wasn't enough security. If this had been the Council headquarters, every square inch should have been crammed with Keepers and constructs, but from what I could see, the defending humans seemed to be mostly if not entirely ordinary humans, and they were losing. *Where's Anne?*

We caught up with Archon at the next intersection. He was standing just short of the crossroads, head tilted as though he was listening for something. 'So?' Rachel demanded as we walked up. 'Where's the control room?'

'Just around the corner,' Archon said.

Rachel began to stride past.

'Look out!' I snapped.

Rachel's reactions are fast. She jumped back as bullets whistled past, as well as something else: a beam of some kind of yellow-orange light, there and gone in an instant. It left behind a strange burning scent, as though the air was on fire. Rachel rounded on Archon. 'Why the fuck is it still guarded?'

'Because there are people there.'

Rachel's face darkened, and she took a step towards Archon. 'I'm getting a little tired of—'

'Wait,' Archon said. It was hard to tell through the helmet and the voice distorter, but he didn't seem concerned.

'Wait for what?'

I looked into the futures in which I took a peek around the corner. In at least two of them I got my head blown off – the people down that corridor were *really* trigger-happy – but I got enough of a look to see that the corridor ended in a T-junction behind which was a steel door that wouldn't have looked out of place on a missile silo. In front of the door, metal tables had been overturned to form a makeshift barricade, and a squad of Council security had set up behind it. There was a body lying in the corridor, not dressed in a Council security uniform this time. Apparently Morden's men weren't having it all their own way.

'Wait for *what*?' Rachel said again.

I wanted to warn the Council forces to back off. They were just doing their jobs, and knowing the Council, they probably hadn't had any warning of what might be coming. But Rachel and Archon were standing right there, and I'd already seen that if I stuck my head out to try to talk to the guards, they'd just shoot me.

I sighed inwardly. *Sorry, guys.*

There was a shout, followed by a flat *wham*. More gunfire erupted; there was the hissing sound of that beam weapon, followed by a scream and an unpleasant splattering sound. The gunfire cut off and there was silence.

Archon was already walking past me and around the corner. 'I'm really starting to hate this guy,' Rachel muttered, and followed.

The barricade at the end of the corridor was gone. The tables had been overturned, and the bodies of the defenders lay where they'd fallen . . . which in some cases meant in several places at once. I avoided looking too closely at the pieces of the body to the far left. Three men in masks were standing in front of the door, but it wasn't hard to identify the tall, slim figure at the centre who'd done most of the work.

'Onyx,' Archon said as he walked up. His voice was as toneless as ever, but somehow I had the feeling he wasn't happy.

Onyx is a force magic user and battle mage, and one of those people who's just plain bad news. When I first met Onyx, he was Morden's Chosen, young and brutal and willing to fight and kill at the slightest provocation. That had been five years ago, and as far as I could tell, the only thing that had changed since then was that he was slightly less young. You'd think he'd have grown a little over the years, but apparently Onyx was one of those people who'd found a thug-shaped hole into which to fit his thug-shaped life and had decided that there was no reason to mess with a winning formula. Looking at him, it suddenly occurred to me that maybe the fact that Morden had picked me rather than Onyx as his aide might be a sign that he wasn't all that impressed with how Onyx had turned out either.

If that was the case, it would give Onyx yet another reason to hate me, as if he needed one. My life would really be so much easier if the Dark mages I've known had been a little more selective in their choice of apprentices.

I sensed rather than saw Onyx's eyes flicker towards me behind the mask; it was only for an instant, but I didn't like what it implied. 'What?' Onyx said to Archon.

'You were ordered by Morden to stay away tonight,' Archon said.

Onyx just looked at Archon and the message was clear. *What are you going to do about it?*

Archon stood quite still. I didn't sense anything in the futures, but for a moment – just a moment – I had the feeling that Archon *was* going to do something about it. Then he walked away.

Which left me alone with Onyx, Rachel and two other Dark mages I didn't know. I tensed silently, but for the moment, all four ignored me. One of the other Dark mages was examining the door. 'Sealed off,' he said over his shoulder.

'Then get out of the way,' Rachel said, lifting her hand towards the door.

The Dark mage turned, then jumped aside. I took one look at what was about to happen and dived for cover.

Green light stabbed from Rachel's hand, and blades of force flew from Onyx. They struck the door and bounced straight back. Rachel's disintegrate spell missed Onyx by a couple of feet, turning a section of wall into dust, while Onyx's force blades whined lethally as they ricocheted all over the corridor. One of them barely missed my head; another slammed right into Rachel, making her stagger as her shield took the hit.

'Are you crazy?' the Dark mage who'd been at the door shouted.

'What the fuck was that?' Rachel demanded.

Reflector shields, I thought. They're designed to bounce ranged spells back at the caster; they're more common in duels, but it wasn't the first time I'd heard of them used to secure a location.

'Reflec-shields,' the Dark mage said.

'So what are—?' Rachel began.

Onyx fired again, and this time *everyone* ducked. Rachel rounded on Onyx as the echoes faded away. 'Are you out of your fucking mind?' she snarled.

'Stop it, you idiot!' the other Dark mage shouted.

Onyx moved forward to inspect the door. As far as I could tell, it wasn't even scratched. 'Now what?' the second Dark mage said.

The first Dark mage frowned at the door. 'There are people in there.' His eyes went up. 'And they're watching.'

Rachel and I followed the Dark mage's gaze to a small sphere mounted on the wall: a camera. Rachel lifted a hand to destroy it.

'Wait,' I said.

'For what?'

'Let me try talking.'

'About what?'

Onyx was still at the door and I could sense some kind of force magic. I didn't know how long it'd take him to find a way through, but I was pretty certain he could smash through sooner or later. I stepped directly under the camera, making sure it could see me clearly, and spoke up towards the microphone attachment. 'This is a message to the Council security force defending the control room,' I said. 'You don't know me, but please listen to what I have to say. You need to evacuate the control room as soon as possible.'

Rachel stared at me with an "are you serious?" look. I kept going, not meeting her eye. 'I know you'll have some sort of alternative entrance. Or a back exit. I recommend you use it, and fast. The mages outside are looking for a way in, and once they find one – which they will – they're going to kill you. I strongly suggest that you withdraw first.'

Rachel rolled her eyes, turned and stalked around the corner.

Onyx was readying some kind of force spell, and I could sense it gathering power. I spoke hurriedly; I didn't think I had much time. 'Look, you guys are Council security, right? I don't know what the Council is paying you, but it's not worth your lives. It's not like they're here dying for *you*, is it? Just get the hell out. If they kick up a fuss later, you can point to all the dead bodies outside as to why you didn't stick around. They'll have bigger things to worry about than punishing . . .'

I trailed off. Onyx was still working on his spell, but I could sense magic from where Rachel had disappeared. It felt like . . . I frowned. *A gate spell?* I might not know where we were, but I'd already sensed that this place had the spatial wards. Trying to open a gate here would probably lead to the thing either blowing up in your face or—

I felt a gate open and close.

Magic flared from within the control room, sharp and precise, once, twice, three times. There was a muffled sound, just barely audible through the steel door. It might have been a scream.

Onyx looked up from his spell, and he and the other two Dark mages paused, waiting. The corridor was silent. As I listened, I realised I couldn't hear any more gunfire from elsewhere either.

'Was that her?' one of the Dark mages said.

There was a click and the heavy steel door to the control room swung open, revealing Rachel in the doorway. 'What are you waiting for?' she said irritably. 'An invitation?'

The Dark mages glanced at each other and walked in. Rachel looked at me. 'You coming or not?'

I hesitated, then followed Rachel inside. She shut the door behind me with a thump.

The inside of the control room was walled in black. Office chairs sat in front of long, curving desks, and on the desks and walls were more than a dozen computer monitors, showing camera feeds and status reports. A couple of the chairs had been knocked over, and as I turned my head to look, I saw a scattering of dust next to each of them. I looked at Rachel. 'Was that necessary?'

'I don't give a shit,' Rachel said. She tossed something at me.

I caught the object and looked at it. It was black, small enough to fit into the palm of the hand, and radiated low-level magic of some kind, probably universal. 'I'm done babysitting you,' Rachel said. 'Stay in this room and don't talk to me.' She stalked away.

I watched Rachel go with a frown. Onyx was arguing with one of the other Dark mages, while the last was working at one of the computer banks, leaning in to stare at the screen. For the moment, no one seemed to be paying attention to me.

I took a closer look at the item in my hand. I'd seen similar focuses before, and it didn't take me long to figure out how it worked. I placed my thumb on the depression at the top, channelled a thread of magic into it, and spoke. 'Hello?'

There was a moment's silence, then Vihaela's voice spoke up. 'Took you long enough.'

'Where's Anne?'

'You're in the control room, yes?'

I wasn't in the mood for games. 'You know I am.'

'Find the camera feeds. Section twelve.'

Two quick strides brought me to the security desk. None of the Dark mages did anything to stop me, and I bent over the keyboard, scanning the monitors. One of the screens showed a map of the facility. *Okay, definitely not the War Rooms.* It seemed to be some kind of . . . prison? No, those weren't cells; they were security gates . . .

Vihaela's voice sounded. 'Tick-tock, Verus.'

'Found you,' I said curtly. One of the monitors was divided into nine camera feeds. Three were black, four more showed nothing but empty corridors, but one showed the entrance to what looked like a giant safe, and in front of it was a group of four figures. Vihaela was easy to pick out, but standing a little to her left and off to the side was a slim figure with shoulder-length hair. I felt something inside me ease a little. All the same . . . 'Put Anne on.'

'Don't trust me?' Vihaela said. She sounded amused.

'No,' I said curtly.

In the camera feed, I saw Vihaela toss something to Anne, who caught it and turned it over in her hands. There was a moment's pause, then I heard a soft voice through the focus. 'Alex?'

I felt a rush of relief. 'You okay?'

'I'm not hurt.'

'You didn't get caught up in the fighting?' I was looking at the map, and if I was reading it right, Anne was deeper than me into the facility – much deeper. To get to where she was, she'd have had to go past a lot of guard posts.

'There were guards. Vihaela . . . dealt with them. Do you—?'

On the screen, I saw Anne flinch as something flew out of her hands and back to Vihaela. 'Catch up later, Verus,' Vihaela said. 'We've got work to do.'

'So are you going to tell me why you dragged us down here?'

'We're getting through this door,' Vihaela said. 'You're going to help.'

I stared at the door. It looked pretty heavy-duty. 'You want to know if it's trapped?'

'That sort of thing.'

'That'd be a lot easier if I was there with you.'

'Missing me already?' Vihaela sounded amused. 'No, I think I'll keep you right there. Now stop stalling and make yourself useful.'

I glared at Vihaela's image on the monitor. What's she planning now? I scanned and found a local security display. 'The door's got a signature lock of some kind; looks like a retinal scan but there might be another way to bypass it, probably magical. Then there's a key code . . .'

As I spoke I was looking through the cameras, and a set of feeds at the top caught my eye. They seemed to be showing external views of the facility. Several were corridors with people passing by, and something about them made me think of underground tunnels, but the ones I focused on were the three at the top. They showed a roundabout with a steady stream of traffic. It was night, and cars were circling the arches at the centre and moving through the traffic lights. The angle was weird but the scenery was familiar, and I knew I'd seen it before. I just needed to . . .

Something clicked and all of a sudden I knew where I was. The image on the cameras was Old Street Roundabout. And that meant I was in—

The Vault. All this time, he was going for the Vault.

'Well?' Vihaela said.

'I'm working on it,' I said absently. Inwardly, my mind was whirling. So this was what Morden had been planning. He'd lied to me and to everyone else, let them think he was going to attack the War Rooms, when really he'd been . . .

Had he lied to me? A conversation flashed through my head. Vihaela's words: *'Morden promised me both of you.'*

My answer: *'Did he really? Or did he just imply she'd be coming, and let you hear what you wanted to hear . . . ?'*

'Shit,' I said out loud.

'Need that code, Verus.'

'I said I'm working on it.' So that was where the rumours about an attack on the War Rooms had come from. *Morden* had planted them to draw off the Council's defences. All that soul-searching I'd done about whether to tip off the Council had been a complete waste of time. I could have told Morden to his face that I was going to sell him out, and it wouldn't have made the slightest bit of difference.

Everything made more sense now. That had been why Vihaela had kept me away during those last few hours – so that I couldn't glimpse their plans and pass on any last-minute warnings. And it was why they'd split us up. If I didn't help Vihaela, Anne would be on the chopping block.

But some things hadn't changed. My deal with the Council still held, and even if the diversion worked and this attack succeeded, Morden was going to get it in the neck. Attacking the Vault wasn't as big as attacking the War Rooms, but there was no way that the Council would let him get away with it. Once this battle was over, win or lose, Morden was going down.

I just had to make sure he didn't take me with him.

All of this went through my head in less than five seconds. 'You know, if you can't find a way to unlock it, we can just blow it off its hinges,' Vihaela said.

'No,' I said curtly. With Anne next to Vihaela, I had to help, at least for now. 'The doors in this place are reflec-shielded. Put me on to the guy who's working on that keypad and I'll see what I can do.'

Vihaela handed me over and I started working through

the security systems, and as I did I kept watching the other monitors, piecing together what was going on. Morden's forces had taken full control of the facility – the remaining Council forces were either dead or had fled. The Dark mages had broken through into some lower-priority storage rooms and were busy looting them, but the main storage vault was behind the doors that Vihaela was trying to get through now. The doors would lead into a section which had no camera coverage at all, and then into the Vault itself, which did. Live feeds showed lines of shelves filled with crates and pedestals holding sealed boxes.

The security systems weren't enough to keep out the Dark mages, but then, that's what you'd expect. Most security isn't meant to be impenetrable – it's just meant to keep intruders tied up long enough for reinforcements to arrive. The Dark mages must have set off every alarm in the place while they were fighting their way in, and right now, a Council strike team had to be assembling. How long until it got here?

Casually, I took a glance back at the other people in the control room. Rachel and Onyx were arguing about something, and the other Dark mages were busy with the computers. I slid my communicator focus from where I'd had it hidden and slipped it into my ear. This place was shielded, but there was still a chance that I might be able to get through to Vari or Luna.

For the next few minutes, I multitasked, giving advice to the Dark mage trying to get into the Vault while also exploring the futures in which I tried to get in touch with Vari. Divining for two different sets of futures at once is tricky, but I was making good headway . . . until something caught my eye and all of a sudden I had something new to worry about.

There had been a brief and highly unlikely future in which Rachel and the other two Dark mages had all left the control room at the same time, leaving me alone in the room with Onyx. It had vanished almost as soon as it had appeared, but it had been there long enough, and I shot a glance back over my shoulder. Onyx wasn't looking in my direction, and to a casual glance he seemed absorbed in the contents of one of the computer screens, but now that I knew what to look for, I noticed that he was turned at just the right angle to watch me in his peripheral vision. To all appearances, Onyx was just sitting there, but as soon as the other three Dark mages left the two of us alone . . .

Shit. All of a sudden I felt very vulnerable. The tight confines of the control centre was exactly where I did *not* want to be fighting a battle mage whose speciality was hitting things until they broke. I needed a plan, and fast.

'Light on the panel's gone orange,' the Dark mage said over the communicator.

'Means it's on standby,' I said absently. 'Wait sixty seconds, then input the same code again.' What if I tried leaving the room? Anne and Vihaela weren't that far away; I could get to them pretty quickly . . . no, Rachel was going to stop me. *Shit.* I needed help, but I didn't have Luna or Vari this time. What I needed was someone onsite already, whom I could count on . . .

An idea came to mind and I scanned the monitors again. *There.* On one of the screens showing the atrium, I could see a bulky figure that I thought I recognised. I dug around in one of my pockets and pulled out a thin metal probe, then channelled a thread of magic into the communicator. I'd already seen that Vihaela had locked the communicator so that it could only talk to hers, but I'm pretty good at working around those kinds of things. A thread-thin pulse of magic disabled the restrictions for just long enough to send a message ping. *Now I just have to hope that he checks it soon . . .*

'What are you doing?' Rachel said.

I glanced back at Rachel, making the probe disappear into my palm. 'What do you think?'

'Who are you talking to?' Rachel demanded.

'Your boss,' I said. I held up Vihaela's communicator. 'You want to take over? Be my guest.'

Rachel stared suspiciously, then there was a rustle and Vihaela's voice came from the communicator. 'Verus. What's the hold-up?'

Rachel turned away and I let out a breath before speaking into the receiver. 'It's done. Shields should deactivate in a second; you can cut your way through.'

'Good,' Vihaela said. 'Stay on the line.' On the screen, I saw Vihaela give orders and a Dark mage stepped forward, conjuring a blaze of light that made the camera flicker.

It would take them maybe five minutes to get through. I looked through the futures in which I tried using my own communicator, and my heart leapt as this time I saw movement. Casually, I turned my back to Rachel and to Onyx and spoke under my breath. 'Vari, this is Alex. Come in. Vari, this is Alex. Come in.'

For a long moment there was silence, then Variam's voice spoke into my ear, the signal clear and strong. '*Alex?* I've been trying to call you for hours! Where have you been?'

I heard a footfall behind me and knew that Rachel was within earshot. I held Vihaela's communicator to my ear, pretending to talk into it. 'Okay, keep that up. You should burn through in a few minutes.'

On the other end of the line, Variam paused. 'What?'
'Yes.'

'What are you talking about?'

'No, that should be okay.' I could still feel Rachel behind me. *Please, Vari, figure it out.*

'I don't— wait.' I could sense the light bulb going off in Variam's head. 'Is someone listening in and you can't talk?'

'Yes.'

'It's Morden's goons, isn't it?'

'That's right.'

'Shit,' Variam said. 'Um . . .'

'Look, just tell me what you can see from your end.'

I could hear Variam snort. 'What I can see? Everything's gone to shit, that's what. You remember that adept demonstration? Well, it started quiet, just a bunch of teenagers hanging around out in the street. Then the numbers started to fill up. We'd been told to expect a hundred, maybe a hundred and fifty – turns out there were thousands. The Keepers all got deployed, there were security squads around, everyone was ready to seal off the War Rooms if they needed to. Then everything hit the fan.'

'What happened?'

'Hell if I know. Some Keepers were saying that there were Dark mages in the crowd – whatever it was, someone started shooting and it got ugly real fast. A bunch of people are dead, the Council have the whole place on lockdown and the area's being is being cordoned off and searched. If they—'

'Diversion,' I said.

'What?'

'It's a diversion. You're looking in the wrong place.'

'Yeah,' Variam said. 'Landis said the same thing. He's

sure this whole thing is just to pull the Keepers off the real target, keep them busy at the War Rooms, but . . . We were getting alarms from the Vault and Southampton before the lines got cut. You at one of those?'

'Yes.'

'The Vault?'

'Yes.'

'I thought so. I'll tell who I can, but the Council's in panic mode. They're still convinced that this is all some sort of bluff and the real attack's coming in at the War Rooms any minute. It'll probably be an hour before they're done rounding up the demonstrators and—'

'That'll be too long,' I said shortly.

'Anne's there too?'

'Yes.'

'You're both okay?'

'Maybe not for much longer.'

'Shit. I'll see what I can do. Vari out.' The line went dead.

I swore inwardly. In a crisis, the Council is just too slow. The only person I could call who might be able to do something fast enough was Talisid, and that would take time I didn't have.

'There.' The Dark mage at the other terminal straightened up. 'We're clear.' He looked at Rachel. 'You can handle things from here.'

'Where do you think you're going?' Rachel said.

'West wing.'

'You're not going anywhere until we're done.'

'Tough shit,' the Dark mage said shortly. 'We had a talk with you-know-who and he gave us our jobs. We've done ours. You have a problem, ask him.' He headed towards the exit, his companion following.

Rachel scowled but let them go. Feeling my eyes, she turned to me. 'What are you looking at?'

I turned back to the monitors. *Shit.* Now the control room was empty except for me and Rachel and Onyx, both of whom would easily make the top five list of mages I did *not* want to be locked in a room with. The only exits to the room were the door we'd come in by, and a similar one on the far side. Both were reinforced, and auto-locking. If I could get onto the other side of them, then with the reflector shields, even Rachel or Onyx would have trouble breaking through in time . . . but both were a good thirty feet away, and I did not like my chances of making it before they reacted.

On the monitors, Vihaela's team finished cutting through the heavy doors. The centre of the door swayed, then collapsed, falling silently to the floor with an impact that would have shaken the walls if I'd been close enough to feel it. 'Good job,' Vihaela said over the comm. 'See you on the other side.'

'Wait,' I said. 'There are two corridors between you and the main vault. I don't know what's—'

'I'm sure we'll be fine.' The comm cut off and I saw Vihaela gesture to Anne. They walked in, another Dark mage at the front with Vihaela right behind.

I swore silently. I didn't care if Vihaela ran into trouble, but Anne was another matter. Just as bad, Vihaela was now out of contact. If Onyx figured that out . . .

From behind me I heard Onyx straighten, and I closed my eyes silently. *Why can't anything ever go right?*

'Deleo,' Onyx said.

'What?'

'Take a walk.'

Rachel glared at Onyx. Onyx hadn't treated Rachel kindly on their first meeting, and that had been *before* he'd tried to kill her. It had been years ago, but from the way Rachel was looking at him, I was pretty sure she hadn't forgotten. 'Why?'

'So Verus and I can talk.'

'Why should—?' Rachel began to say, then stopped as she got it.

I saw the futures flicker, and I could almost watch the thoughts going through Rachel's head. Her first reaction was to tell Onyx where to stick it, just out of sheer bloody-mindedness. Then a new thought: *Wait, I could just say yes. Why not let Onyx do it for me?* The counter-argument: *Richard ordered me not to hurt him. If I do, I'll be in trouble.* The other voice: *But it won't be you, will it? You just need to say you weren't around . . .*

Slowly, Rachel turned towards me, her eyes watching from behind her mask, flat and unreadable. I saw the futures flicker, and I knew she was making the choice. I held very still, afraid to say a word. I knew how much Rachel hated me; nothing I could say would make things better and the sound of my voice would definitely make things worse. *Come on*, I prayed silently. *Just give me a little luck . . .*

The futures shifted and settled, the other branches winking out. 'You know,' Rachel said, 'I could go for some fresh air.'

'No!' I took a step towards Rachel. 'We're supposed to be on the same side!'

'You've never been on my side.'

'I've been helping Vihaela—'

'You've been helping Vihaela because she threatened to kill your girlfriend.' Rachel's voice was contemptuous. 'You helped Morden because he threatened to kill *you*. You never do anything unless there's something in it for you. I have no idea why Morden was desperate enough to pick you.' Rachel glanced at Onyx. 'Or maybe I do.'

I couldn't see Onyx's expression change, but I saw violence spike in the futures and I knew that that comment had not improved his mood. 'Either way,' Rachel said, 'I figure I'm doing him a favour.'

'I can help you,' I began.

'No, you can't.'

'I can tell you—'

'No, you won't.'

'Will you just *listen*?' I snapped.

'Why?' Rachel said. 'Everything you say is bullshit.'

I took a breath. There had to be something that would get through to her. 'We were apprentices together once. We were even friends, or something close to it. If that means anything to you, if it ever meant anything to you, then help me now.' I paused. 'Please.'

Rachel stared at me for a long second, as though she were weighing something up inside of her. 'Did you really think that would work?' she said at last.

'I—'

'Shut up.' Rachel looked at me in disgust. 'I am so sick of your shit. You've been trying to get to me for months, haven't you? What did you think was going to happen? You'd give me a speech and then I'd go, "Oh, yes, Alex! I want to be a good girl! I'll do anything you say!"' Rachel shook her head. 'Get this clear. I will *never* help you. You might be able to trick the others, but it doesn't work on me. And right now? The way I see it, either Onyx kills you or you kill him.' Rachel shrugged. 'I'm fine either way.' She turned and left the room.

Leaving me alone with Onyx.

'Well, well,' Onyx said, and his lips curved in a smile.

I stood silently, taking in Onyx's stance. The Dark mage was standing relaxed on the other side of the control room, his hands hanging loosely by his sides. He wore a belt with a couple of items holstered, but as far as I could see he wasn't carrying any weapons. He didn't need them. Onyx's force magic can punch a hole through a concrete wall, and his shields are strong enough to take hits from military heavy weapons. Nothing I was carrying would even scratch him.

There were two exits from the control room: the one Rachel had used, and the back way, leading deeper into the facility. Onyx was blocking my path to the front door, but in doing so he'd left me a clear path to the back one. I checked – yes, only locked from the outside. All I had to do was hit the button by the door and yank on the handle.

Except that in the time it'd take me to do that, Onyx could kill me three times over. I needed a distraction.

'Must really suck when even she hates you,' Onyx said.

I rolled my eyes. Onyx was trying to put me off-balance, scare me before moving in for the kill. It might have worked if he hadn't been so bad at it. 'Give me a break.'

'I bet—'

'Blah, blah, look how pathetic I am.'

'You know—'

'Blah, blah, look how smart you are, blah,' I said. 'You think so slowly that by the time you've opened your mouth I've had time to hear the whole sentence. Twice.'

Onyx's mouth twisted in a snarl. No one likes getting interrupted, and Dark mages tend to have even less tolerance for it than most. 'See how fast you think when I split your head open.'

'Right, brutal violence,' I said. 'Your go-to solution for every problem. It ever occur to you that this is *why* Morden's been passing you over? He needs someone whose CV doesn't start and end with "sociopathic killing machine".'

Violence was flashing through the futures, and I knew that Onyx was within a sentence or two of jumping straight to the killing. 'You know what?' I said. 'Fine.' I pulled my knife from my belt sheath and started stalking towards Onyx. 'You want a fight? That's exactly what you're going to get.'

Onyx had been expecting me to run. He hadn't been expecting me to attack, and just for an instant he hesitated before a spray of blades flashed out at me.

An instant before Onyx cast, I switched directions, sprinting for the door. A monitor behind me exploded in sparks, an alarm went off and I dropped my knife and threw gold discs to the left and right. I called out a command word, feeling the force barrier snap up behind me just in time to intercept the next spell; Onyx saw the wall, destroyed it with a spell, sent another volley of force blades to shred the whole area in which I'd been standing . . .

. . . and in that time I'd yanked the door open and ducked out of sight.

The door led into an empty corridor. The distance to the next junction was maybe fifty feet away, and against most people I could have covered that in time, but Onyx is *fast*, and he was already sprinting after me. I knew that I wouldn't make it.

So instead of running, I flattened myself against the wall. Onyx came charging through the doorway, his force shield radiating around him. He passed within two feet of me and I ducked in behind. Onyx caught the movement in his peripheral vision and whirled – too late. I slammed the door in his face and the lock clicked just an instant before Onyx's next spell hit it from the other side.

I heard the *wham* of the force magic and felt the door vibrate. I let out a breath, feeling my heart hammering. *Too close.*

An alarm was beeping, loud and insistent: *meep meep meep meep meep*. Looking around, I saw that Onyx's spells had done a number on the control room: a chair had been cut in half and shards of broken monitors covered the floor. A message was flashing on one of the surviving screens: LOCKDOWN ENABLED.

There was another *wham* and I heard the door vibrate behind me, and that galvanised me into action. Onyx would find a way through that door soon. I crossed the room to the other exit; it was the one Rachel had used, and I'd have to watch out for her, but I'd deal with that problem when—

I paused. The door wasn't going to open.

I hit the button just to make sure; a red light blinked above the panel, but nothing happened. I pushed it again. 'Come on, come on . . .'

Meep meep meep went the alarm. Over the noise, I heard a voice coming from the communicator. '—rus?' The alarm was drowning it out. '—there?'

I grabbed the communicator off the desk. 'Yes.'

'Sounds a little noisy in there.'

'What?' I needed to get that door open before Onyx found a way in. I checked the monitors and found the local security settings. The doors were outlined in red, and I clicked the unlock button. An error message flashed: LOCKDOWN ENABLED.

Vihaela said something that I couldn't hear over the meeping of the alarm. 'Little busy!' I shouted. There was a button marked 'All Clear' and I clicked it. The alarm cut off. All of a sudden, the only noise was the distant *wham* of Onyx trying to blast his way in.

'I said, everything all right in there?'

'I'm just great,' I said shortly. 'Where's Anne?'

'Standing right here.'

I glanced up at the camera feeds. I couldn't see Vihaela or Anne on the displays. 'I don't see you.'

'Oh, we're not in the vault yet.'

There was a weird noise in the background, something like an elongated hiss. 'What's that noise?'

'Hmm,' Vihaela said. 'That's interesting.'

'What?'

'Anne, dear?' It sounded as though Vihaela was speaking over her shoulder. 'Time for you to earn your keep.'

'*What's* interesting?'

'Guardian dracoform,' Vihaela said. 'We should be five minutes or so. Don't go anywhere.' The communicator went dead.

'Guardian what? Where are—?' I realised I was speaking into a dead microphone and swore.

Onyx was still hammering at the door. *Okay, screw this.* It was time to get to Anne and find a way out of the Vault before the whole Council came down on our heads.

The computer menu was demanding a six-digit code. I looked into the scenarios in which I typed every possible combination and saw hundreds of possible futures unfold in parallel, each terminating in the same message: 'Code

Invalid'. I focused, standardising the movements I used to type, zooming out. The hundreds of futures became thousands, the thousands became tens of thousands, the tens of thousands became hundreds of thousands . . . One future didn't fit: a single white ball in a sea of black. I picked out the code, typed it in. The menu disappeared.

The communicator in my ear pinged. 'Vari,' I said absently.

'Alex?' Variam said. 'You guys need to get out now.'

'Why?' I asked. The lockdown menu had disappeared, but the door's icon still wasn't changing from red to green.

'The Council are refusing to release the Keepers to reinforce the Vault,' Variam said. 'They're still afraid that this is some sort of feint and the real—'

'This *is* the real attack!'

'I know! They authorised Sal Sarque to send in a reconnaissance team.'

I paused. 'How big a team?'

'From what I've heard? All of them. You do not want to be around when they get there.'

Sal Sarque was the head of the Crusaders. It was a good bet that the 'reconnaissance team' was going to be composed of the same sorts of people as the ones who'd taken Anne. 'How long do we have?'

'They might be there already.'

Vihaela's communicator flashed. A glance at the futures confirmed that it wasn't Vihaela. 'I'm going to have to call you back,' I said. 'Alex out.' I grabbed up the handset. 'This is Verus.'

'Got your message,' Cinder's voice said through the speaker. 'Trouble?'

'You could say that. I'm locked in the control room and Onyx is trying to smash his way in.'

'Del?'

'Was the one who left us here in the first place. Any chance I could get some help?'

'No.'

'Seriously?'

'Guard duty at the front,' Cinder said.

I swore. 'There's not much time. We've got a Crusader strike team coming in.'

'Where from?'

'Don't know, but they'll probably have some kind of back way.'

'Understood.'

'Wait! Can't you—?' Cinder clicked off. '—help,' I finished, talking to the dead line. 'Thanks.'

I became aware that the control room had gone quiet; the muffled *wham wham wham* of Onyx's force spells had stopped. I couldn't hear what he was doing any more, and that worried me. I glanced up at the cameras that should show the corridor he was in, but they were black. Onyx obviously didn't want me to know what he was doing. Bad sign.

I crossed the room and put a hand to the wall, concentrating. I could feel a force magic source from the other side; it felt powerful, and *sharp*. I looked into the futures of what would happen if I stayed where I was . . .

Great. Onyx couldn't smash through the door, so he'd decided to cut through the wall. He'd break through in a little over ten minutes. I needed a way out.

I scrolled through windows on the computer system, searching for a way to unlock the door. Access settings – no. Network controls – no. Local security – that should be it, but none of the commands were working . . .

The communicator pinged. 'Hello, Verus,' Vihaela said. 'How's it going?'

'Just wonderful,' I said shortly. 'Where are you?'

'Why don't you see for yourself?'

I looked up at the monitors. For the first time, I could see movement on the vault cameras. The Dark mages of Vihaela's team were spreading out, grabbing items off shelves and pedestals and shoving them into bags. As I watched, I caught sight of Vihaela, talking into the communicator. *Where's Anne?* 'So you're in,' I said. 'Congratulations.'

'Thank you,' Vihaela said. 'Though I should really give the credit to your friend. You never told me she was such a combat expert.'

'Yeah, she's a woman of many talents,' I said. I could see Anne over Vihaela's shoulder. 'Since everything's going so well, how about you order Onyx to stop trying to kill me?'

'He's there?'

'Yes.'

'Oh well,' Vihaela said. 'I try to make it a policy not to get between master and apprentice. I hope you're still keeping an eye on things.'

'Are you listening to a word I'm saying?'

'I'm sure everything will be fine. Keep watch for another ten minutes, then you can come join us for extraction. I wouldn't wait around for the Council if I were you.'

'Thanks, I'd figured that out on my own. What kind of extraction?'

'One of the items in this vault acts as an amplifier for piercing gate wards.'

'That's great. What about the fact that Onyx is going to smash through the door in *less* than ten minutes?'

On the monitors, I saw Anne take a step towards Vihaela's communicator; Vihaela gave her a look that stopped her. 'Honestly, Verus, I don't go running to you with all my problems.'

'Wait! I want to talk to—' Once again I found myself talking into a dead microphone.

Okay, Alex, think fast. I had . . . around seven and a half minutes before Onyx cut his way through. I went back to the computer settings with redoubled energy. Nothing, nothing . . . *there.* The lockdown command had reset the security permissions. I clicked the button marked 'Authorise'.

A window flashed up. ENTER THUMBPRINT SCAN.

I looked around and found a thumbprint scanner. And the people who'd be authorised to use it would be . . . the people that Rachel had just turned into dust.

Shit.

An image on one of the monitors caught my eye; Rachel had just walked into the vault. Anne gave Rachel a look but Rachel ignored her, moving next to Vihaela to exchange a few words and— I frowned. *Wait. What's Rachel doing there . . . ?*

The Crusaders arrived.

Every camera feed went dark all at once. I felt the signatures of spells in the distance: gates, fire, air. Gunfire sounded in the distance, followed by muffled shouts. I looked into the futures in which I waited where I was and realised that Onyx wasn't going to be the first one in any more. The Crusaders were less than two minutes away, they were going to open the door from the outside, and they were being led by . . .

Oh, come ON. It was Jarnaff, and he was being followed

by a whole strike team. Was there a single mage in Britain who hated me who *wasn't* in this place?

I scrambled for the controls. The Crusaders had done something to mess with the system, but they hadn't shut it down completely and I managed to find a reset function. With a loud beep, the lights above the door panels went red. It would keep them out, but not for long. My divination lets me mimic expertise, but it's not a replacement, and by my best guess I had maybe three minutes before either Onyx or the Crusaders broke through, at which point it would be a race to see who killed me first. I looked around from one door to the other. I felt like a rat in a trap. I had to come up with something . . .

If you have one problem, you have to solve it yourself. If you have lots of problems, sometimes you can get them to solve each other . . .

I grabbed Vihaela's communicator and disabled the lock. 'Cinder, this is Verus,' I said. 'Come in.'

A moment's pause, then the communicator activated. Cinder spoke over the *whoosh* of flame. 'Little busy.'

'I need your help.'

'Can't get to you—' Cinder broke off, addressing someone else. 'Kyle! Eyes right!' There was the *ratatat* of an automatic weapon.

'Call Onyx,' I said. 'Convince him I'm at the main entrance to the control room talking to the Crusaders.'

'How?'

'Jesus!' I snapped. 'I don't care what you say, tell him whatever the hell you like, just make him think I'm there and not inside!'

Cinder paused, but for only a heartbeat. 'Fine. Wait one.' He cut off.

There was a scratching sound from the front door. I looked up in time to see the light above the door go from red to green, and I stabbed a finger at the keyboard, locking it again just a second before the door would have swung open. *Damn, they're fast.* I hit a command that I knew would buy me a few seconds; the mouse icon spun as the application went into reset mode.

From the other side of the room came the scraping sound of warping metal. I looked and thought I could see a flicker as Onyx's force blade cut through the wall. I held my breath. If it was going to work, it would have to be now. I looked through the futures. *Nearly* . . .

There. All of a sudden the futures in which Onyx came through the back door vanished, and I heard the distant sound of running feet. I stood listening, counting down in my head. To get all the way around the control room from the outside, Onyx would have to run down two corridors, then turn a corner. He should be coming into view of the Crusader team right about . . . *now.*

I felt a flash of force magic from outside. There was a muffled shout, then a scream, and I saw the wall vibrate. The futures in which the Crusaders broke through the door abruptly vanished.

There. I took a deep breath. If I was *really* lucky, Onyx and Jarnaff would kill each other, but at least now I had some breathing room. I put a hand to my ear. 'Anne, this is Alex.'

No answer. 'Anne, this is Alex. Can you receive?'

Still nothing. I frowned. Anne and I had checked those communicators just before leaving to meet Vihaela. What was going on?

I could still sense force magic through the walls: Onyx

was giving the Crusaders quite a fight. I pulled up the camera controls and managed to find the command to get the vault cameras up and running, then looked up, searching through the screens.

The Dark mages were pulling out. Across the camera feeds, I could see the members of Vihaela's team grabbing last items from the shelves and containers and hurrying for the far side of the vault. A gate was already open, one mage maintaining the spell while the others moved through one by one. A figure in a helmet was overseeing them, arms folded: Archon. I was struck by how well-ordered the evacuation was. Dark mages usually don't co-operate well, but these worked together quickly and efficiently.

It took me a second to find Vihaela, and when I did, I frowned. She was with Anne in a small alcove. The alcove contained a pedestal with an open box, and Vihaela and Anne seemed to be having some sort of argument. From her body language, Vihaela seemed to be trying to . . . order Anne? Persuade her, maybe . . .

A chill went through me, and all of a sudden, I had a very bad feeling. I scrolled through the menu, found a volume icon and turned it up.

Anne's voice came from the speakers, faint and tinny. '. . . does it do?'

'It's an imbued item,' Vihaela said. 'A powerful one.'

Anne looked dubious; she said something I couldn't hear. 'Because it doesn't work for Dark mages,' Vihaela told her.

I frowned. Something about that box looked familiar. I'd seen it before, but . . . closed, instead of open?

'. . . to be a tourist,' Vihaela was saying. 'Do something useful.'

Anne was looking down into the box but wasn't moving

to take it. The lid was blocking my view of what was inside, but something was nagging at my memory. Darkness and fire . . .

And suddenly I remembered. The raid on Christmas Eve; the bubble realm and Ares. This was the relic I'd carried out of there. The same one that Morden had wanted the first time . . .

And with that, I remembered what Arachne had said. *'But underneath it, the essence remained. A human who called up the jinn according to the old rituals, with the jinn as a willing partner, could still unlock their full power . . .'*

Dread spiked through me, and horror. *It wasn't me at all.* I hit the transmit key, shouting into the microphone. 'Anne! No! Don't touch it!'

Neither Anne nor Vihaela reacted; the audio feed was one-way. But Vihaela glanced past Anne to the camera, and just for a second I could have sworn she smiled. Then it was gone, and Vihaela turned and called to the remaining Dark mages. 'All right! Last one out, get the lights!'

'Wait!' Anne called. 'Where's Alex?'

'Last I heard, he was on his way,' Vihaela said over her shoulder. 'Hang around if you like, but we're not waiting.' She walked away to join the retreating Dark mages.

I scanned through the futures frantically. Something caught my eye; I brought up the other cameras and hissed under my breath. There were men hurrying down the main corridor, mages striding at the centre, gunmen flanking them and covering the lines of fire. They were only minutes away from reaching Anne.

In the few seconds I'd looked away, the vault had all but emptied. Rachel was one of the last ones out. 'Deleo,' Anne called out. 'Where's Alex?'

Rachel didn't bother to answer. 'Hey!' Anne shouted.

Rachel paused, glancing over her shoulder. 'Crusaders probably got him.' She looked at Anne with an unpleasant smile. 'Too bad for him. Maybe if you stuck around, you might be able to help.' She turned, walked away out of view. Anne was left alone.

'Oh no, no, no,' I muttered. The last Dark mages were leaving through the gate; Rachel stepped as I watched. Anne was the only one visible on her camera now. From where she was standing, she couldn't see the gate; she didn't realise she was about to be left behind. The Crusaders would be at the doors. I started to look to see how long she had—

No. All of a sudden, I knew that was the wrong thing to do. It was what I'd been doing for too long: just standing and watching, looking ahead without *doing* anything. But I didn't have any way of reaching her—

Yes I do. Alone in the control room, I reached into my pouch, pulled out the dreamstone and looked down at it, seeing the facets glint amethyst in the light of the monitors. I'd already scanned the futures in which I tried to get in touch with Anne and I hadn't seen this working—

But that was what Arachne had been telling me, wasn't it? I hadn't been making it work; I'd been looking into the future to *see* if it would work.

For once, I didn't stop to think. I focused all of my concentration on the dreamstone and *threw* my mind into it, picturing Anne in my thoughts.

For an instant, I had a sense of vertigo, like falling across an impossible gap, then there was the sense of something tearing and all of a sudden I could hear voices. It felt like opening a door, as though they'd been there all along and I'd just never found the way.

. . . *where he is*, one voice was saying. There were two of them; both were Anne's, and yet both were different. *He could be coming, maybe she's lying, maybe they're all lying . . . can still feel that dragon, how it felt, no, have to think. Have to think. If he's coming, I should wait; if I leave I'll be abandoning him, he might need me, can't leave him alone if he needs my help, but I hate this place, I want to get out . . .*

'Yes,' I said. 'Get out. Can you hear me?'

. . . *could fight them. No, not fight, kill; but no, I don't . . . you don't have a choice, you remember that house, cutting and tearing . . . No. I can stun, paralyse, I don't want to go back . . . wouldn't be enough, you know what you have to do. I'm afraid of what it does. Take it. No. Don't have a choice . . .*

She can't hear me. I focused my thoughts into a beam, projecting the words. *Anne.*

On the screen, I saw Anne start. *Alex?*

It's me. You need to get out of there.

Where are you?

Don't worry about where I am.

I have to! . . . hurt, nearly dying. Where are you?

Still in the facility. Follow the Dark mages; I'll find my own way out.

No! I'm not leaving you! . . . besides, it's too late. They're gone.

I looked at the monitors and saw that Anne was right. The gate was closed. *Then find a place to hide. The Crusaders are going to reach the vault any minute.*

Can't hide. All of a sudden, Anne sounded weary. On the monitor, I saw her eyes shift down to the open box. *One choice left.*

No! I sent the thought as forcefully as I could. I could sense Anne's feelings, tired and desperate and afraid, but there was something else underneath it, something darker that wanted to be unleashed, and that scared me more than the Crusaders. *Anne, you can't. That's what he wants!*

Anne's hand had been drifting towards the box; now it paused. *Who?*

Richard and Vihaela. This is what they've been planning all along, leaving you here. Whatever you do, whatever that thing is, don't take it!

Planning how? Anne asked. *I don't understand.* But she drew back a little from the box.

I felt a tiny surge of relief. *We can figure that part out later. Right now we need to——*

There was movement on the monitors. Anne and I looked up as one.

The Crusader team came through into the vault. There were nearly a dozen of them with more behind, and they had a direct line of sight to Anne, and for the first time I got a clear look at the two mages in the middle team. It was Lightbringer and Zilean. Zilean and Anne saw each other at exactly the same time.

For a frozen moment Anne was absolutely still, then her face twisted in terrible rage. I heard both voices inside my head snarl as one, and on the monitor I saw Anne's hand disappear into the box.

Every camera inside the vault went black.

I felt a flash of something from the direction of the vaults, powerful enough to sense even through the distance and the walls. Inside my head I felt anger, fear, chaos. *Anne!*

A moment's pause, then a presence, cold and looming and massive. Words reared up like a towering wave. *GET OUT.*

The wave crashed over me and I was hurled back to my body, the connection fraying and snapping. I staggered, caught myself. I was alone in the control room.

17

The dreamstone was dark and silent. From outside, I could hear muffled voices, and I was distantly aware that the battle between Onyx and the Crusaders must be over. They were about to break into the control room, and this time I wouldn't be able to stop them. Somehow, it didn't seem important. Whatever that thing was that had thrown me out of Anne's head, it had felt like it was claiming territory. I needed to get to her.

I scanned the futures, then tapped a command into the computer, pulled out my gun and fired into the computer bank. With a *whirr*, most of the remaining screens went black. I moved to the back door, watching the lights on the panel. What I'd just done wouldn't keep the Crusaders out; the systems had redundancies. They could override the controls. But to do that, they'd have to cancel the lockdown, which meant . . .

The lights on the panel went green. I pulled the back door open and stepped through just an instant before the Crusaders came in the front. I was free.

I ran towards the vaults. The Crusaders had the control room, and it wouldn't take them long to get the cameras back up, and once that happened, they'd know the location of everyone in the facility, including me. I needed to make it there before that happened.

After the earlier battle, the corridors felt eerily silent, my footsteps echoing off the walls. I passed a clump of bodies, cut sideways through an access corridor, then slowed as I drew close to the entrance to the main vault. It was the same door that I'd guided Vihaela through, and it was occupied. I stopped one turning away, listening.

'. . . don't have time for this!' someone was saying. 'Send your men in!' It was the lightning mage, Zilean, and he sounded agitated. *So he's still alive*, I thought coldly. *Pity.*

'No,' another voice replied, this one older and steadier. 'We're holding for Jarnaff.'

'It's one girl!'

'Whatever that *thing* was, it was not a girl.'

'She's using some Dark mage trick. If you'd committed—'

'That *trick* just fucking *ate* three of my men in as many seconds. While *you* turned and ran.'

'I'll have you sent—' Zilean's voice sharpened. 'Wait. Someone's here!'

I was already turning the corner, breaking into a sprint. I didn't know what I was going to find behind those doors, but Zilean seemed convinced that Anne was still alive and that was good enough for me. I had a brief confused image of the Crusaders clustered around the shattered vault door – Zilean was there, and so was Lightbringer – then I threw a condenser right into the middle of them and they disappeared in a bank of mist.

Shouts broke out, three different people trying to give orders at once, but the Crusaders hadn't been prepared for someone behind them and in the confusion I ran straight through their ranks. Shapes loomed up in the mist, then I was through.

I don't remember much about that last mad dash. The corridors between the door and the vault proper held the final security measures that Vihaela and Anne had fought their way past, but I didn't have time to stop and look. I saw a monstrous shape, clawed and fanged, lying dead against the wall, and shattered constructs piled in the first room. Something hissed and snatched at my ankles, but I dodged and kept going, and came out at last into the main storage vault.

My first impression was of size; I hadn't realised just how big the place was. The ceiling was arched stone, and it looked ancient, as though it had been here for a long, long time. Wooden cabinets were tucked into alcoves, and pedestals held boxes and stasis cases. Most were open, broken by the Dark mages in their looting. A couple of the cabinets to the right were smoking and burnt, and a section of wall had been shattered as though by some great force, but my eyes were only for Anne, lying against one of the pillars. Her eyes were closed and she wasn't moving.

I rushed to her side, kneeling down to touch her neck. Anne didn't seem hurt – her pulse was steady and she was breathing – but she wasn't getting up either, and as I looked through the futures, I saw that she wasn't going to. Her hand was clutched around something that looked like a signet ring, the fingers locked tight. There was no sign of the 'thing' that the Crusaders had been talking about, nor of the missing men. Briefly I wondered what had happened here, then put it out of my mind. I pulled out Vihaela's communicator. 'Cinder, this is Verus.'

A pause, then Cinder replied. 'Verus? We're bailing. Crusaders brought in reinforcements. Get to the east wing.'

The east wing was most of the way across the facility. I thought about my chances of making it all the way there, through the Crusaders, while carrying Anne's unconscious body. 'Can't.'

'Where are you?'

'Main vault.'

There was a moment's silence. 'Can't get to you.'

I paused. 'Anything you can give me?'

'That focus Vihaela used still running?'

I'd already checked. 'No.'

There was another pause. 'Got nothing,' Cinder said at last. 'Sorry.'

'Yeah,' I said. There was danger in the futures, coming closer. The Crusaders had recovered from their surprise. 'Guess we'll have to catch up another time.'

'You make it out, I'll do what I can for cover,' Cinder said. 'If not . . . take a few of the bastards with you.'

I switched off the communicator and looked into the futures. The Crusaders were going to be here in less than thirty seconds. I heaved Anne up in my arms; she felt lighter than I remembered from the last time I'd had to do this. There was a partition halfway across the vault which blocked off the view of the back of the room and I carried her behind it, setting her down gently to rest against the wall.

Voices sounded from the other side of the partition. I looked to the right, towards where Vihaela's Dark mages had opened that gate. The focus they'd used to do it was gone and I was pretty sure they'd taken it with them. In theory, they could still use it to come back for us. I knew they wouldn't.

More voices, cautious footsteps. I held still. There was a chance that the Crusaders wouldn't find us. Sure, they were mages, but not every mage has a spell that makes it impossible to hide from them. Okay, so life and death mages can find you through walls, and mind and charm mages can pick up your thoughts and your feelings, and air mages can feel you breathe, and fire mages can follow the trail of your body heat, and earth mages can sense the vibration of your footsteps, but it was possible that the Crusader group didn't have any of those, right?

A voice sounded from the direction of the entrance. 'We are here under the authority of the Council. Come out where we can see you.'

I didn't move. *Maybe they're bluffing.*

'We can see you hiding behind that partition. You've got ten seconds before we blow it down on top of you.'

I sighed. *Not bluffing.* I walked out into the open.

The group of mages standing at the entrance was like a Who's Who of Light mages that I did not want to meet. Zilean was there, his eyes narrowing as he saw me, and flanking him was Lightbringer, his face stolid and expressionless as he held a shield of glowing energy in one hand and a blade of light in the other. There were two other mages I didn't recognise, one surrounded by a shield of flame, the other with eddies of air magic swirling around him. Six men with guns were spread out around the mages; two were watching the back, while the other four were covering me. Unlike the men who'd been defending the facility, they didn't wear the garb of Council security. They looked more like mercenaries, or worse. And at the front, wearing battle armour with his shaven head bare, was Jarnaff, my old friend from the War Rooms. 'Verus,' he said with a tight smile. 'Fancy meeting you here.'

'Jarnaff,' I said unemotionally.

'You know, I thought Morden was going to be a little more discreet,' Jarnaff said. 'Didn't expect him to send his aide.'

'I'm not here because of Morden,' I said. I already had

the feeling that I wasn't going to be able to talk my way out of this, but maybe I could buy some time. 'I came under orders from the Council.'

'Did you now.'

'I've been working for the Keepers this whole time.'

'Bullshit,' Zilean cut in.

'You don't believe me?' I said. 'Sal Sarque signed off on the deal. Go ask him.'

Jarnaff studied me, and I felt the futures shift. They were changing . . . but not enough, and I felt my heart sink. *This isn't going to work.*

Zilean couldn't see what I could. 'He's lying,' he said harshly.

Jarnaff made a soothing motion. 'Easy, Zilean.'

'He knows it'll take too long to get in touch,' Zilean said. 'He's just playing for time.'

'Well, I'll agree that that's a possibility,' Jarnaff said. 'Still, we should do things properly. Once everything's secure.'

The air mage spoke up. He was tall and thin, with a hooked nose. 'Where's the girl?'

I was very aware of Anne behind me, hidden by the partition. 'What girl?'

There was a faint rustle, and the click of metal. All of a sudden, the guns were pointing at me a lot more directly. 'You really don't want to play games, Verus,' Jarnaff said.

'We were both sent here under specific Council instructions,' I said. 'Infiltrating Morden's unit. You've got comms, haven't you? Call them up, right now. Check our story. They'll authorise it.'

Jarnaff just looked at me. So did Lightbringer and Zilean.

'You're not going to call the Council,' I said. It wasn't a question.

'Well, here's the thing,' Jarnaff said. He was smiling slightly and I could tell he was enjoying himself. 'The Council passed an emergency resolution delegating authority to Sal Sarque to resolve the situation at this facility by any means necessary. And I'm his representative. So as far as you're concerned? Right now, I *am* the Council.'

Here's a thing about divination: when someone hasn't made a choice, it's hard to see what they're going to do. Which means that if you look into the future and you *can* get a good idea of what someone's going to do, then you know that they *have* made a choice. Right now, I could see that Jarnaff's men were willing to kill me without warning or hesitation. You don't do that to someone you think might be on your side. 'You're still going to need my testimony.'

'Yeah, that was back when we still thought this whole thing might have been a fake,' Jarnaff said. 'Now that Morden's gone this far? Not so much.'

I should have expected it really. Talisid had told me that Levistus and Sal Sarque hadn't wanted to make that deal with me. If I died, that would get them out of their obligations. 'So what's the story going to be? That I "resisted arrest"?'

'Oh, come on, Verus,' Jarnaff said. 'We don't want to *kill* you. We want to hear what you've got to say. I know some people who'd just love to sit you down for a chat.'

I saw Zilean's expression change very slightly. It might have been a smile. 'I think I've seen how you like to do those,' I said, my voice flat.

'What's the matter?' Jarnaff said. 'Feeling nervous? Why don't you tell me some more about all those assassins you've faced down? You don't seem so cocky now.'

I was silent. Jarnaff nodded to the man at his side. 'Go get the girl.'

'No,' I said.

Jarnaff sighed. 'Can we stop pissing around, please?'

'What do you want her for?'

'That's not really your concern,' Jarnaff said. 'Now, I'm not going to ask you again. Get out of the way.'

I stood my ground.

'Going to do this the hard way?' Jarnaff asked. He smiled. 'All right.' He gestured. 'Keep him alive if you can.'

Some of the mages and gunmen began to advance. Their movements were slow and careful, and they scanned the room as they moved, but I knew the caution wasn't for me: it was for Anne. Except that Anne was unconscious, and I was out of time. I tried to think of how I was going to win this. *Okay, maybe I can hold off the mages to the right, while I engage the guys on the left . . . and maybe the other four gunmen and Jarnaff and Lightbringer and Zilean will all drop dead of spontaneous heart attacks.*

This wasn't going to work.

'Wait,' I said, searching through the futures in which something I said made them stop. There wasn't one.

The gunmen were close now, and I knew that the only reason they hadn't fired yet was that they didn't see me as enough of a threat. I was out of ideas. 'Wait,' I said again.

Lightbringer stopped. The gunmen did too.

'Who the fuck is that?' one of the mages said.

I started to answer, then realised that they weren't looking at me. I turned.

There was a man standing at the other side of the room, black-armoured and wearing a helmet. Archon.

'He's not one of ours,' the air mage said.

'You,' Jarnaff said. 'What are you doing here?'

The guns were split now, with only the nearest of the gunmen covering me. The others were aiming at Archon. I wondered very briefly why I hadn't seen Archon in the futures, but the Dark mage was already speaking. 'Councilman Jarnaff,' Archon said in his flat voice. 'I would like to negotiate.'

'Who the fuck are you?' Jarnaff said. 'Another of the raiders? The only thing you're going to be negotiating with is the inside of a cell.'

'Here are my terms,' Archon said. 'Take your men and depart. I will do the same.'

'Yeah,' Jarnaff said. 'You really don't get to give us orders.'

'It is a reasonable offer.'

One of the mages laughed. They'd been caught off-balance by Archon's appearance, but now they were recovering. 'Who are you again?' Jarnaff said.

I saw what was coming and stood very still.

Archon reached up and unclasped his helmet. It seemed to take a long time. The Crusaders watched, curiosity on some faces, hostility on others. Archon pulled the helmet off to reveal his face, and when he spoke, it was in his true voice at last. 'My name is Richard Drakh.'

The whole room was dead silent. I could sense the Crusaders shifting their feet, one or two of them taking a step back, but all I could do was stare at Richard, my thoughts whirling. He'd pretended to be Archon . . . ?

No. There never was an Archon. Pieces clicked into place, the way Archon had talked, how casually he'd given orders. I remembered that first night when he'd come to meet me in Wales. I'd called Richard to check who he was, and it had been Richard's voice that had answered . . . but if you could build a voice distorter into a helmet, you could add a phone too. I didn't know why he'd tricked everyone then, and I didn't know why he was revealing himself now, but all of a sudden I felt a spark of hope. Maybe there was still a chance for Anne and me to get out alive.

The Light mages were hesitating. They obviously all knew who Richard was. Jarnaff recovered first. 'Bullshit.'

'No,' the air mage said. 'Jarnaff, it's him.'

'Shut *up*,' Jarnaff said under his breath, then addressed Richard. 'All right, fine. You're Drakh. That supposed to impress us?'

'That is entirely up to you,' Richard said. 'However, Verus and Miss Walker are, for the moment at least, under my protection. I must ask that you not take any hostile action against them.'

'Yeah, you're not really in a position to be asking anything,' Jarnaff said. The Light mage seemed to be regaining his confidence. 'You were with the raiders. That means you're in violation of the Concord.'

'Really?' Richard said. 'So you'd be happy with this whole incident being reported in full to the Council?' Richard shook his head. 'I really don't see any need for them to be informed of every trivial detail. Nor is it your business to clear up every straggler. You swept the facility, fought your way through to this room and secured it. I imagine Sal Sarque will be quite pleased.'

'Know what'd make him a lot more pleased?' Jarnaff said. 'If I bring in the ringleader.'

I felt the mood in the room shift. All of the guns were pointed at Richard now, though I couldn't help but notice that not all of the Crusaders looked happy about it. Lightbringer's face was set, but the air mage behind him looked nervous and Zilean had edged away. All of a sudden I had the feeling that if it weren't for Jarnaff, the Crusaders would be backing down.

Even better, from my point of view, was that Anne and I seemed to have been forgotten. One of the gunmen had closed to within ten feet of me before Richard had made his appearance, and now he was caught between us, trying to watch us both at the same time. I measured distances, calculating how long it would take him to bring that gun up.

Richard faced the Light mages, his stance relaxed. If the number of men facing him bothered him, he didn't show it. 'I would advise against it.'

'Unless you've got a whole lot more Dark mages up your sleeve, I don't really see what you're going to do.'

'Councilman Jarnaff,' Richard said. 'Let me make myself quite clear. I will be departing this facility with Mage Verus and Miss Walker. Your choice is whether you will be alive or dead at the time.'

'Really,' Jarnaff said with a sneer. 'You're going to single-handedly kill every one of us.'

'Not all of you.' Richard said calmly. 'Somewhere between seven and ten of you. I expect Verus will account for the remainder.'

Several of the Crusaders turned to look at me and I inwardly cursed. They weren't going to forget about me now.

Jarnaff hesitated. Just for a second, I saw the futures shift and I knew that Jarnaff wasn't as confident as he was trying to sound. He was genuinely considering backing off on this one. But then he glanced very quickly behind him to the other mages and the other paths winked out. 'Lightbringer, Maraxus,' he said. 'Arrest him.'

Richard spoke again, this time addressing the two mages behind Jarnaff. 'Last chance.'

The fire mage – Maraxus – hesitated, but Lightbringer didn't. He started walking forward, his dark face level and set, hammer in one hand, shield in the other. A barrier of solid force shimmered around him, and Maraxus fell in slightly behind him, watching Richard carefully.

Everything started happening very fast.

Richard shifted slightly, and Maraxus shouted out, 'Hands!' and then Richard was throwing something at Lightbringer. It impacted on the centre of Lightbringer's shield and with a sputter of sparks both Lightbringer's shield and force barrier vanished. Lightbringer's hand flicked up and he made a gesture; nothing happened, and I had just time to see surprise on Lightbringer's face before Richard shot him through the head.

The room erupted in shouts and gunfire. I was already moving, closing the distance to the nearest gunman. I caught the rifle by the barrel as he tried to bring it to bear, hit him in the face, then landed a kick which put him on the floor. Another of the gunmen saw me and turned. I sprinted for cover, bullets chipping fragments of stone from my heels, the trail of gunfire catching up with me just an instant before I dived behind the partition.

Richard was fighting on the other side of the room and I could sense battle magic flying back and forth, but I didn't have time to see who was winning. The man I'd knocked down was struggling to his feet and two more gunmen were moving in. I tried to snap off a shot and a volley of fire made me jerk back into cover. I glanced to the right; Anne was still lying there unconscious. *Can't let them get too close.* One was circling, trying to get a bead. A future flashed up where I could get an uninterrupted shot, and I tensed, ready. Fire magic flashed; there was a scream and I leant out, sighting. The gun was an unfamiliar one, some type of assault rifle, but I knew how to make it work and that was all that mattered. The flanking man was still looking in the direction of the scream when my burst took him through the neck.

Blades of air lashed my position, invisible and razor-sharp, curving around the pillar to strike. I jerked aside from one which would have blinded me, feeling it score a line across my cheek, then fumbled out the gold discs of one of my force walls and threw. They clattered to the floor and I called out the command word just before another cloud of razor darts came curving in, slamming into the force barrier and bouncing off. It wouldn't stop them but it would slow them down.

Behind. I whirled to see Zilean backing away from the other side of the partition, lightning crackling around his hands. He was maybe twenty feet away from Anne, and as I watched he turned, seeing both of us.

I already had the assault rifle levelled. I fired, aiming for his chest.

A translucent shield of silver-grey formed at Zilean's fingertips. My burst slammed into it, ricocheted. 'Not this time, Verus!' Zilean shouted. There was a wild look in his eyes, but he held the shield flat towards me with one hand, electricity crackling at the other.

I'd already scanned the futures in which I fired again. I started walking towards him, keeping the gun trained.

Zilean flexed his fingers, electricity jumping in blue-white sparks. 'Any closer and you die.'

I didn't stop. 'From what?' I said calmly. 'If you could

blast me through that shield, you'd have done it already. That's the trouble with lightning magic. Great for hurting people, but it's not so good on defence, is it?'

Zilean hesitated, and I knew my guess had been right. That shield he was holding was from a focus, and it wouldn't be easy for him to hold it up while also attacking. And as long as I held the gun trained on him, he wouldn't dare take his attention off me to blast Anne.

But then Zilean's eyes flicked over my shoulder and without turning I knew I was surrounded. The two gunmen were working their way around the forcewall. I hadn't been able to get it all the way across the room, and in only a few seconds they'd reach the edge.

'You know, you hurt me that last time,' Zilean said. He sounded more confident now, and I knew he was trying to keep me talking. 'Took them a long time to fix me up.'

'Sounds like your life mages are a lot worse than Anne.'

Behind me, the gunmen cleared the wall. I shifted, placing myself between them and Zilean so that if they fired, they'd risk hitting each other. 'Who?' Zilean said. 'Oh. Was that her name?'

A bolt of fury spiked through me and my finger trembled as I fought the urge to shoot. *Have to think.* On the other side of the partition, the battle was still raging, but I knew I wouldn't be getting any help. I looked at the shield with my magesight, recognising the pattern. It was a basic kinetic barrier. *But it's not anchored, is it? Not to anything except his hand . . .*

'You know, she took a long time to start screaming.' Zilean was smiling; he knew he only needed to keep me busy for a few more seconds. 'It wasn't until I put the scalpel in—'

'Hey, Zilean,' I said. I was close enough now to make out the lines on his face. 'What's the energy limit on that shield?'

'More than anything you've got.'

'Good,' I said, and charged. I had an instant to see Zilean's eyes go wide before I rammed the shield shoulder-first.

No matter how powerful you make a shield, you can't get around basic conservation of energy. If something hits a shield, then most of that energy's going to go into whoever's holding it. Against bullets this isn't a problem, because the shield spreads the impact. That means all the wielder has do is absorb the momentum, and there's only so much momentum a quarter-ounce bullet can carry.

Absorbing the momentum of a one hundred and seventy pound body is a little harder.

Zilean stumbled and tripped, the shield dissipating as I fell right on top of the Light mage. We scrambled on the floor, me trying to bring the gun to bear and Zilean desperately trying to fend me off, and I was just about to get him when a future flashed through my mind of bullets ripping through me. I dropped flat; the bullets whistled overhead, and the instant's distraction was enough for Zilean to catch the barrel of my rifle and send a shock through it which numbed my hand.

Conventional wisdom is that grappling with elemental mages is a bad idea, but I'd fought Zilean twice now, and I knew he didn't have much stomach for up-close and personal fights. He could have tried to blast me, but instead the future filled with electrical light and I knew he was about to use his lightning jump to escape.

I hit Zilean across the jaw. The angle was weak, but it

was strong enough to stun him and the futures in which he cast his spell winked out. I hooked an arm around his neck and dragged us both upright.

The two gunmen had closed to less than thirty feet away. Both of them had their rifles levelled and they'd been about to shoot, but I was holding Zilean pressed against me, the crook of my elbow crushing his throat, and they hesitated. Zilean clawed at my arm. Electricity sparked at his fingers, but it sank into my armour and Zilean was too dazed to manage a more powerful spell. 'Don't shoot!' he choked out. 'Wait!'

I kept my grip with my left arm while my right hand reached behind my back to my holster. 'Tell them to drop their guns,' I said into Zilean's ear.

'Do as he says!' Zilean shouted, a note of panic in his voice.

The gunmen stared at us with *is-he-serious* expressions, and I knew they were trying to figure out what to do. As Zilean opened his mouth to give another order, I drew my 1911 and shot him in the back.

Zilean jerked. The gunmen's futures forked crazily as they tried to decide whether they'd be in more trouble by shooting or by holding off. Before they could make up their minds, I brought the gun up over Zilean's shoulder and shot one through the head. The other turned and ran and I shifted my aim, missing two bullets before the third caught him in the small of the back and sent him tumbling to the stone.

Electricity burst blue-white, making my limbs spasm. I staggered back, losing my grip on Zilean as the lightning mage tried to run, but his legs didn't seem to be working right and he stumbled and fell. Zilean pulled himself to his knees, readying another lightning bolt, then his eyes went wide and he screamed.

My gun was levelled on Zilean's forehead, while his hand pointed uselessly down at the floor. 'Go ahead,' I said. Dots swam before my eyes, but Arachne's armour had absorbed the worst of the charge and my hands were steady. 'Try it.'

Zilean didn't try it. He opened his hand and the lightning bolt dissipated. 'Wait,' he said. 'Don't shoot. I'm bleeding.'

I looked down at Zilean.

'We can—' Zilean swallowed. There was sweat on his brow and blood leaking from his belly; I knew the gut wound had to be agonising, but his eyes were locked to the muzzle of the gun. 'We can get you a pardon. A few security men – that doesn't matter. Just get me to a . . .'

'To a healer?' I said quietly. I didn't look at Anne, lying only twenty feet away. 'Like her?'

Zilean's face was white. 'Look, Verus, you have to understand . . . it was just a job. It wasn't personal.'

'It was personal to me,' I said, and Zilean's eyes had just enough time to go wide before I fired.

Blood and bits of skull flew. Zilean dropped bonelessly, lifeless eyes staring up at the ceiling. I stared coldly down at the body, then walked over and picked up the rifle I'd dropped, checking the magazine. Then I ran for the edge of the partition.

There weren't many people still fighting. Richard was still taking on the rest of the Crusader force by himself, and incredibly, he seemed to be winning. I could see at least three bodies lying still, and Richard was engaged in a furious long-range duel with Jarnaff, while the air mage rained missiles down upon him from above.

It's rare to see a master mage fight. For the most part, they don't need to – very few people in the magical world will go up against one willingly, not if they know who they are. When master mages do oppose each other, their conflicts are usually political rather than physical, and if one starts losing, they usually have plenty of time to withdraw. In all my life, I've seen maybe half a dozen master mages in actual combat, and every time I have, it's stuck in my memory. Each has their own style, their own way of moving and engaging. Vihaela is like a dancer, darting and graceful. Landis is the only Light mage I've seen who can match her; he's not as fast, but his technique is so perfect he doesn't need to be. Morden almost doesn't fight at all; he just overwhelms opponents with single crushing attacks which end the battle before it ever really starts.

Watching Richard in action was different from any of them.

It wasn't that he was especially fast. He was quick, but not as quick as an air mage and with nothing like the eye-blurring speed of Vihaela. Nor was it that his weapons seemed especially powerful. He held a pistol in one hand and there was a flickering black shield around him radiating that strange untyped magic that I'd seen him use as Archon, but I could measure its power and it wasn't all that much stronger than my own armour. The spells Jarnaff and the other mage were throwing at Richard had enough strength to cut right through his shield if they ever struck it squarely, yet somehow, no matter how quick the force lance or how well-aimed the air blade, Richard was never quite there when it landed. He moved and fired in a measured, unhurried sort of way, as though it was a shooting range, and one by one, the men facing him died.

One of the remaining gunmen went down to a bullet and the other scrambled away, searching for cover. The air mage sent another flurry of blades which darted out to surround Richard in a star pattern and converge. There was no possible angle to dodge, but somehow in the second it had taken the air mage to prepare the spell, Richard had changed his shield. The black screen caught the blades, whirled them around and spat them out at Jarnaff like a shotgun blast. Jarnaff staggered back and while he was distracted, Richard lifted a hand towards the air mage and four black threads leapt out.

The air mage had his shield ready. The threads weren't powerful enough to break it, but just as they struck, I realised they weren't all the same. Each had a different type of countermagic woven into it, so that no single shield would stop them all. The air mage managed to block two of the threads and slow down the third, but the fourth went through the shield as though it wasn't there. Blood sprayed and the air mage spun from the sky.

Richard turned back towards Jarnaff, killing the last gunman with an almost absent-minded gunshot, and all of a sudden he and Jarnaff were the only ones still standing. 'Stay back!' Jarnaff shouted, backing away.

Richard walked towards him, his expression calm. 'I gave you a chance.'

Jarnaff's eyes darted left and right, settling on the exit that he'd come in by. He put one hand to his ear, talking loudly and urgently. 'Control, we need reinforcements. Bring them in, all of them!'

'I'm sorry, Jarnaff,' Richard said. 'I really would have preferred to do this peacefully.'

'You're fucked,' Jarnaff snarled. He lifted a hand, focusing his shield and layering it, drawing power from the rear to fortify the front. The two layers became three, then four, turning translucent so that I could only barely see his face. He'd obviously seen what had happened to the air mage. 'You're never getting out.'

I still held the rifle in my hands. Both Richard and Jarnaff were focused on each other. I lifted the gun, aimed it between them, hesitated. *Which one?*

'You hear me?' Jarnaff said. 'We'll bring in mages until—'

Richard cast a spell. A thin lance of black light darted not from his hand, but from behind Jarnaff. It struck Jarnaff's weaker rear shielding, pierced it, and punched a neat, small hole right through the centre of Jarnaff's chest.

Jarnaff staggered. He stared at Richard as though surprised, then sank to the ground. The shield winked out.

'I heard,' Richard said to the body. He glanced back at me. 'Have you decided whether to pull that trigger yet?'

'I'm still deciding,' I told him. I didn't lower the gun.

Richard walked across the vault and past me. I traversed the weapon, tracking him. Looking into the futures in which I fired, I saw the bullets spark off, and it suddenly occurred to me that I was trying to threaten him with exactly the same weapon that those dead gunmen had been shooting him with . . .

So many dead men. It hit me that we were literally surrounded by bodies. Zilean was lying just a little way away, sightless eyes staring up at the ceiling, and the two gunmen I'd shot were sprawled further back. The half of the room nearer to the exit was littered with the corpses of the Crusaders who'd attacked Richard. The air mage lay in a pool of blood, Jarnaff was crumpled in the corner, and the bodies of every other member of the strike team were scattered in a gruesome pattern. Blood and bodies everywhere, and looking at them made me dizzy. Richard and I hadn't really killed a whole Crusader strike team, had we? I wasn't supposed to be a battle mage. How had this happened?

I suddenly realised that Richard was kneeling next to Anne. 'Get away from her,' I said sharply.

'She's quite unharmed,' Richard said, and rose, slipping one hand into his pocket. 'But I wouldn't suggest waiting around.'

'You'd rather we go with you?' I said harshly.

'Unless you'd prefer to stay here and explain the situation to the Council.'

I stared after Richard, but he didn't look back. He'd walked to the same area where Vihaela and the Dark mages had disappeared, and was studying the alcove. 'Mind telling me how we're going to leave?' I said. 'Because whatever Vihaela's lot used to gate out, they took it with them.'

Richard didn't turn around. 'Carry her, please.'

I looked – again – into the future where I fired on Richard. Same result. I slung the rifle and picked Anne up in both arms. Her head leaned against my chest and I started to walk over. 'I don't know what you think you're going to accomplish,' I said. 'Maybe you didn't notice, but the gate wards on this place are—'

A gate opened in front of Richard's hand.

I stopped dead. 'How the *hell* . . . ?'

'Not the time, Alex.' Richard stepped through the gateway.

I hesitated for only a second. Whatever was through the

gateway, I didn't think it could be worse than here. I stepped through.

I came down onto firm grass. The air was cool, and stars shone down above the dark shapes of trees; we were somewhere out in the country. I knelt, setting Anne down carefully on the grass, and as Richard let the gate close behind us I saw that he'd dropped his shield.

I moved without thought. Richard didn't quite react in time, and looking back on it, I think I must have caught him by surprise. My fist landed hard enough to make him stagger, and he half-blocked the second punch as I moved in.

Then the futures flickered and slid away. My third strike hit nothing but air, and something slammed into my jaw, stunning me. I hit the ground and rolled, scrambling to my feet.

Richard was standing ten feet away. 'Are you finished?'

I tensed, ready to move.

'Don't,' Richard said. His voice was hard, and all of a sudden I realised that he had his gun out.

I stood very still. Richard was aiming at my midsection, and from looking into the futures I knew he wasn't bluffing, but it was very, very hard to keep myself from going for him anyway. 'You planned this,' I said, and my voice shook with anger.

'If I hadn't stepped in, you and your companion would either be dead or screaming your lungs out in a torture chamber,' Richard said. 'I appreciate that you don't work for me willingly, but this ingratitude is becoming tiresome.'

'Ingratitude . . . ?' Red rage filled me. Only the certainty that Richard would shoot the instant I moved held me back. 'You set this up. You and Vihaela. All so that Anne would pick up that relic.'

'Yes.'

'*Why?*'

'Because matters with the Council are coming to a head.'

'She had nothing to do with the Council!' I shouted. 'The only reason she's even here is because of me, and now she's in deeper! Was this all just some fucked-up game? To make sure that this time I wouldn't run away?'

Richard gave me a curious look. 'Alex, I don't think you quite understand. She isn't here because of you. You're here because of her.'

'You wanted someone who could bond with a jinn to be a pawn in your power games,' I said savagely. 'Except you didn't have one, did you? Because the only people who work for you willingly are psychopaths like Vihaela. So you had to force someone into it who *wasn't* willing.'

Richard shrugged. 'Reasonably accurate, allowing for your personal bias.'

'Then why her?' I shouted. 'You wanted someone to fuck with some more, why her and not me?'

'Because you said no.'

'*When?*'

'Two and a half years ago, in Sagash's shadow realm.'

I stopped dead. I remembered that meeting. It had been the first time I'd seen Richard since his disappearance, more than a decade before. 'You didn't tell me . . .'

Richard sighed. 'No, Alex, for reasons that should be obvious, I did not give you a detailed breakdown of my plans involving the jinn and the Council. If you had agreed to my offer, you would have received further information in due course. You did not.'

I hadn't been alone in Sagash's shadow realm. And Richard had made that offer to two people, not one . . . 'Anne,' I breathed. 'You had your eye on her from the beginning.'

'I did tell you that not everything was about you,' Richard said. 'You really should pay attention. In any case, Anne also rejected my offer, but she did so under your influence. I judged that left to her own devices, she would have said yes. I think subsequent events have proven me correct on that score. Jinn do not contract with an unwilling agent.' He nodded down at where Anne lay. 'She will be an excellent host.'

I lunged.

The gun barked and a tiny, stinging pain flashed through my ear. Richard had aimed it precisely enough to just clip the skin. 'Last warning, Alex,' Richard said. His eyes were cold and set. 'I won't kill you unless I have to, but you'd be amazed what a person can live through.'

I held still.

'Take care of her,' Richard said, and backed away. His eyes and the gun stayed locked on to me until the night swallowed him.

I stared after Richard for a long time, then looked down at Anne. Something about those last words sent a chill through me. The unspoken message had been: *until I come back*.

A cold wind eddied across the hilltop, making me shiver. The starlight shone down from above, Anne's face a pale shape against the grass.

18

It was two hours later.

Luna and I were sitting in Arachne's cave. I'd patched up my wounds with a first aid kit and the healing salve I carry, though it had been a poor job compared to what Anne could do. Arachne was gone. She'd listened to my story, examined Anne, then disappeared into the tunnels. The few words she'd said before leaving hadn't been reassuring. Luna had arrived shortly after, by which time I'd been exhausted and only half coherent from the after-effects of the adrenalin rush. It had taken Luna a long time to get the story out of me.

'What happened at the War Rooms?' I asked at last.

Luna grimaced. 'The Council aren't saying. But I managed to get through to Landis and he filled me in. Short version: it was a disaster.'

'How?'

'Okay, so originally it was supposed to be a protest march, right? Whole lot of adepts all gathered outside the War Rooms with signs. Well, the Council knew it was coming and they'd cleared the area out. No TV crews, a damping field to mess with phone signals, police cordons on the outside, the works. Only it turned out the Council had underestimated the numbers, as in by a factor of ten. The Keepers and the security were jumpy; the crowd started getting angry. And then someone started shooting.'

'Who?'

'The *Keepers* are saying there were Dark mages hidden in the crowd, and the security men fired back. But that's what they would say, isn't it? Not like they're going to admit to gunning down a crowd of innocent people.' Luna sighed. 'I don't know. The EM field messed up everyone's phones, so there aren't any recordings. Sonder and the time brigade are going over the place. Maybe they'll figure it out.' Luna looked at me. 'If they *do* find out it was the Council's fault . . . you actually think they'll admit it?'

'Probably not,' I said. *And that's what everyone else is going to think too.* 'How many ended up dead?'

'They're still counting. At least a dozen.'

I winced. Relations between adepts and the Council had been bad enough already. Even if this *had* been a set-up by Morden and Richard – which seemed likely – no one was going to be in the mood to listen.

Luna's eyes had drifted over to Anne. Anne was lying on one of the sofas, her eyes closed and her breathing slow and regular. 'Is she going to be okay?' Luna asked.

'Physically, she's fine,' I said. 'She woke up while Arachne was checking over her, but I don't think she recognised us. Drank a little water, went back to sleep.'

Luna looked at me. 'Physically she's fine.'

I nodded.

'What about *not* physically?'

'She touched the relic that jinn was bound in,' I said. 'I don't know what happened after that. But I've got an ugly feeling that when she does wake up, we're going to find out that she made some kind of contract.'

Luna looked alarmed. 'You mean like the monkey's paw? If she made a wish . . .'

I shook my head. 'You didn't see the way she was looking

at Lightbringer and Zilean. If it were as simple as granting wishes, they'd both have been dead by the time I got there. But *something* drove off a full team of mages and gunmen.'

'You said you felt something when you were linked to Anne by the dreamstone,' Luna said. 'Was that it?'

'I hope not,' I said. 'Because if it was . . . it was a *lot* more powerful than me.'

We fell silent, looking at Anne's sleeping figure. I didn't give voice to what I was really afraid of. With some things, it's a lot easier to invite them in than to get them out.

'Do you think this was what Morden was planning all along?' Luna asked. 'Setting Anne up in that vault to make her desperate enough?'

'It wasn't the only thing,' I said. 'Those Dark mages looted practically everything in the Vault. God only knows what the consequences of that are going to be. But I'm pretty sure it was why he involved *us*.'

'I was just thinking,' Luna said. 'Remember what Anne told us? About how Morden asked her to be his apprentice, all those years ago? Then when Richard came back, he didn't go straight away to meet you, did he? I mean, he could have done it at any time, but he waited for months. Until Anne got taken into Sagash's shadow realm.'

I nodded.

'Do you think that was why?' Luna asked. 'I mean, when he made you two that offer . . . we thought it was because of you. What if it was the other way around? *Anne* was the one he really wanted, you were just there?' Luna looked at me. 'It would mean they've been planning all this for years. All the time that we were spying on them, *they* were watching *us* . . .'

'There's more,' I said. 'Last year, when that kill order

went out on me, you got out of it by passing your journeyman tests. Vari got out of it by transferring his apprenticeship to Landis. But when we tried to do the same with Anne, it was rejected. We never found out why that happened, did we?'

'But that was Levistus . . .'

'Levistus was responsible for the vote on *me*,' I said. 'But we never found any evidence that he was behind what happened to Anne. Why would he care about her? And even if he did, why hide the evidence? And then Morden swoops in. And because Anne was under the same death sentence, he could put her under his protection as well . . .'

'And we never thought about it, because we thought it was just to keep a lever on you,' Luna finished. Her eyes were angry. 'That *bastard*. All that time we were running around, he was pulling strings to make it worse!'

'Yeah, well, it's not going to do him any good.' I couldn't keep the savagery out of my voice. 'After tonight, Morden is *done*.'

'He wasn't there . . .'

'Onyx was,' I said. 'And then there were those rumours that he was planning to attack the War Rooms. They worked in his favour before, because they drew the Council's attention away from the Vault, but there's no way in hell anyone's going to believe that he didn't have anything to do with this. The only reason Morden's been able to stay on the Council this long is by keeping himself squeaky clean, and now that's over. If there isn't a Keeper team on their way to arrest him already, there will be soon. I've done my last job as his aide.'

Luna frowned. 'But what if he just makes the same threat? You work for him, or . . . ?'

'I'd love to see him try,' I said. 'Last time, he held all the cards. He was the one holding off our execution order, and we had nothing on him. Now it's the other way around. Not only is the execution order gone, but he ordered me to attack a Council facility. If he tries to pull that same shit again, then I can just go straight to the Keepers. They wouldn't have done anything before, but now? He'll be even more screwed than he is already. No.' I shook my head. 'Anne and I are loose from him and away from the Council for good.'

'Yeah, well,' Luna said. 'Morden wasn't the one trying to kill you tonight.'

'No, that was a Council aide,' I said, and sighed. 'And that's another thing. If the Crusaders decide to go public and accuse me of being party to Jarnaff's death, then I'm dead, and probably Anne is too. Our only chance is that they might have too much to lose. I've seen too much of their own dirty laundry now for them to be comfortable bringing it to a Council trial, not to mention that it'd mean publicly admitting that their elite black ops team just got slaughtered by one Dark mage and one diviner. The loss of face might actually scare them more than a trial would.'

'Is there anything we can do either way?'

'Wait and see.'

Silence fell again, and this time, neither of us broke it.

It was late into the night when Variam finally arrived, and when he did, the first words out of his mouth were, 'Have you heard?'

Luna and I shook our heads.

'The Council passed an emergency resolution ordering

Morden's arrest,' Variam said. He was still wearing his battle gear, but from the looks of things, he'd had an easier night than we had. 'They sent a whole freaking battle group over to his mansion to get him. Keepers, constructs, the works.'

'Faster than usual,' Luna said.

'Because they all agreed for once,' I said. 'Go on, Vari. What happened?'

'You might want to be sitting down for this,' Variam said. 'Morden surrendered. I wasn't there, but from the sound of it he just walked out into the middle of the Keepers and demanded to see their warrant. When they did, he went along quietly. Wasn't a shot fired.'

Luna's eyebrows climbed. '*Seriously?*'

'He's demanding a full trial,' Variam said. 'Lawyers and prosecution and everything. Says the evidence will prove his innocence.'

'Are you sure about this?' I asked.

'Landis saw the whole thing.'

'Can they even *put* a Council member on trial?' Luna asked. 'I mean, who'd he be tried *by?*'

'Christ knows,' Variam said. 'They were running around looking up the laws when I left. I don't think they've even figured out what to charge him with yet.'

'They won't, not anytime soon,' I said. I remembered how long the Council had dragged their feet on Cerulean's trial, and he'd only been a Keeper. A Council member being charged would be the legal event of the century. This was going to take months.

'You think Morden is actually nuts enough to believe the Council's going to find him *innocent?*' Luna asked.

'Of course they won't,' Variam said. 'Everyone knows he did it.'

'And even if he didn't, they'd find him guilty anyway,' I said. I shook my head. 'This is crazy. First Morden loots all those items from the Vault, then he just gives himself up? All the imbued items in the world won't do him any good inside a Keeper cell.'

'Then that's it, isn't it?' Luna said. 'Morden's off the Council. It's over.'

'Not quite,' Variam said.

We both looked at him.

'So like I said, they were still looking up the laws when I left,' Variam said. 'Turns out there hasn't been a Council member arrested like this in living memory. But they did find *one* thing.'

'What?'

'So, Morden's under arrest, right?' Variam said. 'But until he actually dies, or until he's sentenced and stripped of his position, then he's still a Council member. They can't assign his seat to anyone else.'

Luna shrugged. 'Who cares?'

'Oh?' Variam was looking at me and grinning, and I held quite still. I had a sudden horrible suspicion where this was going. 'Think you're about to start caring soon. Turns out, when this happens, then until the trial's over, then Morden's place on the Junior Council goes to his second. Which means his aide.'

Luna stared at Variam, then slowly turned to look at me.

'You're now Acting Junior Council member and official representative of the Dark mages of Britain,' Variam said to me, still grinning. 'Congratulations. Oh, and when you have a free moment, the other members of the Council would like to have a chat. As in, all of them.'

I just stared.

'I think you just broke Alex,' Luna told Variam. She turned back to me, her expression curious. 'What are you going to do now?'

I sat down heavily. I did not have the faintest idea.

Look out for book nine in the Alex Verus series!

extras

www.orbitbooks.net

about the author

Benedict Jacka became a writer almost by accident, when at nineteen he sat in his school library and started a story in the back of an exercise book. Since then he has studied philosophy at Cambridge, lived in China and worked as everything from civil servant to bouncer to teacher before returning to London to take up law.

Find out more about Benedict Jacka and other Orbit authors by registering for the free monthly newsletter at www.orbitbooks.net.

if you enjoyed
BOUND

look out for

CHASING EMBERS

by

James Bennett

Behind every myth there is a spark of truth . . .

There's nothing special about Ben Garston.
Or so he'd have you believe. He won't tell you, for
instance, that he's also known as Red Ben. Or that the world
of myth and legend is more real than you think. Because it's
his job to keep all that a secret. But now a centuries-old
rivalry has resurfaced, and the delicate balance between his
world and ours is about to be shattered.

Something is hiding in the heart of the city – and
it's about to be unleashed.

ONE

Once upon a time, there was a happy-ever-after. Or at least a shot at one.

Red Ben Garston sat at the bar, cradling his JD and Coke and trying to ignore the whispers of the past. The whiskey, however, was fanning the flames. Rain wept against the window, pouring down the large square of dirty glass that looked out on the blurred and hurrying pedestrians, the tall grey buildings and sleek yellow taxicabs. The TV in the corner, balanced on a shelf over the bar's few damp customers, was only a muffled drone. Ben watched the evening news to a background of murmured chatter and soft rock music. Economic slump to the Eagles. War in Iran to the Boss. The jukebox wasn't nearly loud enough, and that was part of the problem. Ben could still hear himself think.

Once upon a time, once upon a time . . .

He took a swig and placed the tumbler on the bar before him, calling out for another. The bartender arrived, a young man in apron and glasses. The man arched an evaluating eyebrow, then sighed, poured and left the whole bottle. Ben could drink his weight in gold, but Legends had yet to see him fall down drunk, so the staff were generally tolerant. 7 East 7th Street was neither as well appointed nor as popular as some of the bars in the neighbourhood, verging on the dive side of affairs, but it was quiet on weekdays around dusk, and Red Ben drank here for that very reason. He didn't like strangers. Didn't like attention. He just wanted somewhere to sit, drink and forget about the past.

Still Rose was on his mind, just as she always was.

The TV over the bar droned on. The drought in Africa limped across the screen, some report about worsening conditions and hijacked aid trucks. Strange storms that spat lightning but never any rain. What was up with the weather these days, anyway? Then the usual tableau of sand, flies and starving children, their bellies bloated by hunger, their eyes dulled by need. Technicolor pixelated death.

Immunised by the ceaseless barrage of doom-laden media, Ben looked away, scanning the customers who shared the place with him: a man slouched further along the bar, three sat in a gloomy booth, one umming and ahhing over the jukebox at the back of the room, all of them nondescript in damp raincoats and washed-out faces. Ghosts of New York, drowning their sorrows. Ben wanted to belong among them, but he knew he would always stand out, a broad-shouldered beast of a man, the tumbler almost a thimble in his hand. His leather jacket was beaten and frayed. Red stubble covered his jaw, rising via scruffy sideburns to an unkempt pyre on his head. He liked to think there was a pinch of Josh Homme about him – Josh Homme on steroids – maybe a dash of Cagney. Who was he kidding? These days, he suspected he looked more like the other customers than he'd care to admit, let alone a rock star. Drink and despair had diluted his looks. No wonder Rose didn't want to see him. And in the end his general appearance, a man in his early thirties, was only a clever lie. His true age travelled in his eyes, caves that glimmered green in their depths and held a thousand secrets . . .

That lie had always been the problem. Since his return to New York from a six-week assignment in Spain, his former lover wouldn't answer his calls or reply to his emails. When he called round her Brooklyn apartment, only silence answered the buzzer on the ground floor. Sure, he'd hardly been the mild-mannered Englishman, leaving her high and dry, dropping everything to run off on the De Luca job. And it wasn't as if he needed the money. He'd been around a long time. He got bored. He got restless. He *went into his cave*, as Rose would've put it. The jobs were a way of keeping in shape, and of course, his choice of clientele meant that no one was going to ask too many questions. Now he was paying the price for this diversion. A week back in the city and Rose was another ghost to him.

But once upon a time, once upon a time, when you didn't ask questions and I could pretend, we were madly in love.

Outside, the rain lashing the window, and inside, the rain lashing his heart. April in Insomniac City was a lonely place to be. Ben took another slug of Jack, swallowed another bittersweet memory.

A motorbike growled up outside the bar. The customers turned to look. Exhaust fumes mingled with the scent of liquor as the door swung wide and the rain blew in – with it, a man. The door creaked shut. The man was dressed completely in black, his riding leathers shiny and wet. His boots pounded on the floorboards, then silenced as he stopped and surveyed the bar. His helmet visor was down, obscuring his face. A plume of feathers bristled along the top of the fibreglass dome, trailing down between his bullish shoulders. The bizarre gear marked him out as a Hell's Angel or a member of some other freeway cult. The long, narrow object strapped to his back, its cross-end poking up at the cobwebbed fans, promised a pointed challenge.

As the other customers lost interest, turning back to their chatter, peanuts and music, Ben was putting down his tumbler of Jack, swivelling on his stool and groaning wearily under his breath.

The man in the helmet saw him, shooting out a leather-gloved finger.

"Ben Garston! This game of hide-and-seek is over. I have some unfinished business with you."

Ben felt the eyes in the place twist back to him, a soft, furtive pressure on his spine. He placed a hand on his chest, a faux-yielding gesture.

"What can I say, Fulk? You found me."

The newcomer removed his helmet and thumped it down on the end of the bar. It rested there like a charred turkey, loose feathers fluttering to the floor. The man called Fulk grinned, a self-satisfied leer breaking through his shaggy black beard. Coupled with the curls falling to his shoulders, his head resembled a small, savage dog, ready to pounce from a thick leather pedestal.

"London. Paris. LA." Fulk named the cities of his search, each one a wasp flying from his mouth. Like Ben, his accent was British, but where Ben's held the clipped tones of a Londoner, the man in black's was faintly Welsh, a gruff rural borderland burr. Ben would have recognised it anywhere. "Where've you been hiding, snake?"

Ben shrugged. "Seems I've been wherever you're not."

Fulk indicated the half-empty glass on the bar. "Surprised you're not drinking milk. I know you have a taste for it. Milk, maidens and malt, eh? And other people's property."

"Ah, the Fitzwarren family wit." Through the soft blur of alcohol, Ben looked up at the six-and-a-half-foot hulk before him, openly sizing him up. What Fulk lacked in brains, he made up for in brawn. Win or lose, this was going to hurt.

The whiskey softened his tongue as well. He made a half-hearted stab at diplomacy. "You shouldn't be here, you know. The Pact—"

"Fuck the Pact. What's it to me?"

"It's the Lore, Fulk. Kill me, and the Guild'll make sure you never see that pile of moss-bound rubble you and your family call home again."

But Ben wasn't so sure about that. Whittington Castle, the crumbling ruins of a keep near Oswestry in Shropshire, was in the ancestral care of a trust. The same trust set up back in 1201 by King John and later bestowed on the Guild of the Broken Lance for safekeeping. The deeds to the castle would only pass back to the Fitzwarren estate when a certain provision was met, that being the death of Red Ben Garston, the last of his troublesome kind. The last one *awake*, anyway. Of course, the Lore superseded that ancient clause. Technically, Ben was protected like all Remnants, but he knew that didn't matter to Fulk. The same way he knew that the man in front of him was far from the first to go by that name. Like the others before him, this latest Fulk would stop at nothing to get his hands on Whittington and reclaim the family honour, whether he risked the ire of the Guild or not. Vengeance ran in Fulk's bloodline, and his parents would have readied him for it since the day he was born.

"The Lore was made to be broken," Fulk Fitzwarren CDXII said. "Besides, don't you read the news? The Pact is null and void, Garston. You're not the only one any more."

"What the hell are you talking about?"

Before he could enquire further, the man in black unzipped his jacket, reached inside and retrieved a scrunched-up newspaper. He threw it on to the bar, next to Ben's elbow.

It was a copy of *The New York Times*. Today's evening edition. Warily lowering his eyes, Ben snatched it up and read the headline.

STAR OF EEBE STOLEN

Police baffled by exhibition theft

Last night person or persons unknown broke into the Nubian Footprints exhibition at the Javits Center, the noted exhibition hall on West 34th Street. The thieves made off with priceless diamond the Star of Eebe, currently on loan from the Museum of Antiquities, Cairo. Archaeologists claim that the fist-sized uncut gem came from a meteor that struck the African continent over 3,000 years ago. Legend has it that the Star fell into the possession of a sub-Saharan queen.

According to a source in the NYPD, the thieves were almost certainly a gang using high-tech equipment, improvised explosive devices and some kind of ultra-light airborne craft, a gyrocopter or delta plane. Around midnight last night, an explosion shook the Javits Center and the thieves managed to navigate the craft into Level 3, smashing through the famous 150-foot "crystal palace" lobby, alighting in the exhibition hall and evading several alarm systems to make off with the gem. The police believe the thieves took flight by way of another controlled explosion, fleeing through the Javits Center's western façade, out over 12th Avenue and the Hudson River, where police suspect they rendezvoused with a small ship headed out into the Bay, across to Weehawken or upriver to . . .

God knows where. Ben scanned the story, plucking the meat off printed bones. The details were sketchy at best. Between the lines, he summed them up. No fingerprints. No leads. No fucking clue.

The bar held its breath as he slapped the *Times* back down. No one spoke, no one chewed peanuts, no one selected songs on the jukebox. The rain drummed against the window. Four-wheeled fish swam past outside.

"Clever," Ben said. "But what does this have to do with me?"

"More than you'd like." Fulk grinned again, yellow dominoes lost in a rug. "You're reading your own death warrant."

"If this is a joke, I don't get it."

"No, you don't, do you?" The man in black shook his head. "I've travelled halfway around the world to face my nemesis, and all I find is a washed-up worm feeling sorry for himself in a bar. Is it because of your woman? Is that why you returned? She won't take you back, you know. Your kind and hers never mix well."

"You came here to advise me on my love life?"

Fulk laughed. "You're asleep, Red Ben. You've been asleep for *centuries*. The world holds no place for you now. You're a relic. You're trash. I only came here to sweep up the pieces."

"Yeah, your glorious quest." Ben rolled his eyes at their audience, the men sat in the booth, the guy with a palm full of peanuts frozen before his mouth, the one shuffling slowly away from the jukebox. "You need to get over it. Mordiford was a very long time ago."

A storm rumbled up over Fulk's brow, his deep-set eyes sinking even further into his head. Obviously it was the wrong thing to say. The ages-long river of bad blood that ran between Ben and House Fitzwarren was clearly as fresh to the man in black as it had been to his predecessors, perhaps even to the original Fulk, way back in the Middle Ages.

Muscles tense, Ben sighed and stood up, his stool scraping the floorboards. Despite his height rivalling the slayer's, he still felt horribly slight in Fulk's shadow. The whiskey could make you feel small too.

He didn't need this. Not now. He wanted to get back to the Jack and his heartbreak.

"It was yesterday to us," Fulk said, the claim escaping through gaps in his teeth. "We want our castle back. And Pact or no Pact, when we have it, your head will hang on our dining room wall."

The bartender, cringing behind the bar, guarded by bottles and plastic cocktail sticks, chose this moment to pipe up.

"Look, fellers, nobody wants any trouble. I suggest you take your beef outside, or do I have to call the—"

The sword Fulk drew from the scabbard on his back was a guillotine on the barman's words. The youth scuttled backwards, bottles and cocktail sticks crashing to the floor, panic greasing his heels. He joined the customers in a scrambling knot as they squeezed their bellies out of the booth, tangling with the other guys pushing past the jukebox to the fire exit at the back of the bar. In a shower of peanuts and dropped glasses, they were gone, the fire exit clanking open, a drunken stampede out into the rain.

Ben watched them leave in peripheral envy. He grimaced and rubbed his neck, a habit of his that betrayed his nerves. Then his whole attention focused on Fulk. Fulk and the ancient sword in his face. There was nothing friendly about that sword. They had met before, many times. Ben was on intimate terms with all fifty-five inches of the old family claymore. Back in the Middle Ages, the Scots had favoured the two-handed weapon in their border clashes with the English, and while this one's saw-toothed edge revealed its tremendous age, the blade held an anomalous sheen, the subtle glow informing Ben that more than a whetstone had sharpened the steel.

"Who're you having lunch with these days? The CROWS? That witchy business has a nasty habit of coming back to bite you on the arse." Ben measured these words with a long step backwards, creating some distance between the end of his nose and the tip of the sword. "House Fitzwarren must be getting desperate."

"We are honour-bound to slay our Enemy."

"Yeah, yeah. You're delusional, Fulk – or Pete or Steve or whatever your real name is. Your family hasn't owned Whittington Castle since the time of the Fourth Crusade, but you dog my heels from Mayfair to Manhattan, hoping to win a big gold star where hundreds of others have only won gravestones. And as for this," Ben nodded at the gleaming blade, "tut tut. Whatever would the Guild say?"

"I told you, snake. The Lore is broken. The Guild is over. And now, so are you."

The sword swung towards him, signalling the end of the conversation. The step Ben had taken came in handy; he leaned back just in time to avoid an unplanned haircut. The blade snapped over the bar, licking up the tumbler and the bottle of Jack, whiskey and glass spraying the floorboards.

Fulk grunted, recovering his balance. The weight of the claymore showed in his face. His leathers creaked as he lunged forward for another blow, the blade biting into beer-stained wood. Only air occupied the space where Ben had stood moments before, his quick grace belying his size as he swept up his bar stool and broke it over the man in black's head.

Cracked wood made a brief halo around Fulk's shoulders. His strap-on boots did a little tango and then steadied as he regained his balance, his shaggy mane shaking off the splinters. He grimaced, his teeth clenched with dull yellow effort. The sword came up, came down, scoring a line through shadow and sawdust, the heavy blade lodging in the floorboards.

The stroke dodged, Ben rushed through his own dance steps and elbowed Fulk in the neck. As the man choked and went down on one knee, Ben leapt for the bar, grabbing the plumed helmet and swinging it around, aiming for that wheezing, brutish head.

Metal kissed fibreglass, the sword knocking the helmet from Ben's grip. Sweat ran into his eyes as Fulk came up, roaring, and smacked him with the flat of the blade. If this had been an ordinary duel, Fulk might as well have hit a bear with a tooth-pick. The Fitzwarrens' attempts to slay their Enemy had always remained unfairly balanced in Ben's favour, and over the years he had grown complacent, the attacks an annoyance rather than a threat. Now his complacency caught him off guard. This was no ordinary duel. Resistant to magic as he was, bewitched steel was bewitched steel, and the ground blurred under his feet moments before his spine met the jukebox. The air flew out of his lungs even as it flew into Jimi Hendrix's, a scratchy version of "Fire" stuttering into the gloomy space.

The song was one of Ben's favourites, but he found it hard to appreciate under the circumstances. He groaned, trying to pull himself up. Stilettos marched up and down his back. His buttocks ached under his jeans. He tasted blood in his mouth, along with a sour, sulphurous tang, a quiet belch that helped him to his feet, his eyes flaring.

Across the bar, Fulk's eyebrows were arcs of amusement.

"Finally waking up, are we? It's too late, Garston." The man in black stomped over to where Ben stood, swaying like a bulrush in a breeze. "Seems like my granny was wrong. She always said to let sleeping dogs lie."

Fulk shrugged, dismissing the matter. Then he brought the sword down on Ben's skull.

Or tried to. Ben raised an arm, shielding his head, and the blade sliced into his jacket, cutting through leather, flesh and down to the bone, where it stuck like a knife in frozen butter. Blood wove a pattern across the floorboards, speckling his jeans and Doc Martens. They weren't cheap, those shoes, and Ben wasn't happy about it.

When he exhaled, a long-suffering, pained snort, the air grew a little hot, a little smoky. He met Fulk's gaze, waiting for the first glimmers of doubt to douse the man's burgeoning triumph. As Fulk's beard parted in a question, Ben reached up with his free hand and gripped the blade protruding from his flesh. The rip in his jacket grew wider, the seams straining and popping, the muscle bulging underneath. The exposed flesh rippled around the wound, shining with the hint of some tougher substance, hard, crimson and sleek, plated neatly in heart-shaped rows, one over the other. The sight lasted only a second, long enough for Ben to wrench the claymore out of his forearm.

Hendrix climaxed in a roll of drums and a whine of feedback. The blood stopped dripping random patterns on the floor. The lips of Ben's wound resealed like a kiss and his arm was just an arm again, human, healed and held before his chest.

"Your antique can hurt me, but have you got all day?" Ben forced a smile, a humourless rictus. "That's what you'll need, because I'm charmed too, remember? And as for my head, I'm kind of attached to it."

Flummoxed, Fulk opened his mouth to speak. Ben's fist forced the words down his throat before he had the chance. The slayer's face crumpled, and then he was flying backwards, over the bloody floor, past the bar with its broken bottles, out through the dirty square window that guarded Legends from the daylight.

Silvery spears flashed through the rain. Teeth and glass tinkled on asphalt. Tyres screeched. Horns honked. East 7th Street slowed to a crawl as a man dressed head to toe in black leather landed in the road.

Somewhere in the distance, sirens wailed. Ben retrieved the newspaper from the bar, thinking now was perhaps a good time to leave. As he stepped through the shattered window, he could tell that the cops were heading this way, the bartender making good on his threat. Who could blame him? Thanks to this lump sprawled in the road, the month's takings would probably go on repairs.

Stuffing the *Times* into his jacket, the rain hissing off his cooling shoulders, Ben crunched over to where Fulk lay, a giant groaning on a bed of crystal. He bent down, rummaging in the dazed man's pockets. Then he clutched the slayer's beard and pulled his face towards his own.

"And by the way, it isn't sleeping dogs, Fulk," he told him. "It's *dragons*."

Then he took flight into the city.

Enter the monthly
Orbit sweepstakes at

www.orbitloot.com

With a different prize every month,
from advance copies of books by
your favourite authors to exclusive
merchandise packs,
**we think you'll find something
you love.**